THE
Last Life
OF
Prince Alastor

THE
Last Life
OF
Prince Alastor

ALEXANDRA BRACKEN

Disney • HYPERION

LOS ANGELES   NEW YORK

All rights reserved. Published by Disney • Hyperion, an imprint of
Disney Book Group. No part of this book may be reproduced or transmitted
in any form or by any means, electronic or mechanical, including photocopying,
recording, or by any information storage and retrieval system, without
written permission from the publisher. For information address
Disney • Hyperion, 125 West End Avenue,
New York, New York 10023.

First Edition, February 2019
10 9 8 7 6 5 4 3 2 1
FAC-020093-18355
Printed in the United States of America

This book is set in Adobe Caslon Pro, Caslon Antique Pro, Edlund/Monotype;
Bad Neighborhood Badhouse Bold/House Industries; Blossom/Fontspring
Designed by Marci Senders

Library of Congress Cataloging-in-Publication Data
Names: Bracken, Alexandra, author.
Title: The last life of Prince Alastor / by Alexandra Bracken.
Description: First edition. • Los Angeles ; New York : Disney-Hyperion, 2019. •
Series: [The dreadful tale of Prosper Redding ; 2] • Summary: "Prosper's
adventures continue when he ventures to Alastor's home, the demon world"—
Provided by publisher.
Identifiers: LCCN 2018016913• ISBN 9781484778180 (hardcover) •
ISBN 9781368002332 (ebook)
Subjects: • CYAC: Demonology—Fiction. • Blessing and cursing—Fiction. •
Supernatural—Fiction.
Classification: LCC PZ7.B6988 Las 2019 • DDC [Fic]—dc23
LC record available at https://lccn.loc.gov/2018016913

Reinforced binding
Visit www.DisneyBooks.com

SUSTAINABLE FORESTRY INITIATIVE   Certified Sourcing
www.sfiprogram.org
SFI-00993

THIS LABEL APPLIES TO TEXT STOCK

For Susan Dennard—
a true witch with words

DECEMBER 1690
TOWN OF SOUTH PORT
PLYMOUTH COLONY

A voice cried out through the darkening snowfall.

It was a wisp of a sound, so very pitiful and weak. At first, Alastor had merely been surprised it survived the journey through the mirrors at all. And yet, that whimper had wrapped around his senses. It held on as he sat before his hearth of crackling green magic, dining on his evening feast of banebats and pumpkin mash.

Help me. . . .

He might have mistaken it for a foul wind cutting through his tower, except that the words were laced with alluring pain.

With delicious desperation.

With the promise of powerful magic for the taking.

Help me, I beg thee!

I shall, the malefactor thought with a smirk. And gladly.

And so Alastor, Prince of the Realm, had set his silvered knife down and risen to find the tether of magic already awaiting him on the surface of the mirror. When a mortal's desire was strong enough, it created a shimmering ribbon of emerald power that Alastor could then trace back to its source.

He lifted a silver chain off its hook on the wall, dropping it over his head. The small lantern dangling from the necklace clacked against his coat's spider-shaped buttons. Alastor relished the shiver of the mirror's glass as he passed through it.

Help. . . .

He followed the begging voice through the winding tunnels of the mirror pathways. The essence of that grief, that anger, only made the tether burn brighter through their smog and shadows. Excitement licked through him at the sight of it glowing.

What sort of mortal wormling, he wondered, might carry the potential for so very much magic? Someone with immense responsibility, surely, with tremendous power over the lives of other humans. A king, perhaps? An *emperor*, even?

Oh, how he would lord this over his brothers until their black hearts burst with jealousy and outrage! He'd make sure the bounty of magic from this deal would make them rue the day they ignored this particular summons. His brothers often relied on their many minions to go out and gather magic *for* them. They were far too busy hosting balls and dueling with trolls to do the very thing that they were born to do—that is, aside from ruling lesser fiends.

As Alastor had learned, if one wished for power, one had to seize it for oneself.

Only, the second he reached the portal into the human world, he knew his fantasies had been little more than delusions.

The human mirror was small, no bigger than what most of those flea-bitten men used while shaving their faces. Alastor had never understood that custom, as facial hair often improved their otherwise ratlike features and made them somewhat bearable to a fiend's refined eye. This one, however, was not currently in use at all.

He gripped the frame of the mirror. Considering. Watching from behind the glass, hidden. A frigid gust of wind reached him, coating the surface of the portal like frost. The warm, damp heat of Downstairs was at his back, urging him to return.

A shaving mirror, of all things! One that served as a window into what appeared to be a bleak shack of dark wood, not a gilded mirror gazing upon a suitably glittering palace hall.

Help . . . help us all. . . .

He ought to have gone back to the comfort of his tower and pumpkin mash and left the mortal to his suffering. Yet his hands were fixed to the frame, his claws digging into the wood. He had already come this far, hadn't he? And regardless of what rank of troublesome scab this human was, the strength of his desire had lit the tether like a torch.

Alastor supposed, with an indignant sniff, *all* humans, whether peasant or king, longed, hated, feared, and suffered, only to different degrees. That was the dance of human existence. They swung from one misery to another, trading partners and rivals as they spun through their ever-dwindling years.

The potential for strong magic was still there, if Alastor could discover whatever desire had been powerful enough to summon him in the first place. He would wring it out of the man's pitiful heart like the last drops of ooze from a rotbeetle, until he had his contract.

Pouring himself through the tight constraints of the mirror's frame, Alastor shifted into the form he took in the human world, that of an ivory-coated fox. Humans had a general distaste for darkly ferocious creatures, but the shifting also served the purpose of avoiding the glamour enchantment that plagued all fiends in the human realm. That curse of invisibility in their true forms had been a parting gift from the Ancients, before they walled themselves up inside of their own realm.

The fact that only malefactors could shift was proof of their superiority, Alastor thought as he dropped silently onto the floor. Other fiends were forced to rely on noise and shadow to provoke fear in the hearts of humans. While fear could be powerful, the magic the lesser fiends milked from that human emotion was a mere flame compared to the wildfire generated from each deal a malefactor made.

Wind screeched through the gaps in the home's slanted walls. Cold pierced him from all sides, like a thousand arrows. The frigid air alone almost made him turn back, but as soon as his paws had touched down, he was struck by wave after wave of agony. *Anguish.* There was so much of it in the house around him, it might as well have papered the walls. Alastor reached up with his paw, opening the small lantern that hung around his neck.

The air wept magic. The power glittered and swirled as it flowed into the enchanted container. As he waited for the gathering to finish, he took stock of his surroundings.

The only source of light in the room had been from the dying fire in the hearth. His own hearth was a mighty structure, dominating the room like a glowering giant. He'd instructed the goblins to craft it from the finest dragonglass and encrust it with petrified elf hearts. This one, however, was little more than a pile of scorched stones, and the figure that sat before it was even less impressive by his estimation.

It was a shapeless creature, wrapped in a faded quilt—a woman? The magic now seemed to be streaming solely from her. It rose from her shoulders in great, shuddering waves. A fearsome pain, indeed. It would be a simple thing to make a deal with a creature so vulnerable.

Yet the tether did not lead to her. It led outside. Her desire, it seemed, was not within his power to fulfill, or else he might have heard her voice through the mirror as well.

He knew not to dally here any longer, but it was a curious sight, and Alastor found the curious to be irresistible. A pot for food had fallen onto its side beside her, as dry as a bone.

Human fire was so strange—so very inefficient compared to the magic they used for heating, cooking, and lighting Downstairs. Far more feeble and needy as well. The last of the fire survived on a few thin branches and what the woman fed into it. Bits of lace. A knit bonnet, too small for her own head. A pair of shoes, no longer than a human thumb.

Alastor did not wish to look any longer, and did not have to. Exhausted, the woman released a soft sigh and slumped down onto the ground.

The wind threw the door open with a terrific roar. Freezing air exploded around him, momentarily blinding him with a wall of endless white. Reluctantly, he slipped outside.

The humans called this . . . snow. His lip curled back from his fangs. How he *loathed* snow. How the flecks of it caught in his coat, how it stung his eyes, how it made him shake like a hob about to have a horn removed. The only thing in its favor was that it better disguised this form; a white fox could travel far to find its prey unbothered when it all but disappeared into the landscape.

By the time he found the tether again through the driving wind, ice had frozen onto the pads of his paws. But there wasn't much farther to go. Within moments, he realized he was no longer hearing the cries of the man inside his mind, but in his pointed ears.

"Sorry—so deeply—my daughter—"

The man's shape was dark through the veil of the winter storm. His black hat and cloak provided no shield from the flurries, but the man did not seem to care. He did not so much as look up as Alastor approached him from behind. The emerald glow of the magic in his lantern spilled out over the snow, but the man could not see it. Alastor did not think he would care about that either.

Before him was a small hole in the ground, rapidly filling with snow. Beside that, a small wood chest. The name CHARITY had been carved into its lid with careful strokes.

They must not have been far from the ocean. Even with the sharp scent of frost in the air, Alastor's refined nose detected the brine of its churning waters. The dirt piled beside the man was mixed with sand and rocks.

His pleasure at this prospect deepened. Such soil, he'd come to learn over the centuries, meant little could grow. Little food meant little hope. Strangely, though, there seemed to be dozens of small growths, leafless saplings almost buried beneath the snow.

No, he realized. A breath momentarily caught in his throat.

These were not saplings. They were grave markers.

He waited until the man had lowered that box, which was so very small, into the ground. Until he had covered it again with dirt-stained snow. Alastor half expected the man to begin weeping again. Ice had crystallized on his lashes and flakes of snow had caught on his wet cheeks. The man sat back, his hands raw and red from the cold, his hard breathing forming white clouds around him.

"Such loss," Alastor said, at last.

The man looked up, his expression like that of a human lost in a nightmare. Seeing the magnificent creature before him, however, did not fill him with the appropriate awe. Instead, he threw an arm over his face with a horrified cry.

"Begone, devil!" he moaned out. "A fox—speaking! Perhaps the fever now is upon me as well. . . ."

Closer now, Alastor could see the wasting in the man's form. Skin clung to his bones, chapped and seemingly bloodless. His already beady human eyes had sunk farther into his face. Hunger and suffering had hollowed him out, leaving, Alastor knew, more room to consider the offer now before him.

He reached out to touch the tuft of fur on Alastor's head,

then yanked his hand back as if scalded. "Thou art real. . . ."

"Indeed. However, I am no devil," Alastor said, because it was, for all intents and purposes, true. "A devil would not come to thee in thy time of great need."

"That is precisely when a devil would come," the man said, his voice hoarse. "When my heart is weak, and my faith shaken."

Hmm. Fair point, well made. Alastor shifted strategies ever so slightly.

"I am no devil, but I am a creature of business," he explained, miming innocence as he licked his paws. "I heard thy cries and came only to offer thee my services. I am Alastor. What is thy name?"

The man did not give it. Instead, he sat stone-faced, staring out at the hill of graves before him. One of his hands stroked a gash in the fabric of his cloak. Then, without a word, he unknotted its strings from around his neck and draped the wool over Alastor's small form. Though it was damp from the snow, the fabric was still warm and reeking of the man's body.

"Wh-what is the meaning of this?" Alastor spluttered, too shocked to move out from beneath it.

"You are freezing, creature," the man said simply. He rubbed at his thin shirtsleeves, all stained with soot and dirt. "Only one of us need die of this cold."

Alastor momentarily lost his ability to speak.

The mortal's voice lowered. "It is for the best, you see. There is but enough food to see my wife through the winter. She will need to keep her strength, to fend off the sickness."

"Thou has lost a child," Alastor said, recovering. "Others, too, it seems . . . How heavy the heart sits, with that knowing. How it sickens. And yet you do not have to lie down and die beside them."

"Thou art a devil," the man whispered, his face crumpling. "What dost thou know of pain?"

"Only," Alastor said, "that I have helped many out of its darkness."

"Can thou bring back those that this desolate wilderness has taken from me? Can thou make it so they never followed me across the sea?"

Ah. Alastor understood now why his grief had felt so powerful, similar to those kings and queens and generals he had encountered in his life. Woven through it all was the weight of his responsibility for the others. His guilt.

"I cannot bring back the dead as they once were," Alastor said. "And you would not wish to disturb them."

Realizing that he was still under the man's cloak, Alastor stepped out from beneath it. The cold bit at him once more. His own breath fogged the air as he rested one paw against the rip in the fabric. The other he used to open the lantern, and let out a small bit of magic. The man's eyes widened as the fabric stitched itself back together.

"Witchcraft," he breathed out.

Alastor gave a sharp shake of the head. "*Possibility.* I mend. I grant wishes and good fortune. That which your soul most desperately desires is within reach. Release thy notions of *good* and *wicked* and see the gift before thee. Make the choice to seize it . . . what is thy name?"

"Honor," the man said. "Honor Redding."

Somehow, Alastor swallowed his noise of disgust. What a perfectly repulsive name. Humans and their irony. As if honor existed among them.

"It is . . . a business transaction?" Honor said, his voice weak.

Alastor threaded the needle quickly. "Yes. Business. I will merely provide services in exchange for something of value to me."

Honor shook his head, snow falling from the brim of his hat. "I have nothing of value to trade."

"Thou hast thy life, dost thou not?" Alastor asked.

Honor looked stricken.

"I do not need *this* life," Alastor told him. "Merely a promise of service in my realm after your life in this one is finished, before you move on to your next. Domestic things, really."

Honor closed his eyes, as if he could imagine it. "How . . . how long would I be in this service?"

"Until I am satisfied," Alastor said simply.

He, of course, was never satisfied, but this was the joy of toying with humans. They often did not know the right questions to ask, and never seemed capable of following a possibility down its many avenues.

"It's only . . . such a thing . . . I've been taught such bargains are evil," Honor said, his voice hoarse. But there was hunger in his eyes. A need to survive. A need to care for those around him, the ones who had followed him to this bitter land.

Alastor smirked inwardly. It was a familiar protest, and he knew precisely how to answer.

"What evil can come from a choice made with a pure heart and the best of intentions?" Alastor asked. "Will thou allow this suffering to continue, when thou has the ability to end it? When thou might stop these needless deaths?"

The frail man looked upon the new grave, brushing away the snow that had fallen on it.

"Honor Redding," Alastor said, "who will be left to bury thee, when all those thou love are gone?"

The man released a shaking breath.

"Could thou prevent anyone in this town from dying of sickness?" Honor asked.

Mortal fool. At least a worse sort of human would have known to ask for more. He might have negotiated until he arrived at no one dying an untimely death before old age. It would have taken more magic, however, and Alastor might have asked for more in return.

"Certainly," Alastor said. Malefactors dealt in curses and left spells and enchantments to witches. It was simple enough to adjust to fit more . . . wholesome needs such as this. He would cast a curse that eradicated any sickness from entering the town's boundaries, make it so fever and infection could not set in.

Snow fell silently between them. The sky darkened with oncoming night.

"Do we have an agreement?" Alastor asked.

Honor took a deep breath and said, "Tell me what I must do."

A Fiendish Arrangement

The mirror's surface rippled, exhaling a puff of warm, sour-smelling air. The overhead sprinklers were still putting out the last of the candles Nell and her father, Henry Bellegrave, lit to perform her spell.

The darkness inside the watery glass glowered back at me as I took a step forward. My face distorted in the reflection, until it looked like I was snarling.

If only my family could see me now. *Poor little Prosper,* my aunts used to say, *scared of his own shadow.* They wouldn't believe for a second that I'd be willing to follow Pyra, or that I was capable of finding Prue, my twin, inside of whatever shadows were waiting Downstairs.

They didn't know me at all. I'd made mistakes, I'd been misled, but I wasn't some helpless victim in this story.

In that moment, the only thing I felt was anger. At myself. At my family. At Nell. At Alastor. At the fiends who couldn't leave the human world alone.

Wait.

I took a step back, frustrated. "What now?"

The deal. We must set the terms.

"*Seriously?* Now? We're going to lose their trail!"

Yes, "seriously," you craven rumpwart. An understanding up front will prevent later troubles. And, Alastor said, somewhat grudgingly, *I require the magic generated from the deal to open a direct portal to the mirror we'll arrive at. The mirror pathways have been cursed so that any humans who find their way inside will be trapped there forever, and I rather thought we had more important things to do than float around in perpetual darkness, Maggot.*

Okay. That was fair. "I want your help to save Prue from Downstairs, no matter the circumstances—"

That is acceptable.

"I'm not finished," I said. "I want you to also guarantee that you will help us get back to the human realm and not strand us down there or in the mirror pathways."

Well played, Maggot. You are learning the ways of a fiend.

I set my jaw hard enough that it was almost painful. "I'm *nothing* like a fiend. I won't ever be. All you do is hurt others and destroy good things. I just won't be your plaything anymore."

Alastor was silent.

"I also want you to end the grudge you have against my family," I said. "And leave them alone."

He sneered inside my head, making my skin crawl with the sensation of it. *No. I will grant your first two requests in exchange for the promise of your eternal servitude Downstairs upon your mortal death.*

I choked a bit at that. Forever . . . was a long time. Actually, it wasn't a long time, it was the thing past the standard of *a long time.* My afterlife would consist of licking his boots clean and cooking him whatever disgusting things they ate Downstairs.

Oh no, Maggot. I have hobs to do such things. No, you would tend to my fireviper nests, and then, after you've proven yourself, you'd have the privilege of preparing my favorite fairy crisps. They screech and bite as you pluck off their wings, but the oven is always quick to quiet them.

I rolled my eyes, letting my hands curl into fists at my side. The punishment wouldn't be doing any of those jobs. No, the real prison of misery was knowing that I'd be forced to listen to him going on about his "dark magnificence" until I'd probably wish I could die all over again, just to escape it for a few seconds.

I couldn't believe I'd ever been stupid enough to think, even for a second, that he might turn down my offered contract. Like, *You know what? I'll take the moral high road just this once and help you and your sister out of this dastardly situation I'm directly responsible for putting you in.*

But that was the difference between humans and fiends. Humans had the capacity for good. Fiends didn't.

How your courage crumbles at the prospect, Alastor said. *It is the only thing I ask, and yet you squander the passing seconds as though you have nothing to be concerned about. As if knowing for certain that your sister's heart is strong enough to survive the dark rigors of Downstairs.*

My own heart suddenly slammed against my ribs.

While she'd undergone several surgeries and had been given the all clear by doctors, Prue had been born with a heart condition that had nearly killed her. There was no telling if it was just the doctor's skill and her own innate strength that had helped her survive, or a touch of the unnatural, magic luck the Reddings possessed.

If it was the latter . . . what would happen to her if Alastor finally broke free from my body and took all of our family's good fortune away? What if it was so terrifying Downstairs—

No. I shook my head, flinging the horrible thought away. Prudence was strong. She'd always been the better of the two of us, in all the ways that mattered. She'd rescued me from any number of mess-ups. It was my turn to save her, and I would.

I will help you save your sister and ensure you return here together. In exchange, I'll have your shade. Do you accept these terms?

Wait. The thought of Alastor's vow of vengeance on my

family stirred up another one. Honor Redding had already promised all the shades of his family and descendants centuries ago, including mine. I wasn't giving the fiend anything more than he already had.

Confound it all—Alastor spluttered, clearly hearing my thoughts. He'd been so in love with the image of tormenting me that he really *hadn't* realized it. This time I was the one smirking. *No! I require something else, then*—

A heavy pounding on the storage room's door startled me out of my thoughts. My head snapped around, stomach plummeting as someone called out, "Is anyone in there? Stand back from the door, we're coming in!"

"I accept your original terms!" I said. "Just hurry!"

A flash of green light gathered at the center of my chest, then billowed out in tendrils. I startled, jumping back from the mirror as the shimmering strands knotted themselves together over my skin and seeped into it.

Magic. I'd never seen a shade of green like this before, not in all my paint sets or colored pencils; it wasn't one found in nature, that was for sure. It looked almost . . . electric. The last few traces of magic floated around me like sparks, drifting into the mirror.

Fine, Alastor said, sulking. *Clearly my time inhabiting your puny mind has temporarily dulled my own. The sooner I escape, the better.*

Yeah. We'd see about that.

A surge of prickling heat went through my arm as he

took control of it. Somewhere behind me, the pounding on the storage room's door intensified like a booming heartbeat. I couldn't look away from the mirror, though, not when my finger touched its shivering glass and a spark of that same green magic leaped from it. I took a deep breath and closed my eyes.

Do you always close your eyes when frightened? Alastor asked. *Open them wide, stare down your fear until it obeys you.*

I gritted my teeth. "I'm not afraid."

Not yet.

By the time the door burst open and the firefighters spilled inside, the mirror had already closed behind me.

Where Fiends Dwell

Passing through the mirror portal is like being caught between one heartbeat and the next. For that single disorienting second, there is nothing but pure black—no air, no light, no sound. You're not falling, or flying, or moving at all.

You're not even sure you still have a body.

And just when you know to start worrying, when the soggy edges of your thoughts start to make less and less sense, it all explodes.

Something reached out and gripped me by the throat, yanking me forward so hard that I felt my cheeks and lips peel back from my teeth. Rainbow prisms of light whirled around me, spinning faster and faster. My stomach heaved, and I couldn't close my eyes; tears streamed from them. A roar filled my ears, drowning out my thundering pulse and Alastor's gleeful laughter.

In the end, I didn't get off the ride—I got ejected.

My eyes and mouth snapped shut as all that spiraling air suddenly detonated, releasing me with a thundering *crack*.

"Al!" I managed to choke out. My knees hit wood and splintered it. When I finally landed, it was with a loud, queasy-making *splat*.

Brown mud and something that smelled suspiciously like what came out of the wrong ends of humans sprayed up around me on impact. It pooled around my waist like I was in the most disgusting of swamps. I coughed and gagged. When my palms skimmed over the water, they caught on floating pieces of . . . something.

Ahhhhh, Alastor said wistfully. ***It is the essence of "home," is it not?***

It was the essence of puke, actually. Days-old puke, left outside in the heat.

Holding my breath, I managed to push myself fully onto my feet, closing my eyes as the reeking watery substance dripped off me. The ground was compact beneath my feet, at least, and when I stood, whatever steaming poison was roiling around me only reached my knees. Better. Ish.

I moved forward gingerly, craning my neck back to peer into the shadows over my head. There was only a thin stream of green light illuminating the space, just enough to make out the basics.

We *had* fallen through some kind of wood bench. I grasped up the two biggest pieces of it, holding them together to reveal the telling circle that had been cut into it.

Oh.

No.

This was . . .

I started to bring my hands up to cover my face, only to remember what was on them. I started to wipe them against my shirt, only to remember it was on that, too. And then, because the only other option was screaming, I took a deep breath.

"Al," I began.

Yes, Maggot? he asked, all innocence.

"Why," I said, the word tasting like vomit, "did you bring us through a mirror in an outhouse? Why? *Why?*"

*Not that I must explain my every decision to you, but I brought us here because it is **my** private facility. It is cursed so that only I may open its door. It is the only mirror in all the realm that I could be sure was not watched by Pyra or her crew of filthy traitors, as no one else is aware that it exists.*

"You put your emergency escape in your toilet?"

While many lesser fiends and peasants aspired to my station and adorably mimicked my finely tailored outfits and demeanor, no fiend would ever desire to look in here, would they?

There wasn't a lot that I could—or would—praise

Alastor for, but I had to give him this: he could rival any cockroach for self-preservation.

"You really don't mind your subjects seeing you for the first time in over three centuries covered in . . . *this*?" I couldn't bring myself to say the actual word.

Fie, Maggot. I wouldn't dream of announcing myself in such a hideous and humiliating form as a mortal boy. No, I shall wait until I am free of your prison and in my true, ter-rifying form before I allow the realm to rejoice at my return. It will be soon enough.

"How soon?" I asked, unease prickling over my skin like thousands of spiders.

I felt the curve of his smirk in my mind and shook my head.

No—I had my own answer to my question. How soon? Not one second before I rescued Prue and got us back to the human world. Figuring out how to break my family's contract with him to save us all from his vengeance had to come second.

The Reddings: just your average all-American family who made a deal with a demonic parasite to destroy their rivals and pave their future with gold, and then were stupid enough to try to break the agreement to avoid its conse-quences. As much as I loved my parents and sister, the finger I was pointing at Alastor was crooked, and curled back at me.

If Alastor was a cockroach, then my ancestors had been the Black Plague. Alastor might have darted away from trouble to hide, but the Reddings hadn't been happy until they'd wiped out anyone who had dared to stand in their way.

"You better hope you never escape my head," I swore, "because the second you do, I am going to wring your fluffy white neck for all of this."

It would endlessly amuse me to watch you try, Alastor said. *Do you intend to stay down here and bask in the moist offerings, or shall I help you jump out?*

I don't need your help, I thought back. Eyes burning with the fumes, I stretched up, feeling for the ledge the seat had been balanced over. My fingertips brushed stone. Solid ground.

Now, how will you do this, Maggot? Alastor wondered. *I seem to recall your trepidation at the prospect of having to climb a rope ladder in—what do you humans call it? Ah yes. Physical escalation.*

The soup of waste and mud shifted around my knees. My foot found a groove in the wall. I kept both hands up on the platform.

Physical education, I corrected. I would have rolled my eyes, but they felt like they were on the verge of melting out of my skull.

Education? What is there to learn? Some creatures, like myself, are born with physical prowess, and others, like

yourself, are not. You must accept the hand Fate has dealt you
or make a deal with me to rise above your station.

That wasn't true at all. Even the best athletes had to
build endurance over time, and with almost everything
else, you just developed a tolerance. You suffered through
your extended family calling you worthless until it no longer stung. You learned how to stay silent as your teachers
berated you for another failed test. You got used to a fiend
talking inside your skull enough to keep functioning and
not curl into a tiny ball of torment.

I had a high tolerance for a lot of things. And I was
not going to be the Redding Who Died of Starvation and
Dehydration in an Outhouse, thanks.

My arms shook as I dragged myself up. The soles of
my wet sneakers slipped against the wall, struggling to find
purchase. By the time I finally flopped onto the flat, hard-
packed dirt floor, my heart was pounding and I couldn't feel
my fingers.

The outhouse itself was no bigger than a coffin. There
was a small crescent-shaped cutout in the simple wood door
through which that eerie green light was filtering. I stood on
my toes and peered through it.

A long alleyway stretched before us, curving into darkness. Foul, pale vapor hissed from cracks between the
cobblestones on the ground. The walls on the buildings
beside the outhouse seemed to lean over the pathway like
vultures, waiting to see what prey might scurry by.

When nothing melted out of the nearby shadows, I slowly pushed the old door open. There was only one way to go—forward.

I stripped off my sopping-wet sweater and tossed it aside. By the time I reached what I assumed was the end of the alleyway, the smog thickened, glowing green under a nearby streetlamp that flickered with magic flame. That electric shade of emerald fell over the whole realm like a coat of slime. They didn't seem to have real fire here, and I wasn't sure why that surprised me.

I took a deep breath, studying what I could see of the kingdom. Painting it would be simple. I'd only need three colors: sinister black, dull silver, and that fluorescent, unnatural green.

I don't think I ever truly appreciated how many bright, vivid colors existed in the human world until I came here, a place stained with overwhelming darkness.

There's a stone at your feet, Alastor said. ***Take it in hand and toss it against the wall to your right.***

I already knew I was going to regret it before the rock even left my hand, but I did it anyway. It clacked against the other stones, and just like that, the structure dissolved into a thousand inky bats.

"Gah!" I sputtered. Throwing my arms over my face and head did nothing. Their wings fluttered against my skin, prickling like cactus needles. "Why did you—why did you tell me to do *that*?!"

I bit back a small cry of pain as one of their tiny clawed wings hooked into my earlobe and tugged. "Get *off*!"

These bats made whatever we had in the human world look like flying mice. They were the size of hawks, and I could not have been less surprised when I felt a set of fangs puncture my arm and the drag as it pulled at my blood.

I gripped its squirming form with my free hand and wrenched it away, throwing it toward the others. The beat of their wings sent the vapors spiraling up, lifting its heavy cover to let me see what was beyond it. My eyes widened as I looked up.

And up.

Because of this, Alastor said, pride swelling in his voice. ***Welcome, Maggot, to Downstairs.***

The Kingdom of Dark Towers

The kingdom glared back at me, inky and seething against the glow of magic from the streetlamps and lanterns in the city above us.

Alastor inhaled sharply. It was the gasp of someone who was seeing home for the first time in three hundred and twenty-five years.

We stood at the base of what appeared to be a small mountain, one that was curving in on itself like a rotting apple. Aside from the one we stood on, there were three other levels—streets—that ringed around it, connected to each other by a labyrinth of stone steps and ladders. With each layer, the buildings grew taller and thinner.

The buildings were all made from the same black stone and mortar. I brushed my hand against the side of a pub—Grim Grayscale's, if its crooked sign was to be believed. The building's stones had each been carved into the flat rectangle of a brick, but they were smooth to the touch. Actually, now that I was really looking at them, the pub, and the other structures like it, just seemed like gloomier, more sinister cousins of the colonial homes you'd find in Salem. In Redhood.

But the difference was that in Downstairs, everything was just that little bit off, like someone had tried to read someone else's homework upside down and copied it. Windows had been installed at a slant. The doors were too narrow and too tall. It was like looking at a shadow version of home.

Yes, well. If one lives in the Flats, one generally does not have the currency to buy the finer homes on the upper steps, in the Scales or the Crown—the third and fourth steps, you see? The Horned Palace sits at the head of it all, behind the veil of the fog.

Steps meaning *streets*, I guessed. The street right above ours looked roughly the same, with a few strange, shadowy shapes I couldn't fully make out. The third step, the Scales, had neater versions of the homes down here, but they were stacked on top of each other—three, four, five stories high. Each level of each teetering house had its own roof, all of them curling up like grasping claws.

You are overawed by the dark majesty, Alastor said. *I understand. Look upon my kingdom and tremble, mortal—*

"What's up with the street at the top—all of those massive trees?" I interrupted, pointing. They looked taller and wider than even the redwoods in California, only without any leaves.

It might have been the distance, but the bark on them looked like it had petrified into stone. Whole sections of the trees were missing chunks, as if they'd been picked at by massive crows. Their long, spindly limbs protruded up into the sky, like the legs of a dead spider on its back.

Not trees, you treacherous rag, Alastor said, exasperated. *Nothing so disgusting as plants grows here. That is the Crown—see how the towers ring around like the peaks of a diadem? It is where the noble fiend families reside. It is where my own tower remains, waiting for me. That one, right at the center. Only . . .*

"Only what?" I pressed. His tower was taller than the rest, of course, the dark prongs spiraling up and up into the hovering vapor until they disappeared into it. There looked to be some kind of metal staircase winding up the side of it, too, like a snake trapping its prey.

There are . . . far fewer towers than I recall. They did not lean quite so. And this is truly odd—

"I don't know what could *possibly* be odd about any of this," I said.

Odd, he began again, ignoring me, *because at the head of each tower there should be a glowing mass of magic, like watchful eyes over the realm. That is where the families kept their hoard, to keep it far from the envious peasants in the Flats.*

"Wow, you're serious about this peasant thing," I muttered. The condition of the buildings on this step showed neglect and wear in a way that made my stomach twist. The fiends down here must have lived smog-ridden lives, constantly afraid their sloping roofs would fall in over their heads.

Not that I cared about the living conditions of fiends. At all.

Of course, we occasionally stoop to come down and enjoy the merriment of mingling with lesser fiends. You cannot find a better glass of beetled juice anywhere in the realm, largely because it contains the tears of the wretched creature pouring it.

I ignored him. My eyes had finally adjusted to the dark, and high up on the Crown, I could now make out lines of chains that wrapped around several of the towers. Most seemed to run from the tops of the structures all the way to the ground below. Between them, fading in and out of the vapor, were structures that looked like they had been carved from single, massive stones. In the shadow of the grand towers, they seemed so simple. Almost primal.

"All right," I said. I'd wasted enough time gawking, but it *was* hard to look away. Every time I blinked I seemed to catch something new. The stone-dragon gargoyles curling around the roof of a house. The glinting blades at the peaks of each building, waiting to pierce the soft belly of any creature that dared to land on them. A metal fence capped with skulls of different shapes and sizes. Distant orange banners.

For once, I was seeing something—I was *doing* something—no other Redding had done. Not just the Reddings, but *all* humans.

I'm not at all sorry to disappoint you, but twenty-seven humans have accidentally found themselves Downstairs after falling through open mirror portals. You are not the first, nor are you the only.

"Really?" I asked, gazing up at the towers. "What happened to them?"

One was eaten by a troll, one managed to escape only to be dragged back by a howler, and the rest—

"You know what?" I said. "Never mind. I can live without knowing."

Finally, I tore my gaze away, returning it to the empty street around us. I'd just have to commit as much as I could of this place to memory and try to sketch it later. And then bury those sketches so no one got worried I'd taken a turn for the dark and strange, and locked me in my room forever.

Time to get going, I thought. Prue was waiting. Every second that passed was another one in which Prue could be *hurt*. Or, I guess, eaten by a troll. I really missed those few precious moments before I found out that was an actual possibility.

"Let's get out of here before the resting hour or whatever is up," I said. "Do you think that Pyra would keep her at the Horrible Palace?"

Horned Palace, Maggot. Though it truly is horrible in its majesty—

I turned to find the nearest stairs to start what looked to be a long climb, only to stop. Realization hit me, slowing my steps along with my blood. I looked again, squinting. But as the cloud of vapor and dust drew up into the air, something else seemed to be missing.

"Is the palace cursed or something?" I asked. "Is the human eye not supposed to be able to see it?"

The step above where the towers had once sat was rimmed with a low stone wall, with nothing but sky beyond it.

No, Alastor said weakly. *'Tis not.*

The palace wasn't there at all.

"Al? Still with me?"

I kicked a chunk of stone down the street, watching it disappear into a pile of mauled metal baskets. Whatever food they'd held was long gone, devoured by rot or the dozens of rats scampering along the edges of the street.

Without wood, everything—from the empty, animal-less carts to doors to signs to the skeletal vendor stands—was hammered out of metal.

Of course, Alastor was still with me. The malefactor talked about human emotions as if they were flavors—a sour pain, coppery anger, salty defiance. But I felt *his* emotions like the changing of the seasons. Right now it was winter in my mind. Every last one of his thoughts seemed to have iced over with dread.

Will you ever cease with that pernicious nickname?

Finally. If there was one thing I could count on to rally, it was that ego. "We don't have time to mope. If the palace is gone, where would Pyra keep Prue?"

Mope? I'm no fool—

"No, I mean, we can't just walk in circles while you feel sorry for yourself."

He sneered. *Of course a mortal would not understand.*

"I *do* understand," I said. "But—hey, look. There's a rat eating another rat. You *love* that kind of thing. Doesn't that make you feel better?"

He sniffed. *It does, just.*

One of the rats unhinged its jaw like a snake and devoured the enemy rat whole. I took a generous step back, then crossed to the other side of the deserted street. Folding myself into the shadows, I leaned back against a stack of massive empty cages. Nearby, a new crack split the cobblestones, sending up a hissing wall of vapor. I jumped as a piece of faded parchment tore off a nearby door and slapped me in the face.

CLOSED BY ORDER OF THE QUEEN. REMAIN IN THE FLATS AND RISK THE DEVOURING OF THE VOID, I read. There was a black wax seal of a horned skull with a crown above it at the bottom, followed by the words LONG MAY SHE RAGE. "What's the Void?"

Alastor took away something else entirely from the parchment. *How dare she present herself as queen when, under her so-called reign, the Horned Palace has fallen for the first time in over five thousand years!*

Now that I was looking, I saw the broadsheets everywhere. Tacked onto doors, papering over windows, blowing like tumbleweeds under the urging of the vapors streaming up from the ground. Alastor was wrong. The fiends weren't resting. They weren't on this step at all.

"This is so creepy," I whispered.

Thank you, Alastor said.

"Unintentionally creepy," I corrected. "You really don't know what the Void is . . . ?"

A cold prickling broke out across my skin, turning the hair on the back of my neck to needles. The moment sharpened, and the vapors quieted just enough for my ears to detect the sound.

Footsteps.

I spun around, eyes frantically skimming the buildings nearby. All the doors were chained up, with metal gates covering the alleyways. There was nowhere to hide.

Another step, closer now.

"What do I do?" I breathed out.

Into that barrel, Alastor said, his own fear igniting mine, *quickly!*

Two metal barrels had been overturned in the street. I

pried the cover off one, choking on its pungent vinegar-like stench as I crawled inside and frantically pulled the lid shut behind me.

A thin ray of green light filtered in through a split at the barrel's seam. I pressed my eye against the crack and held my breath.

A long, dark snout appeared through the vapor and drew in a deep sniff. Drool dripped over its protruding fangs, catching in its shaggy black coat and hissing like acid as it hit the cobblestones.

My pulse began to trill like a violin as the massive dog passed by the barrel, its blade-like claws clicking and scraping against the debris in the street. Another one followed close behind the first, stopping only to snap up one of the crimson rats. I cringed at the agonized screech that followed.

The words seemed to ooze out of them like blood from a fresh wound. *"Hunt Alastor. Take boy. Hunt Alastor. Take boy. . . ."*

Howlers.

Nell and I had been chased across Salem by a pack of them. They'd been sent to search for Alastor.

Be still, Alastor told me. *Be calm.*

I clenched my hands into fists to keep them from shaking. One of the howlers had the sweater I'd stripped off in its jaws.

Oh, *crap*. Why hadn't I just taken it with us? All they had to do was track the scent of waste and mud—

This barrel once contained beetled juice, Alastor said. ***The smell is still potent enough to disguise your own.***

I managed to take in a small, shaking breath as they finally passed, lumbering down the street. My eyes watered from the stench of the vinegar, and I risked looking away to wipe them against my arm. When I looked back, there was a different fiend standing in the street.

The shape of it was humanlike, only it had to be almost eight feet tall—and growing. I pressed my hand against my mouth as its long torso contorted, stretching out like putty to inspect something on the ground.

A drop of blood.

I clamped my free hand down on the wound that the bat had left. *Stupid, stupid, stupid!* If they could track me by my human smell, like Alastor had said, they could do it by my blood, too. And in all that walking, I must have left a handy trail for them.

One of the fiend's long fingers swept down to collect the splotch of it off the stones. His mouth nearly encircled his whole head, and it opened wide, like it was on a hinge, to reveal rows of jagged teeth. A black tongue snaked out, licking at the blood. The fiend purred at the taste.

Every inch of his wrinkled skin was a sickly green. He was entirely hairless, save for the long, thin black strands that drifted down over his shoulders to the dried-out snake serving as his belt. The blade strapped to his hip was serrated like a saw. Glowing moths clung to the back of his long black trench coat, gnawing at the holes and slashes already there.

As the fiend turned, I saw that he had a small bottle tied to the leather band he wore across his bony chest. It glowed with a few wisps of fluttering magic.

A slate roof tile fell from the pub, smashing against the ground. The fiend spun toward the sound, two flaps of skin on his face peeling back to reveal eight eyes. The howlers pounced back to his side, growling.

What . . . is that? I thought at Al.

A ghoul, he said. ***Be wary. They regard humans as little more than fleshy dumplings.***

"Thinskin . . . I know that you are out there," the ghoul said, his voice gurgling. "I know this, too: you can only hide for so long. Surrender to me now and the queen may allow your sister, she of the bloodred hair, to keep her life—or, at least, the rest of her fingers."

Anger surged through me, and it took every last bit of control I had to stay there, curled up and powerless.

Resist, Prosperity. Do not give in to your fury at his taunting words. Pyra knows she may only use your sister as leverage so long as she is unharmed. Resist.

I forced myself to breathe out through my nose, closing my eyes. It felt like a full hour passed before the ghoul's shuffling footsteps finally faded and I could no longer hear the heavy pants of the howlers. By then, my muscles were cramped and I was feeling a little light-headed from the smell. I started to rise, only to hear a distant thundering.

What now? I asked, another wave of anger washing over me. We couldn't keep wasting time here hiding like a mouse in a hole. I couldn't see anything through the crack in the barrel's seam. It must have been a storm.

No, Alastor said. ***Wait. The ground trembled, as if with steps. Be silent for a moment more.***

Which was, of course, the exact moment my empty stomach didn't just growl—it roared.

That was you! I hissed.

That was you! Alastor hissed back.

The lid creaked open. Dim green light spilled inside the barrel, only to be blotted out as a massive hand reached in and locked around my throat.

Vampyre on a Pyre

Fiends had an array of responses to terror—a whole world of them. Spitting, launching poisoned quills, melting, turning themselves invisible, transforming. Humans, unfortunately, were limited to two responses: fight or flight.

Alas, the boy had neither of these options available to him as the ogre lifted him out of the barrel and held him dangling in the air. Prosper's nails and puny mortal fingers were useless as they tried to scratch their way to freedom. Her grip tightened as she drew the boy closer for inspection.

The boy had thought ogres resembled the frogs of the human world, and Alastor supposed that he could see a passing resemblance. Their skin was smooth and a highly becoming mixture of gray, brown, and green. Freckle-like spots covered the place where her mouth jutted out sharply, like a beak. Two small tusks curled up on either side of it.

"Can you not read the signs, fiend?" the ogre said. "Did someone place a deathwish on you that compelled you to return here? The Void will be on this place within days, perhaps hours. Quicklance—look! I told you we would find fools scrounging around down here. This one reeks of beetled juice. Too out of his mind with it to realize the danger he's in!"

Alastor startled at how fine the ogre's speech was, how carefully the words were chosen, even if they were slightly distorted by her oversized fangs. Ogres, with their extraordinarily dim wits and sturdy frames, had only ever been given mindless tasks, such as stacking stones and supporting collapsing buildings with their shoulders. It was all their tadpole-sized brains could manage. Why had anyone bothered with the thankless task of *educating* them?

Another ogre appeared farther down the road, stepping out from the abandoned building he'd been inspecting.

Like a jolt of a fire scorpion's poison alighting through him, a half-realized thought finally came together. Alastor realized what was truly behind his growing shivers of dismay.

The ogres each wore near-impenetrable dragonhide armor and an orange spidersilk sash that stretched from shoulder to hip. In other words, the uniform of the *King's Guard*. The ruler's most trusted and deadly warriors, elite fighters who would not hesitate to put down a threat or offer up their lives in his defense. His father's Guard had been composed mostly of lycans who had survived their first bout of moon sickness and emerged on the other side of it with clear, highly trainable minds.

To think that Pyra had given such an honor to *ogres* . . . Alastor wanted his physical form more than ever now, if only to vomit. Were his father's old forces so depleted that she'd grant this power to lesser fiends? What was next? A hob overseeing the royal vaults?

Al . . . Al . . . AL—ALASTOR! The boy's voice finally intruded on his thoughts. *Help? Maybe?*

"Say . . . what manner of fiend are you?" the ogre demanded.

Not a word, Alastor warned. The boy was crusted in dung and the tangy scent of beetled juice. The ogres would not necessarily be able to identify him as human until they took the time to scrub him.

Another ogre lowered his face to peer directly into the boy's. Putrid breath fanned out between his fangs, making the boy wince. "See his pale skin? Beneath the dung? *Vampyre.*"

You do have the pallor of the newly dead, Alastor observed.

It's not summer, the boy said indignantly, *of course I'm pale!*

"Oooooooh," the others said.

"But his teeth—" The female ogre gripped Prosper's

face, forcing his mouth open with her thumbs. "These couldn't cut a worm. I've seen bigger fangs on a blood viper."

"No, no, this makes good sense, don't you see, Orca?" said the other. "He has shaved his fangs down. He has smeared dung on himself to pass by unnoticed while the rest of his kind have been taken. He thinks he tricks us—that he is smarter than us—but he is wrong! He is a leech!"

"Er," Prosper began. "Wait a second—"

Being mistaken for a noble vampyre is an honor, Maggot.

Orca tightened her grip on the boy's collar enough to make him choke.

Should we run? the boy asked. *Can you use your power?*

Not without revealing myself, Alastor said. *Give me time. I will find a solution.*

Alastor felt the boy's conflict, his lack of trust, but brushed it aside. He was cunning, the most cunning of all of his siblings, perhaps even his kind. Surely, if Alastor could do nothing else in this wretched time of his life, he could outfox three ogres.

"Splendid," Orca said, her smile growing. "If we hurry, we will make the fire."

"Anytime with that plan, Al," the boy whispered. "Aaaaany-time."

The cart swayed over the cobblestones as it took the long, winding path around the mountain. Rather than extend the journey by passing around the second step, the Boneyard, the road split in a way that Alastor did not remember. The new, paved path was as flat as those of the human world and he found himself hating it just so that he might have somewhere to place the anger burning inside him.

What was that step? Prosper asked, trying to crane his neck around. The ogres had thrust the boy into the back of a cagelike cart and chained his hands to its roof.

The Boneyard—the markets. You may buy all manner of things there, from clothing, to poison, to shades. The stands are built inside the bones of the many enemies who tried to launch assaults against the Horned Palace. Not one has made it past the Blood Gates, which separate this street from the next, the Scales, and their skeletons remained where they fell.

At least the Blood Gates were as deadly and gleaming as he remembered. Black metal joints reinforced the rocks and bone fragments that formed the wall itself. Sitting atop it were rows of teeth that had once belonged to his great-grandsire's favorite pet dragon, Squiggle. Alastor was comforted by the fact that they were still stained red with the blood of countless nemeses. At least he could rely on *some* things not to change.

Every time the cart swayed, Prosper's arm sockets stretched painfully. Alastor eagerly lapped up the magic the hurt created. It would not be long now. Being in his kingdom, with all the magic its inhabitants mined from the land

and air, would give the last push he needed to manifest a physical form.

The boy did not yet know to be afraid of that swiftly approaching moment. He was too caught up in his uneasiness at his surroundings, and could not stop looking over his shoulder at the two stone lizards hauling the cart. They were low to the ground and crawled forward at a steady clip, their bodies twisting and wriggling as they made the near-vertical climb with ease.

Are those dragons?

Alastor decided to humor the boy's curiosity. ***They are little more than distant cousins to the dragons that once ruled the sky. The last two great dragons killed each other in a fight to the death.***

The boy tested his restraints again, his gaze sliding over to the ogres huffing and puffing to keep up with the cart. Alastor found himself irritated by the boy's lack of awe. He began again, ***Ah, now see, to your right are the Black Dagger Mountains, renowned for their glowering beauty.***

The boy turned to stare out through the thick haze.

Alastor waited for the desolate peaks to reveal themselves through the thinning vapor.

And waited.

Not to be rude, Prosper began, *but is it supposed to look like* that?

All that the boy's inferior eyes could make out was a wall

of darkness that stretched from the sky to where the ground beyond the Flats ought to have been. It ringed around the city, and it was impossible to see through or past it. Rather than reflect the light of the realm back at them, it seemed to devour it.

It must be . . . That must be a new fortification.

The wagon's metal wheels creaked to a stop at the entrance to the Scales.

This level of the kingdom had always been for fiends who were neither noble nor lesser. It was made up almost entirely of minor vampyres, businessfiends who were flush with coins and magic, but could not claim nobility.

Many thought the name of the step referred to the scale-like roof tiles of the homes. Rather, it was a nod to the act of fiends attempting to *scale*—climb—the hierarchy of society like invading vines.

But the fiends emerging from the homes weren't vampyres. They were lycans, ogres, hobs, grims, squelchers, goblins, and even gutterboos. *Gutterboos*, who were meant to do nothing but eat whatever garbage fell into the streets.

Alastor watched in growing horror as these fiends retrieved brooms and buckets. A ghoul stretched up, lighting the streetlamps of the step with *matches* and *kindling*. All things that a proper fiend would have used magic for. Others began scrubbing down the sides of the homes and set out platters of misshapen, charred food they had clearly prepared themselves . . . to . . . *share*.

ALEXANDRA BRACKEN

The announcement banners hanging from the street-lamps rattled as one hour turned to the next. They unfurled with a snap, all revealing the first message. THE FLATS REMAIN CLOSED. They curled back up again, then unrolled with a new one: MAGIC RATIONING IN EFFECT UNTIL OTHERWISE STATED. WE SHALL RISE TOGETHER!

"Whoa," the boy murmured, watching as the banners curled once more. This time, when they unfurled, it was to display an etching. Alastor's sister, in her dark natural form, stood over the prone figure of a copper-haired child, the girl's neck beneath Pyra's blade-studded boot. YOUR QUEEN IS VICTORIOUS!

Each new reveal brought another image: the human brat strangled, strung up by her toes, stretched out across spikes. Boring, really. But the boy's silent fury coiled around Alastor, tighter and tighter, until the boy was shaking with the need to strike something.

She only means to distress you, Alastor said, taking pity on him. *Do not rise to her baiting.*

You fiends are really something, the boy said, the words brittle and laced with what tasted suspiciously like hatred. Alastor balked at the strength of it. The last etching revealed the boy's face—the nose too much like a knob and the ears looking more like wings—alongside the words IF YOU SEE THIS SNIVELING MORTAL, REPORT IT TO THE QUEEN'S GUARD!

Beside the wagon, the door of the Poisonmaker's Inn exploded open. The boy jumped as two thin fiends, roughly human-like, were thrown out into the swampy gutter. They spun around, crawling away on their hands and feet as two more ogres strode out after them. One of the ogres tossed a silver coin in the direction of a lycan wearing a tattered apron.

"No, pleassssse, you have the wrong fiendssss," one of them said, his voice wispy and faint. "Have merccccyyy."

These fiends had taken care to coat themselves with something that looked like mottled gray paint. What was left of it on their faces had been smeared away, revealing the bone-white skin that lay beneath it. Everything about their features was pointed, from the sharp tip of their chins to the cut of their mouths and their long bladelike ears. Their eyes were red beads glinting beneath their lids.

Vampyres.

Meantongue! Rotlash! Alastor sputtered, unable to help himself. *Do not let them treat you in such a manner! You are fiends of noble houses!*

"I am sssssssorry," the other said. "Sssssso ssssssorry!"

The boy raised a crusty brow. *You know them?*

We attended school together. Their families own the finest spidersilk mills and oversee the treasury. Yet they dress like peasants? Why, they've painted themselves—goblin silver!

It was exactly what the ogres had accused the boy of.

"H-have merccccccy," the ogre imitated, pretending to cower. The fiends walking around them did not stop to so much as dump their buckets of waste and soured beetled juice on the humiliated vampyres. They simply moved on to their next tasks.

Inside of Prosperity Redding, Alastor felt as if he were a feather blowing in the wind, never to find solid ground again.

One of the ogres stomped a foot down on Meantongue, ripping the black bonnet off his head. "As you've shown my kind mercy, spitting on us for centuries from your tower? Take a look around, *milord*. This may be the last glimpse you'll have of the kingdom."

He yanked the vampyre up, ignoring the fiend as it bared its needlelike teeth and hissed. Prosper turned to face straight ahead and tried not to flinch as the wagon rocked.

Look at them, Alastor fumed, *cowering like fleas beneath a thumb!*

The ogres clamped metal collars around the vampyres' necks, hooking them to the bars that made up the sides of the wagon.

Rotlash sniffled pitifully, chewing on his lower lip with a fang. "I'll have your hidessssss."

The ogres only laughed. One jabbed a meaty finger at Meantongue, who had gone all but boneless with terror. At the touch, the fiend jerked against his restraints, trying to turn. "Take him and ssssspare me! I will help you find the otherssss who hide!"

"Meantongue!" the other cried, kicking weakly at him. "You gorbellied, crook-plated measle!"

With one last look at the vampyres, the ogre breathed in deep, smiling as he said, "How delicious. I can already smell the smoke."

"Beast!" Rotlash was the one dressed in the puffy-sleeved shirt and billowy trousers, not the dress and bonnet. He snarled beneath his breath, "This was your brilliant plan to begin with. What do we do now, Meanie?"

"We should have escaped with the others while we had the chance," the other moaned quietly.

"But we might already be dead. No one knowssss where the fiendssss go when the Void clossssesss over them," Rotlash said miserably. "What sssssay you, fiend?"

The boy straightened, realizing Rotlash was speaking to him. But an unwelcome dread had moved through Alastor at the vampyre's words. *Ask what the Void is, Maggot.*

I can't. Then they'll know I don't belong here.

Well, Alastor thought begrudgingly, he couldn't say that the boy was not learning.

"Well?" Meantongue prompted, his ruby-red eyes narrowing.

Alastor was about to feed him a line when the boy opened his mouth and said, in a rush of panic and inspiration, "Meeep boop bedoop. Badadoom."

What in the four realms was that?! Al sputtered.

Part of my disguise, the boy said proudly, *so they don't recognize I'm human.*

Alastor did not know which group was more foolish, vampyres or humans.

Meantongue flicked a dismissive tongue at the boy and turned to Rotlash with a shudder. "The lassssst inssssult. We travel with a wretched ssssludgesssslug."

Alastor had his answer. Vampyres. Vampyres were the bigger nitwits.

"If only the Void had not come for the king," Meantongue continued. "He sssshould have ssssent a minion to collect the magic tax out in the ssssswamps. Then we would not be in thisssss possssition."

The boy froze, and, within him, Alastor did the same.

Interesting. So Pyra hadn't killed their father to steal his magic, as Alastor had assumed.

"The queen knowssss what causssssesss it, but sssshe is too late to ssssstop it, methinkssss," Rotlash said, sounding almost comforted by his next statement. "They ssssshall all die with ussss."

A big green fist slammed into the wagon's bars. "Oy! Shut your flapping maws!"

All of the wagon's occupants fell silent, save for the hissing breaths of the vampyres and the faint clank of the boy's chains as he tried to tug at them again. They seemed to notice it in the same moment—the small, pale flecks that appeared in the clouds of vapor drifting by them.

Ashes. The last traces of the vampyres who'd come before.

The street widened to accommodate Midnight Square and the quiet, almost disinterested-looking fiends who had gathered there. At the center of it, where there should have been a statue of Alastor's father, resided something far more fearful: a long, wooden pillar. Several metal chains and cuffs had been hammered into it, and now swayed, waiting for their next victims.

The boy's eyes drifted down over the platform that had been built around it. There seemed to be . . . It almost looked like . . .

The flat platform *was* formerly a white fence, the sort Alastor had seen in Salem. Beneath that was a mass of more wood: old doors, chairs, small tables, toys, even spoons. Hay poked out from the cracks between them, ready to serve as fuel for the fire. Rings of thorny branches had been placed around it like barbed wire.

Alastor had assumed the ogres meant magic fire, which incinerated those caught in it instantly. But no. They were to be executed not by magic or poison or blade, but with mortal fire. The sort that kept one alive long enough to feel the agonizing heat devouring them.

The very way the Reddings had killed the innocent servant girl. That night, the memory of it, crawled over Alastor, lancing him.

The flames.

The endless, bottomless black of the Inbetween, the

space between the realms, which became his home for three centuries as he slept.

Honor Redding's face.

The wagon groaned to a stop. Meantongue groaned, drawing his fingers across his face.

What's the plan, Al? the boy thought at him, his body giving a small tremor of fear.

I am thinking! Hush!

As the crowd around them grew, another ogre wearing the Queen's Guard uniform approached them. The female pounded the others on the back before leaning down to peer into the cart. "You know what you must do, leeches. Apologize for your abuse of magic, or face the fires."

What! The boy sucked in a sharp breath as Alastor all but screeched, *APOLOGIZE?!*

Are you telling me that all we have to do is apologize to avoid being burned to death? the boy asked. *And there are fiends that don't take that option?*

A true fiend never apologizes! Alastor sweltered in his hate.

"We ssssshall never apologizzzze to the likesss of you!" Rotlash hissed back.

Yes! Indeed, my friends, indeed! Never apologize, never surrender!

"Are you freaking kidding me?" the boy muttered. *"Seriously?"*

"Fine," the ogre said. "Then I'll make sure the fire burns slow, so our queen hears your pitiful cries from the heart of the city."

"Long may she rage," the other ogres answered solemnly.

Who gives a fig about their imposter queen! Alastor let his voice boom through the boy. *Can they not sense the magnificent being who is before them? I'll strangle them with their own intestines! The insolence of it all. Let me out, Maggot. Prosperity, heed me!*

Absolutely not.

The wagon's lock was removed, falling to the ground as heavily as an unconscious body. The ogres reached in through the bars to unlatch the cuffs and collars.

A sharp bark punctured the bored murmurings of the crowd. Prosper turned back just in time to see the ghoul and the howlers from the Flats shove their way up through the square.

The ghoul went right for the nearest ogre, pointing directly at the boy. Prosper's body locked with panic. The howlers snapped their fangs and flung drops of their poisonous saliva, barely restrained by the presence of the other ogres.

"No, Sinstar," the ogre said. "It's a leech—"

One of the ogres marched the boy forward toward the pyre. Prosper struggled against that crushing grip, trying to see what was happening with the ghoul. His heart slammed harder against the prison of his rib cage.

And all the while Alastor fumed. At his sister. At these

ogres. At every fiend surrounding them. The boy's mind was a hurricane of fear and half-formed plans as Rotlash was dragged up onto the pyre first, hissing and wailing. The sight was met with silence by the watching fiends.

Not even an excited chant from the spectators? Not even a murmur of pleasure at the sight? This would not stand!

"I apolo—" Prosper began, but Alastor could not stand it a moment longer. His voice exploded out of the boy. *"Hear me, ungrateful, folly-fallen, ratsbane subjects!"*

Satisfaction curled through him as Midnight Square went utterly silent. The ogres, the ghoul, the howlers—all turned toward the boy.

"It is I, Alastor, First Prince of the Realm, Master Collector of Souls, Commander of the First Battalion of Fiends, your Eternal Prince of Nightmares that Lurk in Every Dark Sleep."

The boy struggled against Alastor's grip. It was well worth the power it took to hold on just that small bit longer.

"You serve a pretender queen, one who has betrayed your kind by elevating you above your natural-born stations. Have no fear. I will restore the proper order to our realm."

Stop it! the boy begged. *They already want to kill us enough!*

The fiends began to shift, their gazes narrowing. Meantongue's mouth fell open, and his actual tongue unrolled with shock.

"Despite your most unjust treatment of your royal heir, I

strive to look on your repugnant faces with affection, my dear, rump-fed subjects. If you bow to me now and grovel to my liking, I shall consider sparing you when I reclaim the Black Throne. Those who attend to me and return to their duties will lose no claws as I seek retribution. Well, certainly no more than one. After all, every crime demands a punishment."

Alastor waited for the rapturous cheers, the shrieks of joy at the prospect of being freed from whatever mundane and magic-barren existence Pyra had forced them into.

Instead, the ghoul, Sinstar, pointed at Prosper and snarled into the silence, "I told you that was the human boy! Take him in the name of the queen!"

Well. That was certainly . . . This was . . . Alastor's thoughts seemed to dissolve like sand, just as the ogre banded his meaty arms around Prosper's chest.

You idiot! Prosper snarled. *You said you weren't going to do this! We were supposed to work together!*

The boy's feet kicked in the air as the ogre carried him forward.

Alastor, it seemed, had gotten his wish. The crowd hissed and chattered their teeth at him—not in excitement, or even relief at the arrival of their savior. In *hatred*. It churned around them like the thunderclouds of the human world, dark and seething.

They . . . the malefactor thought, stunned. They do not want me . . . ? *Me?*

Prosper managed to pivot and jab the ogre directly in

the eyes. They popped like ooze-filled balloons, splattering against his face.

"Gross!" Prosper cried, trying to fling the goop off his fingers. "Holy crap, I'm so sorry—"

The ogre howled in fury, dropping him. "It'll take me *weeks* to regrow those!"

Prosper slammed against the ground, crawling between legs and grabbing hands until he was under the nest of logs and broken wood that formed the pyre.

"I'll smoke you out, you mortal rat!" Sinstar said, snatching a lit torch from a stunned hob. "You won't get away this time!"

Prosper twisted around, his breath steaming in and out of him. The ghoul's arm stretched forward, the lengthening limb threading through the fiends between him and the pyre, holding the torch aloft like a burning needle.

Think, Alastor thought, trying to cobble together an escape for them. Use your power, just this once—

He felt it gathering in his center, ready to unleash itself on his ungrateful subjects. But in that trembling second before he could unleash its might, a wave of pure, crackling green magic exploded through the square, robbing the boy's sight of the others, and stealing that last bit of sense from both of them.

Stranger Danger

The light exploded over us like a star going supernova.

The pressure of the blast rang out in dizzying waves. Then, as quickly as it had arrived, the light was suddenly ripped away, and all that was left was total and complete darkness.

What is this? Some kind of curse? I demanded.

What does it matter? Run!

I crawled forward through the fencing, the broken furniture, wriggling through the pyre. A second too late, I realized that hiding under the incredibly flammable pile of junk was probably not my best idea.

"*The Void—it's the Void!*" a fiend shrieked.

"*My eyes—four of them are burning!*"

"By the realms!"

"The Void!"

Through the tangled knot of the pyre, I watched as paws, feet, and hooves fled. Somewhere behind me, there was the crack of wood as fiends stumbled into the pyre.

"It's not the Void!" one of the ogres yelled. "Calm yourself!"

And it wasn't. The air was already beginning to brighten as the streetlamps reappeared. The unnatural blanket of darkness was lifting.

Which meant my time to escape was running out.

I still had not found the edge of the pyre when I got my first whiff of smoke. Sinstar had lit the woodpile.

"The mortal! Catch the mortal!" Sinstar bellowed over the shouting. The howlers were pawing through the burning wood behind me, searching.

Finally, I squeezed between a headboard and Halloween sign, and found myself back out in the square. My hands slid through the street's grime. I swallowed a cry as a fiend's heeled boot smashed down on my outstretched fingers. The stones bruised my knees and scuffed my skin.

Keep going, Maggot! That alleyway, ahead—there's a ladder that leads up to the roof of the butcher's shop!

"Why," I breathed out between my clenched teeth, "would I *ever* listen to you again?"

Do you have any other choice at present?

A clawed hand swept past my face, shaving off a few strands of my bangs, and I darted right, knocking into the wheels of a cart. *Ugh! Fine.*

I staggered forward as quickly as my beat-up legs could take me.

"The prisoners—seize them!" an ogre shouted. "Watch out for the leeches' teeth!"

The alleyway Alastor had pointed out was a dozen feet away. Between its narrow, crooked opening and me, however, were crates full of screaming crimson rats and a small, wide-eyed female hob clutching a sign that offered said rats for a blackpenny or the equivalent sliver of magic.

I knew the exact moment the fiend spotted me. Her little snout lifted in indignation, dripping with a wad of blue snot.

I lifted a hand, pressing a finger to my lips in desperation. It was like I could see the scream building in her belly, rising up through her like smoke.

Another fiend tripped over my back, falling to the ground with a snarl. I kept going, and going, and going, as the first note of the hob's shriek split the air.

A hand landed on my collar and *yanked*—not back, or forward, but to the side. My eyes must still have been suffering from the explosion, because all I could make out in the easing darkness was a totally-black-garbed human-shaped creature.

The figure tugged at my shirt collar again, this time

hard enough to rip it, and waved me forward with their other hand.

Maggot, don't you dare—

The hob might have been a rat whisperer, but at that moment she didn't just yell for help—she *screeched*. "The human! He's getting away!"

No one heard her, or no one cared. The panic that had seized the fiends was starting to infect even me.

"My younglings! Where are they?"

"—can't stay here!"

"The *Void*! Great Ghoul, save us!"

If you looked past the snouts and the scales, all that was left was a very familiar, very human emotion: terror.

The dark figure was still waiting, their hand outstretched.

I stared at it, my heart hammering, Al shouting, **Run, fool!** over and over like a song caught on loop. I couldn't see the figure's face beneath the ski mask, but their gloves were sparkling with the last traces of magic. Still, I hesitated. After that show Alastor had put on, what fiend would actually *want* to help us?

I don't know why I reached out and took that hand. I felt reckless and wild, like I'd taken a running jump off a cliff in the hope that a strong breeze would catch me. But what I did know thanks to several *super*-awesome years of bullying at school was this: it would be a lot easier to potentially fight off a single fiend than several hundred of them.

We ran, shoving through the fiends as they emptied out

of the square through the many side streets that fed into it. I panted, breathing in lungful after lungful of vapor. I wondered if I would choke on it before we ever got away.

The dark figure seemed to know less about where to go than I did. Their shape bobbed in and out of the last of the panicked fiends, who were starting down one street only to quickly change their mind and try the next. Whatever was inside the black leather sack slung over the creature's shoulder rattled and clanked.

Alastor suddenly jolted in me as we passed an empty lot between tilted buildings. *Stop, Maggot—turn here! You may hide safely here for a time. The smell of the fertilized soil will mask your scent.*

My feet slid to a reluctant stop. I stepped up to the fence surrounding it, peering over the lethal spikes that topped it. All I could make out was a shed at the back of it, and dirt ground that was dimpled with shallow holes.

"Wait!" I called up to the figure in black. "We can hide here!"

The dark figure hesitated, then walked toward me with obvious reluctance, their shoulders slumped.

I pulled back the climbing vines and black flower buds that strangled the gate's latch, ripping them away where I could. But the hinges were so rusted over I wasn't sure a chain saw could get through them.

You've two hands and feet, yes? Climb!

I seized the top of the fence, carefully avoiding the spikes capping it. I tumbled over onto the other side. My savior didn't follow.

"Come on," I said. "You're the one who caused that big distraction, right? At least rest here for a few minutes so I can thank you."

The masked figure didn't respond, but did finally grip the top of the fence to haul themselves over it. They landed with a soft thud on the hard-packed dirt.

I turned around to survey the lot. Its small shed was made of the same stone bricks and roof tiles as the rest of the city, but its surface had been dulled by dust and soot from a nearby chimney. It didn't look like a fiend had occupied it in some time, but I couldn't see through the matted spiderwebbing that covered the windows to be sure.

The lizard-shaped doorknob refused to budge—I had to shoulder my way inside. The door burst open with a cloud of dust and splinters. I stumbled forward, waving my hand to clear my path of webs.

Inside, three of the four walls were lined with shelves, most containing the mummified remains of what might once have been toads and spiders.

The fourth wall had a built-in workbench, one stacked high with wire baskets and large lamps still fizzling with a few embers of magic. I tapped one of them, sparking a little more life back into it. The waves of heat it emitted instantly made me wish I hadn't. I leaned down to study the strangely familiar fragments in one of the baskets. Their white shell-like surfaces were shot through with crimson veins. A bad feeling churned in the pit of my stomach.

"Al . . . what is this place?" I asked.

It's where I used to breed my prizewinning blood vipers.

I closed my eyes, breathing in deeply through my nose. "I hate you *so* much."

It's been centuries since I used this nesting ground, Al said with a small sniff. *I suppose I was hoping that someone might have tended to it.*

Sorry, but I wasn't about to shed tears over monster snakes.

No matter. Once I am restored to my form and my rightful place in the kingdom, I shall name the runt of the first nest after you. It will bear that name for as long as its siblings refrain from eating it.

A faint snap drew my attention away from the malefactor and back to the doorway of the shed. The stranger hovered there, as if clinging to the last shadows it provided.

"Come in and shut the door," I said, taking a seat on the ground. "We might be here a little while."

Nothing.

"Come on, it's okay," I said. "I'm not going to do anything stupid. I just want to know who I'm thanking."

Silence.

Maybe it was another human lost Downstairs, one who'd forgotten how to speak human language?

Impossible. The realm's magic ensures we all hear one another speaking the same language.

They had been quiet for so long, I actually jumped when the stranger finally spoke. "I don't think you'll be thanking me in a second. . . ."

Wait. That voice.

Is it? Can it be?

My savior stepped away from the shed's door, pulling the ski mask off their face and hair. And then it wasn't just the voice that was familiar. It was the face. The glitter glasses.

It wasn't a savior.

It wasn't even a friend.

It was Nell.

Toil and Trouble

"Why are you here?" The words burst out of me.

"Why does it look like?" Nell asked, running her hand over her tight black curls where she'd gathered them into a bun at the nape of her neck. A few strands had already escaped. They bobbed as she tilted her head, giving me a narrow look. "Why are you covered in . . . *that*?"

We stared at each other.

"I'm . . . in disguise," I said. "Why do you even care?"

Her nose wrinkled. "Okay. Definitely had nothing to do with the outhouse I tracked you guys to. Definitely."

"If you knew, why did you even ask?" I muttered, crossing my arms over my chest. I squinted at her through the shadows. "And why are *you* dressed like a spy?"

That was the only way I could think of to describe what

she was wearing: head-to-toe black. Black jeans, black boots, black sweater, and creepy black ski mask. Nell was usually an explosion of color and pattern. Now she just seemed . . . muted.

"Did you decide to participate in Norton's art project?" I couldn't push back against the tide of anger flowing through me. "Let me guess, you're in a black mood after your dad's plans were foiled."

Nell straightened, crossing her own arms over her chest. "I was the one who helped you foil them, remember?"

"You're the reason Prue was taken—that we're even in this mess!"

Even as I said it, I knew it wasn't totally true. But the words just kept boiling over, and I couldn't stop seeing that last moment before the mirror had swallowed my sister whole.

Nell had thrown me her mother's grimoire, knowing it was enchanted so that it burned in the hands of a fiend. She *had* tried to turn the ogres and Pyra back. And she certainly hadn't finished the spell that would have taken Alastor's powers and left us both dead. But:

1. Nell had kept the real plan secret from me.

2. Nell had set up all the ingredients for the ritual.

3. Nell had pretended to be my friend.

"Me?" Nell snapped. "Your family is the one that started all this by going after the Bellegraves. Their *greed* is—"

"Oh, here we go again," I said. "Did you come all this way to have the same argument with me that we've already had five times? You know what? If that's the case, why don't you just *leave*. Go back to the human realm. No one wants you or needs you here."

"Oh yeah, I noticed how little you needed my help back there," Nell said, pushing her glasses up the bridge of her nose. "You'd be ashes in the wind without me."

No. I would have figured a way out of that mess. I was going to figure a way out of this bigger mess, too. "Just go."

"Fine!" she huffed. "I was getting bored with watching you almost get yourself killed. Good luck." Nell turned toward the door, only to spin back again. "I guess you don't even need that, considering all the lives your family destroyed to get a supernatural dose of it."

My breath steamed out of me. Did she really think I wasn't already torturing myself over what my family had done? What was it going to take for her to see that I wasn't like them—I never had been, and I never would be?

The truth was, Nell had never wanted to be my friend. She had never really believed in me.

I'd show her, too.

Delicious. Alastor sighed happily as he watched Nell go. ***The beats of history never fail to repeat. You both think your-selves above it, and yet you are caught in the same minuet as all the Reddings and Bellegraves who came before you.***

That was . . .

I stilled. That couldn't be true. We were fighting because we had a valid, *epic betrayal* kind of reason to fight. Nell and her father had tricked me, lying to my face over and over again about how they were my family and how they were going to help me.

Come on, she tried to help you escape in Salem, a small voice whispered in my mind, *before Prue came, before you were hurt, before she ever summoned Pyra. . . .*

I shook my head, but once the memory was there, it took root.

Maybe you should go, Nell had said. *Leave. Go back to your family.*

And if I had, the story might have ended in Redhood. My family would have finished the spell to remove Alastor from my body and destroy him, and Prue would be at home, safe. The thought made me miss my parents and our house so much that my chest actually hurt with it.

What are you doing? I asked myself.

What were *we* doing? Nell and I weren't fiends. We were better than that—we had the capability to forgive. Alastor was always going on about how weak human hearts were, how easily moldable they were to all his careful manipulations and contortions. But that same quality was the very reason the past didn't have to haunt us.

Nell *had* helped her father with his plan, but only because she'd been told that doing so would bring her mom back to life. And let's be honest, I could have been *a lot* more careful in vetting their identities and accepting their word.

Dad always said that you couldn't tell who a person was

by their words alone, you had to look at their actions for what was really in their heart. Here was a perfect example. Nell had come here to help me, and now I was sending her away because she hurt my feelings?

I rushed out of the shed, hoping I could still catch her before she disappeared into Downstairs's darkness. "Wait—!"

My feet slid to a stop.

Nell was leaning against the side of the shed, her eyes screwed shut. Her throat bobbed with each hard swallow.

She didn't leave, I thought, relief bursting through me. There was still a chance to fix this. . . .

Oh, la-di-da and hurrah, Alastor said, sounding bored. *Try not to make this disgustingly sentimental, will you?*

Nell opened her eyes, and I saw my own misery reflected back at me in them. Her lips parted with something unspoken, only to close again. Over and over, she did the same thing—searching for the right words, then changing her mind.

"Are you sorry?" I asked her. The vapor moved silently over the fence, spreading its long pale fingers along the ground. Somewhere above us, a crow began to cackle. "Are you sorry for what you did, or do you just feel sorry for me?"

Nell's face was a collage of pain, even as she tried to keep it neutral. I knew exactly how I would draw it—the deepened parenthesis around her mouth, the wrinkle between her brows, the way her eyes skimmed back and forth across the ground.

"You have to know . . ." she began, her voice unusually

soft. "I didn't know that it would hurt you, and I didn't know he had offered Pyra our lives if we failed. He—Henry—he told me that you would be happy to have the fiend out, and then we could go back to normal. He *also* told me that the malefactor could bring Mom back."

The deal that had staked her life, and her father's life, on helping Pyra get Alastor's powers. In exchange, Pyra would grant them all the fortune and luck that the Reddings had enjoyed for centuries. But Alastor's sister had lied about her ability to return the mother that Nell had known; her shade would have come back darker, twisted.

My chest squeezed tight, making it hard to get my next words out. "Then why keep it secret? You didn't have to sneak around or pretend to like me. My family may have the moral compass of a rabid, starving zombie, but they're at least honest about how much they hate me."

Finally, there was a flare in her eyes—*that* was the Nell I knew. "We had to keep it secret. If Alastor knew what we were planning, he would have done anything and everything to stop it. And when we found out that he was taking your body for joyrides at night, that only proved to me that Henry was right."

Accept her help, Maggot. Her repulsive sparkle dust and flimsy spells may be enough to distract the other fiends long enough for us to escape. A witch is a rare catch.

Could you stop thinking about yourself for one *second? Just one. Try it.*

Done. Done again. And again. Shall I continue this game? There was another second—

I tuned him out. Nell must have thought my dark look was meant for her, because she hugged her arms closer to her body and looked away again. "I've never hated you. I don't know what else to say except that I'm sorry. And I don't know how to make it up to you, except helping you get your sister back and doing whatever I can to break the deals our families made with the malefactors. There has to be *some* way to do it. I know you won't be my friend again, but . . . we could at least work together to stop Pyra?"

Relief coursed through me.

"Yeah," I said with a smile. "I'd like that."

*You will **never** succeed,* Alastor hissed. ***Only a malefactor can break a malefactor contract. It's our unique power, along with opening mirror portals—wait a dark, forsaken moment . . . how** did the witchling arrive Downstairs?*

I repeated the question to Nell. She slipped the backpack off her shoulder and rummaged through it until she found a small black leather book, the title in gold foil. *Toil and Trouble: A Witch's Guide to Navigating Mischief and Mayhem, second edition,* by B. Z. Elderflower.

B. Z. Elderflower . . . why did that name sound familiar?

Nell thumbed through the worn pages until she found one she'd marked. "'The knowledge of the exact spell is, obviously, forbidden, but a witch may use her powers to guide a fiend through their interlinked mirror passages and lead them directly to her—'"

Nell glanced up, her expression heavy with guilt. "That's what I did back at the school. My— Henry found a record of the spell for me to use. . . . Okay, here it is. 'It is true that a witch cannot open or close a mirror portal, as a wicked, sniveling malefactor can. However, thanks to their titanic ignorance'—I love her writing, don't you?"

"Very evocative," I agreed, feeling Alastor seethe inside my mind.

"'Thanks to their titanic ignorance,'" Nell continued, reading on, "'they do not know that a witch has two easy work-arounds. A witch cannot open a portal, but she may cast a simple looping spell to repeat any curse that a malefactor has worked, including opening a passage. And, of course, open portals are easily banished to the Inbetween with the following incantation'—basically, by the time I got away from Henry and went for my emergency pack in my locker, the portal had already shut. Then I had to wait for the firefighters to clear out long enough to do the looping spell. It's the only reason I fell so far behind you. And then I just used a minor tracking spell to figure out where you were."

A pox on all witches, Alastor said. ***One with rancid boils.***

"Thanks again for that," I said, then eyed her pack. "Your emergency pack doesn't happen to have water or any food to eat, does it? Because guess who didn't even think about that stuff before he dove headfirst through a magic portal into a realm of demons?"

Nell led us back into the shed, where she set a granola bar and a water bottle on the workbench for me and pointed to them in silent command.

"We're going to have to ration the water," she told me. "I didn't realize they didn't have a supply of it down here."

"'Kay," I said around a mouthful of oats and chocolate. "But why did you think you'd need an emergency pack in the first place?"

"In case the Supreme Coven—" Nell cut herself off. "In case of *just in case*, I guess."

She unlatched the backpack's other buckles to reveal more ziplock bags of food and various evil-looking vials of liquid and bottles of herbs. Once again, I felt deeply stupid for rushing into Downstairs without any supplies, let alone a change of clothes.

As she finished rearranging the contents of her bag, Nell cast a look out of the shed's grimy window. The green light filtering through it deepened the color of her dark skin and reflected off the lenses of her glasses. It momentarily hid her eyes.

I studied her as I finished the last bite of the granola bar. For most of my life, Prue had been my only friend. There were other kids that I saw at summer camp, but I always knew they were only being nice to me because their parents had told them to, or because of my last name. That had all changed a few weeks ago, when I met Nell.

"Friends tell each other the truth," I said. "If this is going to work, we can't keep secrets. I'm not going to lie; you're definitely the more useful half of this partnership, and the old Prosper probably would have just slowed you down. But I really do believe we can rescue Prue and figure out a way to break our contracts together."

"What was wrong with the 'old Prosper'?" Nell looked confused.

"You really have to ask that?" I said, mentally tabulating all the times she'd had to save me in Salem. That Prosper had been mostly useless, and this one was determined to save the people he loved—no matter what dangers and poisonous shadows Downstairs threw at him. "So I think we should try the friend thing again." I held out my hand. "I'm Prosper. It's nice to re-meet you."

"Nell Bishop." A smile bloomed across her face as her hand gripped mine hard and gave it a firm shake.

Not Bellegrave. *Bishop.*

How precious. I might just vomit.

"Fiends have their true names, right? Well, Nell Bishop is *my* true name," she declared. "It's the only one that will ever have power over me. I'm not going to let three centuries of squabbling families ruin our lives. It's like Shakespeare said: *It is not in the stars to hold our destiny but in ourselves.*"

"We'll just rewrite a few destinies, no big deal," I said. "But first we have to figure out where Pyra is keeping Prue.

The obvious place—the old palace—doesn't seem to exist anymore. Actually, a lot seems to have changed from what Alastor remembers, so don't expect too much from him on this disturbing adventure."

"I'm not surprised. By the way—" Nell leaned in close, peering into my eyes. "You are the most narcissistic, delusional little worm to have ever wriggled your way through life. That speech you gave—*seriously?*"

I have no notion of what she might be referring to, Al said primly. *I would say, however, the witchling would know a thing about worms, being descended from them.*

"He definitely blew what little cover we might have had," I said. "I hope you've got more of that green explosive stuff. Between that thing they're calling the Void and the fiends, I think we're going to need it."

She cringed. "Aaaactually, I used the last of it just now. I accidentally dropped the bottle, hence the big *boom*."

More like a big *yikes*.

"That's okay," I said. "You've got other magic up your sleeve, right?"

This time Nell let out a long sigh, taking the backpack from my hands. "There's something else you need to know. Do you remember how I told you that a witch's power comes from the moon? That it replenishes our innate magic each night?"

I nodded. "Yeah, what about it?"

"Did you happen to notice that there's no moon here?" she asked.

Every thought screeched to a halt in my brain. I moved to the window, trying to clear enough of the cobwebs away to see the sky again. I'd just assumed the vapor was covering it, or that it moved through phases, like it did back home. But there was, indeed, no moon.

There's no sun, either, Alastor said happily. *Downstairs is a cocoon of everlasting darkness.*

Nell hugged the book to her chest as I looked to her. She was usually the one leading the charge on our plans, and while she'd definitely had moments of uncertainty and doubt in Salem, I'd never seen her look like *this.* Anxious. Unsure. "I know I'll be able to use *some* power, but I don't know how long it'll last before it runs out. It . . . might not be enough."

"Some is better than none," I said, trying to reassure her. I shoved aside the small flutter of worry in my stomach. "It just means we'll have to hurry, and that's fine with me. I don't want to be here a second longer than we have to be."

The scenes on the orange banners kept replaying in my mind. Prue crushed, Prue tortured, Prue dead.

"The little worm really doesn't have any idea of where to look?" Nell asked.

I am never out of ideas, some are merely slower to arrive than others. In fact, I was just about to suggest we go down to the second step, the Boneyard. There, we shall be able to procure more information about the whereabouts of your sister, as well as this Void.

"Have you heard of a place called the Boneyard?" I

asked. "Is there any information about it in your book?"

"Goody Elderflower made secret trips Downstairs to gather information—she's *so* amazing, you don't even know," Nell said, flipping through the chapters again. "There has to be *something* on it. . . ."

The page-turning got a little more frantic with each passing chapter. Nell clutched the book like it was a lifeline in a dark tide. Finally, she looked up and bit her lip. Guess that was a no, then.

It's the step of markets, as I told you before, Alastor said impatiently. *Will the witchling have to check every last detail against that infernal tome of hers? Did she leave her daring behind in the human realm along with her sense?*

Like you're a portrait of bravery, I said. *I've met pigeons braver than you.*

Of course you have, Alastor said. *Scavenger pigeons will pluck the eyes out of a fiend that wanders into their path—*

I shook my head, but the harder I tried to pry Alastor's observation out of my mind like a splinter, the deeper it seemed to sink in. I didn't blame Nell for having some nerves; I had to imagine if Downstairs was dangerous for a human, it would be doubly so for a witch if she were to get caught.

Well, Alastor said, his voice curling through my mind like silk. *It looks as though you'll just have to trust me.*

Yeah. Because he'd given me so many reasons to.

Squiggle and Scum

The Market of Neverwoe had once lived as a legend in Alastor's young mind.

When he had been as small as a cat's whisker, and still in the care of the spider nurses and his nannyhob, he had marveled at the sight of the shining, silver tent from the safety of his web cradle. Time and time again, it had attracted his attention like a stray silver coin at the bottom of a pail of beetled juice.

From the nursery tower in the Horned Palace, all those centuries ago, Alastor, perched on a chest he had dragged over to the window, watched other fiends scurry in and out of the tent. Other markets, such as the Venom Market, the Meats Market, and even the Silk Shops, had either constructed their stands outdoors using whatever bones were available, or had smaller, less grand tents. The Market of Neverwoe was the only one to grow with each passing year, until, finally, its proprietors were able to purchase the best bone lot of all.

That had only driven Alastor mad with curiosity: What could be so marvelous to turn such a profit? The tent's lush fabric kept eyes in the towers and palace from seeing its wares, inviting them to guess what was sold there, to come down to the Boneyard and see it for themselves.

"Highborns do not barter," his nannyhob had scolded, pulling him down from the window ledge. "If thou needs goods, I shall buy them, oh yes, Bonesitter shall."

At night, he'd dreamed of the mounds of gemstones that would surely be inside, as big as skulls. Bawdy shows that mocked his cold-blooded father for being unable to take back the territory of the southern rim from Gotwart, High Lady of the Bridge Trolls. Perhaps there would also be portraits of his fierce, newly departed mother, who had been the kingdom's midnight flame—as beautiful as she was terrible. Cursed weapons that lived and had to be fed a steady diet of blood. So very many possibilities.

But the truth of the market had been so much more delicious than anything he had imagined. Alastor could hardly wait to visit it again.

If it still exists . . . Oh, how he loathed this new, doubting voice in his head. It was coming to resemble a human's conscience, which was as useless as it was unwelcome.

In the past, the Market of Neverwoe had been safe from the lesser fiends who now seemed to run Downstairs—they had not been allowed to go into the human world to collect magic, which served as the price of admission. If his sister had not crushed Neverwoe with her ridiculous magic "rationing," he had no doubt he would find it at least somewhat changed.

And, as Alastor was learning, the only thing he loathed more than that unhelpful voice was change.

But . . . first things first. They needed to pay their entry fee.

Does the witchling have an empty jar or vial in her odious pack?

Prosper repeated the question. The witchling cast a suspicious look his way. "Of course not. I wouldn't bring a random empty jar when I could be bringing potions, salves, or elixirs."

If Alastor had had eyes, he might have rolled them. *Ask her if she brought protective salt.*

The boy, with growing irritation at playing messenger, did. Nell drew her stolen cloak around her tighter, crossing her arms. "Yeah. So what?"

Salt only harms hags, those leeches. It does nothing to the rest of us. We only spread that rumor because salt is so difficult to come by Downstairs and it truly brings out the tangy essence of swamp snails. It's far easier to find in the human realm when it's thrown at you.

The boy sighed as he watched the witchling's face transform with outrage. She pulled the book out of her cloak pocket—no doubt to find the perfect counterargument.

We don't have time for that. Just toss the salt and take the jar in your hand.

The witchling had brought enough salt with her to prune every swamp snail in the realm twice over. She looked positively hateful as she poured it out onto the cobblestones. It gathered in a small pile at her feet, immediately attracting the attention of a few blood rats.

"Do I even want to know what you're going to have me do with this?" the boy asked, sounding pained.

All I require of you is to hold still and not drop it. See if your clumsy limbs can manage that much.

Long ago, in perhaps the only show of cleverness in his cursed existence, Alastor's brother Bune had exchanged a private mirror portal with Neverwoe's Masters for free admission for all eternity. Alastor wished he had thought of the deal first so that he might take advantage of it now. However, having learned his lesson from the pyre, he thought it wiser to remain hidden inside the boy until he was good and truly ready to manifest a physical form.

This was the only way to pay the price, he told himself. A witch simply couldn't extract threads of her magic to be used by others; it was too much a part of her. A fiend, however, merely collected, stored, and used the magic generated from all of those most delightful human emotions: fear, hate, anger.

Reluctantly, Alastor coaxed out the last bit of magic he'd generated with the boy's new contract. The jar warmed with it, proofing the mortal glass to hold the wisps of power that now curled around the boy's arm. The sight made him miss his old lantern that accompanied him on every trip to the human realm.

In shock, the boy nearly dropped it, forcing the witch to dive forward and catch it mere inches from shattering on the stone. Both of them released the breath they'd held in, staring at each other.

Take care, Maggot! Alastor snapped. *I haven't much more left to spare. This ought to be enough to buy us at least an hour's time inside the tent.*

The boy and witch hung back, curling themselves around the edge of an alleyway as a pack of lycans ran by, heading in the opposite direction. There had been an abundance of discarded cloaks and cone hats left in the abandoned Midnight Square after the fright the witch had given them. Both humans had chosen thick ones and were sweating beneath their deep hoods. Alastor only hoped the stench of goblin would be enough to cover their mortal reek.

"Are we going to need more than an hour?" the boy whispered.

It will have to be enough. Now, onward, Maggot, if you dare. Neverwoe awaits.

Alastor guided the human and witchling down a series of stairwells cut into the side of the mountain, all connecting the Scales to the Boneyard. Knowing that Pyra most likely had patrols of her Queen's Guard searching for them along with the tracker ghoul Sinstar, he kept them to the ancient, crumbling paths that had fallen out of favor. All the while he fought the urge to take over the boy's body again and walk him faster.

In a stroke of luck, the secret doorway he'd cut into the stones of the Blood Gates was still there, and opened with only one running charge from the boy's thin shoulder.

"Is that . . . really a market?" Nell whispered, leaning over the stairs. The vapors cleared, granting them a clear view of the Boneyard.

"Whoa," was all the boy's brain could muster.

Indeed. It is a thing of beauty, is it not?

"I think the word you're looking for is actually *morbid*."

Most of the bones had gone toward constructing the frames of the merchant stands. Femurs made the most stable supports, but the occasional skull added a dash of whimsy, in Alastor's opinion. The oldest markets, such as the crimson widows' Venom Market, had claimed the best and largest skeletons. The proprietors draped elaborate fabrics over the rib cages and had built their tables and shelves inside what once had been gargantuan enemies—troll war boars, a few now-extinct giants, and griffins.

The humans kept to the edge of the street closest to the mountain, running behind the empty stands with their CLOSED UNTIL MAGIC RETURNS signs.

Cowards! Running from a profit because of whatever this Void enemy was? Alastor could no more understand that than the boy's love of polishing his flat, useless teeth.

Prosper turned, his attention caught by a movement to their right. As Alastor had expected, the Venom Market was still open; one of the widows was out winding through the cobblestones, taking in the sight of the empty stalls herself.

The crimson widows were tough beasties who feared no fiend. They each had the body of a snake and the arms and head of a human woman, the result of some ancient curse. No one lingered long in their presence out of fear for their lives, or of catching the affliction. The long crimson veils they wore over their faces were to shield other fiends from their deadly gazes, which could stop a beating heart with a single look.

Alastor noticed something else peculiar: this widow wore a small badge pinned to a crown placed over her veil. It was a small portrait of his sister in her true form—a family order, given only to those most valued, most loved fiends.

And his sister gave them to the *widows*? She had accepted them, these twisted creatures, in such a proud and public way?

Now he well and truly felt as if he were trapped in a nightmare. One he was unsure that he would ever wake from.

Eyes ahead, Maggot, he managed to say. *Unless you wish to be crushed like one.*

The boy swallowed and, mercifully, did as he was told. The widow continued on to the massive stall she shared with the others of her kind, draped in their signature red velvet, and the humans continued on past the curve of the mountain, where Neverwoe's silver tent awaited them.

Prosper and the witchling froze as it finally came into view. Alastor wished again he had his own form, just so he could relish their expressions. Instead, he had to settle for sipping on the boy's shock as it poured through him.

"Those are . . ." Prosper breathed out.

They are.

Two dragon skulls, both the size of buildings and painted silver, stared back at them from dark, eyeless sockets. Their mouths were open as if with their final death screeches, though, alas, their teeth had long ago been removed to spike the top of the Blood Gates. The skulls remained as entrances to the Market of Neverwoe, but a wise fiend knew that going through the jaws on the right, belonging to Scum, would result in getting a bucket of slime dumped on your head.

That is Squiggle and Scum. My great-grandsire's pets and the last two of the great dragons. The brother and sister broke free from their pens and dueled for seven days and nights in the sky before finally killing one another and crashing back to the ground—carving out a slice of the mountain on impact, I might add. Their rotting corpses intertwined forevermore. Siblings: you cannot abide them in life, nor avoid them in death, it seems.

The boy tentatively poked the bone, retracting his hand as if scalded by it.

"It looks like we came at the right time," Nell said, nodding to a sign resting between the two heads. ONE FINAL DAY OF MISCHIEF BEFORE THE CURTAIN FALLS AND THE MAGIC IS GONE! COME ONE, COME ALL, AND LEAVE YOUR WORRIES TO THE VOID . . . IF YOU DARE!

"What are we looking for?" Prosper asked.

A fiend called the Scholar. He keeps a booth toward the end of the market, buying and selling information.

"We don't have anything to pay for that information with," Prosper said, as if Alastor were not already perfectly aware of this.

Of course we do. The transactions are on information alone, a secret for a secret. One of his many spies will have told him where Pyra is holding your sister. And, Maggot?

"Yeah?"

Don't get distracted by the marvels inside. You will see many things that will stun and amaze you. Try not to embarrass yourself by losing all semblance of composure.

"Okay," Prosper said, turning back toward Squiggle's entrance. "Now you at least have me curious."

They passed through the opening on the left. Walking down what had once been the throat of the dragon, they finally arrived at a shimmering curtain. Alastor relaxed as the sound of muffled music filled the boy's ears, but he was surprised, very much so, when the boy's mind lit up with recognition at the tune.

"Do you hear that song . . . ?" the witchling whispered, searching for the boy in the dark. "It sounds so much like—"

A long hand stretched out between the flaps of the curtain. Its skin was the color of bruised apples, red and splotched with yellowing browns. All of its long nails had grown around themselves in spirals, hardened by the centuries into something that might rival stone.

Go on, Alastor urged the boy. *Time is short, and we cannot delay. The market will not stay open for the eternity it'll take for you to rediscover your nerve.*

The palm was turned up, waiting. When Prosper did not approach quickly enough, it began to wave him forward, one finger curling at a time.

I hope you're right about this, he thought at Alastor.

I am always right, Alastor said. *There are only degrees of how correct I am.*

Gingerly, as if afraid they might cut his pale skin like razors, the boy reached between the nails and placed the bottled magic inside. Closer now, Alastor could see that the fiend had painted its claws. Each one bore a different word, or a small cluster of stars. *Beware, dreamers, lest you fall asleep.*

The fiend yanked its closed fist back inside the darkness. The witch jumped as the curtain swung shut again.

The boy opened his mouth, most likely to say something foolish. Before he could, the same fiend reached back out through the tent, pushing the fabric aside.

Satisfied with the offering, he crooked a finger and bade them to enter.

The Market of Neverwoe

The fabric swept back into place behind them, bathing them in the chamber's shadows.

The witchling looked for the fiend who had let them inside. The simple fact was that mortals, whether mere humans or witches, were not used to parsing the darkness, looking for the shadows that lurked inside of shadows.

"What now?" Prosper asked.

A metal box suddenly appeared before them, floating on an iridescent cloud of magic. Its heavy lid creaked open, revealing two silver bracelets inside.

The boy's heart leaped painfully as a bodiless voice said, "Put one on. These are your tickets to enter."

Both humans did as asked; only the witch actually bothered to investigate hers before obediently sliding it on.

Prosper gasped as the metal shrank around his wrist, glowing. Nell sniffed at hers.

"It's enchanted," she confirmed.

Prosper held up his arm. "You think?"

It wasn't until the witch reluctantly put her bracelet on that the same voice warned, "You have paid for an hour's time in Neverwoe. Stay longer, and the bracelet will tighten . . . and tighten . . . until you leave with one less body part than you arrived with." The voice sped up as it added, "Standard terms and operating procedures apply. You will be charged for any cleaning that must be done, including mopping of blood, sweeping of feathers, and the tracking down of stray fingers. Please give verbal confirmation that you understand these terms."

"I do," the boy said.

"I do," the witch said, eyeing the bracelet with deep suspicion.

"Marvelous! Then relax, shed your worries and woes, and prepare for the adventure of an eternal lifetime!"

All at once new, unfamiliar strains of music spun up from nowhere and everywhere, the haunting voices of shades rising from the darkness, along with the rather bored-looking shades themselves.

> *"It's a realm of slaughter,*
> *A realm of fears.*
> *It's a realm of terror*

And a realm of jeers.
Come, leave your cares,
But humans beware!
It's a fiend's realm after all!
It's a fiend's realm after all!"

"Wait," Prosper began. "They totally ripped off—"

"Where did they even hear this song?" Nell pressed. "And *how*?"

You know this song? Alastor asked. It was a new addition to Neverwoe, surely, but he found it highly unlikely that the two mortals had encountered such an original, creative tune.

The changes, however, did not end there.

Lights flashed on around them, momentarily blinding the boy with their spiraling prism. The curtain on the other side of the chamber fell, revealing a tunnel of more spinning lights. The walls themselves curved and turned over the platform, which, as the human stepped onto it, began to move forward on its own.

Alastor supposed that in the three-hundred-odd years that he'd been away, the Masters had made *some* improvements to the market, but this seemed a bit . . . much?

He, through the boy's eyes, watched as the silhouetted images of snakes, scorpions, and wraiths spilled over the top of the tunnel. They were so distracted that no one, not even the witch, noticed when a Master stepped out of a shadow pocket and entered the tunnel alongside them.

"Welcome, boos and ghouls!" he crowed.

The witch jumped again, reaching for the pack hidden beneath her cloak. The boy let out a small shout of surprise, and though he would deny it to his own future grave, Alastor did as well.

What—who *is that?* the boy asked.

A Master, Alastor answered, feeling generous now that they were back in a place he loved so well. *A cheerful race of tricksters. They usually remain invisible, save when needed.*

Are they going to try to eat me if they find out I'm human?

As if eating was the worst of what they might do to him. *Of course not. They are businessfiends. They would harvest your organs and bones first to be sold here.*

The Masters seemed to have simply appeared one day; they were nearly human in form, but the quality of their skin, shrunken tight against their muscles and bones, was like worn lizard leather. Big eyes stared out from their signature wild bushes of white hair. The clouds of it wrapped around from the top of their heads down over the entire lower half of their faces.

"Um, hi?" the boy whispered.

The Master floated beside them, his legs tucked up beneath him and his back hunched. He held out a hand with claws so long, they curled into themselves.

"You are on a journey of ghastly wonder, to a place of no troubles, no worries, and yes, no woe!" the Master rasped. "Your every wish shall be brought to life for one day more!

Come, lose yourself in the depths of delight before our magic is taken by the queen. There are no limits to your fun, only a few simple rules we ask you to abide by—"

Another Master opened a shadow pocket and stuck his head out to say, "Mind the rules, mind your manners."

"No pushing," said another Master, this one female.

"And absolutely *no* fighting," added a third, sticking only a wagging finger out of his pocket.

"They're playing with interdimensional travel," Nell whispered to the boy, sounding awed. "They're slicing open and mending the fabric of time and space to move around quickly."

"Wares will be paid for in blood, trade, magic, or coin," said the first. "And at time of purchase."

"And, our fine fiends, if you've got the notion to thieve . . . lose it now, or feel the deadly sting of the magic we have put in place to protect the merchandise," said another, keeping half of her form in and half of her form out of the pocket.

"All sales are as final as the grave, and there are no refunds for fangs, limbs, or lunches lost on the rides," said the first Master sweetly, reopening a shadow pocket. Thanks to the witch's comment, Alastor wondered, for the first time, how it was that the Masters could play with opening and closing pockets the way a witch might banish something to the Inbetween.

Curious, that.

"Keep all paws, claws, and limbs inside the rides at all times," the female said, slipping back inside her own pocket. "Ignore these instructions and you will find yourself in dire peril."

Prosper's bracelet heated, activating as their bodiless voices declared, *"Your hour begins . . . now."*

At least one part of the entrance to Neverwoe was the same: the ground suddenly dropped out from beneath them. The boy hit the bone slide with a hard *"Oopf!"* and was unable to catch his breath as it spun him around and around and around, the witch following close behind with a loud shriek.

When the bodies of the dragons had crash-landed onto the mountain, they'd destroyed a whole section of the second step, creating a sort of half street between the Flats and the Boneyard.

The boy soared off the end of the slide, landing on a strategically placed cushion. Three Masters appeared out of the air, two to lift him onto his feet, one to brush the dust off his cloak. The boy gripped his hood, struggling to keep it up, even as a Master tried to peer under it.

"Don't be shy," the Master said. "We are all fiends here!"

The boy's mouth opened, but no sound came out. Alastor could feel some realization dawning in the boy's mind as he studied the Master, and neither he, nor, apparently, the Master liked it. The fiend released him and spun away dramatically, diving into a shadow pocket.

The witchling managed to land with far more grace, batting away the hands that tried to help her.

"Are you okay?" Prosper whispered, steadying her as she found her footing.

The witchling nodded. "Can we just get this over with? This looks like a fiend's dream, which means it's a nightmare to us."

From where they stood at the entrance, it was already apparent that this was no longer the market to which Alastor had once lost thousands of hours exploring. It had expanded, like a pup to a full-grown wolf, acquiring new teeth and a higher-quality coat. The explosion of trilling, tinkling sounds and colors around them was an assault on the senses and made those simple stalls of curiosities and fun Alastor remembered feel almost quaint in comparison.

The Masters had more visitors, which meant, of course, more magic, which meant, again of course, that they could simply do *more*. They could push the limits of imagination and find distractions to hook fiends again and again until they were addicted to the sensations. That was the point of Neverwoe—to find ceaseless wonders and amusements until, finally, your paid time ran out.

The changes to the market made him feel somewhat uneasy, but Alastor was pleased to see that there were several hundred fiends dashing around, and more were entering behind them. At least *some* fiends were eager to leave behind the problems of Pyra's rule and whatever this Void was. *That* was how fiends were meant to act. Not acceptance, but avoidance, until whatever problem they faced sorted itself out.

This is . . . quite different than I recall, Alastor admitted. It was so very . . . bright. *Loud.* A pack of lycans stood on a platform hanging from the ridge of Scum's spine, howling out a tune, plucking at a battered violin made of troll intestines and playing a wheezing accordion crafted from the lungs of infant war boars. The fiends milling around them cheered as another song started up.

One of the Masters appeared at the top of an enormous vat of whirling, sparkling magic nearby. She took the visitors' bottle and poured in their admission fee. Just that bit was enough to make the strands of magic-powered lights twinkle and for the vat to spit out iridescent bubbles. They drifted toward the two separate corridors, two different avenues of entertainment.

Venturing into what had once been Squiggle's belly, now draped with odd emerald-and-black-striped silk, would lead a fiend into an array of diverting amusements. Attractions that allowed you to magically shape your enemy out of wax and rearrange their parts, fairy-slingshot competitions with an array of prizes to be had, stone-lizard races, ooze pits and slides, dunking for heart fruit in giggle juice—that one was rather tricky business, as you had to snatch a pulpy fruit between your teeth before dissolving into unrelenting fits of cackles thanks to the liquid.

There were signs for new attractions as well. The boy

leaned toward that corridor, eyes widening again as he and Alastor both glimpsed what was inside. There was an enormous bone loop, on which baskets full of fiends were rising and circling around and around at a quick clip. Another contraption allowed fiends to be strapped into fake iron wings and flung around on chains, as if they were flying. They soared above Neverwoe, shrieking, bobbing, diving. Another sign promised a booth in which you could walk inside of your own dreams or visit with a long-dead ancestor.

The bright new paint, the striped tents, the strings upon strings of magic lights where there once had been fairies stuck inside glass orbs—it was quite a bit more flash than Alastor recalled. In fact, the old sign reading THE MARKET OF NEVERWOE had been changed to read THE NEVERWOE KUNEVIL!

"Kunevil," the boy read. "Like *carnival*?"

The sign clearly reads "kunevil," Maggot. I realize some things are beyond mortal comprehension, but do try to keep up. Don't scorn the Masters for their genius.

"This is all very *familiar*," the witchling said, glancing toward Prosper. "Isn't it?"

"That's one word for it," he said. "*Rip-off* is another."

Rip-off *is two words, you abominable, crusty thumb. Will you please just take the path to the right? That's where most of the market stalls were, and where we will find the Scholar if he is still here.*

Before the boy could take another step, a roar of vapor-tinged air and sound whipped over their heads. Small metal wagons raced along a track of bone Alastor hadn't noticed before, picking up speed as their pathway dipped. The fiends riding it screeched in delight as they passed by.

Hey, Al, the boy began. *What did you say happened to those humans who accidentally found themselves Downstairs?*

Don't bore me with irrelevant questions. One was eaten— *Not that one. The other ones.*

They were . . . Alastor reached back through his long memory, trying to locate the humans in question. When nothing came up, he fumbled for a reasonable reply. ***They were lost to the darkness of Downstairs.***

"Uh-huh," the boy said. "Never to be seen or heard from again?"

What is it that you're implying? On second thought, I do not wish to know. Just continue forward along the right path before you squander our hour, will you?

The boy, mercifully, complied.

"Hang on," Nell said, grabbing Prosper's arm when he took a step toward the corridor's opening. Reaching into her bag, she pulled out a small vial of silver powder and clenched it in her fist.

"What is this stuff?" Prosper asked, holding it up. The witch caught his hand before he could give the glass a shake.

"This is an emergency exit," she said quietly. "If we need it. I have one, too. Just hang on to it, okay?"

The market rolled out before them like a serpent's black tongue. This, at least, mostly aligned with Alastor's memory.

Rather than chiseled stone or shaped metal, the shop signs pulsed with the ribbons of magic that flowed through them, illuminating the tables of wares for sale as the green essence traveled along the edges of the booths. Fist-sized fairies sucked at the power on those glowing lines, oblivious to the fiends milling around with wire baskets, frantically buying up the last of each vendor's items.

As expected, the first few vendor stalls were stocked only with food and drink—something Alastor recognized from his time in Salem as being corn kernels that had popped, only this was drizzled with the syrupy blood of bane beetles. Nearby, bats roasted on pikes, waiting to be peppered and then devoured by the lycans hovering nearby, growling with impatience.

A Master stepped out of a pocket directly in their path. He clutched a tray in his hands, one overflowing with glass goblets of iridescent green drink.

"Liquid magic," the Master called out. "On the house! Feast, quench, and be scary, for tomorrow we close!"

He pressed a goblet into the boy's hands and whirled away, skipping through the fiends that rushed toward him to get a sampling of their own.

The boy sniffed at the liquid.

"Are you really going to drink that?" Nell whispered. "It looks like Mountain Dew."

Try it. I must know the taste of pure magic in liquid form.
Prosper sipped at it, then coughed, pounding his chest.

Alastor cringed. How could magic be so disgustingly sweet?

"It *is* Mountain Dew. Seriously, what's going on with this place?"

What is this . . . dew? We have no such thing on our mountains, nor frost.

Setting the remainder down on a booth ledge, Prosper answered, *It's a drink from the human world. All of this seems to be from the human world. The "Masters" are scamming you. Do they have some kind of portal to get supplies?*

They had the portal Bune had offered them. But surely, no. The Masters always sold the most interesting tools and food. Things you could find nowhere Downstairs, and could use to impress other fiends and render them helplessly jealous.

You are incorrect, Maggot. The Masters are clever, they've developed all this by themselves—

"Is that a box of Cheerios?" Nell said, pointing to a booth labeled MUNCHIES AND CRUNCHIES. "And that's a NASCAR sweatshirt!"

The strange garment currently being tugged at by two arguing goblins was the only one like it on a rack that had horrifyingly familiar clothing: shirts made of tartan that were so very popular with mortals, fuzzy jackets, even those devious fake pumpkins. An ogre had looped the hollow pumpkins' black straps around his ears, turning so that his friend could admire them.

"And here, a fine hat!" one of the merchants, a goblin

missing several fingers, said. He threw out his arms proudly displaying a rectangular object that looked to be made of thin brown fabric.

"That's a grocery bag . . ." Nell whispered.

Prosper hushed her, watching as a fiend slapped down gold coins on one counter, ripped what appeared to be some sort of shiny disk out of another fiend's hands, and held it up to the light, twisting and turning it until its surface showed a rainbow.

Another held what looked to be a kind of red baton, only when the hooded fiend clicked the button on its side, its circular face illuminated with a beam of golden light.

What madness is this? Alastor demanded.

Flashlight, Prosper thought back at him. *You didn't tell me fiends loved human crap and food. We could have brought stuff with us to trade!*

All along . . . all these hundreds of years, the Masters had been selling fiends items from the *human* realm. Alastor knew he shouldn't have believed them when they claimed to have found an ancient treasure trove in one of the lava pits.

Truthfully, he had not understood why Prosper had asked about the vanished humans until that very moment, staring at a lycan unsuccessfully attempting to use what Alastor now knew to be a "cardboard" box to sled across the ground. Downstairs, time did not exist as it did in the mortal world. A human could stay in this realm and live an unreasonably long life. Perhaps the Masters had originally wanted Bune's mirror as a means to escape, or had that bargain kept them trapped here?

The boy shook his head. *You said the Scholar is toward the end of the market, right?*

Correct.

He continued on several steps, jostled by the crowd from all sides. Within seconds, they both noticed that the witchling was no longer with them.

"Nell!" Prosper whispered to her back. She had gone rigid beneath her hooded cloak, unable to tear her eyes away from the booth across the crowded walkway.

This stall was nothing more than a wall of stacked glass cages, each containing a different creature. A different . . . oh.

The hob running the booth reached in with a stick, zapping one with a bolt of magic. The creature shifted, momentarily disappearing into a glimmering cloud of light, before returning to its arachnid form.

"The Masters bought them because they thought they could be trained to perform, but they refused," the hob explained to the customer standing before him. "Now they're yours to buy back, if you've got the blackpennies."

Alastor rather recognized that large, hairy tarantula.

And that ball of black fluff attacking the glass barrier with its tiny wings and claws, desperately trying to break out.

"Toad," Nell breathed out.

Toad and Treachery

Nell tried to lunge for the stall's owner—a hob balanced upon a high stool in order to be seen over the counter. I barely caught the back of her cloak in time to stop her. Even then, as I swung her back toward me, I had to fight the urge to keep from lunging at him myself.

"Wait a second," I whispered close to her ear. *"Look."*

The tall, gray-skinned fiend leaning his bony arms against the counter bore a terrifying resemblance to a praying mantis, save for his humanoid face. He was deep in discussion with the hob. They both gestured toward the cages and the changelings within them.

"We can't wait! He has Toad and Eleanor!" Nell hissed back.

The hob had more than just the two changelings: there were eight of them spread out across the glass cases. A parrot, a frog, what looked like a lizard that decided it preferred fur to scales, a snake with unnatural bright feathers around its head, and a pug puppy with bright green eyes.

Nell let out a quiet noise of frustration, crossing her arms over her chest. I drew us back, closer to a stall selling mutilated oil paintings of vampyres and other finely dressed fiends.

Toad and Eleanor had disappeared from the human world in the days leading up to the confrontation with Pyra, but Nell hadn't seemed concerned, so I hadn't been either. Every morning, I'd watched as Toad wandered off through an open window to go catch his breakfast, do his business, or visit Missy at her shop. He came and went as he pleased.

Clearly, we should have been a *little* more worried.

I told you, Alastor said. *The only good use for them is to pickle them and roast them over a blazing fire.*

You also said they were "nothing more than mice" Downstairs, so why are they being sold to the highest bidder?

Alastor was silent for a moment. *I perhaps . . . exaggerated their lack of importance and did not mention their scarcity. They can also be entertaining, under the right forms of torture.*

"Who caught them and brought them Downstairs in the first place?" I whispered.

Nell met my gaze. Even with her face shadowed by the hood, her eyes were blazing. "Nightlock. It has to be. I'll wring his wobbly little chicken neck—!"

Before I knew what was happening, Nell was knocked sideways, slamming into me. I threw out my arms to steady her as another fiend charged past us, marching up to the booth. Their vivid emerald-green cloak stood out in a sea of black, crimson, and glum purples.

The fiend was too small, the top of her head just reaching the counter's edge, to make eye contact with the hob. That didn't stop her from slamming a sack of coins down on the counter and declaring, "I'll take them all!"

One of the changelings, the one who'd chosen the form of a fancy red parrot, began to squawk and beat its wings. Its muffled coos of "Floo-rah! Floo-rah!" could be heard just over the din of chattering voices around us.

The hob peered down over the counter at Green Cloak through enormous spectacles that made his already large yellow eyes look like a frog's. A dribble of blue snot ran down from his bulbous red nose, only to be licked away. He hooked his glasses back onto his two horns. Shaking his head, he shoved the money sack back onto the ground, leaving the little fiend outraged.

"Is this not a place of business?" she demanded.

"This fiend has already repurchased these vermin for his master," the hob told her, pointing to a fiend with long, stick-thin limbs.

A grendel, Alastor explained. ***Good for little else but chimney-sweeping and clearing out banebat infestations from towers.***

With all the attention on what was happening at the counter, no one noticed that a pocket of air opened, and one of the Masters reached a hand through to snatch the bag of coins. He wrenched it back inside the portal and the air stitched itself back up.

My mouth fell open. Oh, so the Masters could steal, but the other fiends couldn't?

"Too late," the grendel purred. "I've already paid full price for them all. My most illustrious employer plans to host a dinner party this eve in honor of the queen."

"I'll turn *him* into minced meat," Nell growled, struggling against the grip I still had on her cloak.

"Changelings are *not* for eating!" Green Cloak's voice was like a toddler's—or a cartoon character's. Its syrupy-sweet tone was totally at odds with the husky growl of the other fiend. "They are intelligent, sensitive creatures who deserve our respect!"

The grendel howled with laughter.

"They are dangerous pests," the hob declared, "yes, they are."

"And such delicacies," the grendel said, bending at the waist to meet Green Cloak's gaze. "They are friends only to witches. Are you one?"

Nell tensed.

"N-no," Green Cloak spluttered. "Of course not!"

"Then there is no problem," the grendel said. He tossed the hob one velvet sack of coins, then another. The squat creature's stool rocked back and forth dangerously as he tried to catch them.

"Have the changelings delivered to my employer's home by midday, Croakswell."

The hob nodded eagerly, already counting the coins in each sack. "Pleasure doing business, oh yes, you are a fine sir, indeed. This hob is ever-so-grateful for your business—"

Hobs are not meant to run any sort of business! Alastor fumed. *The only thing they excel at is scrubbing outhouses! Honestly!*

"The bird—" Green Cloak tried, the words trembling slightly. "At least let me have that one?"

The gray fiend stopped, tapping one of his bone-thin fingers against his pointed chin. "Sure, little one. Come by our home on Grave Street. It's the house with the many spires."

Green Cloak's shoulders slumped in obvious relief. "Thank you . . ."

"I'll have the cook prepare the bird to your specifications. How do you like your meat prepared? Rare? Medium well?"

In the moment it took Green Cloak to process what he'd said, my stomach managed to twist itself into one big knot. Alastor didn't bother to smother a cackle.

The smaller fiend let out a keening wail of distress and threw herself at him—but she didn't get far. The moment her foot lifted from the market's platform, two Masters appeared again, blocking the space between her and the gray fiend.

"No fighting," one of them warned, his voice the echo of an echo.

"Send her out!" the grendel said. "She's broken your rules!"

Both Masters wagged a finger at him. "No one tells us what to do."

"O-of course not," the grendel agreed quickly. "I will finish my shopping and begone. I thank you for one last splendid day at the market—"

One of the Masters leaned forward from under his cloak, squinting an eye at him. The bush of his beard seemed to crackle with sparks of magic. "We like suck-ups less than thieves."

The grendel fled as if there were a river of acid at his heels.

Nell let out a frustrated breath, standing on her toes to see over the heads of the dispersing crowd. Toad had slumped against the cage. Then his bright green eyes went wide, and a moment later he smashed his furry face against the glass—staring right at us.

"What do we do?" Nell whispered, glancing down at the black vial still in her palm.

My head felt like it was spinning as I tried to pin down some kind of plan. We could try to get Toad, Eleanor, and all the others out and risk testing to see if there *was* magic in place to prevent stealing. We could even wait until they had been carted outside the boundaries of Neverwoe and try to grab them then. Both acts could get us caught, and potentially killed, but the thought of the changelings becoming part of some monster's meal—potentially a special one for the queen—made my blood boil.

Every obvious option would take more than whatever time we had left in the market. And once Neverwoe closed, how would we be able to find the Scholar to get the information we needed about Prue's whereabouts?

Not to add to the morbidity, but maybe there was a way to kill two—figurative, non-changeling—birds with one stone by following the grendel back to the house. There, we could save the changelings and potentially tail Pyra back to wherever she was keeping Prue.

There were so many ways that plan could unravel. It was risky, especially when we had a good, concrete option for information a few dozen feet ahead in the market.

I concur.

You also don't care if they eat the changelings, so keep your opinion to yourself.

Nell pushed forward through the dispersing crowd just as the hob reached up and tugged on a rope over his head. The stall's curtain swept down, blocking the cages from sight. A tiny hand reached between the folds and hung a SOLD OUT sign on the edge of the metal counter.

I shook my head. There was only one way to do this, and I liked it about as much as I liked the fiends. "We should split up."

What? No!

"What?" Nell said in a hushed voice. "No!"

Who are we going to throw in front of us if someone tries to stab you?

"Just for a few minutes," I told her. "You stay here and keep an eye on Toad and the others and make sure they're not taken out of the market without us knowing where they're headed. I'll talk to the Scholar and get answers about where Prue is being held. I'll meet you back here—in, like, ten minutes?"

I glanced down, forgetting I wasn't wearing a watch. The admission bracelet stared back at me. A prickle of dread worked down the back of my neck. At some point the bracelet had shifted from silver to a deepening shade of pink. The metal was growing warmer by the second.

That was okay.

This was fine.

Totally.

"Okay," Nell said, tugging her hood up. "Just be quick, okay?"

I turned back toward the milling fiends, the bustle of bags and jars and cauldrons being filled with purchases.

With only the light of the magic glowing bubbles and a few strings of lights, the farthest reaches of the two rows of stalls seemed to bend toward darkness.

"Yeah," I promised. "Real quick."

There was a line out in front of the Scholar's booth four fiends deep. The curtain was drawn on the stall, but now and then it fluttered as a fiend passed in and out of its depths. I stood at the back of the line with my arms crossed, careful not to meet any creature's eye, but it was almost impossible not to look at them.

A fiend with silvery skin and ears like a small elephant stormed out of the stall with an audible *Argh!* I'd seen a few like this one before, but none dressed in a crushed-velvet suit. The gold chains dangling between the fangs that curved down over its pointed chin jingled, emphasizing each of the fiend's words. "You filthy liar!"

Goblins never take ill tidings well, Alastor observed. ***Their tempers have held their kind back for centuries.***

I wasn't sure what he meant by that until the goblin suddenly spun around and pulled a long, thin sword out of the hilt at his side. Instantly, the Masters were there. The hands, with their ropes of nails, clutched a variety of blades, from kitchen knives to curved swords.

The goblin took a step back but didn't lower his sword— he only swung it toward those of us in line.

"He is a charlatan!" he said, his rumbling voice ragged

with emotion. "Do not give him what he asks for! He'll sell you lies in return!"

"Stuff it, you silver-bellied windbag," said the female ogre at the front of the line. She was dressed in a fine dress of red velvet, her wisps of hair braided into loops. She also stood head and shoulders above the rest of us, including a smaller catlike fiend that had to keep darting out of the way to avoid being trampled.

"Next!" a voice called from inside.

The Masters parted to allow the ogre through. The goblin stood clutching his sword, trembling with rage. The lady ogre reached out and flicked him on his snout.

"Beslobbering wretch!" the goblin snarled, and, before the Masters could disarm him, sliced the tip of his sword against the ogre's arm.

Blue blood bubbled along the small gash. The ogre let out a shocked gasp, clamping her thick hand over it with a look like she was dying.

"Wait—wait—" the goblin said, eyes flaring. "I did not mean to do that—I did not mean to—"

The Masters appeared around him, circling in like a noose.

"I'm—!" The rest of his plea was choked off as the Masters swept him up off the platform and dragged him into a pocket. The clamor of the surrounding fiends died off, leaving us in eerie silence.

What . . . are they going to do with him? I asked Alastor, trying to keep my head down. Out of the corner of my eye, I saw the small catlike fiend reach up and bat at the silk coin purse hanging from the ogre's hip.

They'll drop him off a cliff, most likely. Oh no—don't be a fool, fiend!

At the very instant the feline fiend sliced a claw through the bottom of the purse, its admissions bracelet heated to a molten red. The band tightened until the paw was finally sliced clean off.

The fiend yowled, hopping around until a Master reached through a pocket and dragged him inside.

Another Master's hand collected the few coins that had fallen to the ground, unseen by the distracted, raging ogre. Just before the pocket of dark air closed, the Master gave me a meaningful look.

A *knowing* look.

They knew I was human.

The Master must have seen that realization cross my face, even under the cover of my hood. He pressed a finger against his beard-covered mouth and gave me an exaggerated wink. Then he drew back, and the pocket of air sealed itself again.

I forced myself to shut my mouth and look away, even as I began to piece everything together.

The Masters had said that there was a curse in place to prevent all *fiends* from stealing. Was it possible that the Masters had made sure they themselves weren't included in that rule? Or was it as simple as the rule not applying to them because they weren't fiends at all?

Or, Alastor mused, *is it that the curse is attached to the admission bracelets? All these things are possible, but I do not recommend seeking to test them, nor do I believe your sugar-coated heart capable of theft.*

I kept my head down, moving one foot in front of the other, until I was next in line. The fiend that had been ahead of me tossed the curtain aside in a flurry of excitement, literally bouncing over to another waiting creature, this one with matching green scales and ridges along his back like a dinosaur.

"Neeeeeext!"

My heart gave one last hard thump before speeding up into an all-out gallop. I couldn't even swallow the grimy spit in my mouth, my throat was that tight.

Just try not to stare into the Scholar's eyes. Any of them.

I nodded, more to myself than in response to Al. Clenching my fists at my side, I stepped into the stall.

The Scholar

I'm not afraid to admit that if I hadn't taken one look at the Scholar and immediately lost all feeling in my body, I probably would have run right back out through the curtain.

Behind this booth's counter, flanked by teetering stacks of leather-bound volumes that looked thicker than my arm, was a six-foot-tall spider covered in stiff black hair. Eight round, glassy eyes watched as I forced myself to step forward. A dusting of white powder from his old-fashioned wig drifted down onto his shoulders and curved pincers.

His legs didn't stop moving the whole time I stood there. One flipped the page of the massive volume open in front of him; another tugged his wig straight, a third brandished a quill to write, a fourth moved toward a cage perched on the counter beside him. The tip of this leg was thinner than the other seven, and slightly hooked.

It was that leg the Scholar slipped inside that small cage, jabbing the curved end into the ear of a mummified human head.

The skin had basically shrink-wrapped around the skull, withering down to a bloodless, leathery layer. The head was bald, as wrinkled as the bit of neck that connected it to a brass pedestal. Bright green eyes—no, they weren't eyes. They were glass beads made to *look* like eyes. Both eyelids slid open as his mouth cracked a smile, revealing only two yellow teeth and a whole lot of gums.

It was the head, not the spider, that asked, "What do you seek, Alastor the Lost?"

The words were dry and brittle, as if the head were coughing up lungfuls of dust and needed a sip of water it could never have.

Fat white candles floated in the air around us. One drop of hot wax struck the top of the spider's—the Scholar's—wig, making it smoke like the wick of a blown-out candle.

"I'm not Alastor—" I began.

The spider jabbed his leg back into the head's ear hard enough to make it wobble on its stand. I tried not to gag.

"Lies are tedious and tiresome, you pulpy meat sack. I wish to address the former prince, not a lowly, drooling thinskin."

Pulpy meat sack? I grimaced and Alastor's voice rose in me like a nest of hornets.

"Former prince?"

The spider was incapable of blinking and this only added to his air of disdain and disbelief. "Is there another way to describe you, having lost your body, your kingdom, and centuries of time?"

"That was not my decision! I have returned, haven't I?"

"And yet, this realm did not wait for you," the head said.

Alastor blew out a hot, stinking breath through my nose. To my surprise, he seemed to have accepted that—or at least thought it was pointless to argue.

Can we not upset the terrifying spider fiend? I asked. *Please?*

The malefactor seemed to agree it was time to defuse the situation, or at least slightly alter his approach. *"So . . . Scholar. How are the Festering Forests of your youth? Have you been back recently, perhaps to visit your old nest?"*

"You burned the Festering Forests to the ground to drive us out," the Scholar's talking head said coldly. "Your kind needed new caretakers for your nurseries. Or have you forgotten?"

Oh no.

"Ah. Yes," Al said weakly. *"Time, it certainly flies . . . how quickly we forget."*

"I forget nothing," the Scholar said, tapping the volumes behind him. "I know the whole sad story of your life, and I believe I can predict how it will end without much difficulty."

Alastor bristled, but to my surprise, he kept his voice neutral as he cut to the chase. *"I suppose you will sell the information of my appearance here to Pyra?"*

"I heard the whispers of your reappearance, and"—the severed head tipped over, forcing the spider to pause and right it again—". . . and bought and traded many secrets to learn about your accursed form. I shall indeed sell this information later to whoever is willing to pay my price. You may have time to escape, provided your meat pouch doesn't wither and falter."

I pushed Alastor aside long enough to say, "Please don't call me meat pouch. . . ."

The spider and severed head both stared. One of the spider's legs began to tap out a rhythm against the counter, as if demonstrating how quickly it could stab me through skin, muscle, and bone.

"We seek information on the whereabouts of a human prisoner, Prudence Fidelia Redding, brought Downstairs by my sister," Alastor explained. *"This was only hours ago. Do you have this knowledge?"*

The spider's pincers clicked together as he used a different leg to stroke the open pages of his book. "I do possess this knowledge."

"What do you ask in return for this information?"

The severed head's eyes narrowed, likely because the Scholar's eight couldn't. "You know the price, Lost Prince. A letter for an answer."

Why does he want you to write him a letter? I asked, confused.

Al shook my head hard enough to dislodge the hood. *"No, surely there's something else you desire—what about a shop on Dread Lane, or—or a dukedom? It would have to wait until I reclaimed my throne from my wretched sister, of course."*

"Her name is Pyra the Conqueror for a reason. Not because she merely liked how it sounded, as you did."

Sick burn, spider monster. If I'd been in control of my body, I would have cringed on Alastor's behalf.

"How dare you speak to me in such a manner—"

"I can speak to you in any manner I choose now that you have been marked human in the Book of Fiends."

This time Al shuddered. *"No! Surely not that!"*

"Indeed, you have been." The Scholar seemed very excited to inform him of this, his pincers rubbing together. "Stripping you of your title was one of Queen Pyra's very first actions. Now look at you, cowering and afraid."

The Scholar braced his two front legs more fully against the counter. He pushed up so he could tower over us; I saw my pale reflection in each of his eyes.

"I am never afraid," Alastor scoffed.

"Yes, but you have already traded me four letters for rumors and favors. How long *is* your true name? Can you risk the loss of another letter, knowing I might be able to guess the name based on that final clue?"

Oh—alphabetical letters.

Alastor the Idiot was trading away slices of his true name. Anyone in possession of it could compel and control him, if the research I'd done had been right. Which also meant that if the Scholar guessed it now, he'd probably be able to yank me around like a puppet, too.

Or . . .

Or. A small fissure of excitement worked through me. I tried to shield the thought from Alastor, but the malefactor was swirling like a tide pool of static in my mind, clearly caught in thoughts of his own.

If Nell and I could figure out his true name on our own, wasn't that the answer to our problems? We could force him to break the contracts he and Pyra had arranged with our families, saving ourselves and everyone else.

Alastor was a swirl of grim contemplation in my mind.

Al, this is too dangerous, I told him. *We aren't that desperate yet. We can follow the changelings and see if that leads us to the queen. Let's just go before he rats us out and tells Pyra we were here.*

Alastor prickled with surprise. **You would give up so easily? In the face of this taunting vermin?**

To keep us both from being played like violins and to give myself the chance to uncover the name first? Yeah, I'd do that.

But before I could say as much, Alastor's words leaped into my mouth.

"O," Alastor said suddenly. ***"Now tell me where to find the human."***

I felt a twinge of dread deep in the pit of my stomach. Of course. The one time I'd wanted him to do the selfish thing and clam up to protect his hide, he'd done the opposite. If it had come from anyone else, I might have called it selfless.

The Scholar's pincers clicked together gleefully as one of the arms flipped back through the pages of his book and a second one skimmed down its chart of names. He stopped near the bottom of the page and dipped the tip of his leg into an inkpot. I caught a glimpse of what was written there before the book was slammed shut.

Alastor, Prince of Fiends: S, G, B, W, O
  - *Palace hob overheard another who believes the name ends with —blown, or —bones*
  - *Per his uncle, the late duke, there is a family tradition of true names beginning with S. S—gem? S—bone?*

The Scholar leaned against the book, blocking the rest of the page from view. I swallowed a sound of frustration.

S-bone . . . bones? That was familiar—it almost sounded like—

The stink of the spider fiend, like sour milk, billowed around me as he shook flies and dust off his back. I brushed the powdery mix off my cloak, and whatever train of thought I'd been riding on was derailed.

"Well?" Alastor prompted. *"We have a deal, do we not?"*

"Yes," sneered the talking head. "You malefactors and your *deals*. You will find the human in the highest tower of Skullcrush Prison, where the queen was once held captive by her brothers."

Well, "highest tower of Skullcrush Prison" didn't sound like a bag of fun but—

"Poor, wretched mortal," the talking head cooed. "Even knowing this, you shall never get inside. They have destroyed all the bridges to the prison, and the queen has her best guards overseeing its only mirror portal. But . . . there is another way in. One that has been left neglected."

I clenched my jaw. Was there a rule that all fiends had to talk ten seconds too long and in the most dramatic way possible?

"Okay, what is it?" I asked.

The Scholar jabbed the talking head again, and even though the spider didn't have an expression, I could still somehow tell it was giving me a look of disgust. "You take me for a fool, mortal? If you want the information, you must pay. Alastor the Lost's question was not specific enough."

Inside the cloak's long sleeves, my hands curled into tight fists. I should have known—I *really* should have, considering all the experience I had with Alastor's tricks. *Fair* and *right* weren't part of a fiend's vocabulary, and frankly, I wasn't sure they even understood the concept. I'd call them the absolute worst, but they'd only take it as a compliment.

I wasn't sure I'd ever hated anything as much as I hated these fiends. Even my grandmonster looked like Mother Goose in comparison.

A thought came into sharp relief as I stood there, watching the Scholar reach up to adjust his wig again. I would have to be better than the fiends while I was Downstairs. Better, smarter, quicker.

These fiends had the morals of swamp scum. As in, none at all. If they wanted to keep underestimating me, then good. The only way to trick a trickster was to let them think you weren't capable of it in the first place. The difference was, I'd be doing it for the *right* reasons.

Alastor's bright fury scorched through my veins. *"You devious jackal! And for your vast records, I would like it noted that I allowed my father to keep Pyra in the tower for her safety—so my brothers could not harm her before she manifested an animal form!"*

The Scholar did not choose to respond to that. Alastor, deflated, sank back down in my mind.

"I want to know where this hidden entrance is to the

prison," I told the Scholar. "What kind of information would you trade for it?"

Maggot, you play at games you don't understand, Alastor warned. *You have nothing, and know nothing he'd ever desire to learn.*

"I shall humor you this once, mortal, and tell you that the information you seek must be exchanged for something equally important. A long-held secret will vanquish your short-term problems. But know this: I can smell a lie and can easily place a deathwish upon your pathetic life."

It was the way the Scholar—or rather, the severed head—said *something equally important* that stoked the embers of the idea. A secret location for a secret location, perhaps?

You know no secret locations in this realm, Maggot.

Oh yes I did. A surge of satisfaction rolled through me. "I know where Alastor keeps a secret working mirror portal all for himself. Seems like the kind of information that would be *very* handy—er, not that you need hands to find it useful, but with the Void and all that, it seems like having your own personal escape route would be key."

Maggot. Alastor's voice was like icy venom. *I will cut the intestines from your belly and strangle you with them. You will be taken to a new dimension of suffering—*

You cursed it so that only you can get in, I reminded him. *It's not like anyone else can actually use it. But he doesn't need to know that.*

For a moment, Alastor was speechless. *And did it not occur to you that we might need to use that passage back to the human world?*

As the Scholar studied me, I responded with, *Am I supposed to believe that you only have one secret mirror passage hidden away in this kingdom?*

Of course I have more than one! Alastor spluttered. *But this was not your secret to sell!*

What's mine is literally yours, pal. And vice versa.

"You surprise me," the Scholar said. "I accept. Ask me your question."

A pang of something moved through me, but I brushed it aside. What did I have to feel bad about? This had *worked.* If Alastor really didn't think I would do whatever it took to save Prue, he was in for a terrible surprise.

I took a few seconds to carefully craft the question, trying to find the right words so the Scholar had no way of worming out of the answer. "I want to know everything you know about how to get into Skullcrush Prison."

The Scholar pointed to a worn sign above his head that read PAYMENT MUST BE RECEIVED FIRST.

"Fine," I said. "His secret mirror is in an outhouse in the Flats, in the alleyway next to Grim Goo-goo's—"

Grim Grayscale!

"Grim Grayscale's pub," I finished.

The severed head gave a snort. "Of course. It's quite fitting. He would like to be with his own kind."

My mouth formed a perfect O at that insult.

"Here is all the information I have of the hidden entrance: it is a fiercely protected secret, known to only Queen Pyra—"

"Are you *kidding* me?" I interrupted. "I gave you good information!"

"—and any and all hobs who were assigned to work the prison at birth. That means, mortal, any hob with a name ending with *lock*."

I blew out a hard breath through my nose. Any small iota of guilt I'd had about misleading the Scholar dissolved. At least I'd given him something less useful than he'd given me.

"Does my sister truly seek out the dark misery of Skullcrush?" Alastor said, seizing control of my voice once more. *"The monsters of that prison—"*

"Now obey her," the talking head finished, "and love her, in a way that they never loved your loathsome father, who did not understand them and put them there. They will happily rend you limb from limb if she so commands. I suppose, by then, it will have been a waste to try to learn your true name."

"They will never catch me."

With the way things were going with that ego of his, that was somewhat debatable.

"It is them or the Void," the Scholar said. "And she is our only chance of surviving the latter. If you truly love this kingdom as you claim to, you will help, not hinder, her."

So Pyra had a plan for whatever this Void was after all; a memory from the backroom of the theater nagged at me, too vague to hold on to. It didn't matter. We weren't going to hang around Downstairs long enough to find out what her evil plan was.

"This is my kingdom," Alastor said. The words were like ice in my throat. *"It is* **mine.**"

"And that has always been the problem. You are young for our kind, only eight hundred years old. You do not yet see."

Alastor let out a huff, but reserved his words for me. *I see everything, including one rather large problem: How in the realms are we meant to find a hob with* **lock** *in their name?* Alastor grumbled. *There are so very many of them scampering about, and all respond to "you there" and "servant."*

I couldn't believe he didn't see it. *We already know a hob with that name.*

"Nightlock!"

I spun back toward the tent's entrance at the sound of a rising argument outside. I recognized one of the voices at least: it was the fiend who'd bought the changelings.

The Scholar pushed up onto his counter, climbing over it. I leaped back to avoid his massive body, ducking under two of his legs as he stuck his head out through the curtain.

"I warn you, friend fiend, do not insult my kind employer," the servant was shouting. "I'll have you know that he deserves all that he's been given by the queen and more. I demand you relinquish that set of bone china at once!"

The grendel works for **Nightlock?** *That little slobbering weasel?*

No way. *No way.* Those two words kept circling my mind. This was the strangest bout of good fortune I'd ever experienced as the only unlucky member of an exceedingly lucky family.

Even better, it actually made sense. When the merchant sold the changelings to the grendel, the hob had mentioned that the grendel's mysterious employer was buying back merchandise he'd originally sold. Nell was right—Nightlock had had both the opportunity and motive to take the changelings from the human world and bring them down here.

Oh, this was too good. I'd get the changelings back *and* get our key to finding the secret entrance to the prison in one trip?

Nightlock is elevated enough to have his own staff? His own home? Alastor moaned. *How could this day possibly get any worse?*

As the Scholar edged farther outside, I had one very specific idea of how that could happen.

Before I could really think about it, before I could list all the thousands of reasons why it was a bad idea, I was doing it. Keeping my eyes on the spider, I slowly edged back through his legs, carefully avoiding his body's coarse hair.

"You work in the employ of Nightlock now, do you?" the Scholar asked, easing out of the stall completely. As soon as the curtain fell, I whipped back toward the book, my heart slamming so hard, so fast, I could barely breathe.

What are you doing? Alastor demanded.

The Scholar had left his book open to the page of notes on Alastor's true name.

I glanced back toward the tent's entrance again, adrenaline surging through me. I could no longer hear the argument out in the market over the roar of blood in my ears.

The malefactor gasped. *You wouldn't dare.*

There wasn't time to stand there and study it and risk being caught doing so. There was only time to rip the page out and take it with me to show Nell.

If I was wrong about the Masters' curse for thieves not affecting humans, I was about to find myself short one hand. The hand I used to write.

To draw and paint.

My whole body went cold at the thought, but my mind was too scared to actually picture it, or wonder how I could ever possibly explain the missing body part to my parents. But if I was right . . .

A hero wouldn't think, he'd just do it—he'd make the potential sacrifice for the greater good. Which, in this case, wasn't just helping my own family; it was helping to save Nell from her father's terrible deal.

"You demand, do you? I got my paws on it first, which means you best be taking your eyes off it."

"Curse you to the lava pits! I require that tea set and

I will fight in the name of my employer until my dying breath—"

I kept my eyes on my bracelet as I reached toward the page, waiting for it to sense my intentions and flare with molten heat. It was uncomfortably warm, but it had been for the last several minutes as our allotted time ran down.

I sucked in a deep breath.

The paper was brittle with age. It tore easily, as quiet as a whisper. My vision blacked out with panic, but when my eyes cleared, the page was in my hand and my hand was still attached to my body.

Unbelievable! Alastor seethed. *I should expose you for this! And the mischief of the Masters—mortals!* **Humans! Making a profit off fiends for centuries!**

I flipped the book shut. The severed head watched me the whole time, its mouth open in a kooky little smile.

"Don't rat me out, buddy," I whispered to it, stuffing the page into the pocket of my cloak. "Sorry about the whole . . . body situation."

Stop talking to the dead man's head, you rat-brained rump, and leave before the Scholar returns to find what you've done!

My pulse was still thrumming through me like waves of electricity. Each step I took felt more like flying than walking. At least until the Scholar swung around and crawled back into his tent.

"You're foolish enough to linger and test my patience? I've other waiting customers and the market closes tonight."

The spider fiend waved a leg at the curtains. "Do try to stay alive, Alastor the Lost. I have plans for you. Now, fix your garment and be on your way, pulpy meat sack."

I lifted my hood back up and let it shadow my face. And then, before either of us could reply, the severed head opened its mouth and shouted *"Next!"*

Friend or Fiend

Nell wasn't where I had left her.

I found her standing a few feet away from the Scholar's tent, her gaze turned back toward the entrance of Neverwoe.

I looped my arm through hers, trying to tug her forward. She stiffened, gripping my arm like she was going to try to flip me on my back. Not wanting to confirm that Nell could do it—and also not wanting to wait and see how long it would take the Scholar to find that a page from his creepy book of stalkerish secrets was missing—I whispered, "It's me. We have to go. *Now.*"

As if agreeing with me, my bracelet grew hot to the point of pain. Nell let out a small gasp, glancing down at hers.

"Good call," she said. "Is there another exit besides the way we came in?"

Yes, Alastor began, still sounding irritated, *if you continue straight ahead—*

Another voice rang out over the din of the market-place, drowning out Alastor. "Mandatory evacuations of the Boneyard have begun! In the name of the queen, you will close this market at once and bring the remainder of its magic to the collection point! Any and all fiends who do not cooperate willingly will find themselves *un*willingly thrown into a cell!"

Ogres, all with orange sashes across their armor, stormed through the market, their numbers flooding the aisle of vendor stalls. Several of the guards threw open curtains and dragged fiends kicking and snarling away from their fun. Others knocked down the bone structures and tore at the strands of magic lights, leaving only the illuminated bubbles to light the way. The Masters popped in and out of the air around them, trying to stop them from flattening the whole market under their pounding fists and feet.

There clearly was an exit nearby, because fiends were hurrying past us, merchandise piled dangerously high in their arms as they ran. Their fear charged the air. Equally powerful was the force of their elbows, shoulders, and knees bumping into us, threatening to carry us away with them.

"Look!" Nell whispered, pointing just beyond them.

A shaggy black dog jumped up onto one of the emptied

tables, sniffing around. He lifted his head to look right at us, then let out a thunderous bark. Some of the feeling left my hands as another howler jumped onto a chair to see what he had found. Subpar wasn't far behind.

Sinstar! Alastor corrected.

All right, Sinstar. He held up a lantern glowing with real flame, his wicked-edged blade already in his hand.

Rather than ask Al where to go, we followed a twitchy-looking goblin as it scurried through the last of the market's stalls, made a sharp left turn into the shadows, and pulled back a curtain to reveal a wobbly set of bone-inlaid stairs.

"Where are the changelings?" I whispered.

"I followed the fiend through the market and overheard the address he gave to the delivery fiend," Nell whispered back. There was a hitch in her voice as she added, "Their dinner is in five hours."

I took the stairs at a run, but, sure enough, my lungs began to burn and I couldn't keep pace with Nell. She drifted farther and farther ahead of me, until I couldn't see her above the heads of the nearby fiends. I started to call out to her, only to remember why that was an extremely bad idea.

A little help? I thought at Alastor, glancing back over my shoulder for any sign of Sinstar. A goblin climbed between my legs, knocking me off-balance. I lashed an arm out, somehow catching the railing before I took one final tumble.

THE LAST LIFE OF PRINCE ALASTOR

As you have demonstrated today, you are perfectly capable of looking out for yourself, Alastor said snidely.

Below us, Neverwoe was shattering into pieces, the bone structures tossed aside like toothpicks. I squinted, peering through the darkness to where the ogres had gathered around the clear vat of magic at the entrance. One of them directed streams of magic out of that tank and into a series of lanterns, jars, and orbs.

Section by section, the lights of the carnival went out, the rides went still, and silence swept over it all like a blanket.

The Masters were nowhere in sight.

"Move! Get out of the way!"

I swung back around, tracking Sinstar's reedy voice. He and the howlers were pushing up through the thrashing knot of fiends behind me like dark arrows. With as deep a breath in as I could manage, I ducked under the arm of an ogre and tried to weave my way in and out of the fiends bottlenecked at the top of the staircase.

"By the Great Ghoul," a hob said as I stepped over it. "The Void—it will never end, will it? It will take the whole kingdom!"

"No! The queen *will* save us," a lycan growled back. "She has a plan for us all."

Yeah. That plan being my untimely death. The thing I didn't understand was the *why*.

What do you mean? Alastor asked.

She said she wanted to open the gate between Downstairs and the realm of Ancients in Salem, remember? Why does she need you and your brothers' magic and life forces to do that?

The malefactor did not have an answer for me. I felt his presence tighten into a protective coil.

I wriggled my way between an incredibly tall, incredibly hairy duo of fiends, ignoring their grunts. At the very top of the stairs was another tent. I knew the outside world was near when the first whorls of vapor crept in under the fabric of its walls.

Just as I reached for the fabric flaps, a hand latched on to my arm and gave me a sharp tug left, deeper into the shadowed heart of the tent and away from the fiends.

"Here," Nell said, pulling up one of the stakes from the ground and creating our own exit. We crawled under, careful to replace it just as it had been. I stood up slowly, careful not to slice my back open against the jagged face of the mountain. The sliver of space between it and the tent's panel forced us to sidestep away from where the fiends poured from the market. We were in the narrow space between the tent and the sheer face of the mountain.

A whispery sound, a whistle with too much tongue, interrupted us. Nell and I turned, searching for the source. Finally, a small cloaked figure stuck its head out from a narrow crevice in the mountainside and a familiar, syrupy voice said, "Come, come, Goody Bishop! This way!"

THE LAST LIFE OF PRINCE ALASTOR

The fiend who wished to buy the changelings, Alastor noted.

"Don't call me that, Flora," Nell said under her breath. Seeing my disgruntled look, she shot me a reassuring one. "It's okay. We're going to work together to save the changelings. We can trust her."

As you trusted the witchling, hmm?

I ignored Alastor's mocking words and followed the cloaked figure through the large crack in the mountain's face, turning and slowly sliding forward through it. Stone scraped against me from all sides, forcing me to hold my breath until, suddenly, the space widened into some kind of cavern. As my eyes adjusted to the space's deeper darkness, I made out a crumbling set of stone steps across the way. They looked as ancient as the mountain itself.

"What is this place?" I asked.

I have the same question, Alastor said, sounding a little stunned.

"There are many passages like this hidden within the mountain; most have just forgotten they were ever here," the small fiend chirped. "This way, my new friends, I'll take you to my special shelter."

"I'm not going anywhere until you tell me who you are and why you care about the changelings," I called over to her. "And why would we go waste time at your shelter when they're hours away from being eaten? We should go *now.* What was the address?"

Nell raised her brows, nodding toward the fiend. I turned, just as she lowered her hood.

The first thing I noticed was her skin. It was the shade of a young piece of wood—pale brown, shot through with rivulets of soft green. Colors flowed in and out of each other as if they had been painted onto the waxy texture of her skin.

The shape of her head reminded me in a weird way of the flower bulbs Mom always planted in the spring. On the top of her head, tufts of green hair, scattered with small white flower buds, stood nearly straight up.

The severe line of her lipless mouth curled into a grin. She flashed pearly, flat teeth that had to be straighter and bigger than mine.

Alastor hissed at the sight of her. My skin crawled with the intensity of it.

"My name is Flora la Leaf," the fiend said. "We are going to my secret shelter because Goody Bishop says that you haven't rested the entire time you've been here, so you will sleep and I will go find a way into the horrible house to save our courageous changelings."

"Please," Nell said quietly. "Don't call me that. I'm just Nell."

Flora looked confused. "But you're a witch . . . aren't you?"

"And what kind of fiend are *you*?" I couldn't keep the words from bursting out of me. Some kind that released poisonous fragrances, or stalked gardens, stealing children?

She almost reminded me of . . . she *almost* looked like those woodland fairy creatures from Greek mythology—*nymphs*. Or, wait. Dryads?

She is no fiend! Al shuddered.

"'Scuse you!" Flora's eyes, which a moment ago had been a rich emerald green beneath her grass-blade eyelashes, now glowed a vivid, almost toxic shade of slime. "I am an *elf*! Elves create, fiends only destroy!"

"Wait," I said, holding up my hands.

There.

Were.

Elves.

"Elves exist?"

This was incredible—all those years I'd spent playing *Conquerer's Saga*, how many times I'd read *The Lord of the Rings*, the Play-Doh elves I'd made to ride all those porcelain ponies my grandmother gave me, and no one, not Nell, not Alastor, had remembered to be like, *Oh, by the way, Prosper, the one species you'd choose to be if you weren't human and wanted to enjoy animallike hearing and lightning-fast reflexes—*

Are you quite finished?

—those creatures exist, Prosper, and they actually look more like troll dolls than demigods, but they're still great and cool!

I turned to Nell, utterly betrayed. "Why didn't you tell me about the elves?"

Nell squinted at me through her dusty glasses. "You okay there?"

"He looks peaky, like he might start chewing on his own hand," Flora said, in a whisper that was actually not a whisper.

I realized I'd been staring at Flora the whole time. My hand was up and already halfway to touching her wild hair before I yanked it back, horrified.

"Okay, I might . . . be a little dehydrated," I admitted weakly. "And tired."

The elf let out a sharp hiccup, one that shook her so hard that her feet left the ground. The second one made *me* jump.

"Are you all right?" Nell asked, putting a hand on her small shoulder. Even I was a good head taller than Flora.

"Oh, crumbs! Sorry. 'Scuse me." Flora gave a sheepish shrug as she bent to pick up the small flowers that had shaken loose from her hair. Beneath her cloak, she wore a pale, simple tunic embroidered with leaves and vines. No shoes, but judging by the thick, dark soles of her feet, she didn't need them.

"Does that . . . happen a lot?" Nell asked carefully.

"Only when I'm nervous. And angry. And excited." Flora put a finger to her mouth. "Sometimes when I'm happy, too."

"Ah," Nell said after a long stretch of silence. "Well . . .

should we head to your shelter?" She glanced at me, and clearly I was wearing some of my unhappiness on my face because she added, "You can tell me what you learned about Prue and we can work out a plan from there."

I nodded, but pressure was building in my chest at the thought of waiting even an hour to go after the changelings and shake Nightlock down for the information we needed.

"Prue? Like a prune? I love prunes! I cannot eat them, though," Flora said sadly. "They make me create too much music."

I didn't really want an elaboration on what her definition of *music* was, because I had a pretty good idea already.

"Prue, like my sister," I told her. "Who has been captured by Pyra."

"But why would the queen of Downstairs bother with a human girl?" Flora asked. "Everyone knows all she wants is the boy who is hosting her brother— *Oh*."

The quiet that followed was only interrupted by another hiccup.

I stared back at her, taking in the uneasy sight of her eyes as they narrowed. A clicking sound, like small branches brushing together, rose up in a rattle from her throat. "You're a *fiend*?"

"It's a temporary arrangement," I tried to explain.

The rattling intensified. And, suddenly, her teeth didn't seem so flat.

They only eat plants, Maggot, Alastor said, sounding bored. *Tell her that I once slew a hundred of her ancestors and used their wooden remains to warm my tower for a winter and let her cower.*

Yeah. Hard *no* on that one.

"It's okay, really," Nell told the elf. "Prosper is still Prosper. Mostly. Like, ninety percent of the time, at least."

Flora raised a fist, showcasing a bracelet that looked like it was covered in sharp gold thorns. The blood drained from my face.

By the realms, for all these elves tout their superiority because they love joy *and* peace—*ugh!* Alastor shuddered. *This one was clearly pruned off the tree for being too vicious.*

That was why fiends hated elves? Because they liked bright, happy things?

The only good thing about the elves is that their craftsmanship is truly impressive. If we didn't require jewelry or finely forged weapons, the quality beyond what the Downstairs guilds can use magic to create, we'd have run the elves out of all the realms.

Why? I demanded, trying to give Flora some distance as we hurried up the staircase. When we reached the top, and what I presumed was the Scales, Flora turned back to glare at me again, bringing her tiny fist up one more time in warning.

Because they are annoying, Alastor said. *But mostly*

because we have never been able to utilize their limited magic the way we have humans'—they can only control plants, and we haven't much of those to speak of down here. And they insist on "helping" our enemies. Humans, witches, and changelings alike. Surely they mean to destroy us before we can destroy them.

That sounded like some circular logic to me. *Not everyone acts like fiends.*

Is that so? Then why do so many humans aspire to behave as we do?

It was an ugly thought, but . . . it wasn't untrue. It was like the fiends had all the worst parts of humans, and none of their capacity for compassion or change.

Are elves more human or fiend? I asked, following Flora as she led us through a series of cramped tunnels.

Neither. They are something else entirely.

That was the only confirmation I needed that she wouldn't try to eat me or burn me alive or fillet me like everything else Downstairs wanted to. At least not yet.

"So . . ." I said as we crept along. "Is the changeling you tried to save—that parrot—is that yours?"

Flora's eyes were glowing slits in the dark, and Nell's magic light was just bright enough to reveal her look of deep suspicion. My heart sank.

Stop trying to get the elf to like you.

"Those changelings are my *friends*. They are not *pets*.

They do not *belong* to anyone, even the witches who raise them. I've taken care of Ribbit ever since she left her witch and flew into my cozy cabin in the wintry woods."

"Ribbit left her witch?" Nell repeated incredulously. "Changelings stay within families of witches for generations. They must be the most loyal creatures alive. . . . That witch must have really gone dark side or something."

Flora lifted a shoulder in a faint shrug. "Ribbit does not speak of it. It makes her too sad."

"So you live in our world?" I asked. "What's it like for you? Do you see everything in high definition? Can you read my mind? Why don't humans ever see you?"

The breath that had been steaming in and out of Flora's nose eased up, as did the stark lines in her forehead. She stared at the hand I didn't realize I had lifted again to touch her shoulder. "Erm . . ."

"Elves mostly live in our world, Prosper," Nell said quickly. "They take care of nature, but many of them are skilled artisans and craftsmen. There was an elf in Salem who used to make this amazing jewelry. Missy put the glamour on him so he could sell it in the street fairs. I'm actually not sure what happened to him."

I was really starting to hate Alastor's silences. They spoke more truth than his explanations ever did.

Did you kill that elf? Another, blood-chilling thought occurred to me. *Did you make me do it?*

No. But I saw the ghoul who did it. Perhaps . . . do not tell the witchling of it.

I didn't.

Eventually, Flora led us out of the tunnels to what looked like a sewer entrance or storm drain. Nell shook the light out of her fist and climbed up after the elf. Somehow I managed to squeeze through the stone opening, dragging myself onto the cobblestone street.

Vapors hissed through a fissure in the nearby stones. It was the only sound around us.

The houses on the third level had all the same dark lines of the old-fashioned stone buildings in the Flats, but the many-stacked floors made the buildings loom over us. All the windows we passed were dark, save for a few with black lace curtains and glowing candles. There didn't seem to be a trace of magic in sight.

A faint rumble rolled through the air, sweeping past us. The sound echoed as it bounced off the crooked homes and diagonal walls, stretching itself, growing louder with each second that ticked by.

"Is that a storm?" I asked.

It's likely just lava movement far below us, Alastor said.

Lava? In addition to monsters and curses and magic, I was also going to have to worry about *lava*?

Of course. We have no sun, Maggot. How else would the realm heat itself without warmth rising from fissures?

So *that's* what the vapors were. The cast-off heat from lava. Perfect. Maybe I had breathed in too much and had started hallucinating. . . .

Only, the rumbling didn't stop. Something in the thick air began to quiver. It gave the illusion the buildings were swaying, chattering against each other like teeth.

The rumble became a deafening roar, and then it wasn't an illusion. The street rocked beneath us, throwing me to the ground and Nell onto her knees. Chunks of nearby roofs smashed down around us, forcing me to roll hard to the right to avoid being crushed. Glass shattered, exploding out of the homes like a vicious ice storm.

A whip of blue lightning lashed the sky, illuminating Flora's petrified expression. She crawled toward the edge of the street, where the massive metal-and-stone gate that encircled the step was tearing itself apart.

The Blood Gates! Impossible! **Impossible!** *Not even the troll armies could take them down!*

Alastor's terror doubled my own, kicking my pulse up. Pieces of the Blood Gates buckled and snapped, the stone crumbling into dust. As it disappeared over the ledge, that wall of black cocooning the outer wall of the mountain swept forward, devouring the Flats until there wasn't even a single lantern left to mark where they had once been.

No . . . impossible . . . My stomach gave a hard twist at the pained disbelief in Alastor's voice.

As the aftershocks began to settle and the air finally stopped howling, Flora took in a deep breath and released a soft hiccup. Her face was oddly expressionless as she surveyed the bottomless black that now surrounded the Boneyard like an army laying siege.

"What was that?" Nell gasped out. "An earthquake?"

Flora shook her head. "No. It is the Void."

A Forgotten Place

Up close, the strange stone huts I'd noticed from the Flats looked almost like toadstools. With their droopy roofs and gritty stones, they didn't just seem like they'd come from a different time than the other buildings, but an entirely different world. It was no wonder Flora had chosen one as a hideout. The few fiends on this step didn't give them a second glance.

Of course not. They're clearly tombs for the ancient dead. No one enjoys a haunting unless they are the ones doing it themselves.

"I like what you've done with the place," Nell said finally. Both of us were hunched over to avoid banging our heads on the low ceiling.

Truth be told, I wasn't exactly sure *what* she liked. Aside from a blanket on the ground, a tiny potted sprout, and a fading lantern, there wasn't much to see, never mind admire.

Wait.

I rubbed my eyes, clearing the crust from them. I hadn't imagined it: along the mud-packed walls and ground, someone had carved swirling vines. The flowers blooming on them were so detailed that when I reached out to touch one, I half expected the petal to feel soft. There was a sun, clouds, mountains, rivers. It must have been Earth, because it certainly wasn't Downstairs.

"Wow, those are cool," I said, leaning in for an even closer look. "This must have taken you a long time."

The elf was silent, watching me with those glowing eyes. "I did not make them. Fiends do not understand art, so do not pretend you do. They only see beauty in pain."

Not true. I also see it in the gleam of blackpennies, the dark horizon of Downstairs, and the steaming blood of my enemies. Oh! And in hats. A hat of good structure and balance will take you far in this vast eternity.

"I'm not a fiend," I reminded her.

"That is exactly what a fallacious fiend would say—"

"Flora," Nell interrupted. "You were going to tell us about the Void. Do you know what it is? What's causing it?"

Flora gave me one last long look, then moved to sit on her blanket. She stroked the wilting leaves of her plant.

"The Void is the fiends' punishment for what they've done to this realm."

Sensing this might be a long story, I lowered myself to sit cross-legged on the floor, leaning my head back against the wall. Nell did the same, dragging her pack around. She unlatched it, setting out food and water for all of us. Flora gratefully took a bit of water for her plant but did not eat.

"Every realm has its intrinsic magic, which is the magic the Ancients used to create it," Flora explained. "It's a current that flows through everything, binding it all together. It brings up the sun, renews vegetation with passing seasons, and nurtures its creatures. That magic is the deep roots from which everything in a realm flourishes. The Ancients were careful architects and gave their realms no more or less than they needed to sustain themselves."

It almost sounded like the Ancients were creating each realm the way you'd build a world from scratch in a computer game. "Even Earth?"

Flora refused to look at me and instead answered at Nell, as if she'd been the one to ask. "Earth's magic is in its people, in their shades. That is why fiends can draw magic from human emotions—those feelings originate in the very core of who that person is."

This is dull, Maggot. Get her back on the subject of the Void.

But Flora wasn't finished. "The human world is a realm,

but not one that the Ancients created. They found it in their explorations across realities and decided to use it as a seed world to build other realms. That's why all the remembered realms connect back to the human world. Its stability makes it a good anchor."

That wasn't at all how Uncle B—how Henry Bellegrave and Nell had explained the realms to me, and judging by Nell's face, this was truly brand-new information to her as well.

She may very well be lying, Alastor agreed, a note of bitterness in his voice, *but the Ancients loved and favored the elves. They might have the true knowledge that was denied to the rest of us.*

"Wait—but the Ancients gave witches their power and duty," Nell said. "And witches draw their power from the moon."

There was a small tug at the back of my mind at her use of *their* and not *our.*

Flora reached for the lantern, opening its small door. Drawing out a small thread of magic, she stroked the leaves of the small plant.

Feeding it, I realized, in the only way she could in a realm with no water or sunlight. As the plant soaked in the magic, its leaves perked up and its color deepened from an unhealthy yellow to an emerald green.

"Did the Ancients create witches," Flora said, "or did

they merely find them and ask for their aid to protect the human realm? It has all been forgotten by time."

"But they gave witches the changelings, didn't they?" Nell pressed.

Flora nodded. "As companions and fellow protectors, to thank them and to apologize for—" The elf looked up, eyes bright in the dark. "Well, it does not matter. Earth suffers and sickens with malicious misuse by hardheaded humans, but the fiends have done something far worse. They have drained this realm of all of its magic, and so they went into the human realm to steal magic from there, too. It still was not enough to sate their greed. So they dug deeper and deeper into the depths of this realm to find the last traces of magic in its foundations, and took that as well."

No wonder they'd been forced to ration magic.

"The life here has died, and now the whole realm dies with it," Flora said, her expression hardening. "And for what? To avoid having to sew their own clothing? To power their streetlamps? To move their carts? To have their fun in markets like Neverwoe? The ruling fiends imprisoned the others, forced them into service, and held human shades hostage, making them do the rest—all while the magic stored in their vaults secretly dwindled as the so-called king indulged himself fighting pointless wars, rearranging mountains to suit his taste, filling closets with clothing he never once wore."

How dare she! Alastor growled. *It is **our** realm! We can use our magic as we see fit!*

"You know," Flora said with another glance at Nell, "that once magic has been used, it is gone. There is no hope for this realm now. The Void is the world collapsing onto itself when the last bit of magic in those places goes."

That is . . . that is impossible . . . Alastor said weakly. *A realm cannot collapse.*

"No wonder they love Pyra," I said, finally putting all the pieces together. "She's shaken up the old ways and is the only one giving them hope that she can solve this problem."

"She told us that she's creating some kind of key to open the realm of Ancients—to take their magic," Nell said.

Flora sat up straighter. "I do not see how she could create one. A blood key can open a realm otherwise sealed off, but it requires the *sacrifice* of magic—an act these mercenary monsters are incapable of. The magic they possess inside of them is their life force. All other magic they use and control is stolen."

Nell and I seemed to realize it at the same moment. We looked at each other in the dim glow of the hut.

"She's already gotten the 'sacrifice' of her other brothers' magic and life forces," I began.

"Because she used their true names to compel them to sacrifice it," Nell finished. "Wow, that's evil but . . . also kind of genius, I have to say."

ALEXANDRA BRACKEN

It is suitably cunning, Alastor admitted. *I might appreciate it more, were I not an intended victim of it.*

Nell instantly sobered, though, when something else occurred to her. "Pyra said she'd learned Alastor's true name from their old nanny, and that she originally only wanted to take Alastor's magic to manifest her own animal form. She must have given the name to Goody Prufrock or Honor Redding, but the spell didn't work the way she needed it to. As the Void got worse, her need for Alastor's power changed. And now she's realized she doesn't need a spell at all to compel her other brothers into making their sacrifices. She only needs their true names."

"But the spell Pyra asked you to do," I began, trying to push the image of the storage room out of my mind, "it seemed similar to the one Goody Prufrock tried. You were going to permanently trap him inside of me, right?"

Nell looked down, and her expression made my whole chest clench. "She needed a way to ensure that Alastor couldn't escape your body and get away. Now I see she wasn't going to kill you just to kill him. Pyra needed him trapped long enough to compel him to give up his life force—which is all he has right now, until he's strong enough to regain his physical form."

"Oh, so I wasn't going to die after all?" I asked. That was weirdly relieving.

Nell winced. "The extraction probably would have killed

• 155 •

you, too. Because of the nature of Alastor's curse, the two of you are bound together."

Yes, Alastor said darkly, ***but not for much longer.***

Maybe I was imagining it, but the sensation of his anger was suddenly more pronounced, hardening into something with jagged, sharp edges.

"It does not matter," Flora said, pushing up to her feet. "They will never open the realm of Ancients, with or without the key. The fiend realm is lost. We only have to make sure we are no longer in it before it collapses completely."

"How soon is that?" I asked. Each passing second felt like the last beats of a dying heart.

The elf made her way to the door of the hut, drawing her cloak tighter around her and her hood up over her sprouts of hair. "Days. Maybe less."

Singing Bone

The words sank in like a knife between my ribs, but in my head, Alastor spun himself into a thorny knot of denial and rage.

I can save my kingdom, he said, the words simmering in my ears. *And I shall.*

"I'll go see to the house," Flora told us, stowing her little sapling in a pocket of her cloak. "I must find us a way in to search for the changelings."

"We can take care of that for you while you're gone," I offered, "so it won't get jostled as you carry it around."

Flora looked horrified at the thought. "I would never leave such a powerful plant in your hands, cunning creature."

I looked between the finger-length plant and her. Twice.

"I will return shortly with our way in," Flora continued. "Fiend, if you touch anything, I. Will. Know."

I held up my hands, gesturing to the absolute nothing that was around us.

"Don't be too long," Nell told Flora. "If you can't find a place to slip inside within a half hour, come back and we'll all go together."

Flora gave Nell a reassuring look over her shoulder. "I promise to take care, Goody Bishop."

"Don't"—Nell began, but the elf had already climbed back outside and was running—"call me that."

I leaned my head back against the wall, drawing my knees up toward my chest. I tried to process everything Flora had told us, but another worry wormed its way into me. "Are we sure it's safe here? Sunburn could track us and we'd be sitting ducks."

"You mean *Sinstar*?"

"Okay, yes, whatever. Are we okay here?"

Honestly, Maggot. At least remember the names of your enemies so that you might scream them as you land the killing blow.

"I think we're okay for a little while," Nell said, eating some of the granola. "He'll lose our scents where we escaped through the mountain."

She'd better hope that she's right, because being incorrect involves being slit from gullet to gizzard.

I took a long drag from the water bottle, then used a little of it to wipe my face clean. The caked-on grime smeared off, and I almost felt human again.

Almost.

My stomach was still tied up in knots; I couldn't even look at the bag of granola Nell pressed into my hands. That familiar pressure was back, ballooning out from deep in my chest until I couldn't ignore it anymore.

I shot to my feet, shaking out the tightness in my arms and shoulders. I knew that I was being stupid and that I needed to rest while we had the chance. If nothing else, my legs and the soles of my now blistered feet were burning from having walked so far. But it was like a swarm of wasps were unleashed inside my skull every time I tried to stay still. Each one stung me with the same painful thought: *Prue needs my help.*

"Prosper," Nell said, grabbing my wrist. "*Stop.* Seriously. You're making me dizzy with the pacing."

My face heated at the touch. I pulled my arm away, turning toward the other side of the room.

"I can't help it," I said. "I would scratch off my own skin just to have something to do right now. Maybe we should just go find Flora?"

Finally, some sense! I knew you had it in you, buried deep beneath the teetering mounds of timidity.

"Why don't we talk about what you learned from the

Scholar first?" she suggested. "And you should actually eat something so you don't faint from exhaustion and force me to carry you on my back across this whole realm."

As realistic as that situation sounded for the old Prosper, the new one wasn't about to be anyone's deadweight.

"I don't need food," I said sharply. "We need to just go to the house. The Scholar said Prue is in the highest tower of Skullcrush Prison, and aside from a mirror portal that's heavily guarded, there's only one other way into the fortress."

Nell dragged Flora's lantern close enough for the eerie green glow to paint her skin emerald. She pulled her glasses off, wiping them on the one clean cover of her oversized cloak. *Toil and Trouble* was already open in her lap. "He didn't specify where it was?"

"He didn't know," I said, feeling another flash of irritation at the Scholar's deception by omission. "He said only Pyra and hobs who worked to clean the prison do. Hobs whose names end in *lock*."

Both of her brows rose as she put her glasses back on. "Lock? Like our little rodent of a friend Nightlock?"

I nodded.

"Unbelievable," Nell said slowly. "Goody Elderflower says that hobs start working at a young age, but they're assigned their jobs at birth and it all depends on their name? They don't even get a choice? That's so messed up, even for fiends."

That is the way of things! Alastor said defensively. *The proper way of things! And it is not as if they complained about their lot in life.*

I shook my head. *Did you ever ask them if they were happy? Was it ever a choice?*

Of course not. Every fiend has their rightful role. Ogres build. Goblins scout. Malefactors rule. Perhaps the real reason the realm is collapsing is that Pyra destroyed those foundations.

Or, based on what Flora had said, their cooperation and the magic rationing was probably the only reason there was any part of the realm still standing at all.

"I'm sorry we have to take this detour from Prue," Nell said quietly.

"It's not even really a detour," I said. "After we rescue the changelings, we get to kidnap Nightlock from his own dinner party. We'll force him to come with us to Skullcrush Prison—Al, what step is that on?"

The prison sits on the other side of the mountain, on the Crown, Alastor said. His voice sounded thin, as if he were still struggling to understand what was happening. *The step above this one, where the towers once stood. My great-great-grandsire . . . he wished the prisoners to be forced to look up at the Horned Palace at all times and contemplate their own insignificance.*

Well, that sounded about right.

"So we'll have Nightlock show us the way in, restrain him so that he can't warn anyone, get up into the tower, and then I'll get us out of there," Nell said.

"How?" I asked.

Her hands worried the edges of her book. "I know I promised no more secrets, but . . . just in case something happens, I think it's better if the fiend in the room doesn't know."

It was a totally logical choice to make, I knew that. Yet some part of me—the part that still stung a little from what had happened—hated it. I promised Nell a new start, though, and while a Redding might have reason to think a Bellegrave was working a lie, and vice versa, a Redding had no reason to doubt a Bishop. Especially one whose life was equally at stake thanks to the deal her father had struck.

"Can I ask you something?" I began. I sat again, this time directly in front of her. Nell thumbed through her book. "If you help me and work against Pyra . . . does that mean you could die? Because it really sounded like you could die, just based on what your father said. And I really, really, really don't want you to die."

"I really, really, really don't want *you* to die either," Nell said, pushing her glasses up the bridge of her nose. "The truth is, I don't really know. I actively worked against her when I . . . when I threw my mom's grimoire to you and it burned, and I didn't fall over and croak. Maybe as long as she has a chance of succeeding, I'm okay?"

The stolen page crinkled as I pulled it from my cloak's pocket. No time like the present.

"About the contracts," I said. "I may have an idea."

Not this again, Alastor muttered. *I'll drown out every thought you have on the matter, if I must. It's a realm of terror, it's a realm of fears, it's a realm of—*

Even with his off-key singing, I could still focus enough to add, "If we figure out Alastor's true name, *we* can compel him to break the contracts."

Nell's face lit with excitement. "Could he break one Pyra created?"

Being the superior malefactor, yes—that is, no, definitely, assuredly I could not.

"He could," I said, smoothing the page out on the ground between us. "These are all the notes that the Scholar has on it, including a few letters."

"Huh," Nell said, scanning the Scholar's tidy notations. "What information was Alastor desperate enough to get that he'd give away letters of his true name?"

Alastor fell suspiciously silent.

"He gave one more for information on Prue, amazingly enough," I told her.

Nell shot me a look of complete disbelief.

"I know, but it's part of our deal that he has to help me get Prue back to our world," I said. "He didn't have much of a choice. I had to trade the information about Alastor's secret outhouse to get the bit about Nightlock and the entrance."

"And he *agreed* to that?" Nell looked like I could have knocked her over with a flick of the finger.

I shook my head. "Yeah, right. Of course he didn't."

The skin between her eyebrows creased. I didn't understand that look at all. Why did she seem more surprised that Alastor hadn't helped than if he had?

"I think the Scholar is right about his name beginning with an *S*," I said. "I'm almost positive that Pyra was visiting me in dreams in our world, and she was using the name— maybe to try to compel him to wake up from his sleep?"

"Singing Bone," Nell said, her face brightening. "No wonder you were asking about it."

My sister, Alastor began, his voice chillingly low, *visited you in dreams as I slept, and you did not think to tell me?*

"I didn't figure it out until I saw her in her animal form, and, at the time, I think she was only trying to compel you to wake up," I told him. "Anyway, it's obviously not Singing Bone, but something like it. I know that's not much, but it's a start. We just have to make sure Pyra doesn't use it before we can."

"Agreed," Nell said, folding the page and stowing it under the cover of her book. "I can't imagine what information you had to trade to get the Scholar to give you this whole page. *Please* tell me it wasn't anything that could literally come back and bite you."

I shrugged. "I didn't give him anything for it."

Nell looked up, with that same pinched look as before.

The words were slow with confusion as they left her. "You . . . stole this?"

For some reason, heat flushed through me. "The Masters are human. Or were human. Maybe the ones who accidentally stumbled into the realm."

I was almost disappointed at Nell's lack of surprise. "I figured as much. My sense of magic is weaker here, but they didn't feel like fiends. What does that have to do with anything, though?"

"I saw one of the Masters steal something and realized that the theft curse only applied to fiends," I said with a grin. "Meaning, you and I could take whatever we needed, including that page."

"No, I mean, I'm . . . surprised that you would just take it," Nell said slowly, her brow wrinkling. "You being, well, *you*."

My smile faded.

"What's that supposed to mean?" I asked. My hands curled hard around my knees. "You don't think I'm willing to do whatever it takes to save everyone and get Prue back?"

"That's not what I—" Nell looked down at the page, running a finger down its torn edge. "Never mind."

"Don't 'never mind' it," I said. "If you have something to say, just say it. Like you would have before, when you had no problem telling me what a spoiled idiot I am."

"I told you I was sorry about that," she said.

"I know," I said, the words rapidly losing their heat, "and

most of the time when you called me out, I actually did deserve it. I feel like we're fighting right now, but I don't understand why."

Because you're a Redding and she's a Bellegrave, Alastor sighed happily, ***and you are forever fated to circle back to hate one another.***

That wasn't true. Right now I was just Prosper, and she was just Nell, and there was something wrong.

Nell glanced at me, then back at her book. A deep frown settled on her face.

Seriously wrong.

"Nell . . . what's going on with you?" I asked, softer than before. "I know things aren't exactly stellar right now, us being trapped in a demonic realm on the verge of destroying itself and all, but you're holding on to that book like it's a life jacket. Is it being here, Downstairs? Are you worried about the deal?"

She shook her head.

"Does it have anything to do with the fact that you don't want Flora to call you 'Goody Bishop'?" I said, for lack of anything else to try.

Although I'd been the one to ask, I don't think anything could have prepared me for her quiet, heartbreaking, "Yes."

Daughter of the Moon

It was a long time before Nell was able to speak. She seemed to be rehearsing the explanation in her head, testing out all of its different deliveries, the way she might for a role in a play.

Nell closed the book, but her finger kept absently tracing the gold foil letters of TROUBLE on the cover.

"Are you . . . dying?" I managed to get out.

Please, I thought, please no . . .

Nell's mouth dropped open. "No! It's nothing like that. It's just complicated, and I'm not sure where to start."

"Maybe start with the Goody thing," I said carefully, finally taking a small bite of granola. She nodded and took a steadying breath.

"I don't want Flora to use the title *goody*, because *goody* is reserved for witches who have finished their training."

Instantly, the ridge of my spine relaxed. I released a soft breath. If that was it, then—

"And I'm never going to finish my training."

I actually choked on the granola. Nell reached over, pounding me on the back. My eyes were still watering and I was still coughing as I said, "Are you serious?"

Here was a list of the first things I ever learned about Nell:

1. Nell was an amazing actor.
2. Nell loved wearing bright colors and mixing patterns, and somehow it always worked.
3. Nell lived in a legitimately haunted house she loved running.
4. Nell was a witch.
5. Nell was good at being a witch.
6. Nell was super-proud of being a witch.

I will admit to being intrigued, Alastor said, swirling in my mind. *But I'd welcome one less witch in the realms. We have enough of their brand of menace.*

"I know I told you a little bit about what it's like to be a witch," Nell said. "That we inherit the ability from our mothers. But there's more to it than that. All the covens in America are overseen by the Supreme Coven. They set the rules that all of us have to follow, and they administer the trials, which determines if a witch can finish her tutelage and join a coven or begin one of her own."

"Okay," I said. "I follow. Where's the Supreme Coven based?"

"New York City," she said. "That's where Crescent Academy is, too."

"There's an actual witch school?" I asked. "Wicked."

Wicked *is reserved for only the best of fiends. Remove that exalted word from your mortal mouth.*

Not wanting to explain the finer points of New England slang to an eight-hundred-year-old demon, and also seeing the hard expression on Nell's face, I quickly added, "I mean, not *wicked* wicked, like the whole 'wicked witches' thing, I mean it like 'hey, awesome,' because for one thing, you're not green, and wow, I am *still* talking. . . ."

Nell almost smiled. "It's decidedly *not* awesome. Crescent Academy is for 'misbehaving' young witches who need 'the strictest of guidance reform to be functioning members of our secret society.' It's also where orphans or abandoned or even young witches who didn't know about their heritage go. We call them Daughters of the Moon, since they usually don't have a mother or a coven around them to do the teaching. It's where . . . it's where I'll end up. If I'm lucky."

"But you're not an orphan," I said, my brow creasing. "You have Missy and the Salem coven, right?"

"I fall into the first category, Prosper. Misbehaving. I broke the first rule of witchery—"

To always be a cantankerous, tempestuous plague to the four realms?

"I aided a fiend," she said miserably. "I guided three of them through the mirror portal to find us. I *cast a spell* on Pyra's behalf, out of my own mother's grimoire."

Oh. Oh, man. "But you also helped me. That has to count for something . . . ?"

She lifted her shoulder in a faint shrug. "I'm not sure it's going to matter much to the Supreme Coven. If I take responsibility and plead my case, the best outcome is that I'd have to leave Salem and live at Crescent Academy for the next few years to finish my schooling. The worst is that they could put a hex on me that would suppress my magic. Forever."

Wow. Maybe the witches were a little wicked after all.

"But that's so harsh," I said. "You were being told that Pyra could bring your mom back to life—who *wouldn't* take that deal?"

"Would you?" she pushed back.

I pointed at myself. "Who has two thumbs and just made a contract with a demonic parasite to help save his sister?"

Finally, Nell let out a small laugh. "That does make me feel better, in an awful way. Or at least less stupid."

I stared at her. "You are one of the smartest and bravest people I've ever met. That's why I can't believe that you're just going to . . . give up and not fight to finish your training. Is Crescent Academy really that bad?"

"It's miserable. Cold. It's what witches use as a bogeyman—*be bad and you'll end up at Crescent Academy.* But it's more than that," Nell said, pressing a hand to her book. Her voice became tight as she continued, "Going in front of the Supreme Coven and explaining what I did . . . even if they don't take my powers, it would dishonor my mom's memory. She was such a respected witch, the leader of the Salem coven. I can't do that to her. It's better that I . . . discontinue my lessons and go live with Missy. Get on with my life."

Her shame tastes of pepper, Alastor noted.

My whole chest seemed to lurch. I knew a little something about being the family embarrassment. "Nell . . . I don't know what to say. Not that I have any business voicing an opinion about it since I don't know what it feels like to, one, be a witch; two, lose a mom; and three, face a choice like this, but it's just . . . not right."

"It's better," Nell insisted, with that same terrible, thin tone. "I *knew* it was wrong to work with Henry and Pyra, but I still did it because I wanted my mom back so much. What if my judgment slips like that again, because—because something might happen to you? To Missy? To Toad?"

So that is why she clutches the book close, Alastor said. *She relies on it to confirm her thoughts and beliefs, so as not to stray from what these witches have decided is the right and proper course. Life is a blank page on which we write our destiny. A life lived by another's book is no life at all.*

Reluctant as I was to admit it, Alastor was actually pretty insightful about these kinds of things. He could pinpoint a person's weakness within seconds. Of course, his fatal flaw was that he couldn't recognize any of his own.

I wasn't sure what to say, but I wanted to help Nell so badly, I felt it like a knot tightening in the pit of my stomach. "I support you, no matter what you decide. But all of this just happened. . . . You don't have to choose right away, do you?"

She shook her head. "No, but I'm sure the Supreme Coven knows it's happened by now. Every day I wait is a mark against me."

Wow, these witches . . . I guess centuries of being burned at the stake, hanged, and drowned had hardened some hearts.

Whatever Nell was about to say next was interrupted by the sudden reappearance of Flora. She burst into the hut like a clap of thunder, narrowly missing trampling my hands.

Nell surreptitiously wiped her face against the sleeve of her cloak before asking, "Did you find a way in?"

Flora's eyes glowed. "Oh yes. I definitely did."

I helped Nell pack up everything she had taken out, my hands lingering on the bottles and vials of potions and powders.

I didn't know much of anything about this Supreme Coven, or if pushing back against the rules would only get her in more trouble. Maybe it really was as bad as all that, and these weren't just stories meant to give little witches nightmares.

"All right," I said. "Let's get going."

But even as we stepped back out into the empty Scales, I couldn't stop thinking that if something mattered to you that much, you had to fight, and fight, and fight to keep it—to protect it—in whatever way you could.

JANUARY 1692
TOWN OF SOUTH PORT
MASSACHUSETTS BAY COLONY

The truth Alastor had come to learn was this: human misery was fathomless and fed itself, ensuring its survival.

Just when a mortal believed one source of despair had gone, another sprouted up from his or her life like a weed. Some were small, like stubborn itches. Others festered and grew like the deadliest of diseases. Alastor would always have business in this realm simply because there was no end to human suffering.

As it was, he'd *also* discovered another truth over the centuries: once a human made a deal, and had gotten what they wanted from it, it inevitably caused another need to arise, another desire he could tease out. After one success, humans were far more prone to agreeing to another contract.

This, he told himself, was the reason why he returned time and time again to that forsaken land of snow and called on Honor Redding.

Every few fortnights, he found himself watching Honor, his wife, Silence, and their newborn whelp through the crackled window of their ever-expanding home. Some part of him relished seeing his magic work, even if it meant that the humans thrived because of it. Honor had even hung a mirror outside in the trees, to avoid Alastor being spotted by anyone he did not wish to be seen by.

In those instances when Honor noticed him, he would bring out water and victuals and sit with him awhile, speaking of things. Tiresome things, really—one human family moving, the new name for the colony, trade. Sometimes, Honor would seek guidance, and Alastor would catch himself indulging the human without exacting his usual price.

He supposed he liked the simplicity of this human; Alastor had become so acquainted with the secret scheming of fiends, he found it a relief to share the company of any creature who had no aims of killing him.

Always, Honor would first inquire about Alastor's health and relations, a habit Alastor did not understand. Fiends were far more hale than humans, and brought disease, rather than suffered from it. Moreover, their families despised one another as competitors and annoyances.

Even more mysteriously, Alastor would, occasionally, find himself answering those questions honestly as well.

Alastor had a particular question of his own, one he waited until the end of every visit to ask: *What is it that your heart desires most?*

Each time, Honor gave the same reply. *My heart is full, and there is nothing more I could desire.*

Oh, as if that could be true of *any* human.

Alastor knew that it would only be a short while before Honor found himself in need of his services once more. And almost a year to the day after his first visit, that moment finally arrived.

Alastor watched as Honor sat behind a desk he had somehow, with all his dim mortal wits, constructed himself. He pored over what looked to be a letter, turning it toward the light of the candle burning at the edge of the desk. It was late in the evening, nearly the witching hour. His wife and his child—who bore an uncanny resemblance to a mole, in Alastor's unassailable opinion—slept their dreamless sleep in the new, separate room Honor had built.

As if sensing his dark presence, Honor glanced up and turned toward the window expectantly.

Though he looked haggard and thin, a smile spread across his face. He stood, moving to unlatch the window.

"My friend, it has been months! I feared something might have happened to thee," he said, stepping back to allow Alastor to jump down to the floor.

"How many times must I tell thee, I am not thy 'friend,'" Alastor groused.

Honor laughed. "Thou came to me in my time of gravest need. Thou art the truest of friends."

"Aside from fire and poison, few avenues of harm exist for beings such as I," Alastor said.

"Thou seems weary. Come, come in close to the fire and warm thyself."

Against his instincts, all of which seemed to be indicating he was a fool and ought to return home, Alastor did. He shook off the last traces of snow into Honor's hideous rug and went to dry his coat in the warm glow of the hearth.

"'Tis nothing but the same grievances as always," Alastor said. "My brothers torment me, seeking my position as heir, and my father belittles my efforts."

Honor lowered himself onto the floor beside him. "Those complaints of the heart are truly bothersome, for they rely upon others mending their ways, something you cannot do on their behalf."

The lines on the young man's face deepened, as if he'd stumbled into a web of his own thoughts.

"What bedevils thee?" Alastor asked. His coat had dried and returned to its full glory, yet he could not seem to leave the puddle of warmth spilling out from the fire in the hearth.

"Ah . . . it is merely . . ." Honor trailed off. "Do not concern thyself, Alastor. All things shall pass, including these worries. Tell me of thy travels. It has been an age since any correspondence has reached us. I am in dire need of a well-told tale."

Alastor's suspicions deepened. "No correspondence reaches thee? Do not tell me this is due to the meddling of the other family."

Honor had mentioned another family, the Bellegraves, once or twice before. They had made the journey over the sea together and worked first as friends, then as rivals for land and influence. Alastor knew what the next step of this was: enemies.

The blackguards were clearly after Honor's landholdings and had once slaughtered all the Redding animals and blamed it on wolves. They themselves were the predators. Alastor recognized their strategy all too well; driving occupants from their rightful homes through manipulation and fear was a common tactic of poltergeists and direweasels.

After a long stretch of quiet, Honor explained, "It has been some time since we last spoke. Around the turn of November, someone—a Bellegrave—destroyed the food we had gathered and stored to survive the winter. We have struggled to rebuild those stores, but today the first snow fell and our hope of succeeding fades. I fear they will burn the Redding houses next."

"Can thou not confront them?" Alastor asked. "Demand they answer for such acts?"

"The Bellegraves outnumber our Redding men and women—thanks to thee, our children flourish. However, you cannot give a babe a musket."

Fiends were taught to fight in the nursery. It truly

was remarkable humans had survived this long. "If they destroyed thy stores, what hast thou been eating?"

"We have received aid from the local tribes, exchanging wares for grains. But we cannot ask for more than they offer. They are wary of us, for good reason, as many Englishmen have broken their vows to them or stolen their land. Mostly, my wife, Silence, prepares leaves from the pumpkins in our gardens in whatever manner she can. They destroyed the vegetables as well."

Alastor's fur bristled. "Then fight back, man! Return their fire with volleys of thine own! Why dost thou allow them to uproot you like common weeds?"

Honor smiled faintly. His sadness tasted of dust. "It is wrong to seek revenge."

Of all the ridiculous, beetle-headed, dizzy-eyed human notions . . . Thankfully, Alastor knew how to address this human failure as well.

"It is not *revenge* to force upon them a lesson that thou art not to be trifled with, merely good sense," Alastor argued. "Thou art the leader of this small slice of earth. Thou hast solved the woes of many, taken care of its poor and helpless. Will thou let them run you off thy land—allow these errant, clay-brained beasts to harm thee, starve thee, kill thy family out of their own greed? They do not have thy sense of right and wrong. They must learn. Thou must teach them."

Honor shook his head. "I must turn my cheek. I cannot do them harm in return."

It took every ounce of strength Alastor had not to blow out an exasperated breath. Humans! Honestly.

"If thou cannot," Alastor said, finally arriving at the opening he'd waited for, "then allow me."

Honor turned, horrified. "No. *No*. That is not why I seek thy company. Thou dost not have to do such things."

Thou very much did, if thou intended to live the life to which thou was accustomed Downstairs. Alastor felt a twinge within him at Honor's words; an uncomfortable itch of regret, a tremble of uncertainty about all of those things about himself he held certain.

A small part of the malefactor hated Honor for it—for making him feel such things. Now he could not let this go. He would have to approach it from yet another side.

"What if no harm came to anyone involved?" he suggested. "What if every time a Bellegrave works against thy family, all those who carry the Redding name will have their fortune increased tenfold? It will reward thy good behavior, which might very well teach them what thou has failed to."

Honor did not say no. Instead, he watched the fire, his expression transforming from denial to consideration. Alastor tried not to stare at the man's worn-out coat. Its missing buttons.

Despite his apparent hunger, his struggles to survive, Honor still possessed within him a proud bearing. It was no wilting flower that upended his old world to settle in a new one. That took a certain kind of hunger: for freedom, for control, for mastery over the things previously denied to him.

By the measure of human morality, Honor was innately *good*. By the scale with which fiends measured themselves, he would have already have been fed to a dragon to avoid the annoyance of having to listen to his beliefs.

Ambition was the enemy of decency. Alastor wondered which instinct might triumph within Honor Redding.

"Such a thing is within thy power?"

"Of course," Alastor said. "If thou art willing to pay the price. As my payment, perhaps those in thy family, thy dear, dear wife, thy child and any after, they might join thee in temporary service? So that thou might all remain together, of course, for that while."

He did not tell him that luck could not be created, only taken from others. As fortunate as the Reddings would be, the Bellegraves would find their own bled dry. That satisfied Alastor's taste for revenge, and soon Honor would see the benefit of striking back directly rather than cowering like a worm.

"I . . ." Honor began. "It is surely tempting. . . ."

"Believing thou dost not deserve such things shall always hold thee back from thy dreams," Alastor warned. "Accept this gift I offer. *Seize* it. Or art thou afraid of how far it might take thee? How thou might prosper?"

Honor's face hardened like stone. Alastor had dug deep

enough to strike at the pride he'd suspected was there. "I fear nothing. I shall do whatever is necessary to protect my family, no matter the cost."

Alastor turned his face toward the warmth of the fire, licking his fangs in anticipation.

Grimhold

Alastor remained quiet as we trudged our way up the hill, cloaks tied tight around our necks, hoods up. For several long minutes of walking, the only sound was the call of the ravens perched along the streetlamps, or the flap of their broad wings as they swooped down to collect a crimson rat scurrying along the street.

Then, seemingly all at once, the fiends who lived in the Scales emerged from their houses. Some carried trunks and small pieces of furniture on their backs. Others appeared with objects of art, dining platters, statues, and jewelry clutched in their arms.

Nell and I stepped in closer together. My heart kicked up its pace a little more, until it felt like I was wearing a flashing neon sign that read HUMAN HERE. COME GET YOUR DINNER.

I forced myself to take in a breath and relax my bunched-up shoulders. I was doing this. *We* were doing this.

Get into the house, save the changelings, kidnap Nightlock, and then go get Prue.

This was the beginning of the end.

Winding my way up the street toward the Crown, the step where the towers had stood, I felt my confidence building, and my focus sharpening. Prue needed me. My family needed me—

Something heavy—the edge of a mirror—slammed into my skull, knocking me sideways into Nell.

One of the corpselike fiends, a ghoul, looked over its gold frame with a sneer and said, "Apologies—I did not see you there, ghastly sir."

I clutched at my hood, dragging it down farther over my throbbing head. The ghoul gave an apologetic bow and dusted off my shoulder before continuing on its way.

Maybe the sneer was just . . . his normal face?

"Every fiend must remain calm!"

An ogre in armor stood on one of the many sets of stairs carved into the mountain, ushering fiends to the Crown one by one. He had cupped his hands around his mouth to amplify his voice, but it was mostly lost to the clattering of hooves, stomping of feet, and the creak of metal wagon beds as they were loaded.

Nell took my arm and dragged me toward the stairs.

Do not breathe as you pass beside the ogre, Alastor warned.

There was no time to warn Nell besides gesturing toward my face. I sucked in a deep breath, holding it until my whole chest burned. The ogre never once looked down as we passed under his waving arms, keeping between two lycans.

By the time we reached the Crown, my breath was ready to explode back out of me.

Can I release it yet?

Of course. You never had to hold it in the first place.

That little . . . *I thought I had to avoid doing it so they couldn't detect I was human!*

I was merely testing how obedient you are.

Anger burned in me, hot and sharp. *Well, woof, woof, Al—if I get caught or eaten, so do you!*

My power would at least cause terrible indigestion. In the end, you'd be nothing more than passed gas, a brief stink in an immortal realm—

"It's not a competition!" I snapped.

Flora turned around sharply, huffing out a "Quiet!"

Beneath the shadow of the hood, Nell gave me a concerned look. I waved it off, shaking my head. It *wasn't* a competition.

Because no matter what, I was going to win.

"This street must be evacuated, by order of the queen! Move to the shelter of the old prison—you'll be safe there, by the queen's side!" another ogre called out. "She will not let anything happen to you!"

They're evacuating* to *Skullcrush? Alastor asked, suddenly alarmed.

Crap. It sounded that way.

This cannot be . . . Surely, the situation is not as bad as this.

I was focusing on a different, but related problem: if they were evacuating to Skullcrush Prison, it meant every living fiend in the realm was literally standing between me and Prue.

Escaping back to the human world was about to get significantly more complicated, especially if there was only one mirror in the whole prison we could use to travel.

I stepped around a hob dragging a trunk twice his height. Tears pooled in his enormous eyes, clinging to the lower lids. "She'll—she shall save us, Gory, she will. . . . Don't cry, my fellow, no, no, don't cry—"

Gory being, I think, the salamander curled up inside the glass vase the hob had strapped to the top of the metal trunk. It scraped and groaned against the cobblestones, until a lycan bent down and lifted it, salamander and all, onto his shoulder.

"Come on, then, Webslaw," the wolf growled softly, stooping again so that the thick-bellied hob could climb up his arms and perch on his other shoulder. "It's not far to the prison. You'll be safe there."

What is he doing? It's not a fiend's way to help another fiend, and yet . . . A pang of some swift-moving emotion punched at my gut, but it hadn't come from me. Alastor's astonishment lingered longer. *They must know that I will save them from this. I will save them, and my kingdom.*

"You know," I muttered, feeling the seething knot of the demon throbbing inside my skull. "Maybe the problem isn't that everyone else has changed. It's that you haven't."

At that, Alastor's fury puffed out like a blowfish, sending spikes of his anger through me. I staggered at the pain, nearly losing my balance on the cobblestones.

You speak of things beyond the capacity of your feeble mind, Alastor said coldly.

He was only proving my point, but I decided to leave it at that.

The three of us walked the rest of the way in uneasy silence, winding our way through the piles of stone left behind from the destroyed towers.

It wasn't far, once we broke off from the bulk of the fiends. They flowed in one direction around the mountain to get to the shelter of the prison, and we went the other way.

Nightlock's house was nestled between the remains of two towers. The structures, which once must have been massive, now looked like little more than a giant's broken fangs. Their remains curved slightly up over the house, framing it the way I would in a painting.

To reach the manor-sized home, we were going to have

to climb a narrow, zigzagging path of stairs that seemed to stretch on for miles.

Even if I survived the climb without passing out, I wasn't sure where we could even enter. There was one tower that served as the backbone of the house, wide and sturdy. Smaller spiraling towers sprouted from it on all sides like the arms of a cactus. The decorative spikes that jutted out from between the stones only reinforced the comparison.

At its highest point was a weather vane, the iron shaped to look like a human who had fallen asleep—no. Nope, never mind. It had been made to look like a human skeleton with a sword plunged into its belly. Fun.

I stepped back, craning my neck up to make sure that it wasn't an actual human skeleton.

I know this place. Alastor's recognition flared in me. *This is Grimhold House.*

I turned to tell the girls as much—that we might actually have an advantage for once—but they were already disappearing over the edge of where the pathway met the house's empty moat.

My nerves jumped as Nell and Flora dropped into the pit. There was a narrow ledge carved into the wall of the moat, maybe a foot wide. A short distance away, beneath the bridge that served as the start of the house's impossibly long stairway, was a metal door, left open just wide enough for us to slip through.

I do not like this, Alastor told me as I slid down from the street. Nell steadied me until my toes found the ledge. I had to flatten myself against the rough wall in order to inch along it. *This was Bune's abode. And he himself taught me that what appears as a blessing is often really an invitation to suffering.*

There was a faint crack in the words, as if some memory had surfaced in time to splinter them.

My fingertips turned white as I gripped the slight overhang above us. Loose dust and stone scraped under my foot.

Somewhere nearby, a door slammed like a cannon shot. Flora flinched—hard enough for her right foot to slip out from under her.

She leaned forward, trying to regain her balance. Her eyes flashed bright emerald and her mouth parted at the start of a scream.

I threw out my arm, sucking in a gulp of air as her arm slid through my grasping fingers. "No—"

At the last second, her hand clamped tight around mine. My body jerked with the force of catching her weight and absorbing the momentum of the fall. I bobbed back and forth, my toes rising dangerously off the ground, then my heels, teetering there.

Oh no—not now—not right this second—

The edge of the small walkway literally crumbled beneath my foot, whole shards of the stone clattering down into the pit beneath us. I looked down as I tried to hang on to Flora, who couldn't get her feet back under her.

I shouldn't have.

It wasn't far to fall, no. But lining the basin of the moat was stagnant gassy-green water and the sharp, pearly bones of a monster. It looked as if it had simply sunk to the bottom and died, leaving its remains to become a deadly trap to stumble into.

I told him not to overfeed the leviathan! Alastor moaned. *Alas, poor Goober.*

Breath stuck in my throat. Out of the corner of my eye, I saw Nell lift her arm, as if to cast a spell—only to freeze up. Her outstretched fingers trembled, and her face was a mixture of fear and uncertainty.

Do it, I thought, *just cast the spell! Just* trust *yourself!*

Flora's grip on my arm intensified as she tried to pull herself back onto the ledge. Her pale green skin bloomed red with the effort of hanging on.

More heavy doors slammed, and the loud clatter of wheels overhead announced the arrival of what must be the dinner guests. Voices flared as they passed over the bridge.

Let the elf fall and the fates decide the outcome! Let her fall!

What muscles I had in my arms and legs shook wildly as I tried to lift Flora by sheer strength. My world lurched sharply. I couldn't tell what was trembling now: me, Flora, the stone underfoot, or all of us together.

Nell let out a strangled sound, her arm still outstretched.

"Do it!" I whispered. "Whatever it is, just *try*—!"

Al's voice clanged in my ears, as harsh as an out-of-tune note. ***Prosperity, take care—!***

And then, before I could even suck in my next breath, the ground dissolved beneath me and we fell.

The Unliving
Zachariah Livingston

In the second it took for my heart to stop, I realized I wasn't falling. I was *floating*—cupped by a pocket of air that rocked me back and forth like a hammock.

Nell had made it across the ledge to the bigger, sturdier platform below the bridge. Her lips moved, quietly repeating whatever spell was keeping us afloat. Relief poured over her face, but it didn't wipe out the fear I'd seen before. Not completely.

I swung my gaze to the left, finding a softly hiccuping Flora staring at the place where my hand was still clamped firmly around hers.

"Are you okay?" I whispered.

Her eyes widened. Above us, on the bridge, a fiend sang

out, "Madam Badnight! My, you look radiantly hideous! Care to walk with me to the house?"

I pressed my lips together, sealing in my breath. *Don't look down . . . good little demons, keep walking . . . keep walking. . . .* We all remained exactly where we were, suspended in the tense moment.

A growling, gravelly voice called back, "I'd rather eat my boot, you utter cad! How dare you steal my best racing lizards and act as if nothing happened!"

*Now, **there's a proper fiend***, Al said, satisfied.

Nell's face had turned ashen and her hand trembled as her fingers curled in toward her palm. She twisted her wrist as she pulled her fist back toward her chest. The air around us shook in time to each of her pants. A sheen of sweat dampened her forehead and cheeks.

"Don't. Like. Heights," the elf said. The flowering buds scattered in her hair withered in front of my eyes. Tremors raced along her skin. "Why didn't you let me go?"

The heavy, clipped steps of more fiends passed overhead, their voices little more than passing murmurs.

"Flora, hey," I whispered. Nell's magic vibrated under us, and we dipped just an inch closer to death below. I swallowed the lump in my throat and forced myself to unclench my jaw, keeping my eyes on the elf. Apparently, it was easier to pretend to be someone who was brave when you had to do it for another person. "We're okay. We'll be fine. Nell won't let us fall—"

The word choked off as the air beneath us vanished and we lurched down like sudden turbulence. Just as quickly, we were bounced right back up, but not before Flora had managed to climb up my arm and wrap her arms and legs around my head and chest.

"Flora—Flor—ack—"

Her weight made me tip back dangerously. Somewhere above us, I heard Nell grunt with effort and saw a blaze of green magic pass beneath us, smoothing over the air.

But I also felt the telltale hot rush of pins and needles filling my right arm. The way those fingers prickled as they curled into claws, rising toward Flora's arm around my neck, was a clear warning of Alastor's plan.

I gritted my teeth and shoved back against the feeling of the malefactor flooding my nerves. *Stop it!*

She'll sink us! Why die for her?

As I'd learned, you couldn't appeal to a fiend's honor. You just had to put it in selfish terms they might understand: *Why waste your power trying to shove her off when you'll need even more time to get it back?*

That's— Al's voice broke off. **Cunning, Maggot.**

Nell continued to whisper the spell, too quietly for my ears, as we floated forward. Not back toward the remains of the ruined ledge, but to the wider platform just in front of the door.

As soon as I felt my toes touch down, I turned and gripped Flora, steadying her as she landed beside me.

"See?" I told her. "We're fine."

Flora grasped my arm, staring up at me with bright, shining eyes.

"Um, really, we're okay," I said. "You can, you know, let go—"

Flora did not let go.

"You have an honorable heart, and a singular soul," she said, her voice grave. "You are no fiend at all, Prosper Redding. I will save you from your disastrous fate. I shall free you, by fist or blade, from the rascally rake who lurks inside of you. Though it may take centuries—and you will be wobbly and wrinkled and also maybe dead—Flora la Leaf will not stop, not to eat, nor to rest. Should you disappear, I will find you. I will follow you across the realms—"

"Uh . . ." I began. "Maybe . . . I mean, no thank you? But thank you?"

"—and I will slay your enemies, and create jewelry and wares that would make kings fall to their knees and weep at their beauty—" Flora knelt before me, still gripping my hand. She bowed her head and pressed her forehead against my fingers.

"Wow, okay. *Wow*," I tried again. "That is . . . um . . . a lot. And super not necessary."

There was a hard gasp behind us as Nell slumped against the wall. She pressed a hand to her forehead, her eyes wide behind her glasses. "I almost . . . You almost fell because I couldn't . . . I was too scared it wouldn't be enough. . . ."

"What a wonderful witch you are!" Flora declared. The shame on Nell's face only deepened. She tried to twist away.

"You saved us," I said, chest clenching at the sight. "Your magic—"

"*Don't* mention it," Nell said quickly, emphasizing the first word. "Seriously. Don't. I could have . . . I wasn't even sure it would work. You could both be dead."

"But we're not," I said, then emphasized, "because of *you*. You saved us."

Nell turned away, ending the discussion. She seemed genuinely shaken, and I didn't know what to say—if there was anything I *could* say—that would make her feel better.

Best not to console at all, Alastor advised, in one of his few moments of wisdom. ***It is one thing to fail yourself, and another matter entirely to fail friends.***

Nell hadn't failed us, though. That was what I wanted her to see.

Flora dug around inside her bag, retrieving the small seedling from it. A look of relief passed over her face as she held it up, giving it a thorough looking over.

"There, there," she whispered to it, stroking its leaves again. It might have been the failing light or my own nerves playing tricks on me, but I could have sworn I saw the plant shiver. "It's all right. No need to be upset."

Okay, then.

"Where does this lead?" I asked, turning toward the open door.

This is the door the servants used to feed Goober, I believe.

"How well do you know it?" I asked quietly, drawing the gazes of the girls.

Well enough, I suppose. I had to purchase the plans for it in the Assassins' Market for one of the fiends I hired to dispose of Bune. That reminds me, I wonder if I can get my money back....

Nell, seeing my expression, knew better than to ask. She turned toward Flora instead. "Are you sure this entrance is safe? How did you even find it?"

The elf sucked in an enormous breath, gathering the air she'd need to power her lungs through the story, but another voice spoke for her first.

"Because I showed it to her."

"Holy crap!"

I took a huge leap back, stumbling into Nell. She steadied me, looking less surprised to see a shade than worried.

"Marvelous," the ghost said, sounding bored. "I had forgotten how very rude the living are, or *you've* forgotten what few manners you possess."

This ghost—this shade—wasn't a wisp of light or a thunderous feeling of déjà vu or a soft voice that seemed to come from everywhere and nowhere. He wasn't even like the gentle spirit that lived in the House of Seven Terrors.

This was another *kid*.

A kid dressed in what looked like an old-fashioned suit. He wore—was that the right word? It didn't seem like he was wearing the clothes, but that they had simply become part of him.

He . . . displayed(?) a long-sleeved white shirt, a patterned vest, and short pants that ended where the knee-high socks began. There was no color to him at all. His form was like a thin sheet of bone-white parchment, lit from behind. Even his hair, which might have been dark in life, was as pale and transparent as the rest of him.

His hand brightened and solidified, just for a second, as he closed it around the door. Rather than pass through the metal, he was able to open it.

"Hello, new friend Zachariah Livingston!" Flora said, bounding forward. "This is Nell, and this is Pros—"

"You've mistaken me for someone who still has a heart and might actually care," the boy said, his accent's primness rivaling even Alastor's. "Is that the witch you spoke of cowering behind the boy with a face like a rat?"

Ouch.

How dare he slander you so—you are as attractive as a banebat.

"Prosper is the most chivalrous, handsomest human," Flora interjected sternly, her hands on her hips.

"Hey, thanks—"

"It's not his fault that he smells so bad and has ears like a troll," Flora finished. "Don't be so grouchy."

"I am deceased," the boy said, giving her a withering stare. "I shall be as grouchy as I like."

"We are what we choose to be," Flora said, "and you are choosing to be a meanie."

The ghost did not dignify that with a response. "Come in now, or don't. It does not matter to me if they dine on those little beasts. If they notice I'm missing, or if I displease my master, another decade will automatically be added to my time. And I'm already at three centuries."

Holy.

Crap.

This wasn't just a ghost—a shade, as Alastor and Nell called them. This was . . .

Your future, Al supplied, a trace of a smile in his words.

Zachariah Livingston, or someone close to him, had made a deal with a malefactor while he was alive. And upon his death, that deal came due and he was brought into servitude Downstairs.

"I want the witch to cut my chain now," Zachariah said, crossing his arms over his thin, shimmering chest. "I have been in this realm too long to trust the likes of fiends."

I hadn't noticed it at first, not until we followed him into the dark hallway behind the door and he became our only source of light, but clamped around his ankle was some kind of spiked bracelet. A seemingly endless chain glowed behind him, revealing the path he had taken down the hall and up a flight of nearby stairs.

Ah. Alastor sounded as if he'd just pieced something together. *He must have been collected by my brother Bune. When Bune no longer could serve as his master, his contracted time transferred to the house where he was assigned work. If the witch or elf promised that they could break the contract, they are fools.*

Is it possible to break it at all? I asked. *Or are you just mad they're proving that malefactors aren't all-powerful?*

A witch can break a chain of servitude if the original contractor is gone, and the contract has transferred to an unliving object, such as a house. But the magic it would require is far beyond what she has at her disposal without the moon.

Nell was already pulling out her book, checking the table of contents to find the right chapter. I knew the exact moment when she read what Alastor had just explained.

The swampy air around us reached out and fogged Nell's glasses, giving her an excuse to take them off and clean them on the hem of her cloak. Her jaw worked back and forth, as if she couldn't decide what to say.

I'd told her I didn't want lies between us, but this lie wasn't between her and me, it was between us and the shade. And, more importantly, it was *necessary.*

I felt for Zachariah and knew, whether or not he or someone else made the contract, that he was suffering. Right now, though, I had to prioritize the living.

Maggot . . . Alastor said, an odd note to his voice. *It seems you are capable of surprising me after all.*

"Okay," I told him. "Deal. But we need to save the changelings first. And you have to help us get them out alive. After that, Nell will sever your chain."

The witch in question cut me a sharp look.

"I was killed by typhus, not stupidity," Zachariah told me. His thick brows lowered into a dour look. Or a sour one. Or both. Somehow, both.

Enough. We have wasted too much time. Let me speak, just for a moment.

Against my better judgment, I let him.

"Listen, slave—"

I shoved him back down. "Aaaand you're done."

The ghost boy sulked. "I felt there was something different about you. You're one of them—or you hide one."

Tell him there is no way the other fiends will not notice his chain has been broken, the surge of magic will be too great. Moreover, the only way to truly pass on is with the help of my magic, and I will only grant it should he do as you command.

Is that true? I asked him.

Does it matter?

Right now . . . it didn't. I quickly and quietly relayed the message back to the shade. Zachariah shimmered in the dark air.

"Fine. If nothing else, I'll look on in great amusement as you inevitably fail. I'll be trapped here for another two centuries or however long it takes for the Void to devour us, but at least your deaths will be good for a laugh or two."

The Void. I hadn't thought about what would happen to the human shades serving the fiends if the realm collapsed. There was a new tightness in my throat, but I forced myself to ignore it until it went away. I didn't touch that thought again, even as it sat on my brain like an unwelcome blister.

Zachariah floated toward the stairs at the back of the small chamber, his near-translucent toes trailing against the floor. "If the queen succeeds in saving the realm, I'll ensure someone snares your shades so you're forced to help me clean up after the master's pets. The droppings are especially steamy in the summer."

What a cheerful guy. I shared a look with Nell as we followed him inside.

Hushed voices and clinking silver reached us from beyond the door at the top of the stairs. But it was the way the air smelled that got my full attention—how the traces of rotten eggs faded, only to be replaced by something I might have found at home. Pepper. Garlic. And—

My breath caught.

Freshly cooked meat.

Tender Morsels

The hard part wasn't finding the kitchen. It was getting past the constant stream of shades gliding in and out of it.

We hung back, just down the dark, candlelit hallway, waiting. I tried to track their comings and goings to figure out if there was any kind of rhythm or order to them. So far, there was none—it seemed like a rush of chaos, and the shades never once lost the vaguely panicked looks on their faces.

With visible effort, they forced their hands to solidify just enough to carry the weight of a mountain of roasted fruit, pies decorated with what looked like fried bats, and a jiggling, skull-shaped mountain of Jell-O. Gemstone-like insects floated inside the slippery pink mass, shivering with each slight movement.

"Not enough greens," Flora muttered. "No wonder fiends are so rude."

The shades came and went again, their chains of light floating just above the dirty carpets between the kitchen and the staircase that spiraled up to the next floor, where the fiends—and their ruler—were dining.

"What now?" Flora asked Zachariah. "Are any of the shades your favorite friends? Could we ask them for help?"

Zachariah bobbed on the air, as if riding some unseen current. "Of course not, you nitwit. They'll happily report me to the new master of the house for helping you. Tattling on the misdeeds of others will shave time off their own contracts. And before you ridiculous beating hearts ask, I'm assigned to sweep the halls, up and down, all bloody day and night. The house won't extend my chain to go into the kitchen."

I turned to look at Nell. She was rubbing her chin, her brows furrowed as she tried to write the script for how we were going to pull this off.

The smell of food was turning my stomach hollow, and the longer we stood there, the worse my nausea became. They couldn't possibly be serving dinner yet—we were supposed to have five hours, and we'd barely used two to rest and get here. I knew from years of painful dinner party experiences at the Redding ancestral home, the Cottage, that chefs might do some preliminary prep work, but they wouldn't start cooking *this* early—

"I suppose this is the moment I ought to tell you that

you're likely already too late," the shade said. "They moved the dinner up by two hours because of the evacuation. They're already four courses in with only three left."

Nell and I exchanged horrified looks. Flora moaned, wilting down onto her knees.

Cease this pathetic display at once, Alastor ordered. *The changelings would be one of the final courses. There's time yet to save them, if you must.*

I released a shuddering breath, reaching over to grip Nell's wrist. Her eyes focused on me again. "Alastor says there's still time—we *can* save them."

Two more ghosts, both elderly and hunched, rushed in and out of the kitchen's swinging door. Their forms drooped as they tried to balance two trays.

A thought zinged through me.

Zachariah was blocked by the house from entering the room, but we weren't. And if there was one thing I'd learned from living inside a haunted house, it was that if you couldn't be the living dead, you could make a pretty decent show of playing them.

"I have an idea, and you're going to hate it," I began.

"Is that idea me pretending I'm a shade to get into the kitchen?"

I blinked. "Er, yeah."

"I don't hate it," Nell said, leaning in close enough that our heads were bowed together. "But as much as it kills me to pass up a juicy role, it has to be you."

"Me?" I repeated. "What? Why? You're the actor!"

"Yeah, but I'm also the witch, and I need to cast a stun spell on the other shades to keep them from seeing us and raising the alarm," she said, taking out *Toil and Trouble*. "We just need something white and powdery like flour, and you need to do your arty magic with whatever we find to make you look as awful as the rest of them."

"You die of a wasting fever and see how lovely you look," Zachariah groused. "And besides, you can't stun a shade. They don't have physical form."

"No, you technically can't," Nell agreed, running her finger down a page of her book. "But you *can* temporarily dissolve them into a million little particles of light and magic and call it 'stunning' because it sounds nicer." She looked up toward me. "We're only going to be in the clear for however long it takes for them to reassemble."

I tried not to sigh. "How long is that?"

"Fifteen minutes," she said, then added, less confidently, "give or take."

I set my shoulders back, taking a deep breath.

Whatever it takes, I reminded myself.

"Okay. That'll have to be enough," I said.

If you've finished fluffing your courage, look for a store-room to the right of the staircase. I am uncertain about this "flower," but there is something you can use, if your goal is to paint yourself even paler than you already are.

That something was ground maggots.

Really? I asked him.

Bake them in a meat pie, sprinkle them on a stew—it truly is a versatile ingredient.

"Just hold your breath!" Flora coached as Nell lifted the bag over my head. "If it gets in your eyes, you'll be even sadder than the maggots were as they were pulverized."

I squeezed my eyes shut and covered my mouth and nose with my hand. But instead of water, something icy, wet, and reeking of rotten apples was dumped on my head, soaking straight through my clothes and seeping into my skin.

"Ugh—"

What a waste of perfectly good beetled juice!

"To make the powder stick," Nell explained. The apology in her voice didn't exactly ring true as she struggled to hide her smile. "Here come the maggots."

The white powder whooshed down over me. Most of it crashed into the floor and launched an explosive cloud back up into the air. The girls gagged, waving the fine dust away.

Even though I had covered my face again, I still inhaled the dust and began to cough, beating my chest to get the ground-up bugs out of my lungs. The powder quickly caked onto my skin and clothes.

Nell smeared the maggot powder into my face, stepping back to examine her work. "There's no mirror to show you, obviously, but I think it looks fine."

Zachariah floated behind her, arms crossed, looking off at the shelves filled with jars of pickling fairies. "He'll definitely be caught. Don't expect any of us to clean your organs off the fiends' weapons."

"Oh, Zachy, you're so funny," Flora said, forgetting that she couldn't actually punch his shoulder. "But what about his chain? Won't the others notice?"

"There's no time," I said. "I'll just be fast—let them out and move on. Any other advice?"

That last part was directed at Nell, but Zachariah answered. "Chef has eight arms, so best of luck to you."

Nell turned me back toward her. "Just be quick, act like you belong there, don't make eye contact with anyone, and use this—"

She pressed a small satchel into my hand. I unknotted its ribbons and looked at the glittering purple mass inside. It wasn't the same vial she had shown us earlier—the emergency out. Maybe she had more faith in me than I thought.

"Dizzy dust?" I asked.

"No, it's even stronger—I took it from Missy's shop, so you know it's going to be good," she said. Then added, "Don't use it around an open flame, okay?"

"When you say things like that, it doesn't actually make me feel better," I told her.

"Also, in case it wasn't obvious, you shouldn't breathe it in, either," she said, then gave me a firm push toward the door, the hallway, and the kitchen a few doors down. "Also, maybe don't get it in your eyes."

"Please stop talking," I begged.

"Good luck, pasty Prosper!" Flora whispered loudly. "We'll be watching!"

"Don't expect us to bury you," Zachariah said. "And if your shade gets trapped here, you definitely get the toilets."

Wonderful.

I waited until the shades had come in and out one more time before I snuck down the short hallway to the kitchen—I didn't know what the word *skulked* meant, exactly, but I'm guessing it was what I was doing. I skulked like a creep through the darkness.

I glanced back at the sound of Nell's quick whispering and three loud popping gasps, only to find the hallway aglow with a sea of sparkling magic particles.

By the realms . . . Even Alastor sounded a little awed by the display.

Nell and the others ducked around a corner, and she leaned forward only to mouth, *"Glide, glide!"*

I slid one leg forward along the carpet's long embroidered snake, on to the next carpet, along the back of the snake until I reached the swinging kitchen doors. The same garlic smell was even stronger now, mingled with roasted *something* and the tang of soured sweetness. Pots and pans clattered inside, making it seem as if there was an army of chefs and not just one fiend who was many-armed, and dangerous.

Aside from the usual kitchen sounds—and the frantic

chop-chop-chop of a knife hitting a counter—there was a gurgling, muted voice singing.

"Little beasties, see how they gleam, when I chop*! I make them scream—"*

I pushed the door open, roasting with the wave of heat that billowed toward me. The room was smaller than I'd imagined standing outside of it, and much of what space it had was taken by a massive metal stove that looked like a cousin of a pipe organ.

Fire burst from beneath the boiling pots and pans, rocking them on their burners. I held my breath as the exhaust pipes belched out greasy smoke and crispy flecks of food.

"—tiny gristle bits, oh-so-plump, fatten them up to carve their rumps—"

The fiend working the stove was a whirl of thin, slick arms, each with dozens of small suction cups. It had the upper body of a man—a very, very purple man, with a very, very pointed head. So pointed, in fact, the chef's hat perched on it barely fit.

The chef had two large tentacles where a man would have had legs. The other six were all occupied with moving pots around, chopping, or spooning out soup into skull-shaped bowls.

I gave a wide berth to the collection of knives hanging on the wall, all of which clattered together like wind chimes as I passed. They gleamed with bad intent in the low firelight. Beside them was an enormous empty tank that stank of salt water and mold and seemed to bubble with its own heat. There were no fish inside for the chef to cook—

Of course not. Because that tank wasn't for keeping seafood fresh. It was to keep the *chef* fresh. A trail of slime led from it to where he stood by the stove, every spare inch of it covered with roaches.

A scylla, Alastor complained. ***What fool would hire it? Everything it touches will taste of the Poisoned Sea.***

On cue, a glob of purple slime dripped into one of the pots. The mixture splattered and sizzled against the scorching surface.

"Whoopsie!" the chef sang out, patting the smoking embers that had landed on his already scorched apron. *"Crunchy minions, squealing with fright, put 'em in the oven to serve tonight—"*

The chef never once turned around. One tentacle reached down, opening the oven door.

"Nearly hot enough!" he declared, with a glance to the other side of the room. "Just enough to crisp you up, not enough to ash you."

I followed his gaze over to the racks of cages and baskets hooked onto the opposite wall. Here and there I saw lizards and snakes, most blissfully coiled around nests of eggs and enjoying the room's oppressive heat.

Beneath them, a group of changelings cowered at the edge of their cage.

The enclosure must be iron—it's the only substance capable of nullifying their power. Or else they truly are as dunderheaded as I believed them to be for not transforming into beings that could break out.

I saw Eleanor wave her legs toward the chef. The gleam of bright feathers. Fluttering moth wings. The stretch of a frog's gullet as it gulped in air. The shape of a snake's rattle tail.

But I didn't see a small black kitten with the wings of a bat.

My stomach churned.

"Now, now, little morsels," the chef said. Each of his words sounded as if it were traveling across the room in bubbles. A new coat of slime broke out over his skin like pus bursting from a festering wound. "What is there to cry about, hmm? Do you miss your little friend? The little fearsome critter who tried to save you? The master had a very special request for him. He will love seeing you again—just before your crunchy-munchy little bodies are cut up and washed down with a glass of beetled juice. Hee!"

Inside their cage, some of the changelings began to mewl and cry. The rattlesnake's tail shook out a warning of its own against the air.

He must be speaking of the witchling's Toad, Alastor said. *Then it is already too late.*

No, I thought back to him, *the chef's talking about him like he's still alive.*

I held on to that thought and wrapped it around myself like armor. Toad was alive, and somewhere in this house. And he would claw the living daylights out of me if I didn't help the others first.

It was Eleanor the tarantula who noticed me. Her legs began to do a little anxious dance, as if she didn't know whether to be excited or afraid. I pressed a finger to my lips, keeping my eyes on the back of the chef's head as he tossed a whole pot of black noodles into the air and caught it in a different hissing pan.

I took a step forward, feeling something under my foot in the instant before I pressed it down.

Crunch.

My heart slowed to a single, tormented thump. Black guts oozed out of the roach smashed beneath my foot. The rattling in the cages stopped.

The pans stilled on the stove top.

And the butcher's knife came whistling through the air, straight for my head.

A Feast for Fiends

The knife spun toward me handle over blade, blade over handle, its dingy metal glowing like a demonic eye. A rush of painful prickling woke me out of my deadly trance. Alastor took control and threw us to the floor.

The knife *thwacked* into the door, making it sway open and shut.

I jumped to my feet, reaching for the sachet that Nell had given me with shaking hands. A sharp, high whistle was the only warning I had as Al danced us away from the next knife, slamming us into the side of the putrid water tank.

"How dare you enter my kitchen without permission, filthy shade," the chef gurgled. "The master will have a century for this!"

Without thinking, I opened the small sack and tossed its entire contents into his face—and into the flames licking the pots on the stove behind him.

The scylla's two black eyes blinked as he inhaled the dust, each arm quivering before going limp.

He fell against the stove top with a horrifying *thud*, banging his pans around. I saw his sleepy face for only a second before the whole room roared.

An emerald tide of heat and light blasted from the stove, pawing at the ceiling, lancing out far enough to make the water tank crack and burst. The rancid contents washed out, smothering the flames before they could devour the creatures trapped in the cages.

I slapped both hands to my mouth as the chef's charred corpse toppled to the ground. The roaches fell upon it immediately, chewing through the tentacles and carrying off whole chunks to their hidden homes in the walls.

Well done, Maggot!

"Holy crap," I said, stomach heaving. "I'm gonna be sick—"

The changelings stared between me and the melted, warped end of their cage. The parrot hugged the snake close to its chest, its feathers puffed out in outrage.

The doors swung open behind me, and I whirled around, hands still pressed to my mouth.

Nell and Flora stood there, surveying the smoldering

remains of the kitchen. Floating behind them, Zachariah raised one brow.

"I was . . . wondering why it suddenly smelled like fried calamari . . ." Nell said weakly.

"Ribbit!" Flora rushed across the room. The heat from the cage singed her hands. She yelped but didn't let go until she had the latch open.

The changelings spilled out. The parrot carried the frog between its talons, planting it on Flora's head before nuzzling the elf's pointed chin.

"I was so worried!" Flora cried.

Nell stooped to pick up Eleanor, letting the tarantula climb over her fingers and up her arms. "But . . . where's Toad? Weren't there others?"

Flora swiveled around, searching through the cages. Ribbit the parrot made a mournful sound, but the elf continued to search, finding only feathers and tufts of fur. Tears began to leak from the corner of her eyes.

"We weren't quick enough," she whispered. "All the rest . . ."

Alastor, for once, was quiet. It was a good thing, because if he'd had some smart-aleck response to that, I would have found a way to reach into my own body to strangle him.

Now that the shock of the minor explosion I'd caused was wearing off, a sharp feeling of regret buried itself in the pit of my stomach. I'd been wrong after all.

We were too late.

We'd spent too much time arguing and trying to plan when we should have just *acted*. If we were too late to save all the changelings, how could I be so certain that the same thing wouldn't happen with Prue? What if the queen got tired of waiting, or thought we only had to believe Prue was still alive?

What if—

Enough, Prosperity. My sister is cruel, but she is far more cunning than even I knew. As you said, she would not harm the girl, knowing she is the only way to bend you—and therefore me—to her will. Now stop being a fool and see to the witchling, who fears for the vermin. Her devastation tastes of lavender, and you know my dislike of florals.

He was right—Nell's knees looked like they might buckle. She kept shaking her head, staring at that empty cage. I reached out and grabbed her arm, shocked at how cold she could feel in the smoky, scorching-hot kitchen.

"I think Toad is okay," I explained quickly. "The chef said something about Nightlock having a special request for him, and Toad being forced to watch as the others were eaten. I'm going to go look for him right now."

"I'll go with you—"

I shook my head, cutting her off. Adrenaline surged through me. I could do this. "You and Flora can just . . . think of a backup plan. Find a good place to hide until Nightlock separates himself from the others. He's bound to come investigate why no more food is coming, right? We'll grab him then."

"We should go together," Flora insisted. "Together is terrific, especially against many unfriendly fiends."

"*No,*" I said sharply, ending the conversation. We didn't have time for this. I would and could do this. Alone.

Nell looked askance at me, opening her mouth to say something, but I interrupted her again, my impatience finally boiling over. "I'll do it. If something happens and you freeze again, it could be deadly—"

The instant the words were out, I wanted to take them back. Nell flinched like I had slapped her across the face. Flora lowered her chin, her eyes narrowing as she looked up at me.

"I mean," I said, scrambling for a way to soften my words. "Listen, it's just—I was only trying to—"

Do not surrender on what was spoken in truth, Alastor said.

"*Excuse me,*" Zachariah interrupted, glowering at us. "I was under the impression you were in a bit of a hurry. By my count, you've ten minutes left to carry out your next horrifically idiotic plan."

That brought me crashing back into the moment. "He's right. We'll figure it out along the way. Let's go."

Once I was upstairs, the hallway to the dining room stretched on and on. The doorway at the end seemed to grow more distant with each step. The silver tray we'd taken from the kitchen felt heavier than it had when Nell had first helped me balance it on my shoulder.

Flames on the candelabras popped and sputtered as I passed, and cackling echoed down the hall.

I looked back over my shoulder, searching for Nell's form, but the shadows had already cloaked her, Flora, and the changelings. The familiar clatter of silverware against plates and jovial voices slipped through the crooked doorframe. I could have been standing outside one of my grandmother's dinner parties—they were equally likely to have monsters inside, and I was equally unwelcome at both.

"—and of course, the fool—oh, this *fool*—thought I was just biding my time, collecting mortal garbage for my own pleasure!"

The story summoned a fit of laughter. Someone pounded on the table. Another fiend barked, as if to egg the familiar voice of the storyteller on.

"He donned a flag and thought it a cloak! He carried a doll he believed to be his leech friend—"

Wait a moment—

Who is Nightlock talking about? I asked. *You?*

No! No, of course not. Whoever it is sounds like a true fool. Go in, then. Save your flying rodent.

I took one last second to steel my nerves and pushed the door open . . . only to reveal a room brimming with light and color.

The dining chamber was an octagon, each of its eight sides braced by a curving black metal bone. It was situated under a dome made up of countless stained-glass window panels. Each one depicted a different monster, but the images of snarling fangs and claws were softened by the bejeweled gowns the artist had created for the female fiends, and the fine suits the male fiends wore.

They weren't battle scenes, or even ruminations on the many ways a fiend could kill and maim. The images were of *dancing*. Some even looked to be playing instruments.

It was a depiction of gleeful celebration, not war. Candles flickered in rooms on the other side of the glass walls; the movement of the flames somehow made it seem as though the scenes were moving, swaying to some unheard music.

This . . . this had been made by a true artist's hand. Funny. Some part of me had believed real art couldn't exist in a place like this.

This **is** *revoltingly artistic,* Al agreed. *And no doubt created by elves. This room would have been perfect for storing venom, and Bune wasted it so. No wonder he never allowed me inside. He knew I would mock this travesty for centuries.*

Wasn't it also because you threatened to kill him? I thought back.

What's murder to a family such as mine? Bune was a good sport about the assassins, likely because he managed to push me off a tower. Rather evened things out.

Speaking of Alastor's family, there was one notable

person absent from this table: Pyra. Frustration swept through me.

"You there!" Nightlock thundered from behind a stack of plates and animal carcasses stripped to the bone. "We've been waiting an *age* for someone to clear the plates for dessert! Why did you not come when called? Must I add time to your contract?"

I turned slowly, hands tightening around the empty tray balanced on my shoulder.

Decorative glass bats dangled over the long metal table, which split the chamber in two. Plump white candles had been gathered together at the very center, somehow bleeding crimson wax.

Most of the light, however, was coming from above. Glass orbs, all gleaming like black pearls, had tiny fairies trapped inside. They banged their fists against their prisons to get out, glowing with fury.

Dishes had piled high in front of each guest. A grendel stretched and stretched his neck up, the bones and joints of his back popping loudly to accommodate the change. He peered at me as I approached, his long nose resting on the uppermost plate. A line of enormous black crows screeched out a song, accompanied by crickets the size of my head.

Glide, I reminded myself, *glide!*

After a moment, the grendel turned back to the guest at his right. I let out a small, relieved breath, then began to search the room for any sign of Toad.

I slid my feet over to the nearest fiend—a crimson-skinned creature with ears that pointed straight up like a rabbit's. She wore an elaborate dress that seemed two sizes too large for her.

"Finish the story! I simply cannot get enough of it—it's more delicious than anything a dessert chef could whip up. I only wish the queen had come to hear it."

Hobs, grendels, and goblins at a malefactor's table! Alastor fumed. He continued to complain about this hob's theft of that vampyre's signature jewels, and how the grendel had terrible taste in centerpieces, and something about hoping the moths from the Festering Forest would come and eat the skin from their bones, but all those words drifted away.

My eyes latched on to a cramped iron cage on the floor, just beside one of the hobs perched high upon his chair.

Bright green eyes stared at me through the bars, alarmed. I saw the flash of white, needlelike teeth in the instant before I heard Toad's wings flutter.

"Oh yes, yes, I do so wish she had come, but she felt needed elsewhere. We shall toast again to her honor," said Nightlock. He had what looked like a fireplace poker in hand. Idly, he lifted it up over the table, letting its tip rest inside the nearest candle's flame.

Once the sharp edge was glowing with heat, he jabbed it down into the cage. Toad howled in pain as Nightlock traded his poker for a goblet. I lurched forward, nearly upending the tray in anger.

ALEXANDRA BRACKEN

"To our malevolent queen! Long may she rage!"

"Long may she rage!" the others echoed back to him.

My vision went red. The dishes clattered on my tray.

"Now, the rest of the story," Nightlock began, interrupting himself to belch. "You see, he made it so very easy for me. All I needed to do was slip into the house where the boy was staying. . . ."

Though he wore a sharp blue cone hat and his ash-gray skin looked as if it had been sprinkled with glitter dust, I recognized those bulging yellow eyes and that round nose, as red as if he'd spent the day blowing his blue snot into a tissue. He snarfed, nearly choking on his honking laugh.

"And then—and then he told me," Nightlock wheezed, bracing his free hand on his fine velveteen robes. There were golden rings on each of his fingers and around his single horn. "'Thou may refer to me as my lord and master, or My Eternal Prince of Nightmares That Lurk in Every Dark Sleep!'"

Alastor began to stir inside of me, all heat and stinging humiliation. My hand filled with the sensation of burning sand.

Puny . . . clay-brained . . . scut!

No! Al—! But the tray was already tipping forward, its contents sliding right off it and onto Nightlock's head.

The hob let out an ear-piercing squeal as a plate shattered against his shoulder, and shards of the others fell into his lap. The master of the house and guests shot to their feet, their own plates rattling with the force and speed of their movement. My heart clenched in my chest, tightening until I couldn't breathe.

"Impudent shade!" one growled.

"This toad-spotted bootlicker! Nightlock, are you all right?"

"You! Shade! That's another century for you!" Nightlock growled. "Clean up this mess immediately!"

I was already on my hands and knees, though, pretending to sweep the mess back up onto my tray while one hand felt around for the latch to Toad's cage. His black paw pointed to the right, and my fingers skimmed along the metal framing until I found the hooked hinge keeping the door shut.

"Well?" Nightlock spluttered. "What do you have to say for yourself?"

The latch was rusted and dry. I struggled to slide it open. Toad's head butted eagerly against it, urging me on.

Hang on, I thought desperately. Hang on just one more second. . . .

The latch squeaked, finally giving way. Toad's eyes flared, a warning that was already too late. Before I could wrench the door open, a clawed hand reached down and clamped over my wrist.

A Royal Reveal

The grendel's grip was like a branding iron. I squirmed at the heat of it, trying to tug free as his claws pricked my skin, threatening to draw blood.

Hold still, Maggot, Alastor said. ***Let me take the reins. I will deal with this urchin—***

"What've we here?" the grendel said, cocking her head to the side. Her neck stretched into a perfect upside-down U. "This is no shade! It smells like—"

The door I'd come through from the kitchen burst open with a thunderous *bang*. A fiend—one I'd never seen before—strode in, her shoulders back and her nose in the air. A gown of shimmering black fabric, like a night sky back home, flowed out behind her.

All the different types of fiends seemed to have at least one trait that was vaguely humanlike, but this one, *this* fiend, was the closest thing to us I'd seen so far.

The smooth, shell-like quality of her face was terrifying; it didn't wrinkle, even as she bared her pointed teeth. It was the kind of pale that was nearly translucent, as if she had no blood or veins. The lines of her face were nearly nonexistent. A notch for her nose, a lipless mouth, ears that were just slightly too long and slightly too pointed. One eye was blue, one black.

Pyra.

I turned, searching the room for the malefactor's panther form. The fiends around the table shook off their stupors, falling into bows and curtsies. Even the grendel eased her hold on me to smooth out her full skirt.

This is her true appearance. The form a malefactor takes Downstairs.

My knees locked. I glanced over at the grendel, making sure she was still distracted before trying to slide my wrist and hand through her loosened grip. My heart skipped one beat, then two.

Think . . . I could drop down under the table, get Toad out, and then . . .

"Y-Your Majesty!" Nightlock spluttered, sliding down from a carefully balanced stool. With each step toward her, he bowed. Finally, he took her long fingers in his small hand and slobbered onto her knuckles. "We did not expect you. I was told you were busy with preparations at Skullcrush. Shall I have the shade set a place for you?"

"You shall not," Pyra said airily. "I will not be staying! I've come for that strange shade and the changeling. If you would please provide them, I will be on my way."

A queen would never say please, Alastor said, his tone darkening with suspicion.

Maybe it was the distance, or the way the fairy lights were flickering in the glass orbs, but it almost looked like Pyra's mouth didn't move at all when she spoke. There was something off about her.

And her voice is oddly . . . piercing? Alastor noted.

"But of course, Your Darkest Majesty," Nightlock said. He glanced behind her. "Did you come alone? Where are your guards?"

Very off. And we weren't the only ones who noticed.

Around me, the dinner guests exchanged curious glances. The spell of the queen's sudden arrival was quickly wearing off. Unable to get my hand free, I lifted my foot to use the heel of my shoe to get the cage's latch open. Toad tried to help me from inside, holding the sole more firmly against it with his claws.

Almost have it . . . I thought. Just a second more. . . .

Nightlock straightened, taking a step back. "And why did you come up from the servants' floor?"

"Because . . ." That ringing, prim voice wavered. "I chose to. That's why. And furthermore, how dare you question me?"

Pyra's voice was like a thread of dark smoke curling against your senses. It was regal and appropriately demanding, but it was too high, too—

The wall of stained glass across the room burst inward with a ferocious howl. Several of the fiends at the table yelped and screamed, scrambling to get away from the shards as they thwacked into the walls and clattered across the tables.

The grendel finally released me, turning to shield her face from the glass. I dropped down onto my knees beside Toad's cage just as the howlers leaped through the new opening in the room.

From under the table, I watched as Sinstar's lanky form stepped over the edge of the broken window frame and dropped down onto the carpet. His many-eyed gaze swept around the room.

"That's not the queen, you imbeciles!" he snarled. "I just left her—in Skullcrush Prison!"

One second, the queen was there; the next, she was gone with a *pop*. In her place floated a tarantula.

Eleanor, the changeling.

Nell jumped out from where she'd been hiding behind a suit of armor, clearing her throat. Of course. She'd been the one voicing the fake Pyra. And Flora wasn't far behind, bursting in through the servants' door, her fists already raised to fight.

Then the latch on Toad's cage finally gave way.

He wasted no time. The moment he was free of his iron prison, a burst of power swept out, upending the dining room table. The guests ran, shoving past one another for the door opposite the servants'.

One of the howlers charged toward Toad, only to be thrown back by the surge of magic as a monster raged out from the swirling mass of light.

Toad wasn't just huge—he was prehistorically gargantuan. His fangs lengthened so they now escaped his lips. He towered over me, his jet-black coat no longer fluffy, but shining and sleek. With a screech, his bat wings smashed through the stained-glass dome, sending glass raining down over us.

Under the cover of his leathery wings, I turned back toward where Nightlock had been only moments before. The hob had dropped onto his hands and knees and now crawled toward the servants' entrance as the room exploded into chaos around him.

"Eleanor!" I shouted, pointing at Nightlock. "Nell! Grab him!"

Nell was busy smashing a serving tray over the heads of the goblins who rushed at her, dinner knives in hand. The tarantula disappeared with her own flash of light, emerging a second later a hundred times her usual size. She leaped onto Nightlock, wrapping her legs around him until she'd created her own prison.

The other howler raced toward Nell, only to be batted away with a swipe of Toad's enormous paw. The howler whimpered as he flew through the last remaining panel of the stained-glass wall, disappearing into the hallway beyond it.

Sinstar unsheathed his jagged sword, taking a menacing step toward me. "If my mistress did not want you alive, thinskin, you would be dead a thousand times over!"

"Er—I'll go call for the ogre guard, shall I?" another goblin said, stuffing his hat down onto his head and fleeing through the doorway.

"Shades! Attend to your master!" Nightlock hollered. "Attend to me!"

Pathetic, Alastor snarled. ***Tell the overgrown kitten to make ribbons of his guts!***

The other howler, realizing it couldn't take on Toad, turned to a smaller, softer target: Flora. It lowered into a crouch and, with a terrifying growl, charged her, claws fully extended.

"Flora!" I shouted. "Look out—"

A streak of bright red flashed in front of her, momentarily distracting the howler. *Ribbit.*

Startled, the howler misjudged the distance between himself and Ribbit, catching the changeling on the wing instead of mauling Flora's face.

The howler landed hard, skidding into the overturned table. A streak of blood lashed against the broken glass scattered across the floor. The changeling plummeted with a heart-stopping cry of pain.

Horror left an icy coat around my skin as Flora dropped to her knees, clutching the changeling to her chest. "Ribbit! No!"

A *clang* jarred me back to my senses. And right back into terror.

Sinstar rounded on Nell, his sword slashing and slashing as he drove her back across the room. She held up the tray like a shield, her face wild as she struggled. *"Take my light—no, guide my hand, give me . . . give me . . ."*

A spell. She couldn't get out a spell to defend herself. Every time she tried to begin one, it seemed like she'd change her mind midsentence, until finally, it was nothing but a jumble of words and panic. I pivoted, searching the floor for one of the knives I'd seen, heart punching against my rib cage. Finally, my hand closed over one.

No! Maggot, stay put—

"Get away from her!" I shouted, wielding the blade as I rushed forward.

"Come on, boy," Sinstar said, kicking Nell away. She slammed onto the floor, her breath blowing out of her with the force of the impact. "I'll cut me off a piece of that thinskin. You only have to be breathing, not in one piece!"

The knife didn't shake in my hand, not once, but I still

felt the burning rush of needles under my skin as Alastor struggled to take over. *I'm a bonny fighter, Maggot—let me carve my name into his hide!*

Through the racket of the fiends' escape and the growling, a new voice emerged. Thin, warning. "You shouldn't have done that. . . ."

Out of the corner of my eye, I saw Flora flinch. In her hands, Ribbit's feathered chest rose in shallow pants. Blood dripped down over the elf's hands as she carefully removed a piece of glass from the wing the howler had injured.

"You shouldn't have done that," Flora said again, her eyes glowing bright green.

"Flora . . . ?" Nell began, startled. "Are you okay?"

A dark shadow fell over the elf's face, and her skin seemed to harden into a husk of wood. That quickly, she went from a blooming flower of a creature to a wicked thorn. Her voice deepened as if rising from some ancient darkness, and seemed to echo. An involuntary shiver passed over my skin.

"Now," that strange voice said, "you get my distraction."

Her . . . distraction?

She turned toward Nell, her face frighteningly unexpressive. The words rolled out of her like thunder. "Remember what I asked?"

Nell gawked at her but nodded, reaching down to touch the elf's outstretched hand. Magic trailed out from her fingertip, whirling where it collected in the elf's palm.

Flora retrieved the small seedling from her bag, smoothing the glowing essence over its leaves. The plant flared even brighter than it had when she'd fed it a few hours ago.

It trembled as it rose out of her palm, floating there for several long heartbeats. None of us moved, none of us spoke.

What is this? I asked Alastor.

I . . . do not know, Alastor said, sounding almost stunned. *The elf's wrath transforms the plant, clearly.*

The seedling dropped to the floor.

Where it sat, unmoving.

Flora shook herself, her skin rippling over her form as it softened. The glow faded from her eyes, as did the hard look. As she came back to herself, she seemed almost bewildered. "What's happening? Did it work wonderfully?"

I stared at her. "Was something supposed to happen just now?"

The ghoul let out a screeching laugh, cutting Flora off before she could explain.

"Elf, your kind never fails to disappoint," Sinstar sneered. "I'll make myself a flute with your bones. At least then you'll be useful."

"You won't get close enough to try," Nell bit out. "Test me, I dare you—"

The trembling began like a creeping nightmare. The silverware and broken goblets jolted at our feet, then danced across the stones. The metal frame of the dome moaned, its joints creaking. The whole house seemed to shift on its foundation, stones popping out of place as it was rocked by a growing roll of thunder.

For one horrible second, I was sure we were all about to be swallowed by the Void.

Except magic suddenly whipped into a tornado of sparkling light around Flora, all but swallowing her.

"Flora!" I called. "What are you doing?"

"I told . . . you . . ." she called out, that echoing tone edging back into her words, "this realm could use . . . *more . . . green!*"

Her small seedling shot up, rapidly growing as it absorbed the magic. Soon it was the size of a school bus and nothing—and no one—could do anything to stop it. An offshoot curled around the table, crushing the solid metal in its grip like it was only paper. Other vines grew out of it, snaking through the stones, the doors, the walls, strangling anything in their path.

Nell shoved herself up off the floor, grabbing the bundle that was Eleanor holding Nightlock. Toad's tail snared the three of them and deposited them onto his back.

A piece of the ceiling fell and shattered at my feet.

That was all Toad needed to see. He swept a paw out to hook Flora by her cloak, tossing her onto his back behind the others. The other, smaller changelings clung to whatever part of him they could seize.

"Prosper!" Nell shouted. "Come on!"

The stonework was crumbling, and as each floor above

us caved in, more and more furniture and instruments and portraits and weapons rained down.

Sinstar screamed in rage, running toward me through the falling glass and stones.

Toad's leg was covered in dust; I couldn't get a good grip on his fur as his wings began to beat and he lifted off the ground. More of the monstrous vines rose from the earth, braiding in and out of each other, destroying everything they touched. Toad was clear of the dome, but my fingers were sliding, I couldn't hang on—

Nell turned around, trying to climb down over the changeling's back. Her hand stretched toward me, "Come on! Just a little more!"

"No! You're mine, thinskin!" The ghoul jumped from the table to the remains of the dome. His claws hooked around my foot, yanking down.

No! Hold on, Prosperity!

The weight of the ghoul was too much. I kicked, but couldn't shake him—Toad's fur slid through my fingers, and the last thing I heard before I fell was Nell's terrified scream.

The Devouring Dark

My world became darkness, dust, and a loud, insistent voice ringing inside of my aching skull.

—ity!

No. I wanted to sleep. I just needed to . . . to rest. . . . My body felt like one big bruise. Inside, it felt as if I'd been hollowed out.

Prosperity!

Not yet . . .

Awaken! Prosperity, awaken now!

Awaken . . . Awaken the singing bone . . . A familiar voice wove through that thought, and bit by bit, the words began to change. To sharpen. *I awaken thee, singing bone—* no, not singing bone. But close . . .

MAGGOT! I WILL NOT PERISH HERE CRUSHED

LIKE A WORM AND NEITHER SHALL YOU! WAKE! UP!

My eyes snapped open. Two things quickly became very clear:

1. I was somehow still alive despite falling back into a collapsing house.
2. There was a massive wall of stone hovering an inch above my face.

"Holy . . ." I croaked out, *"crap."*

A flickering net of magic was the only thing keeping thousands of pounds of stone from turning me into a bloody splatter. I was too scared to even blink, on the chance it could upset the careful balance of things around me.

Can't . . . hold . . . much . . . longer . . . Alastor warned. *GET. UP.*

Pain sang through me from the top of my head down to a toe that might actually have been broken, but I scrambled out from under the magic. I crab-walked back until I bumped up against the remains of the dining table, cutting my hand on a stray piece of glass.

Alastor let out a heavy sigh of relief as the magic dissipated and the stones thundered down.

"Thanks . . ." I breathed out.

Alastor's voice was faint. *I saved . . . myself . . . do not . . . insult me with your . . . sentimentality.*

I looked around. The plant house had shredded Grimhold down to its foundations; we'd fallen into one of its lower levels, but there was only vapor-filled dark sky over my head. The vines covered nearly every surface of its remains.

A few feet away, rubble shifted. I jumped as stones scattered across the fractured ground, rolling to a stop just short of my feet. Alastor sniffed once, then again.

"Jeez, who's the emotional one now?" I asked him.

Alastor's presence trilled in me like an alarm. *That was not me.*

I turned slowly, only to be met with the sight of a howler pulling himself free from the wreckage. The shaggy dog shook the dust out of his coat, his eyes blazing red as he bared his teeth.

I pushed myself off the ground, heart jumping into my throat.

Up! Alastor urged. *Climb!*

As Grimhold collapsed, it had buckled inward, creating what looked like a staircase for giants. There was nowhere to go *but* up.

I scrambled onto the broken table, then gripped one of the nearby vines and used it to haul myself up onto the next flat section of stone above me. With adrenaline surging, it was easier to ignore the throbbing pain all over my body.

On your right!

I gripped the vine again and kicked my feet off the stones, swinging left. The second howler wailed as it caught only the edge of the debris. Its claws scored the stone, fighting desperately to hang on.

Breath slammed in and out of me as the dog gave one last whimper before its paws slid down and it fell through the vapor, into the pit below.

The other one nears, Alastor warned.

Even if I couldn't see the demon dog, I heard its heaving pants. Its smell, like rotting pumpkins, came next. I fought to find my footing against the house's broken foundation, climbing the vine one hand over the other.

It was the craziest thing, because that whole time, even with the howler bounding from one section of stone to the next, all I could think about was that rope hanging from Peregrine S. Redding Academy's gym ceiling. The one I'd never been able to climb, even with Coach Tyler screaming at me from below, telling me to engage my biceps.

I sank into the task, walking my feet up the side of the stones.

Finally, my fingers found a ledge—the place where the house had once connected to the maze of steps from the street below, I realized. My legs shook with the last quivering effort it took to half crawl, half push myself onto the flat surface of the landing.

A cold hand clamped over the back of my neck, wrenching me up off the ground.

No!

"I knew that the queen's roach of a brother wouldn't let you die," the bounty hunter sneered, "like I knew the realms would not be cruel enough to deny our queen the chance to kill you herself."

Blue blood oozed from a jagged cut down the side of his terrifying face. Up close, his splotchy skin resembled a slowly rotting corpse.

"Listen, Sirsang—" I began.

"It's *Sinstar!*" the ghoul hissed.

"Okay, Simsaw," I said. Panic had drained every useful thought out of my head but the one I needed most of all. That one rose coolly from the depths of my memory, where I'd stashed it years before, back when Grandmother forced Prue and me to take self-defense lessons after someone had tried to kidnap us on the way home from school.

I stopped scratching at his hand and instead reached around, jabbing my thumbs into his eyes.

The ghoul screamed in pain, dropping me to clutch at his face.

Well done, Maggot, Alastor said.

I shoved myself up and ran for the stairs, jumping down them two and three at a time. Sinstar's steps pounded behind me, picking up speed. The remaining howler let out a sharp bark from somewhere behind us, but the stairs were so uneven, and I was moving so quickly down and down and down to the street, I didn't look back.

I should have.

The ground began to tremble once more. Loose debris clattered across the stairs, and the sky boomed with a phantom thunderstorm. The realm sounded like it was about to erupt from within . . . or something mammoth was creeping up to consume it.

The Void.

I'd been scared before when Sinstar had grabbed me, but it was nothing compared to the terror that pumped through me now.

Rats fled up the mountain in a thrashing river of crimson. As the quaking intensified, chunks of the towers' remains smashed down, crushing half of the rats in one bloody go.

Can't die, I thought desperately, won't die, can't die, won't die—my mind fixated on the words with each step, until I couldn't even hear Alastor's frantic cries ringing in my skull. I risked a glance back, unsurprised to find Sinstar closing in, too focused on catching me to take in the wave of pure darkness sweeping in behind him as it devoured Grimhold and the towers we'd already passed.

It's not stopping, I thought, trying to pump my legs faster. But there was nowhere to go.

I threw one last look over my shoulder as the Void rolled over Sinstar, devouring him with a satisfied growl.

Air swirled around me in a sudden hard gust. Something snapped in place around me, and my feet left the ground.

Dead—I was dead—

"Prosper! *Prosper!*"

My gaze shot upward at the sound of my name.

Toad had grabbed me between his two enormous front paws. Nell leaned around the side of his neck, shadowed by the dark sky.

"Are you okay?" she called down. "Hold on!"

Toad flew in a wide, smooth arc around the curve of the mountain. A castlelike fortress came into sight, magic fires roaring inside the imposing lanterns hooked along its jagged gates. Rows of skulls clattered and bobbled from where they balanced on the pikes above them.

It was as if the Void saw the magic burning at the same moment I did. As quickly as the stormy force had arrived, it abated. The quakes eased off, but not before one last tremor sent a bolt of power up through the street, fracturing it.

The Void had spilled forward like ink, consuming everything but the back half of the Crown. The fortress sat on the end of a long offshoot of the mountain. There was a deep ravine between the street and where the structure was situated, making it impossible to cross the distance on foot.

A few stones at the edge of the street marked where the old walkway must have stood. With the prison's facade carved to resemble a screaming human skull, I could almost picture how the bridge must have passed through the circular gate that served as the mouth, swallowing inmates forever.

Skullcrush Prison. It was the realm's final hope, and it stared down the Void with all the reckless courage that came with being the last of its kind. Enormous glass containers of magic burned bright like gemstones in the sockets of the facade's skull, its presence the fiends' only defense against the encroaching darkness.

But the Void was satisfied—for now.

21

Fate's Stage

Toad flew low, setting me down in the shadow of a former tower before landing himself.

"Prosper!" Nell said again, sliding down the changeling's side. "Are you okay? I saw you fall, I was so sure you were dead—"

"I'm okay," I told her. For now. When the shock of everything that just happened a second ago wore off, I might be on the ground curled into a little ball and weeping, but for now, I was alive and in one piece and the prison was *right there*. Prue was *right there*. And we had our blue-slobbering ticket in.

I went to help Flora down. The elf clutched a small bundle of feathers to her chest, the whole of her focus on the wounded changeling. At the same time, Nell wrapped her arms around Toad's massive head. The CatBat obliged her, purring loudly as it nuzzled her with its face.

"I was so worried about you!" Nell said, her voice tight. "You're not—you're not allowed to leave. You hear me? You can't leave me."

The last changeling on Toad's back was Eleanor, still struggling with a squirming Nightlock in her arms. I held up my hands and called to her, "Roll over the edge. I'll catch you."

Three weeks ago, I probably would have crawled under a table to hide if you told me that I'd be talking to a spider that was almost as tall as me, and urging it to swan dive into my arms.

I absorbed Eleanor and the hob's weight with a grunt, landing on my backside. The spider's pincers gave a little twitter of gratitude as Nightlock snarled, "I demand to be released! I shall scream until an ogre guard comes—"

Eleanor jammed the tip of one of her hairy legs in his mouth, silencing him.

"Can you hang on to him for a few more minutes?" I asked her. The tarantula gave a full-body bob, which I took to be the arachnid equivalent of a nod.

The other changelings had flocked to Flora's side, circling around where she held Ribbit in her arms, softly stroking her feathered chest. Big, fat tears hung at the corner of her eyes, ready to fall.

"You'll be all right, fearless friend," she whispered. "I

know you will be. I will be very brave for you, if you will be very brave for me."

"Nell," I called, gesturing to the changeling in the elf's arms. Toad let out a soft, inquiring *meow* as Nell came to stand beside Flora. When she reached out to lift Flora's green hands away, the elf spun around, curling over Ribbit protectively.

"I'm not going to hurt her, not even a little," Nell said. She slid her backpack off her shoulders and set it down in the dust and rubble to search through it.

"Aha, here we go. There *is* some left," Nell said, shaking a small red vial.

"What is that?" Flora asked at the same time I did.

It smells like roses. Poison, clearly.

"It's a healing ointment," Nell explained. "My mother— my *other* mom made it, so it's the very best. There's no one like her when it comes to the healing arts."

I shifted uncomfortably from foot to foot. The parrot in Flora's hands was soaked in blood. Was an ointment really going to be enough to save it?

No. Death creeps ever closer. I can smell the cooling of its blood.

I didn't want to know what that meant.

"Not just the ointment," Nell corrected herself, pushing her glasses back up her nose. "I've got a spell to work with it. If that's okay, Ribbit?"

The bird changeling turned its head toward her weakly, then looked up at Flora with its glossy back eye.

"It's okay," Flora whispered with a small hiccup. She held the creature away from her body, where Nell could examine it.

Nell unscrewed the cap on the vial and used the dropper to pull out a line of crimson liquid. I was surprised to see her hand shake as she released one, two, three drops over the worst of the changeling's wounds.

"By the power that is my own, mend this wounded skin and bone. By the power of the moon, grant this needed healing boon."

I took the vial of ointment from her and returned it to the safety of her backpack. Ribbit didn't move.

"Is she . . . ?" I began, my heart giving a hard thump in my chest.

Flora screwed her eyes shut and shook her head. "No. No. She would have returned to her natural form. She won't be able to hold her chosen one for much longer, though, I can feel it."

A pity.

It took me a moment to realize that there hadn't been an ounce of sarcasm in Al's comment. *You going soft on us?*

I felt him shift inside me, shivering at the thought. ***I can respect valor and fighting prowess. It is indeed a tragedy to lose a bonny fighter, regardless of the species.***

Nell rubbed at her forehead, muttering to herself as she

scanned *Toil and Trouble*, reading and rereading the spell, but I couldn't take my eyes off Ribbit, or the blood that coated Flora's skin.

Two words circled inside my head, clawing at me: *my fault.*

This was *my* fault.

I'd been the one to take charge, I was the one who had promised we could save the changelings. And I'd failed Ribbit, just like I'd failed Prue.

If I had power—*real* power—I would have been able to prevent this. Maybe it wasn't such a bad thing to long for it, magical or otherwise. I could save the people and creatures I cared about. I wouldn't have to stand around and feel as useless as I did now.

"By the power that is my own, mend this wounded skin and bone," Nell repeated, moving her hands over the bird. Over and over, she tried the spell, her voice strained with fear. *"By the power of the moon, grant this needed healing boon."*

I suppose this is the one thing I shall never understand— the desire to save one another, even at the expense of your own power. But the witchling lacks the moon, Al observed. **She has already wasted too much magic.**

I shook my head, fists clenching at my side. *Don't underestimate Nell.*

"Why isn't it working?" Nell said, scrubbing a frustrated tear off her face before it fell. "My mom never slipped like this. She would be so embarrassed watching me—so ashamed—"

Ashamed. Pain crimped in my chest.

Flora's head bowed as she drew Ribbit closer to the warmth of her chest. "Nell, you tried. . . . It's . . . it's . . ."

The changeling let out a series of whimpers. Flora's eyes widened as she leaned down, bringing her ear close to the changeling's beak. "No, no, it's all right, just rest—save your strength."

"What is she saying?" I asked.

"Ribbit is . . . She's trying to explain that she overheard ogres discussing your sister . . . something about when Pyra will make her move."

It felt like my whole body was dissolving in panic and desperation for whatever information Ribbit had. I bit my tongue—this moment wasn't about me, or Prue. It was about Ribbit.

Nell took a step back, hugging her book to her chest. There was no expression on her face, as if she were so deep in her thoughts she'd become trapped there.

Lemons, Al said quietly. *She tastes of lemons yet again. . . .*

Lemons meant sadness. Devastation.

This is the thing about pain: it never stays exactly the same. Just when you think you've beat an old hurt, or that you've finally sent grief packing, it circles back wearing a new, more terrible face. Nell had suffered through losing her mom, believing she could have been saved, and believing that she could still return. Now it felt like she was trying to keep her alive in a different way: by walking in her mother's exact footsteps.

"Nell," I said, taking her shoulders and turning her toward me. "Look at me."

She couldn't. Time was beating out a too-quick rhythm, and Ribbit's breathing had fallen out of sync with it. It slowed, labored and wheezing.

"Take it from someone who has been told every single day of his life that he wasn't good enough, and that he would never live up to his family and their name," I said. "All those voices in your head telling you that you're worthless, that you'll never be as powerful as your mother, that you won't be forgiven for what you did—they're lying to you."

At that, Nell finally looked at me. Her eyes were red with unshed tears.

"Your mom sounds like an amazing person. You told me once that she encouraged you to be who you wanted to be. There will never be another person like her, just like there can only be one Nell. And that Nell is awesome."

I took the book from her. "There's no shame in making mistakes unless you never try to fix them. I think the only way you could ever disappoint your mom is if you gave up on yourself and tried to be someone else."

Toad's head bobbed in the air. He licked the side of Nell's face, surprising her enough that she let out a startled laugh. His green eyes flashed in my direction as he lifted a paw and motioned for me to continue.

"Listen, I know we don't have time," I said. "And honestly, I don't know all that much about anything Downstairs, or even upstairs in the human world. You could tell me witches eat their own warts for breakfast and I'd believe you at this point."

"No," Nell said, "but they do use them to tell fortunes."

"Okay, see?" I said, not missing a beat. "Here's what I do know, though: *All the world's a stage, and all the men and women merely players.* You just have to believe in yourself."

Nell's face lost its hollow look. A deeply confused one replaced it. "That's not what that Shakespeare quote means. He's saying that we're all pieces in Fate's great plan and we don't really have control over any of it."

"Well, that's the only Shakespeare quote I know, so pretend it's encouraging you to remember that you're a witch—*the* witch of the House of Seven Terrors—and just because the moon isn't out, just because you've stumbled, it doesn't mean that it's not true, and that you're not powerful."

Aim for a swift conclusion, Maggot.

"So even though I know nothing about pretty much everything, I do know this: I saw you use magic in Salem. It worked every time, and I think it was because you weren't afraid it wouldn't. You never doubted what you could do," I said. "So even if you doubt yourself now, I know that I believe in you. I will always believe in you."

Nell stared at me, and slowly, some of the pain began to fade from her expression. She looked down at her hands, spreading her fingers apart. Her lips flattened into a determined line, and I recognized the way she set her shoulders back.

"I'm not going to fail," she said, her voice sounding stronger. "I was born with this power. It's mine to use." She took a deep breath. "I'm ready."

22

The Whole Truth

None of us moved. I clasped my hands behind my back, squeezing my fingers together to work out the last of my fears. Ribbit was beginning to fade in front of our eyes, her feathers glittering as, bit by bit, they dissolved into glowing flecks of magic.

"I'm going to try it a different way," Nell explained. "I learned about this other healing spell, and if I try combining the two . . ."

"Just try," Flora whispered.

Nell placed her hands around where the elf cradled Ribbit and closed her eyes. Her voice was slow as she spoke, and as cool and soothing as the light of a full moon. *"I call upon the seven sisters of the night, the ones who carry the moon's healing light. . . . By the power that is my own, mend this wounded skin and bone—"*

She hadn't even finished the spell when magic started to radiate from between Nell's and Flora's hands. The luminescent haze became more compact, narrowing into threads. As if Nell had threaded it through the eye of a needle, the magic wove in and out of Ribbit's small form. It skimmed the edges of her feathers, caressing her with its gentle power.

A thin strand of magic seeped out of my chest, worming its way through the air. It dissolved into the greater glow wrapped around Ribbit, intensifying its radiance.

Shock rippled through me. Alastor . . . ?

The healing spell lacked the raging heat of some of Nell's more explosive ones. The magic surrounding Ribbit was opalescent, carrying in it a thousand tiny rainbows. It was as soothing as moonlight.

Nell never stopped chanting, not until the magic faded and its shimmering particles caught the wind and scattered.

For a moment, no one moved.

"Ribbit?" Flora whispered.

The changeling let out a soft sigh of contentment. I leaned forward over Flora's shoulder, watching as the parrot lifted her formerly battered wing and pillowed her beak against it. A moment later Ribbit began to snore.

"That was—" I began, elation soaring through me.

"Absolutely amazingly awesome!" Flora said, jumping up and down. When she realized she was jostling Ribbit, she stopped. "Nurturing Nell! Mother Elf was wrong—witches are *not* a self-serving, neglectful malady upon the realms!"

The exhilaration faded from Nell's face. "Say what now?"

Can we return to the matter of gutting Nightlock? Alastor asked, pleasantly enough. *I would so hate for the kitten to eat him before we get the chance to show that maggot what his innards look like.*

Maggot? I thought that was my special nickname.

A special name would require you to be special . . . Maggot.

I looked to Flora again, knowing it was selfish to ask, and that Ribbit needed rest, but the changeling was through the worst of it. Prue wasn't. "Can Ribbit finish what she was trying to tell you about my sister and Pyra?"

The elf didn't look particularly happy about it, but she woke the changeling just long enough for her to chirp a few words.

"The ogres said that Pyra has to enact her plan within the next two days," Nell translated for me. "And that if she doesn't find us before then, she'll start hurting your sister."

It felt like my skin had iced over. "Then we'll have to move even faster."

I stalked back toward where the hob was caught beneath Eleanor. The tarantula loosened its hold on Nightlock, but kept her legs close together, effectively caging him against the ground. Toad leaned down onto his front paws, edging his claws between Eleanor's legs. Toying with Nightlock.

"Sucks, doesn't it?" I said, crouching down to the hob's level. "Being caught in someone's trap?"

"R-release me at once!" Nightlock spluttered. "I am Her Majesty's special adviser! You shall all be arrested for mistreatment—well, not you, witchling, you shall be killed, of course. As will you, human boy, to complete my mistress's plan. And the elf, too, I suppose—well, it's very dire for you all, actually."

"Let him up, El," Nell said, patting Eleanor on the leg. The changeling swung her head around, giving Nell an uncertain look, but did as she asked. The hob brushed off his rumpled suit, then dashed to the right. Toad extended a paw and caught him by the collar of his jacket, then dragged Nightlock back over.

Nell crouched beside me. "You have two options: You can take the easy way and tell us where the secret entrance is to the prison and we let you go, unharmed. Or you can choose the hard way."

Nightlock's mouth turned up, revealing yellow nubs of teeth. "You are in my realm, witchling. I do not have to tell you a thing, no, I do not."

"Oh yeah?" Nell said, smiling sweetly down at him. A swirl of green magic gathered around her wrist and hand as she touched the tip of her finger against his neck. *Toil and*

Trouble stayed on the ground, leaning against the backpack.

What is she doing?

A spell?

Alastor seemed to recognize the magic, because he inhaled sharply. **No. Worse.**

"Tell the truth and tell it well, for lies shall cause your throat to swell," Nell chanted, grinning in a way that scared even me, just a little. *"Tell the truth and tell it true, for lies shall no longer be spread by you. Tell the truth and tell it well, otherwise your throat shall swell. Tell the truth and tell it straight, except about those you hate."*

The hob spluttered again, clawing at his throat as it was ringed with Nell's magic. "A curse! You cursed me! You"—the words choked off, only to be replaced with—"beauteous witchling—no! I mean, yes! This hob, he—"

His eyes began to bulge. He sealed his mouth shut, gurgling in dismay.

"Did you just . . . ?" I began. She lifted a shoulder in a shrug. She *had*. Nell had cursed the hob to do the one thing that came unnaturally to him: tell the truth.

Not only that, Alastor said, begrudgingly impressed. **She specified that he cannot tell the truth about us, so that, even if he should escape, he cannot tell others he saw us or where to find us. It is . . . clever.**

Dang, Nell.

"How long will it last?" I asked her.

"Oh, I don't know. Maybe"—she leaned down, looking the quivering hob in the face—"for-ev-er. I can be convinced to reverse it, provided you become a team player."

Nightlock sucked in a breath, quivering with the effort to hold it in.

"He thinks you're beauteous," I told Nell. "Looks like someone has a crush—"

She threw out her arm, catching me in the chest. *"Focus."*

"Okay, right," I said, then addressed the hob. "Do you know where the secret entrance is?"

The hob's cheeks puffed out like a bullfrog's throat with the effort not to say anything. I reached over and poked one cheek. *Hard.*

The breath and word exploded out of him. "Yesssss!"

He clamped both hands over his mouth, his eyes frantically tracking back and forth between us. "Though you will not find it, no, you will not! It cannot be found through words alone!"

Ah, I love this curse, the Show Not Tell.

What is it? I asked.

One of my ancestors was clever about protecting this entrance. The way in cannot be spoken, it must be shown to you.

"And that means what?" Nell asked.

"He has to show us the way in," I explained. "The explanation is cursed. He can't just describe where it is."

Nightlock let out a noise like a hot kettle.

"Has that passage already been swallowed by the Void?" Flora pushed into that space between Nell and me.

I glanced down at her. "You're coming? I thought you'd want to take the changelings back to the human realm."

"The last mirror is inside the prison, yes? Besides, you have helped me, Prosperity Redding, and now I will help you," Flora said. Turning back to the hob, she brandished her thorny ring again, waving her fist in front of his bulbous nose. "Answer me, horrid hob."

"Easy," I said with a nervous laugh. "We don't want you to get angry again. . . ."

"Again? What do you speak of, Prosper?" Flora asked, confusion settling into her face once more. "I do not get angry. I go to the sparkling place."

Now I am certain she is one bud short of a bloom.

"The voice and power thing at the house—" I shook my head. "Never mind. Just answer her, Nightlock."

Nightlock's face was glowing blue with the slobber and snot dribbling over his hands. "Itisnearbyitisstillopen—no, I meant—gah!" The hob bared his teeth in outrage. "I will not go down there. I—it is—so very dark."

He fears the entrance. Inquire why.

"Why are you scared of the secret path into the prison?" I asked.

The hob flushed with the effort to repress his answer.

"My father hob disappeared in it, as have many other hobs sent to clean it. There is no light to see."

A distant rumble rolled across the sky.

We were running out of time.

"Show us where the entrance is and we'll let you go," I said quickly. "You won't have to come with us."

Fool! We need him to guide us inside of the prison as well!

I know that, I thought back at him. *It's called lying.*

Alastor fell silent, and I took that as my cue to proceed.

The hob stared up at me, considering. Behind him, Nell looked like she had something to add to the conversation. I gave her a sharp shake of the head, but her confusion only deepened.

"You . . . will not make me attend you in its depths?" Nightlock pressed. "This hob shows you the entrance and then he is free?"

"Yup," I said. "See how easy it is to do the right thing?"

"Yes, 'tis the right thing," Nightlock said with a nod. "I will be delivering you directly to my mistress and queen, and she will be most pleased with me."

"Okay, sure," I said, rolling my eyes. "Lead the way to our doom."

The hob straightened, brushing himself off again. The changelings and Flora fell into place behind me, and as nervous as I was about trying to break into a secure prison with a whole troop of creatures, the changelings were bound to be a lot more useful than I was in rescuing Prue. We'd all find the mirror and go back to the human realm together. No one left behind.

Nightlock walked a step in front of me, navigating the rubble of the destroyed towers with his snub nose in the air. He crossed the road and gestured to a storm drain cut into the street. Given that this was a realm where rainstorms didn't exist, I suddenly had a very bad feeling about the entrance.

They've built sewers!

These didn't exist before, the last time you were here?

No. The fiends who lived on the steps below the prison must have finally complained enough about the filth being flung off the sides of Skullcrush onto their homes and heads to merit one being built. This likely connects to the whole drainage system of the mountain.

"Here," Nightlock said. "This is the entrance you seek. Good riddance to you all."

"Is there anything down there that we should be concerned about?" I asked him.

The hob held in a breath, considering his words. "The darkness."

Having learned the art of question loopholes and the need to be specific, I rephrased. "Is there anything dangerous down there that could kill us?"

The hob was quicker to answer this time. "The sludge. Do not fall into the sludge."

Hmm.

"Are you sure about this?" Nell asked, grabbing my arm. "Maybe we should just be more direct—have Toad fly us to the tallest tower?"

I stepped away. "I'm sure. That place is crawling with fiends—they all evacuated the lower streets and came here, remember? The only way we're going to find Prue is if we sneak in."

She shook her head, still not convinced. "If you say so . . ."

Nightlock backed away from us, keeping a suspicious eye on Toad. I lunged forward, grabbing him under his armpits and dragging him back toward the narrow drain.

"W-what are you doing?" Nightlock spluttered, fighting me as I lowered him down through the gap. "You said you would free me! You said this hob would not have to go down into the darkness—please—please! I beg you, mortal!"

"Just because *you* can't lie," I told him, releasing my grip on his hands, "doesn't mean that I can't."

The hob plunged down, landing with a squawk of pain and a hard *thud*. Good. That meant there was some kind of platform or walkway right beneath us.

"Prosper!" Nell stared at me in shock. Even Flora was shaking her head. Defensiveness prickled through me. We didn't have time to argue about this.

"He'd run off and alert the other fiends about us coming," I told them. "This is the only way."

Precisely.

Why was Alastor the only one agreeing with me? I'd be a total idiot to let Nightlock go just because he was a little scared of the dark. I didn't have to justify my decision, especially when Prue's life was hanging in the balance. Maybe it wasn't the nicest thing, but I was doing it for the right reason.

I slid down through the small opening next, not wanting to see the unhappy look on Nell's face anymore.

The platform was slimy and uneven. I had to brace myself to keep from sliding off it as I looked around. There was just enough light filtering down from above to see a walkway along one side of the tunnel.

The sludge moving beside the walkway inched forward, all filth and dung. It smelled a thousand times worse than the rest of Downstairs, redefining the word *rancid* for me. Clumps of garbage and mold coated its surface, threatening to clog the tunnel as it curved behind the platform, heading deeper into the dark belly of the mountain.

You must be loving this, I told Al, reaching up to help Flora down. If sunlight and peppermint turned his demonic stomach, then this must have been the sweetest potpourri.

But Alastor was very still. Very quiet.

"Ugh," Nell said, covering her nose and mouth as she landed. The changelings were right behind her. Toad had to return to his usual size in order to fit through the drain, and he looked none too pleased about it.

Nightlock crouched a few feet ahead on the walkway, his hands over his protruding ears. His eyes caught the traces of light and flared the way a cat's would as he watched me. Pure hatred hardened his face.

A thick bubble of sewage rose on the surface of the muck, only to pop like bubble gum as some thin creature with glowing bones swam beneath it.

"This isn't so bad . . ." I muttered.

Another disgusting bubble burst to my right.

A few steps later, so did another.

And a few steps after that . . .

The sludge began to gurgle, as if set to boil.

Nell shuddered, rubbing at her arms. "It feels like someone just walked over my grave—"

As the changelings moved off the platform and onto the walkway, they burst into small clouds of sparkling light. Their original forms. Flora gasped in alarm, reaching for them. They swarmed together like a hive, swirling in panicked pulses.

"In the darkest night, bring to my hand undying light," Nell whispered. Nothing happened. Her breath hitched in her throat. "It's gone. My magic is gone!"

The sewer sludge thrashed beside us, forcing us back against the tunnel's wall as it lapped up over the edge of the walkway. Nightlock let out a low laugh that echoed along the stones.

"Is there anything else you didn't tell us?" I snarled.

There was just enough light to see the slow smirk on Nightlock's face as he told the truth. "Yes."

The Sewer Selkies

I lunged toward the hob, but Nell caught my arm, dragging me back. Nightlock scampered forward, ducking into a small alcove along the walkway. His laughter was delirious, mocking.

"I told you to fear the dark! I told you to mind the sludge! Only the boy need survive!" he sang.

"You little weasel!" I growled. "I'm going to toss you into the sludge—"

Do it! Pull off his ears! Cut off his other horn!

"Prosper, *look*," Nell said, pointing down the tunnel. A pale figure stood there, without a stitch of clothing or, it seemed, a single hair on its body. But its shape was familiar. In fact, it was terrifyingly familiar.

After everything I'd seen, I still gasped. "Is that . . . a human?"

"No," Flora said, her voice trembling. "That's a selkie."

Wait. I actually knew what a selkie was. They were mythical seal creatures that shed their seal skins and became human when they walked on land. The Redding family had a crash course in the folklore when one of my great-uncles had experienced a break with reality, declared he was a selkie, and tried to live naked on a public beach in Cape Cod for a while. He was doing much better now.

The pale figure came toward us. It swayed as if uncertain that each step of its bare foot would hold his weight. The selkie cocked its head as it watched us, rubbing its webbed hands up the length of its arm, to where small, scaly fins protruded just below the elbow. Its waxy skin was tight against wiry muscles and bones.

The eyes, though. The *eyes*.

They were perfectly round, lidless, and crimson.

"H-hello, slimy—er, special selkie," Flora said, forcing a cheerful voice. "My name is Flora, of the Greenleaf elf clan. Do you remember elves? Your ancestors and mine were friends. They got along wonderfully well. Should we do the same? I love new friends. What about you?"

A drip of sewer slime landed right on top of my head, making me shudder.

Has this fool forgotten that the elves forced the selkies out of the human realm and into this one?

Why? I asked, taking one step back, then another, until I was up against the wall next to Nell. Nell's hood fell back as she pressed up against me. The rotting smell grew worse the closer the creature came, stirring up one horrible suspicion after another.

The gray-skinned, hairless humanoid smiled at Flora, flashing every one of its hundreds of knifelike teeth.

They discovered that they enjoyed the taste of human flesh.

I threw myself forward, snatching Flora's cloak and yanking her back. The selkie snapped and clattered its teeth, swaying as he lurched toward us. The black water, covered with moss and garbage, rippled with violence. Bald gray heads rose out of its depths, surfacing like hollow, forgotten bones.

"'Scuse you!" Flora said, wagging a finger. "That is *not* how you make friends!"

Alastor's voice leaped to my throat. *"**They are not here to make friends! They must have gathered here because the wardens of Skullcrush throw bodies down into the sewers when fiends expire. It is an endless supply of newly rotten meat!**"*

I pulled Flora back again as the selkie took a vicious swipe. A wet hand slithered out of the water and locked around my ankle. This selkie hadn't fully transformed—the rest of its body beneath the surface was that of an enormous seal. I kicked and spun out of its slimy grip with a grunt of effort.

The sludge wasn't just dark because of the dim light, or the filth. It was packed nearly solid with seals. The mass of them writhed, working themselves up into a feeding frenzy.

There was nothing the changelings could do. They zipped in and out around us, fluttering anxiously. The selkies twisted and turned to avoid them, snapping their teeth in their direction.

"Does *anyone* have a single idea of what to do?" I yelped, beating the creature with the heel of my other foot until it released me with a piercing shriek. "Literally anyone—*any* suggestion welcome!"

"I don't know anything about them," Nell choked out. "Goody Elderflower said selkies were one of the fiends that went extinct!"

"They are not *fiends*, Nellie," Flora said patiently. "They are descended from fae, who are descended from the Ancients directly—"

"Great history lesson, tell me again when we're not about to die!" I cut in.

I saw something shift out of the corner of my eye—a selkie, crawling up onto the platform, slithering on its belly toward the alcove where Nightlock was hiding. The hob had literally backed himself into a corner, squealing as the selkie snapped its teeth inches from his nose.

Good, Alastor seethed. ***It's what he deserves.***

"Prosper!" Nell's shout was tinged with anger. I turned

just as she shoved past me, throwing one of her empty bottles at the selkie. The shards embedded themselves in its eyes and back. As it howled out its misery, retreating into the depths of the sludge, Nell scooped Nightlock up into her arms.

"What are you doing?" I demanded.

She whirled around, anger marring her face. "What are *you* doing? Were you really going to stand there and let him die?"

The word rose in my mind like a shadow.

Yes.

Sudden shame burned in the pit of my stomach, but it was quickly drowned out by anger.

You were in the right, Alastor insisted. **It would have solved the matter of him revealing our presence. He is a waste of precious air.**

I shook my head, even as some part of me whispered *yes, yes, yes.* Nightlock was the reason Prue had come to Salem, which made him one of the reasons she'd been taken Downstairs. . . . But did he deserve to get torn apart and devoured by a murderous creature?

"What is going on with you?" Nell said as the hob clung to her neck like a child.

I flinched, my stomach turning with her words. "You don't understand—"

"I don't know who the 'new' Prosper is trying to be," she

said, "but right now all I see when I look at you is the last thing I expected: a Redding."

Anger seared through me. I kicked one of the selkies away, cramming my heel down hard enough to hear the snap of a broken bone.

Nell didn't understand—it wasn't her sister's life at stake.

"I'll do whatever is necessary to protect my family," I told her. "No matter the cost."

Inside my mind, Alastor recoiled. *What . . . did you just say?*

"What?" I demanded, frustration flaring in me again. "Now you—you of all awful creatures—have a problem with me?"

No . . . you have only . . . it's merely that you are not the first to say such words.

I ignored him, just like I ignored the look of anger and pity on Nell's face. I knew what I was doing, and, more importantly, *why.*

"You really want to fight about this right now?" I snapped, dodging a selkie as it slid toward me. "When we're about to die?"

"You are not about to die, warmblood," came an exasperated voice from above. "Though you might yet, if you don't do exactly as I tell you."

24

To the Tower of No Return

His buckled shoes appeared first, followed by his stockings and short, puffy pants. Zachariah slipped down through the darkness of the sewer like a falling star. His translucent form glowed all the brighter as he hovered just above the rush of fetid water.

"Zachy!" Flora cried. "You survived!"

He cocked his head to the side, giving her a hateful look. "I am already dead. Nothing can change that state of being, you lubberwort."

His form brightened with annoyance, singeing the darkness, until it flooded the tunnel with light.

"Wait—" Nell called. "Keep going, Zachariah!"

I didn't understand what she meant until the shrieking began. As the light touched them, the selkies writhed in pain. The same one that had been trying to sink its teeth into Flora's throat threw a waxy arm over its eyes and flung itself into the water.

The stewing muck thrashed and lapped up onto the walkway as the selkies tried to cut through, around, and over one another to escape Zachariah's intense glow.

Nell set a trembling Nightlock down, and the hob collapsed onto the walkway.

"M-mortal m-monsters," he spluttered.

"This monster saved your life," Nell said, thrusting a thumb into her chest. She gave me a sharp look as she added, "And according to Goody Elderflower, hobs honor life debts."

Nightlock snarfed his snot back into his nose, but he didn't dispute this.

"You owe me," she said, gripping his soiled suit jacket and lifting him until he was eye level with her. The changelings swirled around her, flashing to underscore her words. "And I demand payment. You're going to guide us through this tunnel, and you're not going to reveal our location, even if you find a work-around for my curse."

The hob trembled in rage but nodded.

Nell set him down on the sludge-slick stones. "Is this sewer cursed?"

Nightlock gave another jerky nod. "Yes. It strips magic from those who step inside it, leaving them defenseless. If you survive the journey to the prison, it releases."

Good. The changelings streaked down the length of the tunnel, eager to reach the end of it and return to their chosen forms.

"Well . . . come on, then," Zachariah said mulishly. He floated inches above the muck, making the selkies trapped there shriek as he passed over them.

"Wait—wait," I said, jogging to keep up with him. "What are you doing here? How did you even know how to find us?"

"I came because we have a deal, do we not?" The ghost boy looked over his shoulder.

Guilt stung me again, making my chest tight. I'd done what I had to, but both Nell and Flora didn't seem to understand that. They looked at me with such a potent mix of disappointment and worry that I felt poisoned by it.

With all the chaos that came in trying to flee Grimhold as it crumbled, I hadn't even thought about Zachariah. About what would happen to any of the shades bound to the house.

All I see when I look at you is the last thing I expected: a Redding.

Nell's words sank into my mind like teeth. They weren't . . . they weren't true. I was nothing like my family. I was just trying to be—

Braver. Stronger. The kind of person they wouldn't mock.

"I, too, completely forgot about him," Flora whispered loudly to Nell.

"You know, when you whisper something, it's usually because you want it to stay secret," Nell said. "That's kind of the whole point."

Flora's eyes widened. "I thought it was because it was more fun to talk that way. Really?" She lowered her voice into a raspy whisper. "Are you sure? See, that's *definitely* more fun."

"Oh, boy" was Nell's only comment.

"You ran away from our bargain, but in the first instance of luck I've had in three centuries, the destruction of the house voided my contract and freed me," Zachariah said icily. "I will now require something I've yet to decide upon."

Of course, Alastor said as the memory dawned on him. *A contract may end early if its contractor dies, or whatever location the shade is bound to is destroyed.*

"A word of warning you do not deserve: I will haunt you until I come up with a new demand, and you shall not sleep so long as it goes unfulfilled."

"Sounds fair to me," Nell said. "Can I ask you something? How did you know about the selkies and their aversion to light?"

The shade never lost his sour look. "I knew because shades are made to dump the waste of their masters into the various sewer drains and the beasts always recoil at the sight of us."

As we made our way down the tunnel, toward the waiting changelings ahead, Zachariah's form seemed to crackle every so often. It reminded me of our fireplace back home—how the heat and flame would begin to fade, only to burst back to full brightness as the fire fed on a new section of the wood.

"Sorry," I mumbled to him.

"Many people have said that word to me," Zachariah began. "My mother, as she and my baby brother lay dying upon their sickbeds. My father, as he indentured me to a farmer who liked to strike out with his fists. Even the farmer himself, who made a deal with a malefactor, exchanging my afterlife for a bottomless barrel of ale."

"That's . . ." *Rough.* The word felt too trite to say aloud.

Bune always made deals with the brutes of the realm, Alastor said in distaste. **He found them easy prey.**

"I'm just trying to save my sister," I told him, tucking my chin down against my chest. "I'm just trying to do the right thing."

Zachariah crossed his ghostly arms over his chest, staring straight ahead. No one, it seemed, wanted to look at me. Even Alastor was quiet.

"Remarkable, isn't it?" the shade said, the words echoing against the dark stones. "We do things we never thought possible when there appears to be a good enough reason for it."

At the end of the tunnel, Nightlock reluctantly pointed to a hatch disguised by the curve of the stones.

"Where does it go?" I asked, finding its handle and giving it a firm yank. It took me, Flora, and Nell to get the heavy door open wide enough for us to slip through. The changelings in their incorporeal forms floated through it first, illuminating the spiral staircase waiting there for us.

I was out of breath by the time I reached the upper landing, where another door stood ajar. I peered out through the crack, counting out fifteen heartbeats before shouldering it open—

And coming face-to-face with an ogre.

I leaped back, throwing my hands up to defend myself. Instead of seizing me, the ogre only slapped its hand over my mouth. It leaned down, its eyes glowing a familiar, unnatural shade of green.

"Twoawd?"

The ogre licked at its protruding lower fangs, nodding. Ogre Toad released me, just as the other changelings *popped*, shifting their forms to a variety of fiends: ogres, lycans, and ghouls.

"Good idea," I told them.

"What do you see?" Nell whispered, sticking her head out. "Anything?"

Nothing much beyond the gray stone walls and floors, and the lanterns burning with their dim green magic flames. Metal clanged against metal somewhere nearby, but even the voices I had heard before retreated into nothing more than a dull murmur.

I shook my head, waving her forward.

"Where are we?" I whispered to Alastor. "Do you recognize it?"

I have only ever entered Skullcrush through the front door, Maggot. A guards' corridor beneath a level of cells, I imagine.

A moan carried down through the low ceiling. The hallway was so tight around us it made me feel like it had been dug out by some long-ago prisoner who'd managed to escape.

Still, not even the dire and chilling conditions around us could keep my growing excitement at bay.

We were finally here. Prue was within reach. And the human realm was only a mirror away.

Is it? Alastor asked quietly. *How simple it must be for you, knowing your realm is whole and waiting for you.*

I set my jaw. *I had nothing to do with what's happening here. It's not my fault your kingdom is disappearing.*

I didn't want to think about what it would mean for the Void to destroy Alastor's realm after we escaped back home. I didn't want to think about the thousands of fiends who were here. I didn't want to think about what would happen if we failed, and Pyra succeeded in killing Alastor and me to save everyone else Downstairs.

I just wanted to find Prue and go home.

"Okay, my guess is that we follow the voices," Nell said, turning to the right. She lifted one of the lanterns off the wall, even though Zachariah was still glowing beside her.

I shook out my shoulders, trying to ease the sensation of Al's presence from my body. When I'd first realized he was inside me in Salem, he'd felt like nothing more than a wisp of air against my nerve endings. Now it was like being brushed across the face with the soft tail of a fox.

I wonder why that is, Maggot? he taunted. *If I hadn't expended my power to save your worthless life, I'd be free right now. As it is, you have only hours left.*

We'd see about that.

A roar sounded from the far end of the hall, bellowing down to us across the stone. Something pounded in response, each hit booming loud enough that I felt the echo of it in my bones.

Prosperity, Alastor said quietly. *I think we'd best leave this level of the prison. . . .*

Zachariah stopped a few hundred feet ahead of us, lingering beside a massive wall of dark metal. The door and all its chains rattled, exploding their thick coat of dust over them into the air. I slapped my hands over my ears as whatever was inside howled again.

"Holy crap," I breathed out. What could be big and heavy enough to move the cell door an inch, never mind leave an indentation in the sheet of metal, near where Zachariah floated? The door squealed again as the prisoner rammed itself into that same spot—as if it could tear through it by will alone. The shade stared at the warped metal, emotionless.

Nightlock cowered behind Nell as he said, "There are things here older than memory, and darker than the deepest night. Many hobs have been sent to clean these deep levels. Few have ever returned."

As his name indicated, he'd been born to serve here, in this terrible place. No wonder . . . no wonder he'd tried so hard to avoid coming back.

I felt Nell's gaze land on me again, but refused to meet it.

The next door we found led to stairs. I pushed it open a few inches against the protests of its rusted hinges. We just had to keep going up, didn't we? Eventually we'd reach the right tower.

Prue, I thought, rubbing the scar our grandmother had given my left arm. That night in the dungeon felt like a lifetime ago. *I'm coming. I'm almost there.*

She would be in for the surprise of her life when none other than her unremarkable tragedy of a twin materialized out of the darkness to save her from the mess the centuries-old fiend inside him had created.

Oh, please. As if you bear no responsibility. She was your sister to care for. I merely took advantage of your carelessness with the lying Bellegraves.

I set my jaw. *The way you cared for Pyra, letting your family lock her up in that tower?*

How ironic that his sister had imprisoned mine in the same place.

Ironic . . . or intentionally baiting.

"I think your sister is trolling us again," I said quietly.

My sister is many terrible things, but a troll is not one of them, Alastor said, disgusted.

"What should we do about the hob?" Flora whispered to Nell, clutching her cloak tighter. "Won't he reveal us?"

"I shall not," the hob said. "I made my vow."

We'd passed a few empty cells. Maybe we could just . . . leave him down here.

I concur. A wise plan.

A bolt of irritation shot through me. *Stop agreeing with me!*

"Eleanor? Will you make sure he keeps his word?" Nell asked. Ogre Eleanor nodded, trying to scurry the way a spider would with her new, lumbering legs. Nightlock let out a gasp as he was scooped up.

"There is nothing a hob takes more seriously than a life debt—" he began, only to be cut off as Eleanor seized him again, pressing the hob to her chest, and covering his mouth. "Mmmh! Unmand me!"

"I read the fine print in Goody Elderflower's chapter on life debts, you tricky little worm," Nell said. "It said that you only owe a debt to *me*, which means you could happily let the others die."

Nightlock slumped in defeat, glaring at the back of Nell's head as she turned and continued on.

I took the stairs up to the next level two at a time, up and up and up through the levels of the prison, until finally, the voices drifting down like raven feathers were just on the other side of another door. This time, when I peered through the bars, I didn't see a set of stairs—I saw fiends. Everywhere.

The room was massive, divided by a staircase that itself split as it went up in either direction. There had to be at least two hundred fiends sitting together on the soot-covered floor. Stacks of their possessions were spread around them.

Many clutched armfuls of robes, their shoulders shaking as they wept or growled loudly into the plush fabrics. A few goblins tried to stack a series of portraits on top of hastily assembled piles of clothing. Beside them, a lady ogre lay stretched out on bedding, a baby ogre nestled against her chest. I looked away, only to quickly look back.

The ogre wasn't *sleeping*. Another fiend, this one with two necks and two heads, leaned over her, wrapping a long pale bandage around her bleeding forehead.

She wasn't the only one injured either. With what dimly burning light the non-magic lanterns around the entrance provided, I finally noticed the fiends helping the wounded, or clearing out the rubble and debris that had fallen from the nearby statue and walls.

At the very center of what once must have been a dark, cavernous space was a statue of a snarling lion. The upper half of its body had cracked and fallen off, leaving only four legs behind for small fiends to cower beneath.

The despair . . . Alastor said, his voice hollow. A storm of barbed pain and featherlight wonder moved through me like winds shoving at each other. Whatever Alastor was feeling at the sight of the fiends around us, it was many things at once. *The suffering I tasted in the sewers, the same I gladly fed upon . . . it wasn't from the prisoners.*

"I *hate* fiends, and this is even horrible to me," Nell whispered.

"Why?" Zachariah asked. "Why would it bother you? Witches and fiends are mortal enemies, are they not?"

Nell whipped her head around, quietly snarling, "Witches are also in possession of hearts. Not every fiend goes after humans, or tries to enter our realm."

I shushed them, just as a voice beyond the door began a deep-throated wail of misery.

"It won't stop," a goblin said to everyone and no one. A few of the nearby fiends looked over, nodding in agreement. The goblin, his pewter robe matching the glimmering of his silver skin, clutched a hand to his bleeding ear—half of which seemed to be missing. "The Void won't ever stop."

"Don't say that!" another hissed back. "The queen will save us all!"

Inside me, something began to quiver. The depth of Alastor's pain took on a unique texture, one I'd never felt before. It sliced at me, leaving thousands of shallow cuts on my heart.

They help each other, he said, his voice small. *They*

encourage one another. I did not think it was possible for beings such as us.

It's always possible to help others, I told him, the inside of my skin prickling with his barbed pain. In that moment, with Alastor caught in the surge of his feelings at the undeniable evidence around us, I actually felt sorry for him.

"Long may she rage," another fiend called back. "She will push back the Void. She *will*!"

But could she do that without Alastor's powers—without killing me?

How do I get to the Tower of No Return? I asked Alastor. He was silent.

Alastor! I barked out in my head. *Up those stairs?*

The malefactor spoke after another unbearable stretch of silence. **Yes. Up those stairs and countless more.**

There were hundreds of fiends between the tower and me, but I could make it. I could.

"Okay," I whispered, crouching down under the doorway. I lifted my hood over my head and repeated that same word again, both to myself and to the others, "Okay . . . Al, you're going to have to guide me there, but the rest of you should stay here—"

"Prosper," Nell began.

"No, don't try to argue," I said. "I can do this."

"Prosper," Nell said again, this time a little louder.

Ogre Toad turned me toward the door's window again.

"If you're done being a stubborn idiot, look at the guard at the base of the stairs," Nell whispered.

I peered through the fiends milling around, and knew exactly when I found the guard she was referring to. The dark scaled armor seemed to swallow its small form, and each time it turned, its helmet slid crookedly on its head.

The guard turned, scanning the room. In one hand it clutched a short sword, and in the other, a candle lantern. Its frail light was more than enough to highlight the long curl of bright red hair that had escaped from under the helmet.

Relief burst inside of me like a sparkler. And yet in the moment that followed, a very small, very ugly feeling crept in. I felt myself, and my vision of being the hero, deflate.

"She returned from the Tower of No Return," Flora said, her eyes wide and glowing.

Of course she had. She was Prudence Fidelia Redding.

She had rescued herself.

A Ruined Reunion

"What do we do?" Nell asked, taking a step back from the door. I leaned against the wall, thinking. "We can't call her over here without someone hearing. . . ."

"If we can't get her attention," I said, "I'll go grab her and bring her back. There have to be enough fiends moving around that no one will notice a cloaked figure, right?"

No. Lurking, cloaked figures are **never** *suspicious.*

Nell did not look convinced, either.

Before anyone could offer an alternative idea, Ogre Toad linked his massive arm through mine and marched us through the door and into the entrance hall to the prison.

Oh—*oh. Nice, Toad.* He was providing the cover I needed—literally with his massive body, and figuratively by giving us a story for being there. We were just a guard and his prisoner. Out of the corner of my eye, I saw something long, silky, and black stroke the air.

"*Tail*," I reminded him. He shuffled back a few steps and, with a second, quieter *pop*, the cat tail disappeared.

The sobs and moans of the fiends accompanied us as we made our way through the piles of salvaged belongings. They were distracted by their grief, but each step I took rattled through me. So many eyes. So, so many opportunities to be seen. I mentally willed Prue to turn toward us, but she kept her face angled stubbornly away.

And then, without warning, she turned and hurried *up* the stairwell, not down.

My mouth fell open, ready to call out to her, but there was no way to do it without signing my own death certificate. I spun toward where we had left the others, but they must have seen what had happened and were already on the move.

Ogre Eleanor led the way, holding a squirming and likely gagged Nightlock under a cloak. The other changelings trailed after them, still looking uncomfortable in their fiend forms. The second they reached the stairs, we were all running. Zachariah blew past us in a streak of light.

At the top of the grand staircase was a long hall of empty prison cells. Waiting for us at the far end were three massive metal doors, the middle one left slightly ajar.

"Is that the door to the Tower of No Return?" I asked Alastor.

He didn't answer.

"Al," I whispered again. "Which one?"

I don't know, he said faintly.

"Which one is it, Nightlock?" Nell said.

The hob released a heavy sigh and confirmed, "The middle door."

I stepped forward only for Nell's voice to stop me.

"Wait," she said, swinging her pack forward and untying the laces. It took her only a moment to find the familiar dark vial. Its silver contents shimmered at me.

"Our emergency exit?" I said.

"Just in case," she whispered, still not elaborating.

I lifted the door's heavy latch and, with Nell's help, dragged it open. Beyond it, the staircase looked like a twisted spine, its steps as white as bleached bone.

"Prue?" I called. "Prue!"

Nell hushed me. "Where are the guards? And now that I'm thinking about it, why did she come here?"

"That *is* weird," I agreed, glancing back to make sure we hadn't been followed. "Al, should we be worried?"

The malefactor's silence vibrated in my ears, tempered only by the sound of everyone's panting breaths. It nipped at my senses and stirred up a warning at the center of my chest.

By the time we reached the top of the tower, my legs felt like they were on the verge of melting into mush. Nell and I leaned against either wall of the stairwell, dangerously close to rolling back down all those steps we'd just climbed.

Flora breezed by us, practically skipping up the last few steps.

"This is so . . . creepy," Nell said, glancing around.

"Prue?" I called again. "It's me—we've got to get out of here—"

The only response to my words was the screech of a rat as it ran back into a hole in the wall. Overhead, thousands of tiny spiders swarmed the ceiling, crawling over each other to slip in through the doorframe to get into the cell.

Strange crimson light filtered down from a hatch in the ceiling. Nell held out a hand under one particularly strong beam of it, as if she could catch it in her palm like a stream of water. As high as we were in the dark sky, the air around us was sweltering with the heat of what I recognized was magic.

A rickety metal ladder leaned against the metal hatch overhead, inviting us into the tower's only prison cell. I gripped a rung and started climbing.

"Are you sure you want to . . ." Nell began. "Never mind."

As strange as it had been to find no guards posted along the tower's stairs, some part of my mind recognized that it was even stranger that there was no lock on the door. With one last surge of strength, I drove my shoulder against it and almost crowed in triumph as it slammed open.

I shielded my eyes with my hand, trying to give them a moment to adjust to the flood of bloodred light. Crawling off the top rung of the ladder and onto the floor, I drew onto my knees. And froze.

"What . . . is that?" Nell whispered from the ladder, her face lit by the crackling power above us.

Alastor gasped. The sound of his shock whirled in my ears, tightening fear's clawed grip on me. I couldn't tell if he was talking to me or to himself as he said, *The pain here is immense. The stain of it echoes through the centuries.*

The cell was the largest of any we'd seen, but it was filled with lightning bolts of that same unsettling crimson power. They raced over our heads, firing toward the orb hovering like a small sun below the tower's turreted roof. The mass of magic throbbed like it had a pulse of its own, flashing dangerously with each shudder.

"Prue?" I called, searching for her. "Where are you?"

This power is that of malefactors. . . . It feels familiar, almost as if . . .

"Prue?" I called out. "Where are you?" We must have taken a wrong turn somewhere, or there had to be another hidden exit. She just wasn't here.

I crossed the room to look out through the lone window, searching for Prue's shape on the edges below.

From up here, the effects of the Void were even more pronounced. But, at one point in time, Pyra must have been able to see far and wide.

It would have been the worst kind of torment, wouldn't it? To have your whole realm spread out beneath you, and still be too distant to touch any of it. To look down at everything you could never have, every single day. Of course she was the way she was—this cell was her villain origin story.

She is not a villain, Alastor said coldly. *She is . . . she is . . .*

"Where is she?" Nell asked.

"I don't know," I said, frustrated. "Everyone spread out. There must be an escape route somewhere."

Behind me, Flora and the changelings followed Nell as she climbed the ladder. Seeing them all bathed in the eerie light made me feel like my skin was crawling. That feeling only intensified as I watched Zachariah shoot into the air, toward a narrow stone platform that ringed the room. The shade went still, and for the first time I saw something other than disdain on his face.

I saw horror.

I took step after step back, trying to adjust my line of sight to see what he was staring at. "What's wrong?"

Four statues loomed on the platform like gargoyles. Their faces were carved with agonized expressions. Even the shapes of their bodies looked tortured, as if the stone had once been alive and had felt every chip of the chisel. They were horrifying to look at, but even stranger were the streaks of magic that seemed to drain from them. Each glowing wisp sizzled as it passed overhead and fed into the orb.

Those are not statues, Alastor said hoarsely. *Those are my brothers.*

"Your brothers?" I repeated. "No, they've clearly been—"

Nell rushed over to my side. I only pointed up at the walkway, too horrified to speak.

"Mmmpf!" A muffled sound rang out from the other side of the room. "Promper! *Promper!*"

I turned slowly, my eyes following the curve of the tower's upper level until, finally, they landed on Prue.

Prue wore the same clothing from Salem. Her face was streaked with sweat and dirt, and she had been bound and gagged.

But that was impossible. . . . We had seen her. . . .

The smoldering orb throbbed in earnest, squealing like metal being cooled too quickly. It folded down onto itself, wrapping one of its layers over another, and another, and another—

A sharp, blinding pain cracked my skull. I staggered back against the nearest wall, jamming the heel of my palm against my forehead. The girls kept their backs to me, staring at the show of light and power. I stumbled toward the opening in the floor, frantically trying to pull the ladder up through it. I had to get to Prue—

"It's hardening into stone," Nell said, looking up at the orb.

"Like a diamond," Flora said solemnly. "Heat and pressure shaping it into something new. The blood key."

"How is this a key?" Nell asked, turning to the elf. "How could she use this to enter the realm of Ancients?"

There was a hard tug at my core. My feet slid across the floor as some invisible force dragged me toward the calcifying orb. When I held up my hands, their edges seemed runny, as if I had painted them with watercolors.

We must . . . get out . . . of here . . . Alastor panted. *She wanted us here. She knew we would come. My power—I feel it draining—*

I fought the pull, trying to wrench myself free from its grip. The world around me blurred. Then, somehow, I was falling, hitting the ground hard with my knees. I barely felt the impact. Beneath my fingertips the floor was scarred with marks. They smudged and came into focus with each heartbeat.

It wasn't simple scratching, but *words*. I traced their shapes with my hands, fear spilling through me with each jagged shape. Some of the grooves were cut deeply into the floor, put there with patient, vicious hatred. Others had been worn away by feet or time, or had simply been crossed out.

The words spiraled out, the only shadows in the bright room. DAGGER and FLINT and ROT and SCALED and GRAVEN and HOWL—more I couldn't make out. There seemed to be lines connecting some of them together, while others had scratches through them. They were meaningless when combined: ROTSCALED, DIREHEART, FLINTDAGGER, GRAVENHOWL, and . . .

My blood began to fizz in my veins, my pulse slamming so hard inside my head that my vision began to go dark. The pain flourished behind my temples again, and this time it made me groan.

Pay attention, I ordered myself. *Look—look—*

One combination of letters was written over and over again, scattered across the floor. The trail ended just between my two palms.

"Prosper, are you all right?" Nell asked, sounding like she was far away. "Do you know what this means? Wait—what's the matter?"

Alastor hissed. The hot rush of pins flooded my right arm as he brought my hand to my eyes and tried to push my thumb and index finger into them. I shoved back against the pressure of him, the sting of his burning magic.

***Leave this place! Leave* now!**

"At last you've arrived," a silky voice said from the shadows on the far side of the tower. I must have been hallucinating, because . . . because the speaker looked like Prue. It *was* Prue, dressed in the oversized fiend armor, only . . . one of her eyes was solid black and the other blue. Beside her, a crimson widow slithered out, her hands carrying a silver tray with a single vial on it. The serpent woman's face was masked by her ever-present veil.

"Once I heard that you had impersonated me," Not-Prue said, "I couldn't resist returning the favor."

She opened the vial and downed its contents in one go.

The crimson widow collected the glass again and slithered past us, heading for the opening in the floor. She hissed, her long tongue flicking against Nell's cheek. The witch stared straight ahead, her hands fisted at her side.

Not-Prue began to jerk, her limbs straightening, her skin bulging, as if her blood boiled beneath it. Within seconds, her face, her hair, her skin melted and slid to the ground in a puddle of gore.

"Now," Pyra said in her true, disarming form. "Shall we begin?"

Alastor screamed in my ears, the sound like spikes driving through my brain. *Run!*

There was a *thud* and clattering as Nell dropped her backpack to the ground. It was the last thing I saw before everything began to fade to black. As I collapsed onto the unforgiving stone, my cheek pressed against one of the words scored into the ground by Pyra's claws, long ago. I clung to the last bit of consciousness, fitting the last of the puzzle pieces together.

The notes written in the Scholar's book in the market . . .

My nightmares . . .

Maggot, the malefactor began, his voice vibrating with panic. *Prosperity—*

I couldn't tell my excitement from his terror. It all mashed together inside me until my heart was racing faster and faster and faster.

The dreams I'd had—fiends used dreams to communicate,

Nell had told me so. I'd had that nightmare so many times, the one with the panther. It would stalk back and forth, watching me with hungry eyes. And those words it had growled to me, over and over. *Awaken the singing bone. . . .*

I'd seen that same panther in real life, only a few days ago. It was Pyra, and replaying her words without the veil of sleepiness, I heard them differently. So similar, and yet so crucially different.

I was right. The words hadn't been a clue Pyra had slipped to me, but a command to her brother. Awaken.

Awaken.

She had been commanding him to return the only way you could compel a fiend to act against his will.

By using his true name.

You know nothing! Alastor said, his voice tight with anxiety. *You know nothing!*

And now I knew it, too.

Memory Lost to Time

For far too long now, Alastor had grown used to the sensation of being trapped inside a dark room, with only the thoughts of a human for company. Now, he realized, there was a far worse sensation waiting for him: that of being slowly dissolved into granules of power, blown back into the darkness of the Inbetween as little more than dust. He dug himself deeper into the boy's mind, struggling against the blood key's ever-sucking pull that threatened to sap the very life from him.

Not yet—I am not finished yet—

"—*up! Wake up!*"

Prosperity's thoughts had misted into clouds of color and uncertainty, and his pain and fear were not nearly enough to replenish what the blood key had drained.

That agony wormed through the boy's head again. He slapped his hand against his skull, as if he could drive the sensation out by force.

"I think I'm going to be sick. . . ." His words were slurred with pain, and something twinged in Alastor at the sound.

"He feels the effects of the blood key," the elf said, her voice edged with ice.

"Indeed he does," Pyra said. "And now you've brought me the last piece I need to pass into the realm of the Ancients."

Nightlock wormed his way out of Eleanor's arms, slipping to the floor. "All thanks to me, Your Majest-eeeeee!"

Pyra threw out an arm, sending the hob sliding across the floor until he fell through the trapdoor.

Ogres, with their bright orange sashes marking them as the Queen's Guard, squeezed through the small hatch. As one, the changelings returned to their chosen forms, magic storming around them as they stretched and popped into larger, more monstrous sizes. The ogres only held up their swords, grinning.

"It has been an age since you've been here, hasn't it, brother?" Pyra purred. "What do you think of my new decor for the cell of my youth? I find it to be gloriously grim."

I must speak to her, Alastor told the boy. *Let me speak.*

The boy was groggy, but agreed to the request. *All right. Nothing else. Not yet, at least.*

"You came to visit me once in this cell, do you recall that?" Pyra asked. She began to pace beneath the hovering bloody key. "I woke to find you watching me from the walk-way above us, having entered through a door I did not know existed. You never spoke, not once, in all the times I pleaded with you for help. To release me."

"It was for your own protection," Alastor told her. *"Our brothers wished to kill you, believing that you shamed the family. They did not believe you would ever manifest an animal form."*

Pyra flicked a hand toward the husk that had once been Bune. "They screamed louder than I ever did when I locked them in here. But their sacrifice is what's allowed the realm a second chance. A way to push back against the encroaching Void."

Alastor glanced sideways, to the far side of the room, where the witchling and the elf had backed themselves up against the wall. The changelings formed a protective wall between them and the ogres, but the accursed CatBat launched itself up into the air and retrieved the boy's flame-haired sister. With her bindings cut by a single swipe of the changeling's claws, the girl gratefully climbed onto his back.

"This is the only way, brother," Pyra said. "I know you see it, too. Why not tap into the realm of those who hide, who have hoarded their magic for thousands of years, leaving all others to wither?"

Alastor curled the boy's right fist. The truth in Pyra's words stirred something in him, a sense of certainty that fluttered like a moth's wings.

His realm was in torment. It was in ruins. Alastor saw the choice so clearly now: either he would fade into the darkness, or his realm would be devoured by it. A king without a kingdom ruled nothing and no one—he was a fool wearing a silly, meaningless hat.

"The Ancients are wise and all-knowing," the elf called out, furious. "You've squandered the realm! You could have changed your ways centuries ago, distanced yourself from your need of magic, but you were too greedy—too—"

Toad dropped Prudence Redding beside Nell, who had to hold the Redding child back to keep her from rushing toward the boy.

"Prosper! Prosper, can you hear me?" she called, struggling to free herself. "What's the matter with him? What have you done?"

Pyra glanced back over her shoulder at the ogres. "Shut that one up, won't you? You're welcome to dispose of the elf, but make sure you save her ears. They'd look fetching dipped in molten silver and worn as earrings, don't you think?"

The changelings growled and screeched in protest, closing ranks around Prudence.

Flora narrowed her eyes in the same way she had before unleashing her monstrous plants upon Grimhold. Alastor might have warned his sister not to test the strength of Skullcrush, especially after the shaking the Void had given it, but another squeaking human voice interrupted him.

"Try it," Nell warned. "Also, gross. Earrings made out of ears? What is *wrong* with you?"

He prickled at the insult. There was nothing wrong with *his* sister, unlike the human boy's. Nothing like outrageously red hair or spotted skin. She was fearsome and fearless.

Pyra turned her impassive face toward the witch, her laugh like the scream of banebats across the starless sky. "Look around you, child. This is the place that created me. Forged me into something strong. It is beyond your understanding."

"You think you're the only one who got locked away and was forced to watch as the world went on without you?" Prudence Redding asked, her voice trembling. "Living each day never knowing what would happen to you—if you'd go to bed one night and not wake up, or if you'd ever be able to make friends and see beyond the tree in the yard of your house?"

Pyra narrowed her black eyes. "Human lives are insignificant, coming and going in the blink of an eye. Your struggles do not match my own! Not now, not ever."

No. A human could not understand the life of a fiend— the small eternities they were given to create havoc and unleash mayhem. Every realm played its role; the fiends had always been intended to test and best the humans, and that was why they had been given the gifts they had. Their superior strength, their incredibly handsome visages, their innate magic—they were granted for a *reason*. Humans could only generate power through the strength of their emotions, particularly fear. What was the point of their existence?

Why did the human realm stand while the fiend realm fell?

Pyra turned, flicking her fingers in the direction of Prudence and the others again. One of the ogres stomped forward, clutching the handle of his ax in his hands. The bird changeling spread his wings, shielding the witch and girl.

But not before Alastor could have sworn that he saw the witch lean forward to whisper something to Prosper's sister. That she pressed something into her palm.

"Brother, I know you feel as I do—that you've seen the suffering of our subjects. Would you have our world destroyed simply because we did not dare greatly, out of fear of reaching for vast power that could, and should, be ours?"

Al, you can't be serious, came Prosper's incredulous voice. Alastor felt the boy begin to rise again, struggling to regain control of his mind and body, but the malefactor was not finished.

No. He was merely beginning. And he had questions of his own.

"Taking power from the Ancients threatens the order of things," Alastor said. ***"It would risk all of the realms collapsing, would it not?"***

Pyra made a noise of disgust. "Are you human or are you fiend, brother? If this does collapse all of the realms, then good riddance, I say. If we do not get to live and thrive, then no one does."

Al, tell me that you aren't buying what she's selling, the boy said. *The lady's lost it—risking destroying every living thing on the chance her plan works? It's totally senseless.*

No. It was *fiendish.* A new sort of fiendish Alastor rather appreciated.

It felt as if the veil of quiet, lingering doubt had been lifted from his mind. Alastor could see things clearly now, lay out all his options as he might have set out his finest bone-handled utensils for dinner.

More importantly, he understood his sister. He understood now that she had done everything to save the realm, when no alternatives presented themselves.

The time of helping the humans and the elf was over; he could no longer do so while it was potentially at the expense of his kingdom. The matter of who would sit on the Black Throne could be taken up again later, after the question of their survival was answered.

Alastor gripped the boy's voice, ready to wield it again, but a curious thing happened.

The elf, that spritely, hideous creature with the too-quick smile, transformed once more. Her skin hardened into a dispassionate mask, her eyes glowing like magic flames.

She opened her mouth, and instead of the syrupy-sweet voice that Alastor had come to expect, a deeper voice, like the soothing flow of a river, emerged. "You will never succeed."

The witchling jumped, spinning toward the elf in surprise. The human girl could not stop staring at the creature, taking in her flowering hair and wrathful expression with disbelieving eyes.

Even Pyra's breath caught, just for a moment, but she recovered smoothly with, "An elf would know a bit about failure, hmm?"

The elf's face did not betray a flicker of emotion at Pyra's taunt. In the silence that followed, a slow, triumphant smile spread over it.

"It has been so long now . . . thousands of years have turned the treacherous memories to dust. You malefactors have cursed your kind to forget. You have cursed *yourselves*. You could not handle the truth of your existence." Flora turned her burning gaze over to the boy. To Alastor. "The time for *our* vengeance has finally come. Foolish fiends, an Ancient stands before you, telling you that your plan will not succeed. The blood key will not open the Ancients' realm— for you stand in it now, and you already have ensured its destruction."

Alastor, possibly for the first time in his life, truly could not think of anything to say. He barked out a laugh, but the sound died as no one joined in. The ogre guards shifted restlessly, unsure of what they were hearing.

"Liar!" Pyra snarled.

"Elves . . . are the Ancients?" Nell squeezed out.

"I don't understand," Prudence Redding said, glancing between everyone in the prison cell. "I thought there were four realms?"

"No, there have only ever been three," the elf said with relish. "Ages ago, the elves created new realms, crafts-creatures planting the seeds of new worlds. Designing the landscapes, measuring out the mountains, dreaming of the creatures we'd create to inhabit them. When we found the human realm in our travels, we loved it so. Its wild green. Its sparkling waters. We used it as the anchor for the realm we would design to be our own. A perfect world for elves, with trees as tall as towers, with burrows to raise our young. Each stone lovingly carved, each flower carefully nurtured. This was once a realm of peace. Of light. Until the fiends arrived."

"This is pure fantasy," Pyra said, pointing a clawed hand. "Guards, seize the meddlesome elf!"

Flora held up a fist, magic crackling over her knuckles. The ogres stepped back in alarm. Cowards!

"If I lie, tell me—why do you not remember the founding of your realm? Why is the account not recorded in your Book of Fiends, or any tome at all? Why do none of you malefactors recall why and how your ancestors came to rule?"

"They—they were born into the role," Alastor protested. Yes. Obviously so.

Pyra, however, was strangely silent. As a young male-factor, she had once voiced similar questions to Alastor. At the time, he had dismissed them—the fiends' history was shrouded in secrecy, he had said, so that no one could question their legitimacy and might. But he had only repeated their father's explanation.

"You fiends believe so deeply in your power, your right to devour magic," Flora explained, "but you were nothing more than a mistake the elves made in our otherwise perfect plan. You broke our design, our beautiful realm."

"What do you mean?" Nell asked.

"We so wished to trade with, and befriend, the humans," Flora said. "But there was a darkness to them. Anger. Hunger. Greed. That is not the way of elves. We thought we could save them—improve their design—by removing these hideous feelings from them. But . . . it was a deep rot. The darkness always grew back. And the feelings we split off from the humans somehow manifested into beings. Monsters."

Fiends.

No . . . no . . . this was impossible. Fiends, the castoffs of wretched humans? Alastor's pride shuddered.

The boy had been quiet for so long that Alastor had begun to hope it was because he'd been rendered unconscious and could be kept that way.

But Prosper spoke slowly now, working through the realization. *This makes perfect sense, actually. I know you don't want to believe it, but maybe that's why fiends can only create magic from human emotions like fear and anger. It's like . . . you're resonating with those feelings because you were born from them.*

Do not speak of things you will never understand!

"We tried to teach you fiends our ways," the elf continued. "To protect the humans, we forbade fiends from entering their realm, and cast a glamour curse upon all fiends so that no human would be able to see you."

What a stupid strategy, the boy said. *Everyone is far more frightened of what they can't see.*

That was a surprisingly perceptive observation for the boy to make. Alastor had assumed the witches were the ones who cast the glamour and kept human eyes from seeing the fiends, but the why of it had hardly mattered, as malefactors could get around the curse by manifesting animal forms. The other fiends had simply learned how best to use their invisibility to terrify humans and take what magic they could from their fear.

"But you fiends grew restless, destructive. You murdered my kind in order to seize the realm," the elf said darkly. "Those of us who survived were forced to flee into the human world using our mirrors. The malefactors who led the revolt took the knowledge of how to create the portals and hoarded it, ensuring only they could create them. But that was still not enough for them. They cast a curse of forgetting on the other fiends to ensure they would not remember what had occurred. So no fiend could question their rule."

Well . . . that did sound quite a bit like his kind, if Alastor was being honest. But his sister was shaking her head, a scream of denial and fury working its way up her throat. She released it in a roar.

"Do you not believe me?" the elf continued. "Then how else would I know that your first ancestor had no animal form, and that she blended her line with a mere pooka and destroyed all the other true shapeshifting fiends so that her children and heirs would have no rivals?"

Alastor felt as if he were balanced on the tip of a match-stick, poised to tumble into numbed shock. No one . . . *no one* outside of his family knew of this. The presence of a pooka in the few remaining malefactor bloodlines was his kind's most closely guarded secret.

Pyra, of course, knew this as well. The others might have seen her silent, still form as the effect of her being stunned, but her mood was shifting, flowing through her like a raging river of lava. She was *furious*.

"You *are* an Ancient," she growled. "And still, you will not fix the realm? You'll let it be devoured and the creatures you created destroyed?"

Flora's eyes narrowed as she took great relish in saying, "*Yes*. It is what you deserve. You were a mistake. You have always been a mistake."

Something in those words stirred a surprising anger in the boy, but Alastor himself felt oddly calm. His realm was collapsing, his sister despised him, and an elf—an *elf*—had just upended his understanding of the order of things. But there was one thing Alastor never truly lost in the face of confusion and chaos: the upper hand. His ability to improvise, to shift plans at a dizzying speed, had always served him well.

And now it would save him.

"Sister," he began, his thoughts swirling like sand through an hourglass. *"You may take my power, however* **weakened**"—he spat out the word—*"it might be. As a sign of my willingness to work together, I will voluntarily sacrifice most of my power now, keeping only enough to stay alive. Even incomplete, the blood key can serve a different purpose."*

Al? Prosper's voice was faint but growing. Alastor felt his thoughts scatter almost as quickly as he could piece them together.

"Go on," Pyra said, crossing her arms over her chest.

"We only need a new realm, do we not?" Alastor said. *"The blood key has more than enough magic to tear open a hole between our realm and the human one."*

"No!" Nell gasped.

Alastor! The boy struggled for control, trying to wrestle his body back from the fiend.

"The humans are weak, and their world is far vaster than our own," Alastor said. *"Could we not remake it? Fiends are*

meant to rule. It is our destiny to bend humanity and their shades to our will."

Pyra's smile was like the curve of the deadliest blade. "I had not considered that. How *quickly* the hideous blue sky would blacken at our command, staying that way forevermore."

"The humans will be easily dealt with. They are so very susceptible to plague and fear. . . ."

It felt like old times, mocking the lowly worms of the realms this way with her. Alastor, finally, was able to drag the boy's body back onto its feet. Perhaps they would be able to work something out, with her serving as his adviser. . . .

As Alastor watched his sister's smirking form, he recognized it as a new destiny unfolding.

He had not suffered humiliation at the hands of the Reddings without reason. He had not lost centuries of his life to the darkness of the Inbetween for no purpose. All of it had been like a winding path of black spidersilk. The way forward glistened with potential.

Alastor would not merely have his revenge on the Reddings. He would force all humanity to pay their dues.

The elf woke up from her trance, shaking the last vestiges of the power from her body. "Did I tell my story?" Her eyes shifted to the boy, and Alastor despised her cloying look of concern. "Prosper . . . ? What happened?"

"Now, Prue!" the witchling shouted.

Alastor and his sister whirled toward the cluster of

cowering humans just as the girl drew her arm back and hurled a black vial down to the ground.

"Silver of old, silver of fate—come together as a gate!" Nell shouted. She raised both arms, a flickering ball of green magic growing between her hands, and threw it down onto the mess of powder and glass.

The air filled with clogging smoke. Stones dislodged from the walls, and ceilings came smashing down in a torrent as the tower rocked. Pyra was thrown back several feet, landing hard enough to momentarily stun her.

The witchling and elf clambered onto Toad's back, drawing Prudence Redding up behind them.

No, Alastor thought, fury weaving through him. They weren't about to ruin his plans, not after he'd finally found a way forward with his sister—a way that would allow he himself to save the realm and win back the fear and respect of his kingdom.

"Stop him!" Pyra shouted. Above them, magic sizzled around the blood key. It burned with an intensity that would kill a living thing at first touch, surging through their veins and burning out their body.

To Alastor's surprise, the mortal fools didn't try to touch it or steal it away. No, they were only concerned with their escape.

"Prosper!" Nell called. "He has to open it—tell Alastor to open the mirror!"

The tendrils of molten silver merged on the ground,

pooling into a glossy mirror. Clever, clever witchling. She'd known they might not have easy access to a mirror in different parts of Downstairs, and she'd found a way around it: using a spell to create one of her own.

But what she had not accounted for, it seemed, was Alastor's response.

"No."

27

Shattered Spells

No.

The thin illusion I'd been holding on to that there might be a different end to this story finally shattered. That single word was as much a statement as it was a promise; from this moment on, there would be no more working together, even just to survive.

Alastor had chosen his realm over mine. I knew, eventually, something like this would happen. I wasn't disappointed. I wasn't even surprised. But I had hoped . . .

What? I'd hoped that he'd wake up and decide to do the right thing? That we were friends?

The ogres thundered across the cell, jumping onto the walls to try to scale them. The other changelings sprouted new wings of their own, joining Toad's and Ribbit's massive forms as they soared around the blood key. The fiery knot of magic pulled at me, weakening my body more with each moment that passed. We needed to get out of here. *Now.* Toad flew the others higher and batted one of the ogres to the ground.

"Break their mirror, Clockworm!" Pyra shouted to the other ogre. "Shatter it!"

"Prosper!" Nell called down. "Tell him to hurry!"

Alastor wormed through me, threading in my veins like a trail of dancing fire.

He wasn't going to let go.

With what strength I had, I tried to shove him down. If I could subdue him, twist him back into submission, I might—

Wait.

Realization surged through me. I could *order* him to do it. I knew the secret name his mother had given him at birth, the one that would let anyone—fiend, human, elf— bend him to their will.

Do it, Alastor growled, seeing my thoughts. *Finish becoming what you were always destined to be: the inheritor of Honor's legacy.*

My blood beat out a hard, fast rhythm. That was power— that single word was power itself. It was the magic wand that could wave everything away, if I chose to use it. The trump card that I only needed to flip over to use.

Power.

A name. I just had to say a name, and I could order an eight-hundred-year-old demon to do whatever I wanted him to do, including nullify the contracts on Nell and me.

I'm doing this to save my world, I shot back. *I'm doing what I have to—*

For the right reasons? Alastor finished coldly.

Ice crystallized around my heart. Zachariah's words echoed back to me. *We do things we never thought possible when there appears to be a good enough reason for it.*

I was— All along, the entire time we'd been Downstairs . . . I'd justified the things I'd done by reminding myself they were all adding up to the rescue of Prue. Even now, I'd be using the name so we could escape, to remove Alastor's power from Pyra's grasp for just long enough for Downstairs to disappear once and for all. The human realm would never have to see another fiend.

All I had to do was use that name. It was right there, on the tip of my tongue, burning like I'd stuck a cinnamon candy on it. One word. Three syllables.

Say it, Alastor seethed. **Just say it, you filthy Maggot. You think yourself to be so good, so kind, that humans have all the scruples that fiends lack. . . . In the end, you are no better than Honor was.**

That wasn't true. I shook my head, and with a deep breath, I ripped through the hazy darkness of my own mind.

I slammed back into my own body, sliding into control

as if I were tugging on a fresh set of clothes. Alastor had dug his claws into my brain, and as he receded, he tore at it, burrowing the pain in deep. His simmering resentment boiled the contents of my stomach and made bile burn up my throat.

I'm not Honor, I told him. *I have never been like him, and never will be.*

He merely possessed what you did not until this moment, Alastor said darkly. **Power always comes at the expense of others, Prosperity Redding. That is the choice you make—the knowledge you live with.**

I shook my head, trying to clear the echo of his words. *I'm not like Honor.*

It was only a matter of time.

Honor had killed an innocent girl. He had destroyed a whole family to fatten his pockets and spread his influence.

All to save his own. As you intend to do now. Go on, Maggot. Bend me to your will.

What was going too far, when we were talking about the end of the world? Couldn't I do this one thing—this one small thing? He was a fiend. He lived to torment . . . so why did it matter if he was served some of his own medicine? It wouldn't be any more or less than what he was planning to subject me to after he got his tiny claws on my shade—

My shade. *The deal.*

"Get my bow!" one of the ogres barked to another. "I'll shoot them down."

"There's no time for that," Pyra snapped. She closed her eyes, raising her arms over her head. Wisps of magic rose from the orb, wrapping around her feet, letting them rise off the ground. Flying without wings.

Which seemed really unfair, all things considered.

You have *to do this,* I told Alastor. *Getting Prue back into the human world was one of the terms of our deal. If you don't open the mirror portal, you're breaking your own contract . . . which means my end of things is null and void.*

I wasn't sure about the meaning of all those business words, but I'd heard my mom and dad use them on conference calls and they sounded official.

Alastor let out a strangled noise.

"Hurry!" Zachariah shouted. "What are you waiting for? An official summons?"

"Help us now, or break the contract," I told him quietly. Pyra swiveled toward us, but I kept pushing, kept digging. "You said you never break a contract. What happens when you do? Do you lose the magic created when we agreed to it?"

You will just use my true name to command me to break the contract.

Am I using it now? I said. *I could, and if you do this of your own volition—if you uphold our deal—then I won't.*

You lie.

Somewhere above us, Toad screeched and dove toward an ogre, all claws out like knives.

My thoughts raced. *The deal was that we get Prue back to the human world. If you don't open that mirror now, you violate the terms of the agreement. You lose the magic that came with it. And you need it, right? To break free from me?*

Alastor groaned.

"What are you saying to him?" Pyra demanded. "What has he promised you, human?"

"Prosper, hurry!" Nell called. She clung to Toad's neck as he reared back, away from the slice of an ogre's barbed ax blade. Prue kicked another guard in the face as he leaped toward them.

Shouts came from the stairwell below. Metal clacked against stone as the approaching soldiers ran up the endless stack of stairs. Closer and closer, until the floor vibrated with the force of their drive.

Alastor's voice was oddly formal, almost stilted, as he said, **I will uphold my terms. Approach the mirror and touch it.**

My legs felt as heavy as lead, but I half crawled, half ran the short distance between the mirror and me. I slammed down onto my knees, pressing my whole hand to the still-hot glass.

"Alastor!" Pyra cried. "I expected betrayal from you, but even I'm surprised it took less than two minutes!"

A surge of magic rushed through my arm, flowing out through my fingers. Alastor was silent as the glass rippled and the portal opened.

Toad and the other changelings wasted no time. Before I could so much as shout up to them, they dove for the mirror. Flora and Prue both screamed at the steep angle of his descent. The ogre's ax swung out again, nearly catching another ogre who dove for the changeling in the chest plate.

"Hand!" Nell cried, leaning to the left and stretching her arm toward me.

Her fingers locked around my wrist. The force and speed of Toad's dive nearly ripped my arm out of its socket as I was dragged headfirst through the mirror.

Dark, cold air blasted at us from all sides as we corkscrewed through the blurred, dim passage around us. Before I could draw in enough breath to scream, we shot out of the other side of the portal.

Nell's grip on me finally broke, and I rocketed by her, slamming into the edge of something mercifully cushioned. The others weren't as lucky. They crashed into a baby-blue rug, limbs locked around each other until they looked like one of those many-legged Chimeras from Dad's book of Greek mythology. The changelings shifted back to their usual sizes in a symphony of *pop*s.

"Ouch! Flora—!"

"Toad, your leg is crushing me—!"

"What sort of room is *this*?"

Zachariah floated above them, spinning in circles around the familiar striped wallpaper, the bookshelves, the tall white dresser that used to have all the pictures and trinkets on it, the ones now scattered across the floor. The Heart2Heart posters.

The still-rippling full-length mirror in the corner of the room, just beside the door to our shared bathroom.

My blood turned to ice.

Alastor began to laugh.

"Wait . . ." Prue began, sounding dazed. "What are we doing in my room?"

"You . . ." I began, worry devouring all other thoughts. "You opened a mirror back into Redhood?"

I connected the open portal to this mirror because I thought you would enjoy a visit home. To see it one last time.

Nell clambered to her feet, breathing hard.

"Mom?" Prue called out, heading for the door. "Dad?"

I caught her shoulder, holding her in place. Then I pointed to the mirror. To the still-open portal, its quicksilver surface gleaming with malice.

Dozens of dark shapes appeared in its depths, marching forward through the curtain of vapor—the roar of their voices as they shrieked and crowed with excitement made my skin feel like it was trying to peel itself off my bones.

"Close it!" I shouted. "Alastor!"

Our deal stipulated that I help you rescue your sister and open a portal for her back to the mortal world, Alastor said, his voice like venom. *I said nothing of closing the portal again.*

I ran my hands through my hair, clutching fistfuls of it. This wasn't happening. This couldn't be happening.

"He won't do it," I told the others. I could have punched myself in the face for all those wasted, stupid seconds I'd thought I'd finally managed to put one over on him.

One fiend became a dozen, and a dozen became a hundred. Ogres. Lycans. Ghouls. Green, silver, red, gray, purple. Scaled, furred, fanged, clawed. Magic illuminated the sneering glee on their faces.

Don't do this, I begged him. *Please!*

Your desperation is exquisite on my tongue.

Nell dove for her bag, turning it over to shake out the remaining contents. Only two empty vials clattered down onto the carpet. The mirror began to rattle against the ground, the surface rippling at a boil as an ogre's claws brushed it, testing.

"Someone do something!" Prue shouted, picking up one of her equestrian trophies and wielding it like a club.

"I can . . . Only the malefactor can shut it, but I can put it in another—I can put it in the Inbetween!" She rubbed her hands together briskly, as if to spark the magic. *"Open to me, door of wonder—"*

Even I recognized something was wrong when the usual glow of magic didn't appear in her palms. Nell looked down at her fingers, then toward the sunlight streaming through the window, horrified. And I knew. I knew without a single word of explanation that Nell had finally run out of magic.

So now the fun begins, Alastor said gleefully. **Abandon hope, Prosperity Redding, for it has abandoned you.**

The ogre's hand passed through the glass, its fingers dancing in a taunting wave.

"Run," I gasped out, grabbing Prue's arm and pulling her toward the bedroom door. *"Run!"*

But it was already too late. Behind us, monsters burst through the passage like a cloud of furious hornets, and there was nothing I could do but watch as my nightmare came home.

JANUARY 1693
TOWN OF REDHOOD
PROVINCE OF MASSACHUSETTS BAY

After a year away to deal with the matter of aspirant trolls who, for the thousandth time, had tried to seize his father's throne, Alastor arrived back in the mortals' realm.

And promptly realized he was lost.

The path he'd always taken through the mirrors to call on Honor Redding had, for the last two years, opened to the forest near to his humble home. Now, however, Alastor found himself in a dark library of sorts. He turned around, wondering if he'd somehow taken a bad turn and accidentally come through the wrong portal. But he recognized the stench of the place—the familiar human reek of Honor and his family. It was only everything else that had changed.

The mirror's wood frame, the same one Honor had

carved, was now a finely crafted gold. The foggy surface of
the glass bore a familiar crack down its center.

This room was nearly as large as the entirety of Honor's
first home. Handsome shelves lined three of the walls, and
the fourth was covered with expensive cloth paper that
seemed to shimmer with the firelight from the hearth. The
desk at the center of the room gleamed with polish. Alastor
leaped to the top of it, padding across its clean surface until
he found a stack of correspondence neatly piled beside a silver inkpot.

All were addressed to Honor Redding.

Alastor moved from the chair to the large window, surprise alighting through him. Outside, the moon was bright,
and if he turned just so, he was able to see the way the house
had been enlarged and refinished with stone. He could make
out the shape of nearby stables. A carriage.

"It is remarkable, is it not?"

Honor stood on the threshold of the room, his eyes
bright. Shutting the door behind him, he made his way
across an ornate rug—one he'd likely surrendered a small
fortune to import.

"All of this, in only a year," Honor said, coming to stand
beside him at the window. "Imagine where we shall be by
next year. Thy magic held true. As the Bellegraves' hatred
and jealousy grew, so did their acts against us, which only
brought us greater fortune."

Alastor should have felt some pride in what his magic

ALEXANDRA BRACKEN

had accomplished, but now he only seemed capable of staring at the man. An unwelcome, growing uncertainty began to stir in him. Honor was neatly groomed, and his suit was finely tailored. Alastor was sure that if he looked directly at the man's shoe buckles, he would see his face reflected back at him.

Yet, there was . . . a kind of hardness to the man's face, one that hadn't been there before, even as he'd suffered through the perils of mortality.

"This is . . ." Alastor searched for the right word. The man's gaze narrowed the longer Alastor allowed the silence to stretch, and despite his status as the superior creature, Alastor's skin prickled with instinctive dread. "Remarkable, indeed."

Unexpected was the word he'd meant to say.

"Shortly after thy last call, I was offered a partnership in a trading company. A storm came up along the coast, ravaging all ships but ours. The profits have been immense, and Redhood has flourished as a result."

Alastor straightened. "I thought this was the town of South Port."

Honor shrugged, leaning against his desk. "I have remade it, building new structures for the community to enjoy, adding new homes and families, increasing our crops. Should I not also rename it?"

"Of course," Alastor allowed. "It is only right."

It was what any fiend might have done.

• 325 •

Tension left the man's shoulders and his face returned to its usual smile. Alastor was sure the usual questions were coming, and had prepared entertaining stories for all, including the one about his brother becoming trapped in a barrel of beetled juice. After the tiresome warring with the trolls, Alastor was hoping for a few tales of human foolishness as well.

"I've some ideas for thee," Honor began, eyes growing fever bright with excitement. "I have waited so long for thee to return, it has given me months to make plans of how I might secure this wealth. *Nurture* it. Immortalize the Redding name in stone. Now, more than ever, the Bellegraves grow suspicious of how I have changed our fortunes. They must be dealt with before word of our new-found prosperity spreads north."

Alastor stilled.

Ah. So this call would be all business. For a moment Alastor truly wondered if he was dreaming this encounter. That vague prickling sensation turned to thousands of needles, all stabbing through his skin. He could not understand why. Was this not what he was after, always? The escalation in the number of contracts, each containing grander terms that would keep him flush with magic?

And yet . . .

And yet, he thought. This was Honor Redding. The one mortal who had felt different to him.

"Why would that be bothersome?" Alastor asked,

keeping his tone light. "Would it not benefit thee to warn off potential enemies by spreading stories of your might?"

Honor shook his head. "There is hysteria sweeping the colony, a rabid fear of the unnatural and devilry. Whispers are enough to condemn a man or woman to death. It only worsens with time. They may accuse me of witchcraft."

Alastor let out a prim noise of disgust. "I am no witch."

"I know this, but the world does not," Honor said. "I must take care."

"What dost thou have in mind for the Bellegraves?" Alastor asked, curling his tail around him. "A curse so that they may not speak of thee to anyone else?"

Honor's brow creased as he absently stroked his fine desk. "No. I wish for them to perish. All of them."

Alastor's stomach quivered. "Thou mean for me to kill them?"

"They do not have to die by thine hand, but rather . . . a pestilence, perhaps?" Honor suggested. "Something that will neither arouse suspicion nor cast blame on our reputation, of course. We will act as though we are nurturing them, aiding them, and then we shall bury them. All of them."

Alastor turned to gaze out of the window, his hardened heart suddenly rising in his throat. Casting deathwishes was an ugly undertaking, certainly, but one he had done before—albeit not on so grand a scale.

"I must confess, my—" Alastor caught himself before he

could say *friend*. "I must confess that thou surprise me with this request."

The cold mask slid over Honor's face again. "I do not see why. Thou was the one who instructed me in pursuing my heart's desires."

The malefactor tried not to flinch. It felt as if he were splitting at his center. Why should he feel any ounce of regret now, when this human was finally proving his own worst suspicions about mortals? There were no exceptions to be found, not even among those who professed to believe in a better way.

All were corruptible in the end.

"What thou hast provided is not enough," Honor pressed. "I require more. For myself. For my family. For our future."

More, more, more—the human appetite was voracious.

"As part of this new contract, I also desire that thou make this prosperity of the Redding family permanent, for as long as Reddings walk this earth."

Alastor's lips parted. "Such a long-standing boon would require more than thou art willing to give."

"Such as?"

He could not possibly mean for this to occur, Alastor thought. Honor would see reason, once he heard Alastor's price.

"The shades of your entire family, all those who possess a drop of Redding blood now and in the years to come. Upon their deaths, they will serve in my realm."

The man did not so much as catch his breath. "Agreed."

Alastor's eyes widened. "Truly?"

Honor crossed his arms over his chest, glancing to an unfinished portrait of himself on the other side of the library. "Everyone who shares the benefit of this blessing must also share its cost."

The malefactor knew that he could cast this curse and it would be a beautiful, terrible thing to behold. He knew that he could make the Redding name known the realm over. He knew, too, that the amount of magic this contract would generate would mean his brothers could not ever challenge him. He might be able to use some of it to help his sister manifest her animal form, if such a thing was possible.

And yet, he thought again. And yet.

"Do we have a contract?" Honor asked, all eagerness.

"Yes," Alastor said. "We do. I shall grant thy wishes."

Honor smiled. Alastor could not stand the sight of it. He leaped down off the windowsill and quickly padded across the room. Before Alastor passed through the mirror, Honor spoke one last time.

"Thou will not become a problem for me as well," the man said, his voice hardening, "Will thou, Alastor?"

Alastor knew he could not return to this place. There was nothing left that Honor could offer him now. Their business, and whatever else had existed between them, was now at an end.

And yet, when he heard Honor's voice calling to him

through the mirrors three months later, he hesitated only a moment before attending to it. Perhaps he would find a man returned to his senses, one who would seek to nullify their last contract. Perhaps the human wished to talk of things, as they once did.

But when Alastor arrived in the town of Redhood, he was met only with death, and with fire.

The Fiends of Redhood

Every Saturday and Sunday, come rain or shine, snow or heat waves, the people of Redhood, Massachusetts, gathered in the gazebo located in the town square. Supposedly, they came to sip coffee and listen to a string quartet play the same five songs and enjoy the "atmosphere" of their pretty little home. In reality, the gatherings were used to mine for gossip.

Juicy tidbits of drama and betrayal had always been a currency in Redhood, and there was no gossip more valuable than the happenings of the Redding family.

What the old lady was up to now with her unending, unbending rules. Why so many of them had come out of the woodwork for a Founder's Day that seemed just like any other. And if I had to guess, where the Redding twins had gone that was so important they'd miss school for nearly two weeks.

Every weekend, without fail, the charming houses with their historic home markers would empty themselves out into the very heart of Redhood. With the sun shining and the autumn air crisp, no one would dare miss the opportunity to comment on the weather before breathlessly sharing intel about their neighbors and friends, trading those stories for others that would give them the illusion of being powerful and in the know.

It also meant that no one would miss the sight of the two youngest members of the Redding family running down Main Street, looking like they had come straight from a Renaissance faire, the yellow sulfuric dust of a demon realm still rising off them.

At least, I thought, the townsfolk couldn't see the changelings, Flora, or Zachariah. But the glamour also meant they wouldn't be able to see the fiends when they finally decided to spill out of my house, and I wasn't sure if that was a good or bad thing.

"The—string quartet—" Prue managed to squeeze out between pants. "I totally forgot what day it was—"

"Just look for Mom and Dad!" I called back to her.

Even I knew that the chances of Mom and Dad sitting around enjoying music while their only children were missing were slim. The better bet was that they were in the Cottage, with Grandmother and all the others, but we had to pass through the gazebo and square to get there. And if they weren't in the Cottage . . . they'd have an awful surprise waiting for them back at our house.

I'd been too much of a coward to look back as the sound of shattering glass and gleeful screeching chased us down the driveway. The smashing of furniture and the singsong of Pyra's "Run, humans—see how far you get!" had only spiked my fear.

The air shivered around us, making every hair on my body stand at attention. Nell spun, her eyes searching the street. If I had blinked, I would have missed it. A blanket of magic coated the air like a camera's flash, turning my view of the world momentarily photonegative.

"What did you do?" I demanded. "Alastor! What was that?"

He was silent, but I felt his own confusion rub like sandpaper against my mind.

"That couldn't have been good," Prue said, looking to Nell. The witch only shook her head and turned to Flora.

Who was no longer standing with us.

"Flora?" Nell called out. "Flora! Where are you?"

She'd been in the house with us, and I'd made sure she was keeping pace. Toad meowed in concern, pointing toward the woods beyond Main Street. He was the last of the changelings with us. The others had shifted into bird forms to fly out in every direction, searching for help. Eleanor was heading straight to Salem to alert Missy and her coven. I wanted to believe the witches would make it in time, but by the way the day was going, we'd be lucky to still be breathing in ten minutes.

Now the Ancient has abandoned you as well.

I squeezed my eyes shut, shaking my head as a wave of anger passed through me. After all we'd been through, I couldn't believe Flora would just vanish and leave us to our fates. "Come on. We don't have time for this. If she wants to find us, she will."

We slowed as we approached the gazebo, the sweetly singing strings carrying on with a song that promised spring, not the oncoming winter. Clusters of baby strollers were parked at the edge of the grassy park, the babies themselves sitting in the laps of their parents on the wrought-iron park benches or plaid picnic blankets.

I gripped the back of Nell's cloak, drawing her closer to the protective cover of the trees that lined Main Street. Nearby, the bell from Pilgrim's Plate jingled as someone stepped out from the café.

"Wait," she said suddenly, glancing around. "We lost Zachariah, too."

I spun, searching the air and nearby buildings. She was right. I didn't see his crabby face anywhere.

Your allies abandon you. How long before the witch does, too?

The din of music and chatter from the nearby park

floated between us. I breathed in another deep gulp of air, relishing the sweetness the nearby stand selling roasted chestnuts added to it.

The painted wood signs hanging from the shops began to squeak, swaying back and forth on their metal hinges. On their cooling tray, the sugarcoated chestnuts began to dance away from each other. Harry, the roaster, looked up, pushing his tidy uniform hat back out of his eyes.

Oh no.

Oh yes, Alastor hissed.

The music from the violins suddenly cut off. The gazebo creaked, shaking loose a shingle from its roof. It dented one of the carved jack-o'-lanterns that circled the structure as it fell and bounced away. A few people stood up from their blankets, searching for the source of the distant, fast-approaching thunder.

The crowd let out a collective gasp as their coffee and cider spilled over the rims of their cups. Parents dragged their children away from where they'd been playing, swinging their gazes around.

"Do you hear that?" someone asked.

"Earthquake?" another suggested. "It sounds almost like . . ."

And then, as if a lit fuse had finally found its way to an attached bomb, a roaring sound detonated in the distance. Wind littered with dust and shredded red leaves, bits of pumpkin, decorative witch hats, and strings of ghost-shaped lights crashed through the town's square like a tsunami.

I threw myself over Prue, covering her as a piece of white picket fence dislodged and flung itself at her.

Like one final, dying exhale, every tree in the town square threw off their remaining leaves. The blast knocked several of the older residents clear off their feet, and many of the people around them rushed to their aid. Others merely stared at one another, bewildered.

They're coming, Alastor sang. *They're coming!*

I sucked in a deep breath, summoning all the courage I'd managed to muster Downstairs. Then I turned and darted into the street that separated us from the town square.

"Run! Everyone needs to get out of here!" I shouted.

If this had been a real plan, I might have stopped to think about:

1. What I looked like.
2. What I smelled like.
3. How the people of Redhood, with their perfectly styled hair and cashmere sweaters and scarves, might react.

They stopped what they were doing, all right. They stopped and stared at me.

"Is that . . . is that Prosper Redding?" someone asked.

"It can't be," her friend said back.

"Get out of here!" I shouted. "It's not safe! Go!"

A drumming sound, uneven and wild and ancient, filled the air, growing louder, faster, until it infected my heartbeat and sent it racing, too.

Now, Alastor said, *the fun begins.*

Home Again

The terrible vapor arrived before they did—yellow and noxious, as if Downstairs had belched out the rotting contents of its belly.

Then came the chanting, the mocking singsong of their *"Nah, nah, nah, naaaah, nah, nah, naaaah!"*

They sang like a poorly tuned violin missing half its strings as their dark shapes parted the fog. The vapor stroked the cobblestone road with foul fingers.

The metallic *slam-slam-slam* of a grendel clashing two silver trash-can lids set their marching pace. They were merrily, monstrously uncoordinated. Some barreled forward on all fours, others hopped, and few took unnaturally long gliding strides. Pyra, however, was nowhere in sight.

The ogre at the front of the horde rose up to his full

height, thrusting his battle club into the air. Immediately the cackling and caroling stopped.

Prue grabbed my shoulder, her grip tightening until it ached. "There's so many of them. . . ."

It took me a second to realize it, and it was only after Alastor let slip a surprised, *Impossible, she—*

Now that we were back in the human world, under the glamour that kept the fiends invisible, Prue, as a person without magic, shouldn't have been able to see the fiends. Now that I was thinking about it, maybe it was something in our blood, or something to do with Honor's bargain, because she'd been able to see the fiends in Salem, too.

But the real problem was that Prue wasn't the only human who saw them.

When the tide of crimson rats swept up through the fiends' feet, writhing and squirming as they raced toward the town square, the residents of Redhood opened their mouths and let out a soul-chilling collective scream.

Nell and I spun toward each other. I couldn't even get the question out.

"I don't know!" she said. "That must have been what we felt before—the glamour's been removed!"

The *who* and *why* of it fell away, trampled by the terror of the moment. With only one exit and entrance into the square, the residents of Redhood charged forward blindly, desperate to find an escape. They crushed their ornately carved pumpkins into pulp underfoot, slid through the wet leaves on the ground, and shoved each other to get away. The musicians clung to the railings of the elevated gazebo as if they were on the bridge of a sinking ship.

Every muscle in my body clenched at the horrible sounds of their terror. Kids—little *babies*—began to cry. I couldn't tell where one scream stopped and another began.

"No. *No!* I hate this stupid town!" Harry, the chestnut cart guy, ripped off his hat and threw it to the ground. "No one even says thank you! You can all save yourselves!"

He ran up the opposite end of Main Street but didn't get far. The rats and a pack of crocodile-sized lizards quickly swept up the street after him, knocking him off his feet and carrying him away. A moment later, his cart toppled over, too.

The fiends broke ranks, scattering with booming shouts. The ogres thundered toward the shops and homes on Main Street, waving axes, clubs, and staffs. The goblins scampered toward the town square, linking arms to block the exit. Though they only reached a little past the humans' knees, they snarled and clacked their teeth, flicking and flapping their fine robes. The few residents that had escaped the bottleneck in the park were dragged back by the scruffs of their necks.

The sight of my teacher Mr. Wickworth hyperventilating as two lycans clamped down on his jacket and carried him toward where the others were imprisoned kicked me square in the ribs. The few people who tried beating the goblins blocking the exit with purses and backpacks were immediately tackled to the ground.

Prue hooked her arms through mine and Nell's, dragging us out of sight behind the fallen chestnut cart. She was panting hard, but her face was set with determination. "Well, they're not eating them, at least?"

That was the thing I'd truly been afraid of. The fiends scratched and nipped at their prey, but only to contain them. It was almost like they knew that making the residents of Redhood watch as their world was destroyed would be a far worse punishment than death.

Or they were planning on using these people for something else.

Lycans leaped up to snap the wooden street signs into pieces. Down came the walls of wood, of brick, of stone. The ogres lowered their heads like bulls and charged through all the rubble. Goblins smashed through the glass of the Fair Lady, Grandmother's favorite clothing shop, emerging a few minutes later modeling their finest dresses and vests.

Hobs climbed the gazebo, tearing the pristine white wood apart plank by plank. The demonic rats ate the roses and other flowers, vomiting them back up on the shoes of the terrified residents around them.

Within minutes, Main Street was unrecognizable.

I stood there, watching it all. Unable to stop them. Unable to even move.

What do I do?

Glass exploded a few feet to the left of me as fiends tore through a storefront. Pain seared my left shoulder, making me fall back from where I'd been standing. The girls both darted to the left, moving to the better shelter of a nearby car.

Maggot! How many times must I tell you to flee destruction before it destroys you! Alastor fumed. *Now look what you've done to yourself!*

I wasn't suffering any more delusions that Alastor had ever cared about me beyond needing to keep my body alive. The vibrations of anger that fanned through my blood confirmed as much.

Biting my lip, I forced myself to look back over my shoulder. A shard of glass as long as my hand protruded from where it had stabbed into the muscle and skin, stopped only by my shoulder blade. The area around the wound was gushing blood. It soaked through my undershirt and cloak in seconds.

You're lucky it missed your lung, you mortal fool! Alastor ranted.

Carefully, to avoid cutting myself on its jagged edges, I pulled out the shard. It made a horrible sucking noise. My vision went hazy.

What do I do? What do I do? What do I do?

"Two for me!"

"Five for me—hit the old bag of bones and it'll be six!"

Shingles smacked into the back of Mr. Davenport's

head, knocking the elderly man forward as he tried to flee down Main Street. The goblins on the roof of the restaurant still had a stack of the shingles, and were already taking aim at their next human victim.

A dog yelped nearby—the McKillip family Lab ran at top speed, leaping over the rats still clogging the street. I recognized the howls that followed; the sound sank through my skin, rattling my bones.

Howlers.

A pack of the massive black dogs barreled after the Lab, yipping and snarling at each other to get to their prey first. The screams from the town square started again as townsfolk caught sight of them.

Pray that Pyra did not summon the warrior ghouls to attend to her in her victorious march into the human world, Alastor said. ***Or else no one will make it out alive.***

I pressed my hand to the cut on my shoulder, reminding myself to breathe in, breathe out. A grendel passed me, pushing one of the abandoned baby strollers. A silver-skinned goblin sat inside, a child's costume crown draped over its ears. It waved to the terrified humans they passed, like a queen.

Another goblin followed, its stroller filled with all the pumpkins it could find. A few of the hobs stood on each other's shoulders to tip the chestnut cart back up, descending on the sweetened nuts—only to spit them back out in disgust.

Within seconds, a horde of sugar-drunk fairies descended on them, bobbing in the air as they carried off armfuls.

"No—you can't, Toad," Nell whispered. "You can't! There are too many of them!"

The changeling struggled in the prison of her arms, trying to wriggle his way out.

Even he was trying to do *something*. All I was doing was just sitting there, watching the dream that was Redhood come crashing down around me.

I couldn't make another deal with Alastor in order to call off the fiends. The malefactor already had everything he wanted from me. I had nothing left to use as leverage.

There was his true name . . . but somehow, using it felt like it would be taking that last step across a bridge that was slowly crumbling behind me. If I went any farther, I would never be able to get back to a place that made me feel good about myself.

Even to save your friends? a small voice whispered. *Your family? The whole realm?*

No. I couldn't force someone to do something against their will. Even Alastor.

I'd told myself Downstairs that I was doing everything for the right reason, but in the process, I'd compromised who I was. I wouldn't do it again.

I pressed my hands to my face, trying to block out the sounds of the people of Redhood screaming, the cracks and smashing of nearby homes and businesses as they were reduced to smoldering rubble.

The truth set in, heavy and unforgiving. Even if I compelled Alastor to order the fiends back Downstairs, it wouldn't do any good. They didn't consider him their leader. They would answer only to Pyra.

"Is there a phone I could use somewhere nearby? I'm hoping Eleanor reached her, but if not, I can at least get the word out to Missy," I heard Nell say. "She and the Salem coven are only a few hours away—they could banish some of the fiends back Downstairs."

Prue sounded as defeated as I felt. "There won't be anything left in Redhood in a few hours. By then, the fiends will have spread out to all the nearby towns, too."

Meaning even more people would be in danger. Would lose their homes. Maybe even their lives.

I did this.

If I had kept better control of Alastor in Salem and figured out his plan . . . if Prue had never been kidnapped . . . if I hadn't ordered Alastor to open the mirror . . .

Yes, Maggot. It is your fault. You have truly lived up to your Redding name. Look at the heartache, the destruction you have brought to those people you claim to love.

All I had wanted to do was the right thing—to save my family—and I'd managed to destroy everything in the process.

Where were my parents? At the Cottage or traveling? Did it matter as long as they weren't here?

I gazed out over the town I had grown up in. The uncomfortable, stiff, perfect place that had always made me feel like I was wearing shoes that were two sizes too small. The people who had called me names and told me I wasn't worth anything—that I didn't deserve the family I'd been born into, and the name I had never asked for.

But if I cleared away those feelings, what was left was something very different. Something that might have been love. I rubbed the back of my hand across my forehead, swallowing the thickness in my throat.

It was like the hidden da Vinci painting they had found in that castle in Italy, masked by twenty layers of white-wash. The dark truth of Redhood and the Reddings had been hidden by time, covered up for so long that a different kind of ugliness had been allowed to grow in its place.

The only way to save it was to start over. There was nothing to be proud of in Redhood's past, but there was something that could be made of its future. If it survived.

If I wasn't going to use Alastor's name, I could only see one other option to save this realm from being torn apart.

Toad finally freed himself from Nell's arms, *popping* into his bigger, meaner form. His growl sent a few of the nearby goblins scattering. A bundle of hobs began to throw raw food at him from inside the broken window of Pilgrim's

Plate. He swiveled his head around, eyes narrowing.

"Toad!" I whispered. Crouched behind one of the last benches still standing along Main Street, I waved him over. The changeling darted to my side, lowering a wing to shield me from the sight of the fiends in the park.

"Can you get the girls to the Cottage?" I asked him. "Prue knows the way. They and anyone there can go into one of the panic rooms."

While those rooms featured top-of-the-line safety equipment, they were meant to protect against very human burglars, murderers, and kidnappers. Not monsters from another dimension. Still, it was worth a try.

The girls had their heads bent together—most likely discussing a plan. Toad's nose wrinkled in a rare show of uncertainty, but he didn't try to stop me.

I took a slow step back from Nell and Prue, then another, until I had ducked around the last standing wall of Pilgrim's Plate.

What are you doing, Maggot? Alastor asked.

By the time they noticed I was gone, it would be too late to stop me.

I'm looking for my parents, I said, keeping my thoughts even. Cool.

The trick was not to think about it, or show my hand to Alastor. This would only work if I could keep him from surging forward to take control of my body.

One step, and then another, and then I began to run. A second after I passed one of the oldest mansions on Main Street, an ogre burst onto its porch, tearing out the door and its whole frame with a swing of its spiked club.

"Again!" an ogre called from inside. She leaped up onto the centuries-old crystal chandelier and brought it down in a rain of glittering glass.

Nell and Prue rushed forward from behind the car, hollering like warriors. They ran toward the place where hobs had encircled several families, spraying their babies with blue slobber.

The youngest meat is always the tenderest.

Toad swept out after them, soaring into the air. He scooped the girls up with his paws and used his tail to whip the hobs away.

I didn't want to see any more of this. I forced myself into an all-out sprint. Before long, I'd turned down Apple Lane, and was facing down my own house at the end of the street.

I'd always liked that we lived at the end of a small cul-de-sac. It meant that I could look out onto Main Street, which crossed ours, from my bedroom window. It had felt like a seat at the top of the world.

The houses on Apple Lane had wide lots, their yards broken up by trees and wild blueberry bushes. Their white, perfectly symmetrical colonial faces were differentiated only by the color of their shutters—some green, some red, some blue. Ours were black.

Those shutters, along with the rest of the front of the house, had been completely torn off.

My footsteps slowed to a stop as I looked up. I pressed a hand to my aching shoulder and the sticky, fresh blood.

It was like looking at Prue's old dollhouse. Somehow, Pyra and the other fiends had blown out the wood, the brick, and the windows, shaving the front of it clear off. The few neighbors who had risked becoming social outcasts by staying home from the concert stood on their front porches, hands clapped over their mouths.

"Prosper, is that you?" Mr. Featherton called. "Don't go down there, son, it's too dangerous!"

I almost laughed. But I already looked like I'd come climbing down a filthy chimney dressed like a wizard, so I thought it was probably best to not seem any more deranged than I had to.

"Gas leak," I told him weakly.

Shoving my hands into the pockets of my ruined cloak, I shielded my thoughts from Alastor as best I could as I continued down the cobblestoned street. One of the lamps flickered weakly, sparking as I passed beneath it. The fragments of siding and glass were scattered across the front yard, curtains and blankets tossed out into the nearby trees.

It is beautiful, is it not? Imagine what we shall do to your world once the rest of the fiends arrive.

I wouldn't.

The blood key was back in the tower, unfinished. If I

returned through the open portal, I could destroy the mirror, and its passage, from the other side. I would be trapped in the fiend world, but so would the blood key as it and the other magic nearby burnt itself out.

When the Void did fall over Skullcrush, it wouldn't just take out me and the key, it would save the human realm from a worse fate.

Maggot . . . what are you truly doing here? Alastor asked, his voice deepening with suspicion. *I've been inside your head long enough to know that a foolhardy plan is bound to be brewing by now.*

I ignored him, passing through the front hall, past the door to the kitchen. The fiends had ripped through there, throwing pots around and splitting bags of dried pasta and flour. The table where we'd all sat together for so many meals, laughing, catching up, had been cleaved in half and tossed into the living room's bookshelves. Priceless paintings were smeared with spaghetti sauce or ripped from their frames. Someone had drawn a smiley face with horns in the dust on the TV.

All the family pictures that had lined our staircase—something Grandmother had always deemed "unsightly" and "plebeian"—were in shreds. I brushed the broken frames off each step with my foot, continuing the climb upstairs. My heart banged in my ears.

This was . . . This was the right thing to do.

It was the only thing to do.

Prue hadn't needed me to save her, and never would. My parents would still have one kid. The rest of my family would be glad if I were gone.

Prosperity . . . ? What are these thoughts? What is it that you mean to do?

I shook my head, clearing my mind. At the top landing, I stopped long enough to glance toward my room, but the door was shut and had stayed that way. Turning right brought me back into Prue's bedroom, to the wreckage, to the mirror.

To the person who had beaten me there.

She rose from where she had been sitting on the only spot on the mattress that hadn't been gutted. Its stuffing, as well as the feathers from Prue's pillows, still drifted through the air like snow. Small flecks had caught in her steel-colored hair, dusting her ever-tight bun. Behind her, the far wall gaped open, revealing the destruction from above.

Instinctively, I attempted to smooth down my hair and wipe my dirty cheeks against my shoulders. It seemed pointless to straighten what was left of my scorched cloak, but my hands still tried.

The room reeked of flowers and vanilla, mingling with the sulfuric stench of the fiends themselves. The smashed perfume bottles crunched under my feet as I bent down to pick up a picture of our family from under the fragments of its glass and frame.

I was exhausted, but when Grandmother turned to me, I met her unflinching gaze head-on.

"Now, Prosperity," she said, folding her hands together in front of her. "I must have a word with you."

Of Grandmothers and Monsters

"What are you doing here?"

My grandmother was standing in front of me—right there. In full color. Breathing. Speaking. But it was like my brain couldn't grasp that reality. It felt like I was stuck somewhere inside the mirror's portal, between destinations, turning and turning in a hopeless tumble. Right-side up was suddenly upside down.

My grandmother was standing *right there*. In the remains of what had been Prue's bedroom. Not in the Cottage's safe room. Not locked away with all of her jewels, furs, and family heirlooms. Right there, dusted with wreckage.

"What do you think I'm doing here?" she said, her voice as icy and refined as it always was. "I am looking after the family. I may not have been born a Redding, but I always understood I would become a guardian of it. I felt the portal open, and I came to retrieve you and Prudence to take you to safety."

The cut she'd made on my left arm using a cursed blade throbbed. I fought the urge to cover it with my right hand.

"The real question is, what are you doing here?" she pressed. "I think I might have a guess; however, I'd like it to be confirmed."

Yes, Maggot. What are you doing here?

"I'm taking responsibility," I said. The wound in my shoulder stung. For a moment I couldn't speak. "For the mistakes I made, and for what our family did three hundred years ago. I'm ending it the only way I can think of."

Redhood had always belonged to the Reddings. Our ancestors had founded it on blood, and everyone who had followed had, wittingly or unwittingly, helped in covering up the truth of how it had come to be. What they did to the girl they'd used to trap Alastor. To the Bellegraves. To anyone who threatened to shatter that life and legacy.

Including me.

To be a Redding was to inherit history, but also the shared responsibility of guilt.

The beginning of this story was Redhood. The end of it would be Redhood.

Sacrificing myself wouldn't restore the lives that had been lost, but I could at least save those who were still living.

"Ah," Grandmother said. "I see."

"No, you don't," I said sharply. "All you see and care about is yourself. About the *Reddings*. Even now, you were only here to get me and Prue, right? Were you going to try to bring the whole town to safety, too?"

She turned, staring at the mirror. The darkness at the center of the portal. "Don't be ridiculous, Prosperity. Family always comes first."

"Don't you get it? That's the whole problem!" I said. "Thinking that way is the reason that we got into this mess in the first place! We can't keep running from what we did—we can't keep trying to hide it by closing ranks to anyone who doesn't share our last name. Redhood is ours to take care of, and that includes *all* the people who live here."

My family had disappointed me so many times, I don't know why her silence now hurt me the way it did. Maybe she was just incapable of changing.

"Where are Mom and Dad?" I asked. "Are they at the Cottage?"

Grandmother shook her head. "They left for Salem this morning. After we'd tracked where Prudence had disappeared to, we were able to piece together what happened. They were to wait for you there, in case you should return through the mirror you used to leave. I, however, had a feeling that the malefactor would bring you back to Redhood."

"Then you knew better than I did," I muttered, swaying a little on my feet. I suddenly felt very hot.

"You must sit down, child," Grandmother said, without a hint of warmth in her voice. "You're about to faint."

"No I'm not—"

Blackness snapped over my vision, drowning out Alastor's frustrated groan of *Not now!*

When I opened my eyes again, I was belly down on the floor, one of the Heart2Heart foundation's fund-raising pillows stuck under my face.

Finally! Alastor snapped.

I couldn't have been out for long. The sunlight filtering into the room was just as strong as it had been before I'd fallen. I shifted, trying to work out the kinks in my sore muscles. A cool breeze from the window slipped beneath the collar of my shirt—meaning that the cloak had been taken off. My shoulder was stiff—too stiff to move. I reached back, feeling the bandage that had been put in place.

What the ...

The last few hours slammed back through my memory and I gasped, twisting around. I hadn't dreamed it. Grandmother was still standing in front of the open mirror portal, humming softly as she arranged a few stones on the floor in front of it.

"Let's banish you, shall we?" she said.

No ... Alastor breathed out.

I jumped to my feet, swaying as all the blood left my head again in one go.

A witch. My grandmother, the one who tormented

anyone who broke her stupid rules or shattered her image of matriarchal perfection. Who never smiled, except at someone else's expense.

This whole time, she'd been *an actual witch*, not just the figurative kind.

This explained so much, and yet . . . this still didn't really explain most things. But when I looked at Grandmother again, I *saw* her.

She wore her usual tight bun, but instead of a dress suit, she was garbed in a long green velvet coat. Beside Prue's bed was her own sewing basket. And just in case anyone wasn't sure who it belonged to, she had monogrammed her initials, CWR, on it.

Grandmother snapped her fingers at me, indicating I should retrieve it for her. I stooped down, surprised at how much its weight strained my already sore arms. Instead of the soft string and pins I would have expected, metal clacked against glass as I passed it to her.

Grandmother flipped the lid open and rummaged through the contents. A single wrinkle appeared between her gray eyebrows as she pulled out a long decorative knife.

I took a generous step back.

Grandmother looked up. "After that speech you gave, I would hate for you to lose your courage now. This blade is used for ceremonial spells only—bring the willow bark, please."

Thankfully, the bottles in the sewing basket were

labeled. I passed the right one to her and watched as she arranged a variety of plants and electric-blue dust across the ground in front of the mirror. The distant shadows of approaching fiends suddenly were not so distant.

She cannot close a mirror I've opened, Alastor said. *I shall enjoy watching her futile attempts. It does not matter, anyway. Pyra has brought the blood key with her. I feel its seething presence in this realm.*

A very bad word my grandmother definitely wouldn't have approved of flickered through my mind. Of course she'd brought the key with her. Pyra wasn't stupid. She wouldn't let something so valuable out of her sight.

My shoulders slumped as I released a heavy breath. "I thought only a malefactor could open and close the portals."

Nell's trick to reopen the portal to Downstairs had worked because she'd been able to repeat Alastor's spell. Casting the same spell now would be pointless with the portal already open. Which made it very curious that Grandmother took her ceremonial blade in her right hand and planted herself directly in the path of any monster about to explode out of the rippling silver surface.

"I'm not closing the portal," my grandmother said. "I'm banishing it to another dimension."

No, she is certainly not! The hot rush of Alastor seizing control of my legs and right arm came on so quick, it burned the air out of my lungs. Before I could wrest control back from him, my arm was swinging up, my fist flaring with snarling power as it came toward the back of my grandmother's head.

No!

Two cold metal bands snapped down over my wrists and locked. Grandmother hadn't even needed to turn around to float the cuffs out of her basket and direct them toward me. Alastor's power faded from my arm, leaving it feeling as if all the blood had been drained out of it at once.

This—this—pig-nosed wench!

Grandmother bowed her head, thrusting the ceremonial dagger forward. *"Goddess of travel, goddess of light, take this accursed object into the darkness, give it flight."*

She dragged the blade around the outer edges of the old mirror's frame. As it moved, the blade lit with emerald magic from tip to hilt. The air around the mirror blackened as it peeled away, curling into itself like damp paper.

"Take this accursed object into the darkness," Grandmother repeated. A horde of lycans took shape in the center of the mirror, clawing at the ground to run faster and faster as their door into Redhood disappeared. *"Give it flight!"*

Grandmother gave one last shove, right in the center of what remained of the mirror, and the darkness swirled, swallowing and swallowing, until only a pinprick of black remained where the mirror had been, then nothing at all.

That is hardly impressive, Alastor said, the words giving a faint tremble.

"Holy crap," I said. "That was *amazing.*"

My grandmother kicked the spell's ingredients aside, strolling through the carnage of ruined clothing and mauled books with her shoulders back and her head held high.

"I need you to understand something," she said, leaning one hand against the post of Prue's bed. "I have never been good with matters of the heart. I have rarely granted myself permission to be soft, not since my own mother died fighting fiends. To protect this family, I have always been on guard. But I have taken things too far, clearly. Even now, I see that you are frightened of me."

"You did come after me with a knife," I reminded her. "Without explaining what was happening. That would alarm pretty much anyone." Except, I realized, her.

"I did. And when I said that I'd hoped it was you who carried the burden of the malefactor, I spoke in anger and fear, and for that, I apologize."

I . . . did not know what to do with that.

"That's not the only time," I told her, hating the thickness in my throat. "Nothing I do has ever been good enough for you or for anyone else in this family."

"All I have ever wanted was for you and your sister to be strong enough to face the trials of life, supernatural or otherwise. I have always feared Prudence's heart condition was a result of the malefactor feeding upon her life. Even after she'd recovered, I remained worried that she did not have the strength to bear the brunt of this unfortunate task, and she might relapse, or we might lose her because I could not figure out a way to stop this."

I released a shaky breath. "And you seriously thought I could handle it?"

"It is one of the few things I have been unquestionably correct about," she said. "That was reaffirmed not just when I learned you'd followed her Downstairs, but this past afternoon, when you were willing to return to that place alone to face its darkness. It made me wonder what I might have done in your position. You have shown me my own monstrous pride, and how it very likely might have caused our fall."

I never imagined I would get an acknowledgment of the way she and the rest of my family had treated me over the years, let alone a true apology. I wanted to live in the moment a bit, and relish it, but there wasn't time. It wasn't that the past didn't matter, it was that the future was at stake.

Tap-tap-tap-tap-tap!

We both swung around to the room's window. Something moved along the edges of the frame, testing.

I strode over to it, waving Grandmother back. She raised her brows in my direction before pushing me behind her, her hand raised and already sparking with magic. The window swung open on its own. Her face lost all color as she stared at the brightly colored parrot that landed on the sill.

"Ribbit," she breathed out.

The changeling turned its head to the side, studying her. Grandmother stared back, her hands trembling as she reached out.

Realization thundered down around me.

Even Alastor sounded shocked. *The changeling was hers?*

For a second no one moved. Then Ribbit let out a quiet cooing sound and floated up from the sill, flying past my grandmother's fingers to land on her shoulder. The changeling rubbed her feathered head against Grandmother's cheek, and I could have sworn those were tears in the woman's eyes.

And to think this whole time I'd thought she'd had her tear ducts surgically removed.

"Yes," she said, clearly agreeing with something Ribbit told her. "I'll summon the coven, apologize for the cruel things I said as I broke from them, and see if they'll come to our aid. Then we'll end this. Together."

"My darling Catherine," came a new voice from the doorway. "We are already here."

31

Dangerous Whims and Irresponsible Curiosity

Elma Hazelwood, the eighty-year-old who lived in the crooked house on Mather Street and was commonly believed to have a pet squirrel, stood in the doorway.

Tucked over her arm was a wicker basket, identical to the one my grandmother had. Her shock of white hair curled up around her forehead and ears, giving her the appearance of wearing an old-fashioned bonnet. "Goodness. It really would be easier if we flew around on broomsticks. Oh, hello, dearie!" Elma gave me a fond smile. "It looks as though you've seen a spot of trouble."

"Elma," my grandmother said, her tone one of shock. "But how did you . . . ?"

"A rather panicked group of changelings found me in my garden. And, well, I heard the screams of terror. The others sent me to suss out your location," Ms. Hazelwood said. "They'll be glad to see you, Catherine."

My grandmother did not look completely certain of that as she raised her chin and gave a curt nod. I trailed behind the two women as we wound our way through the woods behind the house. Five other women were gathered there in their own green coats. All of them fell silent as we approached.

"Well," said one who looked suspiciously like TV chef Agatha "the Sandwich Witch" Dennard. "It's been an age. Is that heart of yours still as ugly as a wart?"

Grandmother stroked a finger down Ribbit's soft feathered chest. "Is your curse work still as sloppy as a burst boil?"

"Aw! Just like old times, ladies!" called a brash voice.

I recognized this woman, too . . . her name was . . . Barbie. That's right. Barbie lived in a town called Glenbrook, which had more trees than people. She ran her own small moving company.

I was less surprised to see her than I was to see her massive flamingo-pink truck parked along the boundary road that divided Redhood from its nearest neighbor. She sat in the driver's seat of her twelve-wheeler, resting her chin on her hand as she watched other members of the coven stacking stones into a small pyramid.

"Don't forget the petals, y'all!" she shouted.

"When have I ever forgotten part of a spell?" Mrs. Wu, the town's librarian, called back. "When, Barb?"

"Ladies," Grandmother said, her tone measured. "Are the other protection cairns complete?"

Ms. Dennard looked relieved to have a change of topic. "Yes, of course. One in each of the town's corners. We only need to complete the incantation."

"Is that the li'l guy the changelings told us about?" Barbie called, hanging out of the driver's side of the semi-truck's cab. Her hair was such a deep red it could almost be classified as a purple. She'd cut off the sleeves of her long velvet coat, baring her truly impressive guns and collection of tattoos on her dark skin. The shirt she wore under the coat was also sleeveless, and bore the same logo as her truck: BARBIE'S SCOOTIN'-HOOTIN' HAULIN'.

Grandmother walked me over to the truck, her hands still clasped around her sewing basket's woven handle.

"This is Mrs. Barbara Elderflower," Grandmother said. "You'll accompany her to retrieve the townspeople and bring them to the Cottage."

"Why the Cottage?"

Alastor blew out a sigh of disgust, which made me that much more curious to hear the answer.

"Thanks to the original contract with the malefactor, the Cottage and all of its land are protected. The fiends cannot cross the boundary walls of the estate."

"How am *I* going to cross the boundary, though?" I

asked. Wait, actually . . . "How *have* I been able to cross it?"

Grandmother let out a small huff of impatience. "I fed the house a drop of your blood when you were an infant so that it would recognize you always as a member of our family."

"Oh. Wait—*what?* You took a drop . . . You fed the house . . . *what?*"

Her eyes narrowed. "I can rescind your invitation at any point, however. As long as you keep the iron bracelets on, we should not have any problems."

I looked between her and the enormous truck and, with a sinking feeling, realized how we were going to collect the townspeople. "What about you, though? What are you trying to do out here?"

"That's not for you to worry about. Go on, now," Grandmother said, turning on her heel to walk over to the others.

Barbie seemed to take pity on me as I climbed up into the cab of the truck. "It's a protection spell on steroids. The fiends won't be able to get out, and nothing else will be able to get in. Now buckle up, we're going off-roading."

"What do you mean, they won't be able to get out?" I asked.

"It's just as I said, hon," Barbie said, turning the keys in the ignition. "We're shifting this town outside the normal flow of time, creating a kind of bubble of vast, physics-defying nothingness around it."

I didn't see how that was possible, but in that moment I didn't care. If nothing else, Mom and Dad would be safe outside of Redhood. Good.

I released a shaky breath as she pulled off the shoulder and onto the road, watching as the rest of the sewing circle raised their arms into the air. A small crocodile with a feathered head—Barbie's changeling—jumped from the dashboard to her sewing basket. Hers looked a bit more worn, but was otherwise identical. It wasn't until I scanned over her initials that I froze.

BZE.

"Wait . . . Barbara Z. Elderflower?" I said slowly.

"Barbara Zelda Elderflower, if you want to be specific, hon," she said. "What's with that face?"

"The author of *Toil and Trouble: A Witch's Guide to Navigating Mischief and Mayhem, second edition*?" I clarified.

"Oh, that old thing?" Barbie lit up. "How'd you find a copy? The Supreme Coven took it out of print—said it promoted 'dangerous whims and irresponsible curiosity,' pshaw."

"My friend is a *huge* fan," I explained. Nell was going to *die*.

Um, figuratively.

"Grand! You'll have to introduce me." The line of bobblehead Red Sox players on her dashboard quivered as she picked up speed. My seat bounced and I was thrown to the left as she gunned the gas. Within minutes, we hit the first cobblestones of Main Street.

"All right, hang on—things are about to get loud and ugly, and if something catches on fire please tell your grannie it's not my fault—" Barbie rolled down her window, leaning out as far as she could. *"Run if you value your evil little lives, you magic-sucking mosquitoes!"*

She leaned back into the cab, reaching over to push the play button on her stereo. Church bells—clanging, beautiful church bells—blared out of the speakers mounted in the truck.

ARGH! Alastor shriveled, thrashing inside my skull.

"Make it louder!" I shouted to her.

Barbie winked, snapping her fingers. The spark of magic jumped from her fingers to the dashboard, and the sound of the bells intensified until I had to cover my ears.

"Hold on!" she shouted.

Ogres dove out of the street as the truck barreled down it. The fiends sorting through their stolen bounty outside the shops crumpled at the sound of the bells. The tires smoked as Barbie hit the brakes and sent us sliding across the cobblestones in a move I had only ever seen in a Fast and Furious movie. The massive truck rocked as we came to a stop at the curb alongside the town square.

"Stay here!" Barbie said, unbuckling her seat belt and jumping down to the blackened sidewalk. "All right, load up, folks!"

The truck swayed as the witch opened the back and people poured into it. I kept watch on the dashboard clock, my fingers tightening around the armrests, my heart rising in my throat. Finally, the trailer's door slammed shut.

"Well, that was a bucket of fun," Barbie said, breathless, as she climbed back inside. I was thrown back into my seat as she floored the gas again.

The roads narrowed as we left the center of town, winding around through the trees. Barbie turned hard and quick enough to make me clutch my chest.

The change came so subtly, it wasn't until we were deep into the woods surrounding the Cottage that I noticed that the world had darkened. The witch in the driver's seat leaned forward, craning her neck to catch a glimpse of the sky through the trees. A green bolt of lightning crackled over the heavy underbelly of the clouds.

"Is that your spell?" I asked, having to shout over the bells.

"'Fraid not!" Barbie urged the truck faster, until the engine was quaking and clattering inside the hood.

"Careful!" I said. The people in the back had no seat belts or anything to hold on to. What was the good of saving them if everyone came out of there with a collection of broken bones?

A screech went up through the forest, shrill enough to drown out the bells blaring from the truck.

Dark shadows raced through the uneven rows of trees around us. Their lanky forms ate up the ground, covering the distance at nearly the same speed as the truck. One veered off from the others, taking a flying leap toward the passenger door of the truck. All I had to see was the long wisp of hair, the eight eyes, and the mouth that nearly encircled its head—my body reacted before my brain could.

I opened the door, twisting in my seat to kick it out as hard as I could. Barbie caught on quickly, veering sharply to the right. The fiend—the *ghoul*—clung to the door, swinging it back out with its weight. Another ghoul bounded toward me, a vicious blade in one hand, the other outstretched. This close, I saw where they had stuffed their ears with cloth and leaves, nullifying the effects of the bells.

Barbie jerked the wheel to the right again, catching the door against one of the centuries-old maple trees. I twisted back toward the dashboard as the first ghoul was knocked off the door like a bug and thrown under the wheels. My stomach turned as the wheels of the truck jumped, taking the unnatural speed bump.

As she made the last turn onto Redding Lane, Barbie didn't wait for the security gates of the Cottage to open. She blew right through them.

The other ghouls were flung away if they'd hit a closing door that we'd been able to slip through. The air around the fence pulsated with power, but it was nothing compared to the light show in the sky.

"Now *that*," Barbie said, pointing up at the blanket of sparkling green magic that burned through the unnatural clouds like an ocean of flames, "is our spell."

Ravenfeather

The residents of Redhood were all a bit green in the face as they were helped down out of the back of the truck. But they were, thankfully, in one piece.

I climbed down slowly, letting the sound of the recorded bells wash over me. It rang out over the wooded land that surrounded the house, driving out some of the shadows. Just not the one inside me.

With a deep breath, I looked up at the grand house in front of us. After the weeks I'd spent going between a legitimately haunted house and jagged, skull-adorned prisons, the three stories of the Cottage no longer sent a trickle of dread through me. As I walked up the gravel of the driveway toward the front door, I wondered if the house had somehow become smaller in the time that I'd been away.

Redhood's residents wandered around the front of the house in a daze. Very few of them had likely ever passed the boundary gate in all their decades of living in town.

"I thought there was supposed to be a gold statue of Old Lady Redding right by the door?" someone whispered.

"I mean . . . there's like eighty percent less gargoyles than I was expecting, given how evil they are," came another voice.

"What are we even doing here? This is *their* fault, isn't it? They brought the monsters—"

"No, *they* have always *been* the monsters."

I glanced back over my shoulder. The people of Redhood hesitated on the drive, even with Barbie's arm waving them toward the inviting open door of the house. Most looked as if terror had drained the life out of them, as they gazed back toward where dark shapes moved beyond the iron fences in the distance.

Three *thud*s from the entryway announced the arrival of the Cottage's white-haired butler. Seemingly unfazed by the scratched, bruised, and filthy masses in front of him, he leaned forward on his cane and cocked his head to the side. His face never once lost the look of mild distaste.

"Dinner has been prepared and sleeping arrangements have been organized. Should you need medical assistance, Dr. Feeny requests that you assemble in the kitchen, where he will treat you in order of need. Mrs. Redding has asked me to tell you that if you prefer to serve as another creature's

dinner rather than dine upon the fine meal we have prepared for you, you are welcome to exit through the same
gate in which you entered. Otherwise, please enjoy your stay
here until the matter of the monsters is settled."

He really hadn't needed to say anything beyond *dinner*.
The residents flowed around him like a river forced to
change its course to accommodate a stone that had been
there, unmoving, from the dawn of time.

Barbie and I waited until the pack of humans had rushed
into the house before starting up the steps ourselves. By
then, the sky was edging toward night, its blue deepening
to a sullen shade. The massive lantern that hung over the
grand doorway flickered on as we passed beneath it.

While Barbie cut a path around the butler, when it came
time for me to do the same, Rayburn stepped directly in my
path. I tried to move, and he shifted with me. This close to
him, the tufts of white hair in his ears and nostrils were very
noticeable.

"Hey, Rayburn," I said slowly. "It's been, ah, a while,
huh?"

If he didn't remember our interaction in Salem, when
Nell had blown a fistful of dizzy dust in his face on the play-
ground, someone had clearly told him what had happened.
Instead of looking at me like a fly that needed to be shooed
away, I was now no better than a poisonous spider that had
to be crushed at all costs.

"Prosper!"

I darted around Rayburn, ducking under his out-stretched arm and moving into the house's warmth and its familiar smell: vaguely musty, polished wood, old carpet.

Nell rushed toward me down the great hall, unbothered by the residents removing their coats and accepting bundles of food from the staff. Toad, back to his usual size, galloped at her heels to keep up.

I barely had a chance to brace myself before she slammed into me, throwing her arms around my neck. Her hair was cold and damp from the shower she must have taken, and she was wearing a set of my sister's clothes.

"Is Prue here, too?" I asked her.

"Yes! Where did you go? It was bad enough Flora and Zachariah wandered off, but we were freaking out when you disappeared! Toad insisted on flying us over here and then kept us here as his prisoners. But, seriously, where did you go?"

I pulled back, deciding to avoid the question rather than outright lie. "Did you get ahold of Missy?"

"The magic is interfering with everyone's cell signal," Nell said. "Our orders are to get something to eat and go to sleep."

I gave her an incredulous look.

"I know. But they're not wrong." Nell let out a soft sigh. "Prue ate a sandwich and fell asleep in the library in the middle of arguing why we didn't need to rest. And it's going to take a few hours at least before my powers are back to their full strength. Also"—she reached up and pinched my arm hard enough to make me yelp—"how could you not tell me your grandmother was part of the famous Ravenfeather coven? How did *I* not put that together?"

"How did you know that?" I asked.

"I recognized the other members—also, Ribbit? Wow. I did not see that one coming."

"Me either," I confessed as we walked back toward the house. "Is the Ravenfeather coven famous or something?"

"Yes! They can trace their lineage all the way back to the founding of Massachusetts! I thought they had moved farther west, but I guess not. Missy is going to be *so* jealous. She loves Agatha Dennard's essays—"

We rounded the side of the mansion and found ourselves on the driveway again. Barbie had climbed back into the cab of her truck to retrieve her sewing basket and was just locking up when she caught sight of us.

Nell froze.

"That's—" she whispered.

"I know," I said.

"No, you don't understand. That's—"

"I know."

Nell looked like she was either going to faint or start clawing at her face.

"Hello again, my slightly smelly dumplin'," Barbie said, coming over to us. "Is this your friend you mentioned?"

Nell kept her hands pressed to her mouth, like she was

too scared of what might come out. Right now all she was managing to utter was a high-pitched note.

"This is Nell Bishop," I explained. "Her mom was a member of the Salem coven, and her other mom still is."

"Oooh, you must be Tabitha's daughter," Barbie said, adjusting the basket from one arm to the other so she could stick out her hand. "I'd heard your sweet mom had passed. I'm awful sorry about that, little witch. I lost my own mom before I took my trials, too."

Nell slowly drew her hands away from her face, her mouth tightening into a pained line. Barbie put a hand on her shoulder, drawing her in closer.

"How about you help me go through my supplies and see what else we might need?" she suggested. "I'd love to hear more about your mom and what's what."

Nell nodded, but caught herself. She turned to look at me.

"I'm just going to find Prue and check on her—make sure nothing truly awful happened to her Downstairs," I said. "You also need to update Barbie on all the new things we found out so she has it straight in her next book."

Over the top of Nell's curls, Barbie winked at me.

The three of us walked into the house together, but soon split off in different directions. Barbie and Nell went to the smaller front sitting room, usually reserved for greeting guests Grandmother didn't like and wanted to make sure they knew it. I continued past the many sitting rooms filled with families wrapped in blankets in front of glowing fireplaces. It reminded me in an uncomfortable way of the fiend families we had seen in the prison.

Prue had mentioned in Salem that the Reddings had spread out looking for me, and it didn't seem like many of them had made it back to Redhood before the fiends invaded. I saw a few second cousins here and there, most of them giving me horrified looks as I passed by, but none of my aunts or first cousins.

I kept my gaze forward as I walked to the stairs, ignoring the press of unseen eyes against me. At the edge of my vision, the candle flames along the walls shivered.

There are no candles lit.

I swung my gaze back, but the glimmers of light were gone. A faint chill crept down my spine as I took each step. Whispered voices carried through the hall, following me up the stairs like a bitterly cold breeze.

I just couldn't tell if they were coming from the living, or the Cottage's watchful dead.

Even with a house full of powerful witches and the protection spell, my mind wouldn't let me sleep. I took a shower, changed, then just walked. Up and down the floors, in and out of rooms, from attic to basement. It had been hours since people had been sent to bed with full bellies and a gentle explanation of what the fiends were. Which was why I was surprised to find someone else awake in the great hall.

Nell sat in the center of the room's plush carpet, beneath the skylight. The soft, silvery moonlight fell over her as she absorbed the full impact of the hundreds of Redding family portraits crammed onto the soaring walls. She glanced my way as I came toward her, her expression unreadable.

"Wow. Your family . . ." she said quietly. "It's so . . . *big*."

"That's one word for it," I said dryly.

Nell didn't laugh. She ran her fingers along the worn carpet. "It was always just me, Mom, and Missy—and their coven, too. Henry claims to be the last of the Bellegraves, but I guess that would actually be me?"

Despite the age of the Bellegrave family and how early they'd been established in America, there would be no walls of storied ancestors for them. There would be no paintings done by the famous artists in the family. There would be no family home for them to gather for the holidays each and every year.

Alastor and Honor Redding had seen to that.

Instead of sitting, I moved to a portrait in a massive gold frame, the one with a section all to itself. The iron bracelet around my right wrist slid down as I reached for the pen resting on the guestbook Grandmother insisted on keeping. I uncapped it, tapping the pen against my lips.

Before I could stop myself, I rolled up onto my toes and drew horns and a curly mustache on Honor Redding's scowling face.

When Nell gasped out a laugh, I added a pointy tail behind him for good measure.

"There," I said. "It finally captures the real man."

I plopped down onto the carpet beside her, admiring my work. For a while, neither of us said anything.

Nell hugged her knees to her chest, looking down at her turquoise-painted toes. "I . . . I talked everything through with Barbie. She convinced me to own up to my mistakes and face the Supreme Coven, come what may. She said she and the whole Ravenfeather coven would put in a good word for me, too."

"That's great," I said, meaning it sincerely.

"It will be slightly less great if they decide to strip my powers rather than send me to Crescent Academy for a while," she said. "But Barbie said something that made me rethink the way I'd been framing this in my head. She told me she knew my mom because they'd both had to go in front of the Supreme Coven on the same day and explain their actions—Barbie had snuck Downstairs but was able to get off with only a temporary magic suppression because her information was so useful. But my mom was there because she'd used her power to help heal a lycan caught in our world, so he could return Downstairs."

"You didn't know that?" I asked.

Nell shook her head. "No. It just made me realize how rigid and outdated the rules are. She did something they'd decided hundreds of years ago was 'bad,' but they refused to see she did it with good intentions and ultimately got the lycan back Downstairs."

"Did they punish her?" I asked.

"Yeah. She had been nominated to join the Supreme Coven—the youngest member ever. But they withdrew that nomination due to her 'poor judgment.' I don't know that they'll have mercy on me, but at least I can tell them what I think of their rules when I see them in person. I can argue for change on behalf of all witches."

"If there's one person that can give a well-reasoned, impassioned, perfectly executed speech, it's you," I said. "Do you want moral support? *Could* I be moral support, or is their building cursed to turn intruders into frogs as soon as they step through the door?"

Nell rolled her eyes, but she was smiling. "You're a good friend, Prosper Redding."

"You're a better friend, Nell Bishop," I told her. "You were right to call me out in the sewers. I'm sorry. I just . . . wanted to be different this time. I wanted to do the right thing, and the only thing I succeeded at was being a jerk."

Nell bumped her shoulder into mine. "I know. But for what it's worth, there was nothing wrong with the old Prosper. If you don't mind, could I have that one back?"

I closed my eyes, wriggling my hands in front of my face. "And . . . done."

When I opened them again, the unhappy, humorless faces of the many Reddings who had come before me glared back from their gilded frames. The lightness in my chest faded as I remembered something.

"Before I forget or another horde of fiends invades, there's something else I have to tell you," I confessed. "I figured out Alastor's true name."

Inside me, I felt Alastor's presence coil tighter.

Nell sat up straighter. "What? When?"

"In the tower. It was one of the names scratched onto the floor. I almost used it to compel him to open the mirror portal. I *could* have used it to force him to shut it. And I didn't. I had to force him using the terms of our deal."

"Why?" she asked.

I ran my hand back through my hair, clutching it in my hands. "I don't know—it was something that he said, about how I was turning into Honor. I just . . . couldn't do it. I'm sorry."

"I understand."

"I know I'm being ridiculous—"

"You're not," Nell said. "I keep thinking about what Flora said, about how the fiends were once part of us. I don't know that they're capable of genuine good, but I know we are. Choosing not to enslave another creature and bend it to your will doesn't make you a bad person. It makes you Prosper. And besides . . . the coven wants to try to get as many fiends as we can back Downstairs and then wait out the Void. Maybe the contracts will automatically be nullified if . . ."

"That whole realm is destroyed?" I finished. "That doesn't feel right either."

"No," she agreed, rubbing at her forehead. "It doesn't."

I lay back on the rug, staring up at the shimmering blanket of the protection spell through the hall's skylight. Nell did the same, resting her hands on her stomach.

"It'll be all right," I said, letting my eyes shut. "We'll figure it out."

Within seconds, we lost our grip on the world and drifted into sleep.

Trapped inside the boy's undreaming mind, Prince Alastor of the Third Realm stewed.

It was an inglorious way to describe his current ignoble predicament, but it would have to suffice until he thought of a better one. The boy and witchling had fallen asleep on the ground and no one had come to awaken them. Now, if Alastor had nothing else, he had time to think. About the boy. About the key. About his family. About his realm.

But even the hours were dwindling, passing by like clouds caught in the wind.

He strained against the iron bonds, testing the bracelet the witch had placed on the boy. Outside, the infernal clanging of church bells continued, and the wards he himself had established centuries ago on this land held.

Alastor supposed he ought to have been proud of that, in a way. There had once been a time when his power was as unquestionable as it was unrivaled. No fiend had dared to challenge him, not until his sister. In the end, Pyra's scheme had been flawless. All she'd had to do was choose the one creature he would never expect to best him—a human—and plant the seeds of betrayal in exchange for what he desired.

Now Alastor found himself again in the grand home that had been built on the foundations of Honor's deceit and greed, his mutilated portrait staring down at him.

When Alastor had first met the man, Honor and his wife had lived in little more than a simple hovel of wood. His requests had started so small, so humbly. Then they had grown fangs, and the price had become darker. Destroy the Bellegraves. Grant us never-ending wealth and prosperity.

Prosperity.

And what had the boy asked him for? *Help me save my sister.*

He tested the iron restraints again, feeling the ache in the boy's shoulder. It was because it was such a nuisance, he told himself, and because it would impede him once he found a way out of the irons that Alastor sent a swirl of healing magic toward the wound. Just enough to close it. The boy would do well with a few more scars.

The witches moving the town out of sync with the mortal realm's flow of time would prove a challenge to overcome, but one he was willing to face in the name of completing his agreement with Pyra and saving Downstairs. Though he had not seen her, Alastor felt Pyra nearby, stalking the perimeter of the estate's vast grounds. She was as unyielding as the black sky back home. The fiends were gathering around her, the start of what promised to be a ferocious storm.

There was precious little Alastor desired more than watching the fortunes of the Reddings wither and Honor's descendants groveling for mercy. Precious little, aside from saving his kingdom.

He had not been entirely honest with the boy. While neither party could violate the terms of a malefactor's contract, the contract could be voided . . . if both parties agreed to it. He had never known a malefactor to consider such a thing, to voluntarily give up potential magic, until now. In trying to destroy him, Honor had made his request to end the contract clear—and now Alastor would answer it.

Outside the walls of the property, the blood key thrummed, starving for more magic. Still not in his true form, Alastor could not send his sister a dream to communicate his plan. His message would have to speak for itself.

He supposed that the Reddings watching their world crumble would have to be enough to sate his centuries-old grudge.

As he reached for the tether of old, brittle magic, Alastor wondered how long he would hear the boy's heartbeat filling his ears, if he might carry it in his mind always, like the echo of a bad dream.

Then, as easily as he had formed the contract with Honor three hundred and twenty-five years before, Alastor severed it.

Into the Woods

The house was calling my name.

The old joints and bones of the Cottage seemed to grow restless as the night wore on, as if it had to adjust its stance to accommodate the new families sleeping inside. The walls loved to play with storms, the old windows whined with each brush of the wind, and the walls caught the thunder, letting it shake them down to the studs.

I'd always hated the nights Prue and I had to sleep over here. I could never shake the feeling of being watched, even after all of the house's many occupants went to sleep. Countless generations of Reddings had lived here, and maybe some just hadn't wanted to let go.

"... *per?*"

My groggy mind registered the voice again, different

from the murmuring of the house. I glanced over at Nell, but she was curled up on her side, pillowing her head on her arm. For a second I didn't understand where I was.

"Prosper? Prosper . . ."

Okay, I hadn't imagined it. I pushed up onto my feet, wiping my eyes. Careful not to wake Nell, I made my way down the great hall, toward the entryway. The voice sounded like it was coming from the bay windows in the informal sitting room. . . .

What are you doing? Alastor asked. **You hear a phantom wind call your name and you rush toward it?**

You heard it, too?

Alastor retreated back into his silence as I searched the room, checking under the sofa and behind the chairs—even inside the armoire.

Never mind, I thought, *you are definitely hearing things. . . .*

I drifted over to the windows, glancing up at the magic spread across the sky. The cold night seeped through the thin glass panes, but it felt good. The contents of my head were blurry and unfocused, and my skin felt ten degrees too hot.

The velvet curtain to the right of me fluttered, and before Alastor could gasp, the cutting edge of a blade was digging into my neck.

I couldn't turn to look without the knife slicing in deeper. But we stood close enough to dark glass that I could see Henry Bellegrave's reflection in it. His long pale hair was wild. He spun me around, keeping the knife on me.

This hedge-born fool, Alastor growled. *Take the iron cuff off, Maggot. Let me finish what I started centuries ago.*

"What are you doing here?" I demanded.

"Finishing this," Henry said, pulling back his fist and letting it sail toward my face.

Lights out, Prosper.

Somehow, even before I opened my eyes, I knew exactly where I was.

The air blew colder here, carrying a hint of smoke from the trees that had never fully recovered from the fire that had happened there centuries ago. The wind played the splotchy gray branches like discordant flutes.

Are you awake now?

I opened my eyes to slits, trying to absorb the sight of the forest without alerting the fiends I heard walking through the mulch nearby. A heavy layer of fog trailed lazily over the ground. Now and then, a shadowed fiend would appear in it, only to vanish again.

The right side of my face throbbed in time with my pulse, and I could actually feel the massive bruise forming. My fingers curled into the soft, wet dirt beneath me.

I think . . . we're going to have to work together, I thought at him. *One last time. It's not too late to change the path we're on.*

Only humans believe in such dreams, Alastor said. *It is now the time of fiends.*

"I can feel your thoughts, even if I cannot hear them," came Pyra's silky voice through the creeping mist. A moment later she herself appeared in her panther form. The blood key rose in the air behind her, casting the forest in bloodred light. "Forget whatever last-minute plan you may be brewing, it's already too late."

Alastor's voice jumped to my mouth before I could stop it. *"At last, you're here and we can begin. I voided my contract with the Reddings, which nullified the protection spell on their property. The humans are yours for the taking."*

"Splendid," Pyra said, signaling to the ogres nearby. They stomped through the forest toward us.

"Why?" I whispered. "Why would you do something like that—there are kids in that house. They have nothing to do with any of this."

Alastor's reply was slow to come. *Yes . . . and their fear will give me the last bit of power I need.*

"Human," Pyra said, looking over her shoulder. "Get on with it. We haven't much time."

Henry Bellegrave stepped out from behind the nearby trees, limping over to me. I pushed myself up off the ground, but before I could stand, a massive hand clasped the back of my neck. I barely got one kick in before the ogre wrapped his other arm around my center and pinned me against his massive chest. The fur of some long-dead animal he wore as a vest prickled against my skin.

"I thought you would enjoy visiting the site of your intended grave three centuries past," Pyra told her brother. "I watched, from just over there, as the witch and the Reddings tried to roast you alive. I would have set another pyre, but I've grown rather bored of them after eradicating the vampyre families."

No wonder this place had never felt right to me. The evil that had occurred here with the death of the innocent girl had permanently scarred this part of the forest.

The blood key glowed brighter, throbbing with menace. That same uncomfortable tug at my center began again, growing in intensity until my head pounded in time with it, and my vision began to swirl, then blur. I tried to push back against the panic, knowing it would only feed Alastor the magic he needed, but I couldn't help it.

I was alone. My chest clenched at the thought. Alastor was still inside me, but I was alone in a way I hadn't been in a long time.

"What do you intend to do?" Alastor asked through me.

"Finish it, Bellegrave," Pyra said. "Then you can consider your contract complete. Not too quickly, however. I want my brother to feed off the pain as long as possible. I need his power restored before his sacrifice."

My head felt like it was twice its normal size. I forced

myself to look up, my neck straining. Through the haze of fog and disorientation, I saw the man's pale hair glowing like flame in the blood key's eerie light.

"I'd say sorry," Henry said, the blade flashing in his hand. "But your family and its contract have killed countless Bellegraves, stomping us out each time my ancestors believed they could build a new life. For that, at least one Redding deserves to die—nice and slow."

"Wait—" Alastor began, the word like lead in my mouth. His presence exploded inside me, all static and sparks.

The knife slid into my belly.

It wasn't the pain that scared me, but the lack of it.

I choked on my next breath, watching as the hot blood spilled out of me and over Henry's hand. He stared down at it, his gray-blue eyes wide behind his thin glasses. His jaw worked silently, back and forth, shock strangling the words before they had the chance to leave his throat.

"I . . ." he began, fumbling over the simple sound. "I . . ."

I, I, I . . . He was only thinking of himself. I was thinking of everyone else.

Who would find my corpse out there, after all the fiends had finished their dark work.

Who would tell my dad what had happened.

Who would hold Mom's hand at the funeral.

Who would reassure Nell that it wasn't her fault.

Who would make sure that Prue . . . that Prue would . . .

It became harder to hold on to the cloudy images. The light in them began to dim, and the bounding in my ears slowed. Every breath hurt.

Every single one.

I don't want to die.

You will not go, Alastor said. **I forbid it!**

A hurricane of pain, fear, and hopeless anger swept through me. It drowned out the last of my thoughts, and kept growing and growing, feeding itself until the pressure inside my chest twisted and tightened and I couldn't breathe; I couldn't breathe.

Agony tore down my center, firing through my blood. It felt like—

I'm being torn in two.

I couldn't tell if the screaming in my ears was my own or Alastor's. Light flared behind my clenched eyelids, and I had to force myself to open them again, to face the strange magic that poured out of the center of my chest, raging through the darkness of the woods.

"Prosper!" Nell's shout sounded like it had traveled from the other side of the world.

Henry stumbled back, throwing an arm over his face to shield his eyes. Fiends began to scurry away from the clearing, squeaking and howling at the intensity of the glare.

What is this? Al? Alastor!

Pyra's lips peeled back, revealing her full set of fangs.

I only had one glimpse of her before the blood key's crimson light clashed with my own, showering sparks of magic between us.

The pressure and pain faded, stealing the light along with them. Bright spots in every color swirled in my vision, as if the power had been tattooed on my retinas.

The ogre finally released me, letting me fall to the damp dirt below. The front of my shirt was soaked through with blood. Whatever strength was left in me drifted away like the last sparks of magic into the starless sky.

Voices—human voices—were calling my name, shouting something I couldn't make out. Just beyond the rows of fiends, the coven of witches, their changelings, and Nell had gathered, staring down the snarling fiends.

Grandmother raised her arms and the trees around us cracked like broken bones, twisting so that their sharp branches surrounded the fiends. Roots rose out of the ground as Barbie guided them forward, making them snap like whips in the air.

And a small white fox sat shivering on the ground, staring up at me with wide eyes. One blue, one black.

"Alastor?" I breathed out.

Threads of power from the blood key lashed out at him, wrapping around him until he choked, thrashing with baby-weak limbs. His form, which only a second ago had been as solid and pale as a pearl, flickered like a flame caught in the wind.

"Marvelous," Pyra said, laughing. "It actually worked. Now, the time has come for you to uphold your end of the bargain. Give your power to the blood key. Prove to me that you are different from our brothers. From our father."

Alastor extended his small claws, digging them into the soft earth, desperately crawling forward even as the blood key dragged him back. "But . . . the boy . . ."

He sounded so young outside of my head.

He sounded . . . scared.

"There, you see?" Pyra sneered to Alastor. She towered over him in their animal forms. One of her paws lashed out, pinning him with the ease of a predator about to enjoy a long-awaited meal. "I knew you would not do it. Coward!"

"Prosper!" my grandmother called from somewhere in the trees. Something brightly colored fluttered at her shoulder—Ribbit? "What is happening? What do you see?"

"I think," Pyra said, the muscles of her neck rippling, "I shall enjoy devouring her first. Not much meat left on her old bones, but destroying a realm rather builds an appetite and I'll take what I can get."

"I've honored my end of our deal," Henry Bellegrave said, his voice tight. "I have, you see? Release me—*release me*!"

Pyra flicked a paw in his direction. "Begone, then."

A flash of pale hair was all I saw before Henry Bellegrave turned and started running for his life.

"No!" Nell shouted. "Stop him!"

Alastor turned his gaze away, his eyes flicking back toward mine. They traveled down my front, to the pool of blood collecting on the fallen leaves below.

Please, I thought. My lips were numb. *Please help them . . . get them out of here. . . .*

The whites of Alastor's eyes flashed. His gaze sharpened, as if he were coming to a decision.

Stay still, Prosperity. We remain connected, but only for moments more.

A faint thread of green magic slowly manifested between us and began to glow brighter and brighter. The end that met my chest suddenly drew back, only to surge forward like a striking snake.

Squeezing my eyes shut, I clenched every muscle in my body to brace myself for the oncoming pain.

It never came.

I forced my eyes open again, watching in shock as that same sparkling thread began to stitch down, weaving itself in and out of my body. Mending. The magic left behind a warm, tingling sensation that was somehow both numbing and soothing.

"As it turns out, Maggot," Alastor said, his voice no more than a whisper, "I have decided to care about one human child."

What . . . ?

The glow around me faded. I looked down, touching the bloodied hole in my shirt. The skin beneath it was the shiny pink of new, healthy skin.

It was impossible, but . . .

Alastor's form trembled and shimmered before me. He tried to unfold his legs and stand, but couldn't seem to catch his balance. I took a step forward to help him, only to be cut off by Pyra, swinging her tail around in my path.

"You human-loving, folly-fallen *hedge pig*!" Pyra snarled. "You give your power away—the magic you promised *me*—to heal the boy? You'll drain your life for *him*? I won't let you! I won't! I command you, Stin—"

A new voice roared out through the night, spilling around the agonized shapes of the trees, blanketing the clearing like a shadow.

"Enough!"

Honor Among Reddings

Zachariah floated down through the trees, willing his hands solid as he reached out to pluck the blood key from the air. The crimson light made his small form flare brighter than it had even in the sewers below Skullcrush. An odd look passed over his face, almost pained, as the veins of magic wrapped themselves around him and began to cut into his shape.

"Zachariah, no!" a high, sweet voice called. "It will absorb you as well!"

Flora darted out of the trees to our right, her eyes flaring with that frightening, ancient green. Zachariah let out a cry of pain as the blood key all but dissolved his arms. Pyra lunged for the glowing stone as it fell, but Flora was closer, and faster.

As if the elf had summoned it directly to her, the blood key raced through the air, arcing down to float between her hands. All traces of the friendly elf were gone, the face hardened with power and hatred returned. The one that belonged to an Ancient.

In one heartbeat, we were surrounded by a dark forest. In the next, hundreds of glowing green eyes appeared in the dark spaces between the trees. The elves—the Ancients—came forward, their steps like soft autumn rain on the fallen leaves. Until, finally, they stopped and formed an unbroken ring circling the clearing, their small shapes illuminated by the blood key's crimson light.

The Ancients came in a variety of heights, shapes, and shades of earthy green and brown. Some carried with them bows and arrows, others were armed with small, bejeweled knives, all of which they raised at the malefactor's approach. The line of them was four or five elves deep in places. Even the ogres, lycans, and ghouls stepped in closer to one another at the center of the circle, backing away from the new arrivals.

"Are you all right?" I called to Zachariah. The boy was still staring at his hands, watching as they slowly re-formed. Finally, he looked my way, raising a white eyebrow at my blood-soaked shirt.

"I think, perhaps, you should be minding your own imperiled, brief life," he said.

The fiends gnashed their fangs and brandished warning

claws at the Ancients. Their backs turned on the gathered witches, and my grandmother, who had never missed an opportunity to seize the upper hand, did not disappoint me.

"*Now*, ladies!" she shouted.

Nell and the women of the Ravenfeather coven unfolded their clenched fists, blowing out a sparkling cloud of dust toward the fiends.

"*Drift deeply into dreams of night,*" they chanted. "*Do not falter, do not fight—*"

One by one, the fiends fell, drooping to the ground in heaps of scales and fur. But not dead. Even from my distance, it was obvious that they were breathing.

"No!" Pyra howled. "*No!* Rise, fiends! Attend your queen!"

But the same monsters that had stormed through the barrier between the realms only hours before did not so much as stir at her words. The mist around them rose and blanketed their sleeping forms. Pyra took a step back, her paws slipping in the forest mulch. Her eyes darted between the Ancients and the coven.

Flora drew the blood key closer and made her way back toward one of the nearby Ancients. This one was taller than her, his limbs gnarled and thin like branches. Unlike Flora's smooth, almost waxy skin, his had the texture of rough bark. The fluttering leaves of his hair had matured to reds and golds.

"This is the elder of the Greenleaf clan," Flora explained, her voice echoing as if we stood in a cave, not open air. "He has come to your aid, Prosper Redding, in gratitude for your assistance in saving the changelings." She turned stiffly to the Ancient again. "Elder, this is the blood key I spoke of."

His voice creaked, moaning like the wind through the battered trees around us. "So I see. It remains incomplete."

"Not for long," Pyra snarled. "This realm is ours, you weed. We'll rip your kind out of this world, just as we did your realm."

"I think not," he said. "We have waited centuries for this moment, when you will be made to pay for what you did to my kind."

Alastor remained where he was, curled up on the soft ground. His form fluttered, weaker now than it had been even just a second ago. The blood key was still leeching off what little magic remained in him.

I pushed myself up onto my hands and knees, and then, finally, my feet. *Hold on*, I told him, scrambling over the ground. If I could get the blood key away from the elder, I could smash it, somehow—

"Do not touch that key, Prosperity Redding," the elder's voice boomed.

"We have to destroy it!" I told him. "Alastor's too frail. It's going to drain him until there's nothing left."

"Flora has told me your tale." The elder did not seem to understand. "Your tormentor lies there defeated by his own wicked deceit."

"Cease this, Maggot," Alastor called back faintly. "I have

ALEXANDRA BRACKEN

always taken care . . . of myself . . . and always shall. . . ."

"Good thing you've got me to help you with that now,"
I said, turning back to the Ancient. The others gathered
around him, looking toward one another.

The elder's eyes flared. "You care about the one that
holds a contract for your eternity? You do not wish him
dead? With his magic gone, your deal is dissolved."

"I knew what I was doing when I made the deal," I said.
"*I* made it. It was my choice, and I take responsibility for it.
I'm not looking for the easy way out. I'm not saying he hasn't
done terrible things in the past, but he's not as evil as you
think he is. He's . . ."

I couldn't use the word *good*, or even really *better*, but
Alastor wasn't the same malefactor I had known in Salem.
Over the last few days, something had changed. He'd saved
me, even knowing what losing the magic would cost him.

The elder held out his gnarled arm, unamused. "These
are wicked creatures by their nature. That cannot be altered.
We removed the glamour over the residents of Redhood to
prove as much, to allow you to better protect yourselves
from their onslaught. Search your surroundings, Prosperity
Redding. See the damage they have done in such a sliver of
time. Imagine it happening all the world over."

So *that* was the snap of magic we'd felt before the fiends
had swept through Main Street.

"So then you'll allow us to be destroyed?" Pyra shouted
as she swiped a claw at the elder, her voice breaking. With a

wave of his hand, the roots of the nearby trees rose from the ground and ensnared the malefactor. She struggled and tore at the restraints, but they only built and built, until she was well and truly caged.

"Insolent fiend!" the elder hissed. "Your kind had over three centuries to understand why the Void was upon you and to save your collapsing realm. Fiends killed our elders, our brothers, our sisters. I do not see why you deserve our mercy now."

Pyra growled, slashing at her cage once again. Every time she broke through a root, another took its place. Still, she refused to give up.

"The others and I had hoped that you might be different from your family," the elder said. "In the end, you merely crowned yourself with the blood and misery of others and proved you were no better than they."

"I punished those who had ruled cruelly over other fiends!" she protested. "Only those who deserved it!"

"You still do not see it, do you? You drained your brothers of their lives and magic and spent centuries gathering the other components of the blood key. You perpetuated a vicious cycle, merely changing the players. Rather than looking inward, and truly examining how thoughtlessly the fiends devoured all available magic, you sought an outside solution: the gathering of more power not meant for you."

"No," Alastor said weakly, struggling to rise. "No . . . that is not true, O great Ancient. She did the one thing my brothers, my father, and even I did not. She took responsibility for what was happening to Downstairs."

"Oh, don't grovel, brother," Pyra snapped at him. "They do not deserve such respect."

"No," I said, "he's right. The fiends did try to change. Maybe it was too late, but they showed that they were capable of giving up their magic. Of helping one another."

"Only to save themselves," the elder said. "It was *hardly* a sacrifice done for the right reasons."

I stood straighter, catching sight of Nell as she crept forward through the trees, trying to get closer. "What's 'right' in this situation? You wanted to make things easier for yourselves when dealing with humans, so you accidentally created the fiends. Then you cast that glamour curse so no human would see them, except it backfired on you. Then you lost control of the fiends because you never tried to accept them for what they were and work with that. And now, instead of being accountable for the creatures you created, you're letting your experiment implode."

"What would you have us do, child?" the elder asked, almost mocking. "Fiends and elves cannot coexist. They have proven as much."

"Are you sure about that?" I said. "Because I'm pretty sure a witch, a fiend, an elf, a human, and a shade all teamed up less than twenty-four hours ago and successfully worked together. If we can do that, why can't you try to start over? Why can't you . . . You don't have to live together with the fiends, but you could try to teach them how to cultivate magic in their own world—how to balance its use so they're never faced with this problem again."

"Think about it, please," Nell said, darting through the sleeping fiends to stand beside me. She gave me a once-over, quickly checking to make sure I was unhurt. I did the same to her. "No one is perfect, but it doesn't mean the fiends can't learn. In fact, you *have* to fail in order to grow."

Alastor pulled on that tether between us, like he was trying to draw on my strength—or feed on my fear. He turned, looking out over the forest, taking in the sight of its rot and ruin.

It began here, I thought. *It has to end here.*

"Do you not see?" Alastor continued, finally rising to his feet. The shape of him solidified just enough for him to take a trembling step forward. "We are all guilty of choices that have taken us far from the roads we intended to travel. I made a bargain with a desperate man in this very forest, a man whose only desire was to save his family from hunger and blight. We begin with the best of intentions and make compromises. When a castle is crumbling, you do not stop to find the crack that began it all, you try to hold all the fracturing walls together in any manner you can, to the best of your ability."

"I see no proof of this change in the fiends you all speak of," the elder sneered, leaves shriveling and falling from around his head.

Alastor turned to look at his sister. Pyra remained crouched and ready to pounce, her eyes on the key hovering between the elder's hands. "You have my sister right before you, elder elf. Pyra recognized something the rest of us could not see—that there were many goodly wicked fiends dismissed and scorned simply for what they were, not upon their merits. Tradition should not stand if its roots are rotten."

Pyra looked toward him. "I have only ever tried to protect the fiends, not just our kind."

The elder shook his head.

"She is a good queen," Alastor insisted.

"Brother . . ." Pyra tried to cut in. "It is no use, they will not hear us out—"

Alastor pressed on: "She has gone too far in this instance. But she is a good queen, who thought of herself second and saving her realm first."

I turned to watch for the Ancient's reaction, my heart pounding at the base of my throat. He turned, fixing his glowing emerald gaze upon me. "Even if we desired to repair the realm, the fiends have ensured that we no longer have the magic to do so."

"You have the blood key, don't you?" I asked, nodding to it.

Inside the cage of roots, Pyra stood, sucking in a sharp breath. I felt a flash of hope when the elder didn't immediately reject the idea. In fact, he seemed to be considering it.

"It is too unstable in its current state," the elder said finally, looking to Flora. She nodded in agreement.

"It is likely to explode if we take it through a passage again," Flora said. "And tear the boundaries of the realms apart. We would need to redistribute its power into smaller, balanced segments."

Zachariah floated forward. "I would like to humbly submit myself to your service. Could I not absorb at least some of its power?"

"What?" I said. "Hold on, that sounds dangerous—"

"Still deceased," he reminded me.

"That very well may work," the elder said, his eyes glowing brighter. "Shades are the essence of magic that humans carry within them. The power would accept you as a vessel because of it."

"Or," Flora said, her voice darkening, "it may incinerate you entirely, never allowing you to pass on."

"No, that's too much of a risk," I began.

"I am still willing to try." Zachariah turned to look down at me, losing the sour twist of his mouth. If anything, he looked peaceful. Certain. "You promised me a favor, Prosperity Redding, and now I call it in, for I tire of your whinging. Allow me to make this choice for myself without your protests."

I had to physically bite my tongue to keep from saying anything. My stomach began to churn and churn until a clamminess settled over my skin. This didn't feel right. Zachariah should be guaranteed safe passage to the afterlife.

"I miss my family," Zachariah said quietly. "I long to see them and know their faces once more. Surely, you can understand that. I wish to be free to move on. To break from this cycle I never asked for."

Break the cycle. Those three words echoed through my mind. *Break the cycle.* The wheels of fate weren't just moving us forward, they were crushing us under them. We had to stop this. Something had to change.

"You aren't going to get to see your family if this goes wrong," I said. "It's too much for one shade to take. There has to be another way."

"Yes, it is too much for one spirit. It is not, however, too much for a family."

The breeze carried the hollow voice toward us, wrapping it around my senses like a sudden chill.

"What in the realms . . . ?" I heard my grandmother say. But even her words died off as the air around us began to brighten. The elves surrounding us shuddered as dozens of shades passed through them. The line of the glowing, ghostly beings extended all the way back to the Cottage, where they'd clearly come from. There were hundreds of them, maybe even thousands.

I sucked in a sharp breath and heard Alastor do the same.

"Holy . . . crap," Nell managed to croak out.

The shades were garbed in an assortment of dresses, bonnets, hats, and buckled shoes. Some wore more modern clothing, others wore nothing more than the thin nightshirts they had likely died in. Memories, stories, photo albums all burned through my mind like a film reel.

Amazement and disbelief tore at me from all sides. My mouth opened, but I couldn't speak. These were the faces in the portraits that covered the walls of the great hall.

These were my ancestors.

Of course . . . Inside my head, Alastor's voice was tinged with realization. With wonder. ***Honor contracted the souls of all Reddings who came after him. While I slept, they could not be retrieved and taken Downstairs. They remained here, all these years, trapped in the land of the living.***

The shade at the front was a woman in colonial dress, holding the hand of a toddler. The child's shade looked up at me, and I didn't see death there. I only saw life.

"Silence?" Prue whispered, coming closer. "It couldn't be. . . ."

But it was. Her shade was nothing like the stiff, miserable portrait of her in the Cottage's great hall, the one that had remained in a small unadorned frame beside Honor's grander one. The shades gathering around us looked to her, waiting.

Silence smiled warmly in my direction, her eyes soft with fondness and her long hair loose around her shoulders.

Silent no more. "We wish to be freed from this accursed land. To be granted the chance to move on. May we assist with this last task to bring an end to this tale?"

Even the elder's eyes were wide. "You may; however, even the blood key's magic is likely only to be enough to restore a fragment of the realm."

"Then, perhaps, we might give a part of ourselves to it?" Silence asked. "We shall help them plant a seed to nurture and grow for the future. We only ask for two things."

I shifted from foot to foot, giving Alastor's flickering form an uneasy glance.

"Go on," the elder said.

"First, thou must make an unbreakable vow to help rebuild the realm to the best of thy ability," Silence said. "And second, we would like the malefactor queen to give the full extent of her own innate magic. As a sign of good faith."

"What? No!" Alastor cried out. "She will not be able to manifest her animal form, nor open mirrors, nor enter into contracts—it may never return to her!"

The elder's hard expression and glowing eyes turned on Pyra. "I accept these terms on behalf of the Ancients. If you do the same, I shall ask the witches to create a mirror for our return to the realm that was once ours."

Pyra let out a low, mournful sound. "Those fiends gathered here . . . they will not suffer the same fate as me?"

"No, they will not," the elder said.

THE LAST LIFE OF PRINCE ALASTOR

"Yes . . ." Pyra's claws dug into the ground. Despite the terrible beauty of her form, and the strength of it, she began to shake. "Yes . . . I humbly submit myself to be punished."

She bowed her head before Silence.

"Then," the elder said, motioning to the coven, "begin."

I gripped Nell's arm as Barbie stepped forward and threw down a similar vial to the one that we had used to escape the Tower of No Return. The power congealed on the forest floor, crackling as it hardened into gleaming silver. Flora strode through the sleeping fiends to touch the shimmering surface, opening a portal.

The elder turned to Zachariah, holding out the blood key. "The shades must gather around as one. I shall help guide the magic into you to carry forth."

A shade floated through me, making me shiver as I stepped back, allowing more room in the clearing for them. One by one, they linked arms, creating rings upon glowing rings, like the lines inside a tree trunk. One by one, their expressions eased into something that might have been peace. All except for a single shade, the last to step forward.

Honor.

He, too, looked nothing like his smug, proud portrait, the one that gazed out of the canvas and dared you to deny his success. This was an old man, broken by a small eternity spent wandering a town that bore his name and the weight of all his dark secrets.

Alastor looked up, meeting the shade's gaze as Honor

stopped beside him. For a long, silent moment neither moved, nor spoke. There was no anger. There was no grief. I couldn't understand it, and maybe I wasn't meant to.

Honor bowed his head. *"My heart was weak, and my faith, shaken."*

Alastor nodded, closing his eyes as Honor went to join the others. He did not watch as the shades reached out for the blood key in unison. Within the span of a breath, its luminescence swirled from crimson to a purer emerald. Magic splintered from it, flying toward the shades like the sparks of a wildfire. They whirled around, faster, faster, until the stone cracked down its center and the remaining magic, trembling with the built-up pressure, exploded out like stardust.

And as the magic kissed their foreheads, their cheeks, the shades retreated to the mirror, slipping through it, until only Zachariah remained.

"I shall likely see you soon," he said, in the instant before he disappeared, "but not too soon, I hope."

I swallowed, and nodded.

The clearing fell dark. Silent.

I stepped back, leaning against Nell. She cast a worried look toward me, but said nothing, not even as the members of the coven made their way through the sleeping fiends and approached us.

"Well?" Grandmother prompted, not one to ever chase a point. "I assume you require our assistance in removing the malefactor's power. The spell Goody Prufrock created will do that, of course, but if you intend to carry the magic forth yourself, I suggest some sort of container, so you will not accidentally consume it for yourself."

The elder gave her a long look that my grandmother chose to return with one of her own. "I assure you, Goody Redding, I am more than capable of doing such a thing."

"That's our gal," Barbie muttered. "Always picking fights with mythological forces of creation."

Flora waved her hands, removing the roots from around Pyra. The panther padded forward, her head held high as she awaited her punishment.

"Wait," Alastor said, stepping forward on unsteady legs. His gaze passed between his sister and the elder. "I would like to offer you a different bargain."

"Do not test my patience, fiend," the elder warned.

"I know a good deal, you see, having made so many myself. I think you shall find the terms to be equally appealing, perhaps more so," Alastor said, "and it will not violate the terms of your vow to Silence Redding."

The Ancient gazed back, unmoving. "Go on."

"Instead of taking Pyra's power," Alastor said, bending his front paws to bow, "I offer you what remains of my own."

The True Name

"What?"

Nell spun toward me, also stunned. "Did I hear that right?"

"Al," I said with a nervous laugh. "You can't. Don't be an idiot."

"*Never*, brother," Pyra swore. "I can accept my own punishment. I do not need your protection—"

"You do not need my protection," Alastor agreed. "And you likely never have. However, the other fiends need *you*. The realm needs you. Perhaps I would have been a glorious king, one held in terror and despair, but even I see that I am . . . extraneous now."

Extraneous? This had to be a trick. He had to have come

up with some kind of clever way out of this, or he'd found a loophole to escape punishment.

"Very funny, Alastor," I said. "This whole time, all along, all you've wanted is to get your kingdom back. That was the whole point of helping me, wasn't it? I still haven't helped you do that, remember?"

"You still wish to end the contract, do you not?"

"Well, yeah, but—"

Alastor just stared back at me, one eye light, the other dark. "Then we are in agreement. I release you from the duties specified in our contract. I dissolve any expectations of service. I release you. I release you. *I release you.*"

A wash of sparkling heat washed from the top of my head down to my toes. "What—Alastor—"

He only turned away.

"I don't think it's a good idea," Nell told him, crouching down to look the fox in the face. She held out a hand, and it passed through his ghostly form. Flora approached behind her, returning to her normal form. This time, she quickly put together what had happened in her other state.

"Maleficent malefactor," Flora said. "All that's left of you is your magic. You have not manifested a full physical form, not yet. If you do this, you will disappear. You will not come back."

Nell turned, looking at the witches for confirmation. They huddled together, a mass of green velvet, consulting. Finally, Grandmother nodded.

"This is ridiculous," I said sharply. "Has everyone lost their minds?"

Toad landed on my shoulder, balancing there. He pressed a paw to my cheek and gave a slight shake of his head.

Alastor angled his head toward the elder. "Is that agreeable to you? Goody Redding, will you stand in place of your family's ancestor and consent to the amended deal?"

"It is," the elder said.

"I will," Grandmother said, her eyes narrowed. "And good riddance to you, I might add."

A sound like static filled my ears. I watched the scene play out in front of me in growing horror, and still it didn't feel real.

"Wait!" I said. Why didn't anyone see that this was wrong?

What is happening? Alastor!

He wouldn't look at me.

"What is the meaning of this?" Pyra asked. "Why would you do such a thing?"

"It is not much . . ." Alastor told her. "I did not have the time to restore it all, but perhaps it will allow something in our home to be mended. And it will, perhaps, serve as my apology for not helping you all those centuries ago, when you needed me most."

"Brother . . ."

"Allow me to do this one thing," he said. "And take a small portion of my magic to revive our brothers. They are depressingly feeble in intelligence and taste, but they, too, deserve the opportunity to change."

No—no—this wasn't right—

"The hour grows late, and this town must be restored to the humans." The elder approached Alastor. "Kneel, creature."

The coven gathered in a circle around them. Nell looked back at me before linking her hands with Barbie and my grandmother. Blood roared in my head until I couldn't make out the words of the spell they chanted.

Magic rose from somewhere inside them, knotting together at the center of their circle. The elves drifted toward the mirror, jumping through it to begin the journey Downstairs. Soon only the elder and Flora remained. The elf gave me a small, sad smile.

I tore my gaze away from her and returned it to Alastor. He lifted his small head, sitting regally on the autumn leaves, his tail curled around him like a question mark. From a short distance away, Pyra released a low, mournful sound.

Nell and the other witches began to chant. I took a step forward, reaching for his flickering shape, but Prue jumped forward, banding her arm over my chest. I tried to shove back against her, to wrench myself free, but she held firm.

"He tried to destroy our family," she reminded me. "He would have killed you."

But he didn't. He hadn't.

"It's not right," I said, my eyes hot and stinging. "It's not right!"

Alastor's shape began to blur. To fade.

Don't go.

The first time I had seen him, Alastor had been reflected in the surface of dark glass. He'd glowed brighter than the flame of the candle in my hand. Alastor had seemed so small then, his fur standing on end, his fangs flashing. He'd been feral with hate.

Now, as he finally turned to look at me, he was as quiet and still as the moon at midnight.

I needed to ask him why. I needed to know why he was doing this—

Don't go, I said again. *Don't go. . . .*

There wasn't enough time.

There was never enough time.

No—there had to be another way—there was—I could—I could save him—

In the last instant before he disappeared, I heard his voice drift across my mind one final time.

Farewell, Prosper Redding. You are not what your family might have made you, and, it seems, neither am I.

36

Neither Here Nor There

It was a strange thing, to die.

Alastor had never thought about it. Not in any true way. He supposed he knew that death would one day lay a bony hand on his shoulder, he'd feel a prick of cold, and that would be that. But he'd always possessed a stubborn denial that he was anything but infallible. He had all but refused to believe that death might run a con he'd fall for. Even as the Reddings had tried to turn him to ash, he had refused to fully relinquish his grip on life.

No, he decided. Never mind. It wasn't a strange thing to die. Eventually, everyone reached the end of their life, whether that was hours, days, years, decades, or centuries. All things that began naturally came to an end. It was, however, a strange thing to give in to the urge to slip away. To take one last breath and surrender to the Next.

Well, if fiends were allowed into the Next. That was another thing he had never thought about, even when he was trapped in the Inbetween, where nothing lived nor died, but was kept like a long-held breath.

For the moment, there was nothing surrounding him— no sound, no light, no air to breathe, no ground to rest his feet upon. He flowed back, drifting and drifting.

Listen to me, a voice whispered in his ear.

He brushed it aside, focusing on the slow current leading him forward. Why did it have to be so infuriatingly slow?

You don't want to go.

Of course he didn't want to go, but he'd agreed to it. It was perhaps the only good choice he'd made in his many centuries, and the many different lives he'd had within them all. He'd been a prince, yes, but in his first century he had been a student, in other centuries a swordsman, and in more recent ones a contractor of shades. There were a number of things he might have tried with a few more lives. Such as . . . a sculptor! A sculptor of fine little ponies, in all sorts of marvelous war poses.

You can live all of those lives. More. You just have to come back.

Ugh. Was he to spend all eternity with an unwelcome, bratty-sounding conscience? Why did it have to sound so much like . . . like . . .

The name was there, on the tip of his tongue. The memory of a face hovered close behind. Mildly ratlike, but then, that was true of all humans.

Alastor! Listen to me! Don't go!

"Why wouldn't I?" he whispered to the nothing. There was no place for him, not anymore. A kingdom that did not need him, a human world he no longer understood or cared to vanquish.

Not everything is handed to you in life—we have to decide who we're going to be and make our own place in the world.

That sounded tedious, and yet . . .

Alastor tried to turn back, to find the source of the words. To tug on the last mental thread that connected them. He grasped for it in the blackness, finding nothing but air. Nothing to slow himself. Nothing to stop the way he felt himself dissolving into air and dust.

I command you to return. The boy's voice echoed through the darkness. *I command you to return to us.*

It wasn't enough. It wasn't going to be enough—Alastor felt one last pull at his center, and then—

Stingingbow, I command you to return.

He heard him.

Stingingbow, I command you to return!

He could not refuse him.

As the endless darkness exhaled, pushing him back the way he'd come, Alastor supposed there was at least one more life left to be lived, after all.

Brothers and Sisters

He took shape out of the fog, swirling together with the flecks of magic that still hovered nearby, refusing to be carried off by the breeze. Alastor, despite being dragged back into the human realm, was fainter than he had been before, and even smaller—the size of a newborn pup. His eyes remained closed, as if he might drift from a deep sleep into an eternal one again at any moment. The rise and fall of his breath came too fast, too quick.

Prue gasped. Her arms went slack enough for me to finally pull myself free. I dropped down to my knees beside him. I didn't even look up as the elder took Alastor's magic and vanished through the mirror, all but dragging a reluctant Flora after him.

"Come on," I breathed out. Alastor was no longer inside me, and his "death" had seemingly severed the last bit of mental connection we'd had. The last trace of his presence, the tether that had let me command him to return to life, had snapped as he'd turned back. The force of it had been like a bolt of lightning racing from the top of my skull to my toes. "Come on, Al . . . wake up and yell at me . . . tell me how stupid I am for not listening to your wishes . . . for breaking my promise that I wouldn't use it. . . ."

"How is this possible?" Nell asked, looking around. The other witches seemed just as startled by his reappearance.

"Is he alive?" Pyra asked bounding forward. She pawed gently at her brother, trying to rouse him. "Brother? Brother, can you hear me?"

"Barely," I whispered.

Her gaze fixed on me. "You summoned him back. You used his true name. Even I did not think to do so."

"I tried," I told her. "It looks like he's about to go again, though—"

The rustling of leaves and sudden deep groans sent a spiky chill down my back. The fiends stirred from their unnatural sleep.

"What happened—?" an ogre rumbled, staggering up from the ground. "Who— *Witches!* What have you done? Where is the queen?"

A lycan beat his paw against his chest, rallying the others around him with a piercing howl.

Pyra threw her head back and shouted, "Stand down at once!"

"The blood key!" one of the fiends cried—a hob. She began scouring the nearby ground, trying to sniff out the fragments of the stone.

"Look—the fox!" another snarled. "It is the lost prince!"

A goblin flipped forward over the heads of the ogres, landing a foot away from us. He brandished his claws for the queen's inspection.

"How shall I gut him for you, Your Majesty?"

Pyra leaped over Al's prone form, snarling. "My brother has saved us all. You will treat him with respect as we return Downstairs using the mirror the witches have provided. The Ancients are there, waiting for us."

It looked like she'd dropped a boulder on the heads of her subjects.

"Dinner?" one of the lycans asked hopefully.

The queen shook her head.

"Your Majesty?" one of the ogres said, glancing down at his club. "But . . . the mayhem? The pandemonium?"

"Is at its end," Pyra said. "We depart now, before the sun rises."

Despite Alastor's insubstantial form, Pyra was still able to pick him up by the scruff of his neck.

"Wait," I said, reaching for him.

The panther looked back over her shoulder. "I cannot. He needs to be returned to our realm to heal. Otherwise, he'll simply fade away once more. Your command is the only reason he held on to a wisp of magic to survive."

"How am I going to know that he's okay?" I asked.

Pyra tilted her head. "Somehow, Prosperity Redding, I suspect you will know."

The fiends filed out of the woods, each visibly more disappointed than the next. A few lunged at the witches for show, growling at their impassive faces. Others scratched at the already damaged trees, petulantly trying to kick them over.

"Oh—witchling," Pyra said, turning just as she and Alastor were about to step through the mirror. "You'll find that your father's contract has been voided. He, however, remains your curse to bear."

"Ah yes," Grandmother said coldly. She strolled past us, following the path Henry Bellegrave had taken as he ran. "I suspect he'll turn up soon enough."

"What will you do to him?" Nell asked, hugging her arms to her chest.

Grandmother turned to her. She wasn't a soft woman; she would never be that snowy-haired granny that baked cookies and taught you how to knit and garden. But she didn't have to be. At her core, my grandmother was made of steel, and that was all the better for protecting the family. "I will hunt your father with all of my resources and bring him to justice, if not in a human court of law then in the court of the Supreme Coven. I cannot forgive him, not after he tried to kill my grandson."

Nell nodded, swallowing.

"However," Grandmother continued, "I would like to try to soothe past miseries by offering *you*, the last heir of the Bellegraves, anything you desire. Any amount of money. Any dream you long to have fulfilled."

Nell looked stunned for a moment, but it didn't take her much longer than that to make her request. "All I want is for him to give up his legal custody of me so Missy can be declared my guardian. Officially. I don't know if even you have that much power, though."

"Regardless, I will try," Grandmother said. "Someone has inspired me to turn the page of our family's long book of history. I am looking forward to the many possibilities of a blank sheet, and all the wonders it may one day hold."

"There are so many good ways to start it off," Nell said. "'Threescore and many years ago,' 'Once upon a time,' 'It was the best of times, it was the worst of times,' 'Now is the winter of our discontent'. . ."

I put a hand on Nell's shoulder as we turned back toward the Cottage. "How about just 'What's past is prologue'?"

But as I glanced back over my shoulder and took in Grandmother's approving nod, the words themselves seemed to matter less than knowing I'd have a hand in writing that history.

Prue and half of the coven returned to the Cottage to tell the townspeople that it would be safe to return to their homes within the hour, though I really didn't see how that was possible given the state of things. Grandmother had only flicked a hand and given strict instructions that everyone there should be served tea steeped at exactly two hundred and twelve degrees and provided with whatever they wanted for breakfast.

Elma had the unfortunate task of coming up with some sort of explanation for what had happened, and the last I heard, she was torn between a mass hallucination caused by an epic gas leak, or the only slightly less believable truth. In the end, the coven agreed against casting a spell of forgetting on the town. What we all needed now was to *remember*.

Grandmother led the other half of the coven through the woods, back toward the remains of Redhood. Nell and I walked a few steps behind, watching as they began the process of disassembling the protection stones and the spell that still burned over us.

"You know," I said, feeling my face start to heat. I cleared my throat, forcing my voice steady. Real casual. "You could stay. Here, I mean. Redhood, the home of Silence Cakes. If for some reason you need a place to stay for the summer or spring break or fall break or winter break from Crescent Academy if they decide to send you there or you *couldpossiblyjuststayforever*."

The cloud of Nell's dark hair framed her look of confusion. "I'd have to use my time off to look after the House of Seven Terrors and decide what to do with it."

Hope deflated in me. "Oh. Right."

"And Missy has her shop," Nell reminded me. "I'll live with her for now, and hopefully your grandmother can help make it all legal."

Right. *Right.* Could I possibly be any stupider?

It hit me then, for the first time, that Alastor would not be answering. I drew in another unsteady breath, rubbing my hands against the sides of my jeans.

"That's great," I said, trying to smile. "I'm really happy for you."

I was. Really.

"You'll miss me," she said, a slow grin growing on her face. "You're going to miss me so bad."

"No, I won't," I said, way too quickly.

"Yes, you will," Nell said, craning her head back to watch as the protective spell disintegrated into a million sparkling fragments of power. They rained down over us, catching in her hair like emerald glitter. "Doesn't matter how far apart we are. You're my friend. I'm your friend. End of story."

"Finis," I agreed.

"Done."

"End scene."

An hour or so later, a frantic Missy had driven into Redhood, right behind the residents who had been locked out by the spell and spent several bewildered hours searching for it. After Nell introduced her to the Ravenfeather coven, they made their way home to begin to prepare for Nell's trial.

As we watched the townspeople mill around, taking in the sight of the magic show unfolding around them, Prue and I sat in the middle of the town square on the steps of the destroyed gazebo.

We'd lifted the pan of roasted chestnuts out of the abandoned cart and devoured them as we watched Redhood magically piece itself back together. The bricks of the courthouse stacked one on top of the other, grinding back into place. The glass front of Pilgrim's Plate shimmered as the shards rose and sealed themselves back into the panes. Above us, magic worked quickly to weave the gazebo roof back together.

"Hey, Prosper?" Prue said suddenly. "I just realized I never said thank you. For coming to get me down . . . there."

I kept my eyes on the chestnuts. "Not sure I did much, except play a huge role in getting you kidnapped in the first place."

"That wasn't your fault. I shouldn't have gone to Salem alone, but I wasn't sure what Grandmother was planning. I really thought she might try to stop me. But I just meant that . . . all of this made me realize that you've been there for me a lot." She let out a faint, sad laugh. "Well, pretty much always, especially before my operation. And I haven't been there for you. Not really."

"That's different," I protested.

"It's really not," Prue said. "And I promise I'll do better."

"I don't need you to take care of me," I told her. "I don't need you to always sweep in and rescue me from my problems or when I mess up. And I know I don't always need to do that for you either. It's okay that things aren't the same as when we were little kids. Nobody and nothing ever stays the same, and that's a good thing."

She nodded. "Yeah. I think you're right about that. But, Prosper, some things won't ever change. The fact that we're twins. Grandmother's hatred of napkins folded into the shapes of animals. Dad singing off-key in the car. And that's a good thing, too."

A familiar blue SUV swerved up to the side of the square. Whichever one of our parents was driving slammed on the brakes, parking crookedly in the middle of the street. Mom's bright head of red hair appeared first as she searched the square. I saw her gasp at the sight of us, and really wished I had remembered to change out of my blood-soaked shirt.

"Finally!" Prue said, brushing her hands together to remove the crumbs and sugar. "I'm *so* ready to go home."

Mom and Dad ran toward us, calling our names, dropping their bags and coats in their hurry to cross the grass and benches that separated us. The fall leaves rose back onto their branches in the early morning's golden light and were ruffled by a crisp breeze.

I smiled and stood. "Me too."

Mirror, Mirror

If there was one thing the town of Redhood could do better than any other, it was keep a secret.

After the coven was finished with it, Main Street and the nearby neighborhoods had been put back together perfectly. Not a brick or wood plank was out of place. The same striped awnings were rolled back out. The hedges and flowers that had been shredded were carefully replanted and groomed to their usual magnificence.

At first, the people of Redhood were eager to discuss what had happened. It was referred to as *the incident* or *that time when . . . you know.* Ghost stories became more prevalent, exchanged in whispers in the grocery store aisles. Amateur photographers roamed the forests at night, looking for proof that it hadn't all been an elaborate shared dream. A trace of that brilliant, crackling magic traced along someone's cheek, or flashed in their eyes.

Maybe everyone's memory of that day faded along with the magic, because life in Redhood soon became as quiet as it had ever been. Town meetings resumed. Parades were scheduled. The school bake sale held its annual Silence Cakes competition.

The only thing that stubbornly refused to return to normal was me.

Before, I'd felt like I couldn't go anywhere without whispers trailing my every step. Most of the time that meant keeping my head down in the school hallways, or finding a hidden place to eat lunch alone, where kids couldn't throw things at me.

I was still alone now, and there were still whispers, but I didn't care what they had to say about me. If I couldn't be myself—if Prosper Redding couldn't hang out in the Redding Academy art room and work on projects, if he couldn't say the things he wanted to say, or do the things he wanted to try to do, then what was the point of going through what I had?

I knew my parents were worried about me. I had told them about what had occurred in the weeks I'd been missing. I left out the worst of it, mostly so they wouldn't lock me up in a panic room for the rest of my life, or be plagued with nightmares. But sometimes, at night, I heard their quiet talk travel from the vent in the living room to my bedroom. *What can we do for him? How can we be sure he's really all right?*

Right now, though, they needed to worry more about themselves. The luck our family had enjoyed for centuries suddenly evened out. Family businesses began to shutter due to lack of support and finances drying up, and the ride to fame and fortune gained unexpected bumps and twists. Nothing truly disastrous or deadly, at least, but our future was no longer as certain as it had once been. I didn't want anyone to have to worry about me, too. I was fine.

I was.

The quiet days turned to weeks, then months. And, just like that, the book of seasons began winter's chapter.

One December night, when the town sparkled like a snow globe with the season's first storm, a hot, reeking gust of air blew across my bedroom.

I opened my eyes to the sight of a small white fox perched on my desk, its long, fluffy tail swishing back and forth over my unfinished math homework. The mirror on the wall behind him rippled.

I closed my eyes again, turning over—only to launch right back up again, slapping a hand against my racing heart.

"Holy *crap*," I said, shock crashing into relief.

I hadn't heard anything from him, had any sign that he was all right, and now here he was. Just like that.

"You sleep curled like a little maggot, as always," Alastor

said with a certain fondness. "It's rather comforting, the predictability of humans."

Around him, artfully arranged like the best of galleries, were my porcelain horse figurines. He took one furred paw and stroked the closest one's long, curved neck. The box they slept in at the back of my closet had been dragged out into the middle of my bedroom floor and left wide open. With only the moon's light filtering in through my curtains, I could see the deep imprint of teeth in its lid.

"Hilarious," I said. "You were watching me sleep? That's creepy, even for you, pal."

"Fiends creep, humans grovel," Alastor said, cleaning his paw. "We cannot deny our natures."

"Can you at least close the portal before something else gets in here?" I complained, reaching back to puff up my pillow. "I'm still finding pieces of fur and feathers around the house."

I lay back down, pulling the covers over me and pretending to close my eyes. If Alastor could hear my heartbeat, it would be a dead giveaway that I wasn't sleeping.

"The temerity!" the fox said. "You will not rest while I am speaking. Do you miss having me in your head? I am certainly not opposed to communicating through dreams."

I opened my eyes and rolled onto my back with a groan. It did seem strange that he hadn't just come to me in a dream, and he'd made the trip up to the human world. Unless, of course, he'd been out contracting with other, unsuspecting humans.

"What do you need, Al?"

"Al! How many times—" The fox's voice cracked, forcing him to stop and clear his throat. "There is a matter in the realm which . . . I might use your opinion on."

The bed absorbed the fox's slight weight without so much as a dip in the mattress. I tried to keep my pulse from stammering in my veins at his words. A matter, huh?

"You don't have fleas, do you?" I asked, pushing up onto my elbows.

The malefactor flashed his teeth. "As I was saying, I would like your opinion on something, if you have time in your tragic schedule of life events. Yours and the witchling's. But the elf is most definitely not invited. Same with the changeling. And don't bring the red-haired superior Redding either. She proved rather unhelpful beyond saving her own skin."

"A matter, huh?" I cocked my head to the side. "Al . . . do you . . . miss us?"

"O-of course not!" the fox spluttered. His blue eye seemed to glow brighter than before. "It is a—it is a boring problem. I am far too busy to handle it, you see. I do not have the time to meddle with rogue shades. I merely thought you, being humans, might be able to reason with them. The elf is *not* invited."

"You already said that." I scratched at my head, trying

to flatten the parts that stood straight up. "Have you asked Nell if she can do it?"

I chatted with Nell every single day. She wasn't allowed to have a cell phone at Crescent Academy, because having to go to boarding school and be far away from your family and friends wasn't punishment enough, but she had enchanted a pair of notebooks that mirrored one another. I could write her notes or draw something I'd seen, and it would show up on the pages of her notebook in New York.

"I thought you might broach the subject with her," the malefactor said, his eyes getting a little twitchy. "The dwellings of witches are rather . . ."

"Well protected?" I finished. I reached for my phone, pretending to type as I said, "Hey, Nell, you busy? Alastor needs us to help save him—"

The fox let out a small screech and dove for the phone, batting at it.

"All right, all right," I said. "I'm just kidding—you can face the end of your world, but you can't take a joke?"

Alastor scowled as he moved to sit on the other end of the bed.

"Hey, how are things?" I asked carefully. "Are you doing okay?"

"I'll thank you to know that I am doing perfectly horrible as chief adviser to the queen," Alastor said with a dignified flourish of his tail. "All of our subjects fear and respect me, and they fall upon their knees as I go by—"

"So they still only listen to Pyra?" I cut in, yawning. The fox's mouth fell open, and before he could splutter out an indignant response, I added, "That's rough. You just have to keep showing them that you care. And by *care*, I mean whatever the fiendish version is of letting them know you hope they don't die."

The fox's eyes trailed off to the side of the bed. "Can you, as a peasant yourself, tell me if your fellow peasants prefer gifts or mercy?"

"Um, both usually," I said. "That goes for both humans and fiends. I would also recommend not calling them peasants. Or subjects."

His gaze snapped back over to me. "Then how shall I refer to them?"

"Try friends? Or . . . fellow residents of Downstairs?"

The fox's lip curled back in pained dismay. "What about serfs? Oh—or swains?"

"Pretty sure those are just synonyms for peasants," I said. "Why don't you just let Pyra be the one who communicates with them and you do the behind-the-scenes work? Earn their love by making sure they . . . you know, are able to eat and aren't in danger of, like, invading lava worms."

"Lava worms are very slow and stupid, Maggot," Alastor said patiently. "But I take your point and shall deign to consider it."

I gave him a thumbs-up.

"What is wrong with your finger?" he demanded. "Is it broken? Why do you hold it in such a way?"

I sighed. "Never mind."

He leaped back onto the desk, stepping carefully around the ponies. "I shall summon you when the time comes, when the moon is full and high and the dark winds blow bitter and cold."

"Do you mean next Tuesday?" I said. "I'm still in school. Can it wait until winter break starts on that Friday? I have to pretend I don't know this town was founded with the help of a demon and finish my history project on the first years of Redhood."

The fiend sighed. "Humans."

"Hey, Al," I called to him as he stepped up toward the rippling mirror. "I'm sorry to tell you this, but you're my *friend*."

His thick coat of white fur fluffed out as the fiend shuddered.

I dropped back down onto my pillow, rolling onto my side, fighting a smile. Outside, snow began to fall, dusting my windowsill, as quiet as my mind.

And when I woke in the morning, the only sign Alastor had ever been there at all was a small paw print in the dust on my desk, and a new, inviting darkness that burned at the center of the mirror's silvered glass.

Acknowledgments

To my favorite puny, rump-fed bugbears—just kidding! Because of the mysteries of publishing (aka the way pages are printed and cut), I wasn't able to include acknowledgments in *The Dreadful Tale of Prosper Redding*, so please allow me to quickly thank the people who helped bring this series to life.

First, thank you to my mom, Cyndi, for sharing all the truly creepy stories about her childhood in Massachusetts. I may have had nightmares about them for years, especially the one with the cemetery fence, but it was totally worth it because they helped me figure out how to write these weird, dark little books of my heart! Also: Thank you for filling in all of the little details about what autumn in New England is actually like, as you forced me to grow up in a state that doesn't experience seasonal change outside of switching between Comfortably Cool and Roast-You-Alive Hot.

Thank you also goes to my sister, Steph, for helping me spread the word about the series and for being such a great support system when I needed it most. Much love to Daniel and Hayley, too, of course.

I'm sending a cauldron full of candy over to Susan Dennard, in thanks for all of her input and brainstorming help as I figured out the logistics of this world. Sooz—thank you so much for reading early drafts of the first book and helping me make the story sharper. Likewise, thanks so much to Anna Jarzab for her amazing early feedback and for not letting me forget that this story was sitting on my hard drive, waiting for its moment.

My ghoulish gratitude to everyone at Disney Hyperion for helping me to . . . wait for it . . . creep it real with these booooo-ks! You are all revoltingly talented and monstrously magnificent at what you do. Laura Schreiber, you are the queen of fiends! Thank you so much for seeing the potential in these books and for helping me figure out how to make these stories both emotional and fun. I toast you with my finest goblet of beetled juice. I'm also so grateful for the input of Emily Meehan and Mary Mudd, as well as the hard work and support of Seale Ballenger, Marci Senders, Dina Sherman, Holly Nagel, Elke Villa, Andrew Sansone, Jennifer Chan, Guy Cunningham, Meredith Jones, Dan

Kaufman, Sara Liebling, Cassie McGinty, and Mary Ann Naples. And sales? You guys are spook-tacular!

Thanks, as always, to my agent, Merrilee Heifetz, for her scary-amazing advice and advocacy. Rebecca Eskildsen, you are unboolievable! Thanks for letting me haunt your inbox and keeping me on track.

And finally, thank you to the many pumpkin-spice-scented candles that sacrificed their lives so that these books could be written in the dead of summer, surrounded by cacti.